ACCLAIM FOR KE

"A compelling and timely story, *Over the Li_____ ___ _____ ___ courage* required to forgive. Irvin paints a vivid picture of life on the border—of loyalty and betrayal, fear and love, hope and despair."

—SIRI MITCHELL, AUTHOR OF *STATE OF LIES*

"*Tell Her No Lies* is true romantic suspense at its best! Kelly Irvin has penned a heart-stopping, adrenaline pumping romantic suspense with an unlikely heroine that tugs at the heartstrings. Highly recommended!"

—COLLEEN COBLE, *USA TODAY* BESTSELLING AUTHOR

"I think I've found a new favorite author! What an exciting read—tense, suspenseful, and masterfully written!"

—CARRIE STUART PARKS, AWARD-WINNING AUTHOR OF *FORMULA OF DECEPTION*

"In *Tell Her No Lies*, Kelly Irvin has crafted a story of wounded characters overcoming and fighting their way to the truth. In a world where so many present one facade externally and another inside their homes, this novel shines a light on the power of truth to cut through the darkness. Wrap that inside a page-turning mystery and some sweet romance and it's a story perfect for readers who love multiple threads. This is a keeper of a story."

—CARA PUTMAN, AUTHOR OF THE HIDDEN JUSTICE SERIES

"With plenty of twists and surprises, this is a story readers will be shocked by."

—*PARKERSBURG NEWS & SENTINEL* ON *TELL HER NO LIES*

"Well-established as a writer of Amish romances, Kelly Irvin's romantic suspense novels promote faith after betrayal and encourage readers to learn to love and trust again."

—INGRAM ON *TELL HER NO LIES*

"Irvin (Amish of Bee County series) creates a complex web with enough twists and turns to keep even the most savvy romantic suspense readers guessing until the end. Known for her Amish novels, this two-time Christy

Award finalist shows that her talents span subgenres from tranquil Amish stories to rapidly paced breathless suspense."

—*LIBRARY JOURNAL* ON *TELL HER NO LIES*

"A moving and compelling tale about the power of grace and forgiveness that reminds us how we become strongest in our most broken moments."

—*LIBRARY JOURNAL* ON *UPON A SPRING BREEZE*

"Irvin's novel is an engaging story about despair, postnatal depression, God's grace, and second chances."

—*CBA CHRISTIAN MARKET* ON *UPON A SPRING BREEZE*

"A warmhearted novel that is more than a romance, with lovable characters, including two innocent children caught in the red tape of government and two people willing to risk breaking both the *Englisch* and Amish law to help in whatever way they can. There are subplots that focus on the struggles of undocumented immigrants."

—*RT BOOK REVIEWS*, 4-STAR REVIEW, ON *THE SADDLE MAKER'S SON*

"Irvin has given her audience a continuation of *The Beekeeper's Son* with complicated young characters who must define themselves."

—*RT BOOK REVIEWS*, 4-STAR REVIEW, ON *THE BISHOP'S SON*

"The awesome power of faith and family over personal desire dominates this beautifully woven masterpiece."

—*PUBLISHERS WEEKLY*, STARRED REVIEW, ON *THE BEEKEEPER'S SON*

"Storyteller extraordinaire Kelly Irvin's tale of the Amish of Bee County will intrigue readers, who will want to eavesdrop on the lives of these characters on a regular basis."

—*RT REVIEWS*, 4½-STAR REVIEW, ON *THE BEEKEEPER'S SON*

"Irvin writes with great insight into the range and depth of human emotion. Her characters are believable and well developed, and her storytelling skills are superb."

—*CBA RETAILERS + RESOURCES* ON *THE BEEKEEPER'S SON*

OTHER BOOKS BY KELLY IRVIN

ROMANTIC SUSPENSE

Tell Her No Lies

AMISH

AN AMISH OF BIG SKY COUNTRY NOVEL

Mountains of Grace (available August 2019)

EVERY AMISH SEASON NOVELS

Upon a Spring Breeze
Beneath the Summer Sun
Through the Autumn Air
With Winter's First Frost

THE AMISH OF BEE COUNTY NOVELS

The Beekeeper's Son
The Bishop's Son
The Saddle Maker's Son

OVER THE LINE

THE

LINE

KELLY IRVIN

THOMAS NELSON
Since 1798

Over the Line

© 2019 by Kelly Irvin

Published in Nashville, Tennessee, by Thomas Nelson. Thomas Nelson is a registered trademark of HarperCollins Christian Publishing, Inc.

Thomas Nelson titles may be purchased in bulk for educational, business, fundraising, or sales promotional use. For information, please email SpecialMarkets@ ThomasNelson.com.

Scripture quotations are taken from the Holy Bible, New International Version®, NIV®. Copyright © 1973, 1978, 1984, 2011 by Biblica, Inc.® Used by permission of Zondervan. All rights reserved worldwide. www.zondervan.com. The "NIV" and "New International Version" are trademarks registered in the United States Patent and Trademark Office by Biblica, Inc.®

ISBN 978-0-7852-2315-3 (e-book)

Library of Congress Cataloging-in-Publication Data
Names: Irvin, Kelly, author.
Title: Over the Line / Kelly Irvin.
Description: Nashville, Tennessee : Thomas Nelson, [2019]
Identifiers: LCCN 2018059444 | ISBN 9780785223146 (paperback)
Subjects: | GSAFD: Romantic suspense fiction.
Classification: LCC PS3609.R82 O94 2019 | DDC 813/.6--dc23 LC record available at https://lccn.loc.gov/2018059444

Printed in the United States of America
19 20 21 22 LSC 5 4 3 2 1

*For my 1980s Laredo Sky Lounge gang, especially
Shellee Bratton, Mike Cisneros, Joanne Cisneros,
Danny Hermosillo, and Larry Burns.
We shared the good days and the bad days.
I'm so glad I spent them with you.*

Love does not delight in evil but rejoices with the truth.

I CORINTHIANS 13:6

Who is a God like you, who pardons sin and forgives the transgression of the remnant of his inheritance? You do not stay angry forever but delight to show mercy. You will again have compassion on us; you will tread our sins underfoot and hurl all our iniquities into the depths of the sea.

MICAH 7:18–19

SPANISH GLOSSARY

abuelo: grandpa
abuelita: granny
antojitos: snacks
aquí estamos: here we are
arroz con frijoles: rice with beans
cabrito: little goat (type of meat)
cállate: shut up (command)
cálmate: calm down (command)
café con leche: coffee with milk
carne asada: thinly sliced grilled beef
carne guisada: stewed meat
carnita: braised pulled pork
cerveza: beer
chancla: flip-flop
chiminea: free-standing, portable fireplace, usually used in backyards
chiquita (o): little girl or boy
claro que sí: of course
¿Cómo te vas?: How are you doing?
con la policia de San Antonio: with the police from San Antonio
corazón: heart
dime: tell me
Dios te ama: God loves you.

ejército: army

ese: slang for homeboy

familia: family

frijoles: beans

gracias: thank you

guero: slang for blond or light-skinned man

hermano: brother

hija: daughter

hijo: son

mamá: mom

mata-policía: kill police (nickname for particular bullet)

mentirosa: liar

mi amigo: my friend

mi amor: my love

m'ijo: contraction for *mi hijo,* my son

m'hijita: contraction for *mi hija,* my daughter

nada: nothing

no llores: don't cry (command)

n'ombre: contraction for *no hombre*: No, man. Slang

No pisar el cesped: Don't step on the grass.

No hablo español muy bien: I don't speak Spanish very well.

No vi nada: I did not see anything.

pachanga: party

paletas: popsicles

papí: daddy

pastel de tres leches: three milk cake

pico de gallo: chunky Mexican salsa

pollo con calabaza: chicken with squash

por favor: please

¿Por qué?: Why?

primo (a): cousin

qué bella: how beautiful

¿Qué haces?: What are you doing?

¿Qué pasó?: What happened?

querida: dear, sweetheart, literally "loved"

ranchera: a style of traditional Mexican music

rubio: blond

señor: sir

señora: madam

señorita: miss

sí: yes

taqueria: Mexican restaurant, specializing in tacos and burritos

te amo: I love you

telenovela: soap opera TV show

tío (a): uncle, aunt

tu mamá: your mama

turista: tourist

un idiota: an idiot

una: a

vámanos: let's go

CHAPTER 1

THE *SLAP-SLAP* OF RUBBER soles against asphalt echoed in the darkness somewhere behind Gabriella Benoit.

Chills hopscotched down her bare arms despite the oppressive August heat.

She glanced over her shoulder.

Nothing.

On the nights she left her restaurant after midnight, Gabriella seldom saw anyone other than an occasional homeless man looking for a place to lay his head for the night. Ignoring the drop of sweat that rolled down her temple and tickled her cheek, she turned the key in the front door lock.

The footsteps trod closer. She fisted her fingers around the keys and listened.

A lone cricket chirped. A fly buzzed her ear. Cars zoomed on I-35 South in the distance, their hum white noise in the night.

Long strides. Nothing furtive about them. Someone out for a stroll? Someone who shared her insomniac tendencies? Her brief career as an assistant prosecutor in the district attorney's office had made her paranoid. Another tendency she couldn't shake.

San Antonio, like any major metropolitan city of its size, had its share of crime. It wasn't the big "small town" older folks liked to claim it once was. Her free hand clutching the pepper spray canister attached to her key ring, Gabriella fumbled for her cell phone in her bottomless leather bag.

Her fingers closed around it.

Get it over with, Benoit.

She sucked in air, let it out, and forced herself to back away from the glass double doors adorned with pale-blue wooden trim and the hand-lettered menu she created herself. Praying the breeze was at her back, she whirled, finger on the canister button.

"Gabs, it's me."

The familiar husky voice filled the night air around Gabriella. Fight or flight? The question she always asked herself now when she heard it. "Eli! You scared me."

Eli Cavazos emerged from the shadows, his hands stuffed in the pockets of his faded blue jeans. "That was my intention, *querida*. How many times have I told you not to close by yourself? It's not safe."

"Last time I checked, what I do is no longer any of your business." When they were dating, Eli would park his unmarked PD Crown Vic on the street during his supper break and watch until she drove away in her Mustang. Then he'd go back to work catching the bad guys and making the world safer. Even though she had no need of his protection—or any man's—she found his concern touching. While it lasted. "I'm not kidding. Please stop."

"I have a question for you." He kicked at a rock with the toe of his well-worn size-twelve Nike, sending it skipping across the dirt and weeds that passed for landscaping on the other side of the sidewalk. "Miss Never-Miss-Church-On-Sunday."

Gabriella refused to take the bait. Eli had never attended church with her during the four years they dated. Nor did he deny his faith. He simply refused to talk about it. She'd been hopeful about changing that. Instead, the opportunity had slipped away while she had her back turned. "I don't owe you any answers."

Quite the opposite.

"Don't you believe in forgiveness? I know from my Sunday school days that God is big-time into second chances. Shouldn't you at least be as gracious?"

He couldn't know she asked herself that same question as she lay in bed at night, staring at the ceiling, praying for sleep, knowing it wouldn't come. She wanted to forgive. It would be so much easier than this impasse, and she would feel less like a hypocrite when she sat in the pew on Sunday morning.

Lowering her head so she couldn't see his face with its dark coffee-colored eyes, bronze skin, sculpted cheekbones, and familiar full lips, Gabriella started toward her Mustang in the middle of the parking lot. She always made it a point to park under a security light. "Go home. Get some sleep. You look like death warmed over."

Eli stepped into her path. His Polo cologne wafted around her, a spicy reminder of what she'd lost. His long fingers brushed a strand of hair from her cheek. She'd once loved those fingers and that touch. Sudden heat replaced the earlier chill.

"Are you ever going to forgive me for being a moron, *mi amor*?" he whispered.

"Forgiveness comes with confessing your sin and repenting. You refuse to do either." Gabriella made a show of looking at her wristwatch. "It was crazy busy for a Thursday today—yesterday. I need to get home before it's time to do it all again."

"I told you I came with a bunch of baggage."

"You didn't mention you were planning to open up a suitcase and dump the contents on my head." Her friends had warned her about dating a homicide detective. She'd rejected the stereotype and took her chances because she simply had no choice. Eli was a force of nature. "I'm too tired for our usual rehash. I'm going home."

She slipped past him, acutely aware of the gray PD T-shirt stretched tight across his broad chest, the five o'clock shadow that darkened his chin, and the fact that he needed a haircut. The feel of his wiry curls under her fingertips and the cool metal of the scissors in her hand as she scolded him about his restless wiggling in her kitchen chair wormed its way into her mind's eye. Every breath brought more of the same familiar ache that radiated from her chest and brought tears to the surface. Six months of this impasse, and Eli still refused to give up.

"Drive carefully, *por favor*." His words settled around her like a favorite jean jacket. "I'm off duty. I could follow you home if you want."

A sudden image of her sister Natalie's expression should she see Eli trailing up the porch steps behind Gabriella made her wince. *Idiot*, Natalie would think before going back to the suspense novels that occupied her sleepless nights. But her kids—should they learn of his reappearance—would be thrilled. What kid wouldn't love a guy who insisted ice cream was a food group and allowed himself to be subjected to camping in a pup tent in the backyard in the middle of July in Texas? "It's one o'clock in the morning. I'm too tired to fence with you. Go home. Sleep. Please."

His lips twisted in a crooked grin. He ducked his head and swiveled without another word. The sound of his swift footsteps on the pavement followed by the slamming of the car door told her he'd received the message. For the moment, anyway. A few seconds later, the engine revved as if he'd jammed his foot on the gas pedal with his Charger still in Park.

Gabriella inhaled. Her shoulders relaxed on the exhale. The desire to bawl like a jilted teenage girl subsided. Glad to be out of Eli's line of sight, she rounded the back end of the Mustang. He'd sit there, mulling his transgressions until she drove away.

She inserted her key into the door lock, careful not to scratch the paint on her '73 classic. Every muscle in her thirty-four-year-old body ached for rest. For a Thursday night it had been busy at Courtside. Searing steaks for the law enforcement crowd paid the bills, but she couldn't fall into her bed until she'd taken a shower to scour the grease from her face and hair. Along with the faint fear of failure. She walked a tightrope every day, trying to keep her restaurant in the black. Starting any business involved risks, but restaurants were at the top of the failure list. Too many options, too much cheap, fast food.

Clean cotton nightgown. Clean cotton sheets. Clean. Maybe somehow she would find the clean start she craved. She grabbed the door handle.

"Gabriella Benoit." A breathless voice unfurled around her like tendrils of smoke wafting from the shadows. "Gabriella."

The effect was the same as if the whisper had been a scream. Her cell phone slipped from her fingers. It hit the asphalt with an ominous cracking sound, then skittered away. She froze. Her fingers went numb around the pepper spray.

"Gabriella Benoit?"

A man stumbled from the portico that sheltered the slender porch in front of the law office doors. His mouth gaped in a brown face that appeared strangely childish in the building's harsh security lights.

In one hand he clutched a gun. The torturous sound of his breathing filled the night air. "Are you Gabriella Benoit?"

Run.

Shoot the pepper spray in his face.

Pick up the cell phone.

Call 911.

Call Eli.

Her muscles refused to take orders. She forced her mouth open. No sound came out.

The young man dropped to his knees. One hand clutched at his chest. His curled fingers were red and shiny in the streetlights.

The gun clattered on the asphalt. He didn't seem to notice. "Por favor, are you Gabriella?"

"You're hurt!" Words, finally. Noise. Her voice sounded like someone else's—someone scared spitless and about to pee her pants. He knew her name. "Do I know you?".

He swayed and groaned.

Gabriella shot forward. She knelt to catch him before he hit the ground. Her knees didn't want to hold her up anyway. "I'll call an ambulance. Or, look, there's a cop parked on the street over there—just let me go get him. He can help you. I promise."

The man's fingers closed around her wrist in a bruising grip. "Jake . . . he . . ."

Jake? Her brother Jake?

The man keeled over.

Gabriella caught him and lowered him to the ground.

Tears rolled down his temples into fine brown hair. His breath came in ragged spurts. "Jake . . ."

"Jake? Jake did what?" She glanced around. Phone. She needed the phone. It was lost in the shadows. She tugged her arm from his slackening grip. "I'm right here. I'm looking for my phone. I won't leave you. I promise. How do you know my brother?"

"He said . . ."

"He said what?" She crawled toward the shadows. Rocks and sticks bit into her palms. Her fingers touched plastic. She grabbed the phone and scrambled to her feet. "It'll be all right. I'll call for help. Is Jake hurt? Where is he? Do I need to send help for him?"

The man didn't answer.

She turned back to him. "I don't know who you are, but—"

His head lolled back. His eyes were open, staring.

Little details stood out in stark relief against the lights. A small scar on his chin, a mole on his lip. His cheeks were smooth. He wasn't even old enough to shave.

With shaking fingers, she called 911.

"Nine-one-one, what's your emergency?"

"A man has been shot."

"Where, ma'am?"

Talking fast, she relayed the information and disconnected. She jolted to her feet and darted down the street. "Eli! Eli!"

He shoved open his door and unfolded his long legs. *"¿Qué pasó?"*

"A man's injured. He's been shot. He has . . . had a gun."

His Smith & Wesson M&P40 already drawn, Eli sprinted past her. It took him a scant few seconds to cover the ground to where the man sprawled. With one foot he nudged the weapon away and then crouched next to him. He touched his neck, then looked up at her, shaking his head.

"He's dead." He rose and pulled his cell phone from his hip pocket. "Are you all right?"

"I'm fine." Gabriella made a supreme effort not to throw herself at him, to that place where she could feel his familiar, steady heartbeat, lean on his solid chest, and inhale the comforting scent of his cologne. "He came out of nowhere. He knew my name. He said—"

"Are you hurt?" Eli grabbed her arm and jerked her from the shadow cast by a scraggly live oak and into the light. "Is that blood? *Are you hurt?*"

"He's a kid. He's just a kid." Gabriella ripped her arm from his grasp. She glanced down. Red stains soaked the front of her white polo shirt. "I tried to help."

"Of course you did, mi amor. You always do." His voice roughened. "He knew your name?"

"My name and Jake's."

Ignoring the blooming concern on his face, Gabriella ducked her head and scrolled through the favorites in her phone until she found Jake's. She punched his name. A few rings and her brother's husky, amused message played. *"Can't talk now. You know what to do."*

She swallowed, determined not to bawl. "It's Gabriella. Call me, Jake. Please. Call me."

CHAPTER 2

————

MURDER TRUMPED NATURE'S BEAUTY every time. Friday morning arrived in streaks of pink and orange in a bank of wispy clouds over the downtown San Antonio skyline in what would've been a beautiful sunrise if it weren't for the dead man lying on the ground.

Detective Eli Cavazos squinted against the light. When he and Gabriella had dated, they both worked nights. More than once in the four years they dated, he picked her up from the restaurant before dawn and they took off for the coast. They watched the sunrise together as he drove too fast on I-37 South. Neither found a need to talk in the face of the astonishing, always-fleeting beauty.

Those epic road trips that began with his Big Red soda and her iced mocha latte and ended with both of them sunburned and covered with sand on a Port Aransas beach stood out as some of the many highlights of the longest relationship of Eli's life.

Trying to ignore the anger that billowed around Gabby like South Texas summer and a gritty fatigue that had nothing to do with lack of sleep, he squatted next to the medical examiner's investigator. "Well?"

"No ID on him. Male, Hispanic, just a kid, no more than twenty, twenty-one, maybe. He was shot at least two times that are apparent in a cursory examination. For once time of death isn't an issue, thanks to your girlfriend." The man's fat face creased in a grin that featured teeth yellowed by coffee stains. "Oops, she's not your girlfriend anymore, is she?"

Eli straightened. "You really are a jerk—"

"Detective Cavazos, you want to talk about the gun?" The CSU investigator nudged the yellow tent next to the dead man's weapon. She stood and stepped between Eli and the ME. "It's a doozy."

Eli rolled an unlit cigarette between his thumb and forefinger, then tucked it behind his ear. "Whatcha got?"

"It's an FN Five-seveN semiautomatic. Kevlar piercing—"

"I know. *Mata-policía*. Cop killer bullets." Eli's hand went to his side before he could stop himself. The pain still kept him awake when he tried to close his eyes and sleep. Which wasn't too often these days. "Serial number?"

"Yep."

The gun, along with many assault rifles and automatic weapons, could be bought in the typical sporting goods store in any town in the country, but not in Mexico. That made it a hot commodity with the drug cartels and made Texas the center of their black-market trade. But this one hadn't made it out of the country. "Let me know what turns up when you run it."

Her black curls bobbing, the investigator nodded and trotted away.

Eli cranked his neck from side to side. He tugged the cigarette from behind his ear, then put it back. Dunbar had finished interviewing Gabby. From the look on his acne-pitted face, Eli's partner hadn't extracted the information he wanted. Eli moved toward him. "You want me to talk with her?"

Dunbar pulled a toothpick from his lips and twirled it between skinny fingers. "She hates you. Besides, I don't think she knows anything more than she's saying. She doesn't know the guy or why he'd show up outside her restaurant talking about her brother."

"She might know something without realizing it." Gabby didn't hate him. She loved him. And she hated him. "Let me try . . . It can't hurt."

Not much, anyway.

Dunbar scratched his long, bony nose and grimaced. The guy had a face only a mother—and his wife of twenty years—could love. "I'm going to see if I can find the location where the shooting occurred. It has to be close."

Eli gave him a thumbs-up and headed toward Gabby. He studied her tense body propped against the cherry-red classic Mustang, waxed and buffed to a high sheen. She looked more like a basketball player than the best dessert chef in town. She was only a few inches shorter than he was, but her black pants and white polo shirt hung on her. She'd lost some weight. That didn't surprise him. When she was stressed, she baked but she didn't eat. Something else for which he could be rightfully blamed.

Her straight blonde hair was swept back in a long ponytail, but her bangs, damp with perspiration, hung in her eyes. His hand twitched with the desire to smooth them back for her. The PTSD counselor kept telling him to give her space. He was wasting a lot of the department's money not taking what some would consider good advice. *Off-limits, buddy.*

Her head bent so her hair hid her face, Gabby studied the cell phone. Eli quickened his pace. "Did you get a hold of Jake?"

"My battery's dead."

"I'm sure he'll have an explanation for all this."

She raked Eli with a look that should've left deep gouges on his face. Her baby-blue eyes were stained red. "Don't patronize me. The guy knew my name. He knew my brother's name." She faltered on the word *brother.* She chewed her lower lip. "He died right in front of me."

"I know, *querida.*" Eli tugged his notebook from his back pocket. "Are you sure you don't know him?"

"As I told Dunbar at least five times, I've never seen the guy before."

"When was the last time you talked to your brother?"

Gabby picked at a hangnail for a couple of seconds. "Two weeks, maybe. He talks to Natalie more . . . because she's . . . you know . . . at home more."

Eli let the painful reference slide. Gabriella couldn't seem to let go of guilt for something that wasn't her fault. "Did you talk about work? Did he say if he was still on the task force?"

"You know how he is. We really didn't talk about his work much, but he was still in Laredo, so he must've been. I teased him about living the life of a gorgeous young bachelor whom all the women swoon over." She stopped, swallowed. "If you'd give me your phone, I'd call him and ask him if knows what this is about."

Her gaze roamed toward the yellow tarp that covered the victim. Eli moved so he blocked her line of sight and handed her his phone.

She turned her back on him and began punching numbers. Her shoulders slumped, and she mumbled something he couldn't hear. Unable to stop himself, he laid his hand on her shoulder and squeezed. She shook it off. "I can't remember . . . I had his number programmed into my cell . . . I can't remember the last two digits." She took a few steps toward the street. "Okay, okay, I've got it."

She straightened, did an about-face, and marked the number. After a pause, the hope in her face drained away, leaving a sick, gray look. "Jake? Jake are you there? Pick up if you're there."

She stuffed her free hand into her pants pocket and bit her lip. Her expression was the I-will-not-cry-in-front-of-Eli look. "Gabs, querida—"

She cleared her throat. "Hey, Jake, it's Sis. When you get this message, could you call me, please? I need to talk to you. Call the house phone. My cell is dead. Call. Please." She disconnected, then turned toward her car. "I'm going to Laredo."

"Give Jake time to call you back."

"Something's wrong. I'm going."

"Not alone, you're not."

She snorted. "Why? I do just about everything alone now."

She never was one to pull any punches. Made her a great prosecutor back in the days when he'd been in vice, before she'd decided to ditch her law degree and cook for a living. "I know that, and I'm sorrier than you can ever imagine. Stop punishing me long enough for me to do my job, and I'll help you."

"I can find my brother on my own." Anger shimmered like lightning in her blue eyes. "You stay here and figure out who killed this man and why. I'll figure out how Jake's involved."

She pulled her keys from her pocket and moved to unlock the car door.

Eli snatched the keys from her hand. She tried to grab them back. Not fast enough. "Give me my keys!"

"If this guy's death has anything to do with Jake, looking for him could be dangerous. You're not going alone." His cell phone to his ear, Eli whirled and strode across the parking lot and along the street toward Main Plaza. Gabby scampered alongside him, still protesting. She was one stubborn woman, but then he'd always known that. "Just let me talk to Dunbar, and then we'll go. Together."

Together.

This case might be his second chance with her.

His last chance.

CHAPTER 3

———

GABRIELLA KNEW THAT LOOK. Still talking on his cell phone, Eli whirled and strode across the street headed toward the Bexar County Justice Center. Dunbar had found something. Something important. The hunt was on.

She raced after Eli. He glanced back and sped up. He darted down the narrow street between the granite facade of the justice center and the old Bexar County Courthouse. He shoved the phone in his back pocket. "Go back to the restaurant. You can wait inside. Turn on the AC. They'll need your shirt for evidence. You can change."

"What did they find?"

"Looks like the primary scene."

"Where?"

"Main Plaza."

The victim had staggered two blocks to her restaurant. Why hadn't he simply parked at the restaurant if he was searching for her?

They might never know.

The crime scene tape was already up on the southeast corner of the historic plaza with its bronze pavers and flat fountains that offered a cooling mist for tourists passing from the River Walk to Market Square.

A uniformed officer guarding the tape lifted it for Eli. When Gabriella attempted to pass through, he lowered it and offered her a stern stare. She stopped, but not without returning the stare with her own. She wouldn't back off. She needed to get closer. She wanted to get closer. She wanted to go to Laredo, but Eli had her keys.

Only a few feet away but totally beyond her reach, he peered into the shattered driver's-side window of a battered maroon Mitsubishi Galant, his arms crossed as if he was afraid he'd accidently touch something.

She tapped her Reebok on the pavement and studied the car. Were those bloodstains? How much of his own trauma did Eli relive every time he dealt with a shooting victim? She manhandled the memories to the ground. It didn't help to relive them. Instead, she studied the scene. What did this have to do with Jake? How did a shooting off Main Plaza connect with an ATF agent? Just after midnight on an early Friday morning, traffic—vehicular and pedestrian—would've been light.

The courthouse and the justice center wouldn't open for another hour. Government workers were just beginning to trickle into the eleven-story Municipal Plaza building. Not much in the way of witnesses.

A homeless man still slept on a bench. An old lady in a ratty green sweater far too warm for August fed bread crumbs to the pigeons. From the look on her face, she probably couldn't produce her own name. The officers would interview everyone, but it seemed unlikely they knew a thing about the shooting.

The scene appeared enticingly normal, until Gabriella's gaze landed on the car. Shattered glass on the sidewalk sparkled in the sun. Was there anyone inside? She inched forward.

The uni squared off in front of her. "That's as far as you go, ma'am."

"There's no body in the car, is there?" She strained to see around him. He leaned into her line of sight. She drilled him with her best prosecutorial frown. "Is there . . . another body?"

Eli turned at the query. Their gazes collided. His eyes were black in the dappled sunlight filtering through the branches of a huge heritage live oak. He shook his head. Gabriella breathed and nodded.

No body. No Jake.

The CSU investigator crowed from where she crouched behind the open car door. "I've got blood. There's blood on the steering wheel, the inside of the door, the handle. There's splatter on the seat and the dashboard." She stood, her face a study in focused enthusiasm. "It looks like a couple of slugs are embedded in the car's upholstery."

Eli joined her behind the open car door. Gabriella strained to see or hear something—anything—that would tell her who the dead man was and what it had to do with Jake.

Another officer began rolling crime scene tape from meter to meter. Gabriella slipped inside it. "Huh-uh." The officer slapped a hand on her arm.

"Don't touch me." She shrugged away, rubbing her wrist.

"I don't want to have to arrest a fellow officer's girlfriend for interfering in a crime scene investigation." Something about the officer's tone said he really wouldn't mind at all. Eli's buddies had closed ranks around him, and somehow Gabriella had become the bad guy in their scenario.

"We're no longer dating, and you know it."

She stomped back a few feet, then stopped. Eli strode toward her, a backpack in one gloved hand, his gaze assessing, like he was approaching a dangerous criminal. The grooves at the corners of his eyes and mouth spoke of the pressure he put on himself with every case. "Did you get an ID?"

Eli nodded at the officer, who immediately backed off. When he turned to her, Eli's features were opaque, his eyes unreadable. He'd retreated into that far, far place of cop. Cop first, cop second, cop third. That was the Eli she truly knew. "The car is registered to an Alberto Garza. He has a Laredo address. His billfold was in the backpack. From the looks of the photo on the driver's license, it's our dead guy. Age twenty-two. Does the name ring a bell?"

Twenty-two. A baby. "No. I've never meet him before."

Eli pointed to an advanced calculus textbook without touching it, confirming the horrific thought. "It appears he was a student at UTSA and enrolled in summer school."

The sound of the trunk popping stopped Gabriella from saying something stupid, like he was just a kid or how could a college student end up dead at her feet? How did any of this happen? She knew how it happened. On paper. She'd never lived it.

"It's weird, though. The one thing we didn't find was a cell phone. What college kid doesn't have a cell phone?"

"Everyone has a cell phone."

"Exactly. And a laptop. No laptop found. But that could be in his apartment or dorm, wherever he lived."

Phones were a gold mine of information. Texts, emails, social media. Especially for a college kid. "It didn't slide under the mats or fall into the backseat?"

"They've been over every square inch of the interior." Eli shrugged. "We'll get warrants for his cell phone records if we don't find it. We can still trace his social media activity online, but I want to see who he's been texting."

"Like Jake."

"Exactly."

The CSU investigator's face appeared over the trunk lid. "Jackpot. Detective Cavazos, over here."

Eli left Gabriella standing there, outside the circle. Just as she'd always been.

No, not this time. This time, it involved Jake. She would bulldoze the inner circle if necessary.

A series of flashes indicated photos were being taken behind the trunk lid. Then the investigator laid her camera in her bag and smoothed a plastic tarp on the ground next to the car. Gabriella stood on her tiptoes to see. The crime scene investigator disappeared behind the trunk lid. Reappeared and gently laid a weapon on the tarp. Two more followed.

Between the four years Gabriella had spent in the DA's office and the four years she dated Eli, she'd absorbed a wealth of information about the endless array of weapons available in a right-to-shoot state. She sold her own gun when Natalie and the kids moved in with her. The first weapon looked like a Walther G22 assault-style rifle.

Gabriella rubbed the goose bumps up and down her arms. What was a college student doing with this kind of firepower in his trunk? Did it somehow connect with Jake's involvement in the ATF task force? He never shared about his work, and that was fine with her. When she opened the restaurant, she'd wanted nothing more than a clean, fresh start. No more nightmares about home invasions and murders of retired schoolteachers who came home and interrupted a burglary in progress by a bunch of drugged-out teenage thugs.

"Hey, Gabriella."

The familiar voice jerked her from her thoughts. Either shock or exhaustion had made her oblivious to the approach of Deacon Alder. She turned and smacked into the *Express-News* reporter's open arms. His hug was quick, hard. He smelled of spearmint gum and spicy aftershave. "Are you all right? I heard some guy died in front of the restaurant. What happened?"

"I'm fine. Really." Gabriella eased back from his space. "What are you doing here? Aren't you off on Fridays?"

"A little birdie told me there was possibly a drug-related hit." His gaze still concerned, he squeezed her arm and let his hand drop. Deacon could slay with his sapphire-blue eyes fringed by long, dark eyelashes. His wiry build and innocuous polos and khaki pants didn't attract much attention, but one look in those eyes and he had a person's full attention. "I happen to be working on an enterprise piece on how the cartel wars are slopping onto San Antonio. Then I find out the victim stumbled around in front of my favorite steak joint and accosted the doctor of dessert. How could I not rush to the defense of the high priestess of pie?"

"That's sweet of you. How could you find out so fast?" Gabriella let her gaze sweep the mass of law enforcement personnel that swarmed the scene. Homicide, the crime scene unit, the medical examiner's office, traffic control. Which one among them thought it would be a great idea to call the paper's number one—at least in terms of enthusiasm—investigative crime reporter? "Who tipped you off?"

"Don't worry. It's not them." Deacon flipped open his notebook and tugged a pen from behind his ear. "They heard the call go out for the CSU at the former mayor's legacy plaza. Plus a homicide. Crime on Main Plaza is really going to irk him. The weekend guy called me. Tell me what happened. Did a guy really keel over and die at your feet in front of the restaurant? Did you know him? Did he try to hurt you?"

"Too bad the chief is out of town." The chief of police felt it was important to show up for impromptu news conferences whenever a high-profile crime attracted media. "You'd have your story without breaking a sweat."

"I don't want the official line. I want a firsthand account from an eyewitness."

Avoiding the questions would do no good. Deacon's tenacity made him excel at his job. Gabriella laid out the bare bones, leaving out the salient detail regarding the mention of Jake's name. Deacon was a friend, but he also wrote articles for a newspaper that put more than a hundred thousand copies on the street every day and reached many, many more through its website and social media.

Absently rubbing the bridge of his nose, Deacon shook his head. "That's really bizarre. He didn't—?"

"You need to get a life." Eli stepped between Gabriella and Deacon. He clutched an unlit cigarette in one hand. When Gabriella opened her mouth, he stuck it behind one ear. "Seriously, why are you talking to this ghoul?"

Eli didn't like reporters, but he particularly hadn't liked Deacon since he'd done a series the previous year on SAPD's increased citizens' complaints regarding police brutality. In addition to his articles, he wrote a blog called *Crime Beat* that allowed him to express his editorial opinions, and he was nothing if not blunt.

Or maybe it was because Deacon so often sat at the counter in her restaurant, eating her desserts and debating politics, religion, and life with Gabriella two or three nights a week.

"Is this your case?" Deacon's pen danced over the notebook. "What can you tell me about the victim? What was the cause of death? Do you know why he contacted Gabriella?"

"That's Miss Benoit to you. Ongoing investigation. Call the PIO."

"Come on, Detective, cut me some slack." Deacon gave him a sad puppy-dog look. "We're on the same side. Good guys against the bad guys."

"Why would I want to help an ambulance chaser like you?" Eli rolled his eyes at Gabriella. "Not to mention a woman chaser."

"No one is chasing anyone." Heat crept up Gabriella's neck and across her cheeks. Great. Like some teenager in a love triangle. "Don't make it personal—"

"It's okay, *Miss Benoit*. I imagine it must be incredibly hard to move on after dating a woman like you. I know I couldn't." Deacon's lips curved in a smile, but his tone said he was dead serious. "Of course, I can't understand going out for hamburger when you've got steak waiting for you. Or in this case why go out for store-bought oatmeal cookies when you've got tiramisu within arm's reach."

Gabriella caught Eli's arm as his fist went up. "Eli."

He stared at her, his eyes blazing coals in a stony face. "It seems like you've talked to everyone in this town about our problems—everyone but me."

He whirled and walked away.

Trying to get her equilibrium back, Gabriella studied her shoes. She hadn't talked to Deacon about Eli. Deacon lived and breathed crime reporting. He talked to cops regularly. And cops were like old biddies, always gossiping.

"Are you okay?" Deacon's expression softened. "Sorry, I didn't mean to make things harder for you."

"Antagonizing him won't help you get a story." She forced herself to meet his gaze. His face was smooth and clean shaven. He had none of the lines Eli's face bore. Lines that came from living on the edge of a razor blade for three years in vice before he moved to homicide. "He could make it really tough for you to get information. Besides, you know there's nothing going on between you and me."

"It's not my fault if he's seeing something that's not there." His eyes blazing with undisguised anger, Deacon squeezed her hand, his palm warm. "He's the moron. I would never do what he did. It's a shame you can't let him go. You could do so much better. I promise you that."

"What makes you think I can't let him go?"

"It's written all over your face whenever you look at him." The anger flickered and turned to ashes. "I've never understood why smart women allow men to treat them badly. There are plenty of good men out there who know how to treat women right."

Gabriella breathed into the onslaught of emotion. Deacon was smart, funny, handsome, and a decent human being. Still, he was a good friend, nothing more or less. "I appreciate your friendship and your willingness to be my guinea pig for new desserts."

He grinned. "In that area, you can do no wrong. Now, is there anything I can do to help? Do you want a ride home after I finish here?"

"I can't leave . . . not without my . . ." She bit her lower lip, already raw from a night of chewing on it. "You could let me use your phone, however."

"Anything for you. Just promise me there's a slice of pineapple-upside-down cake in my future." He dropped the phone in her hand and wrapped his fingers around hers. His gaze probed hers. "I'm serious, anything you need. You can count on me."

Swallowing the sudden lump in her throat, Gabriella nodded. "Thanks."

The single syllable escaped in a whisper.

He nodded and strode away.

Aware of damp perspiration collecting on her neck and face now that the early morning sun was in full bloom, Gabriella sought the shade of the biggest tree in the plaza and contemplated the phone. Natalie had an extra set of keys, but Gabriella didn't want to wake her sister. Or make her drive downtown with the kids. Not in her condition.

She'd call Victoria Richards instead. Vic didn't have keys to the car, but she did have keys to the restaurant. She could take care of getting the place open and ready for the Southtown crowd that came in to grab breakfast on their way to work on Friday morning.

Groggy with sleep, it took Victoria a few minutes to comprehend the story. When she finally strung a few sentences together, it wasn't the murder she seemed interested in. "So you want me to open the restaurant for you today so you can go to Laredo to look for Jake—once you get your keys back from Eli, who insists he's coming with you?"

"Right." Gabriella ignored Victoria's obvious curiosity. "He thinks he's going with me to find Jake, but he's not. No way."

The pause on the line told Gabriella her employee was considering how much she could say and not lose her job. Considering Victoria had been her second-in-command for two years and weathered the blow-out arguments and the aftermath of the breakup, they both knew she could say quite a lot. "He's a detective, he solves crimes for a living, and you don't want his help? Come on, sister, what's the real problem? Are you afraid a couple of hours in a car with him will change something? You broke up six months ago. You keep saying you're over it. Put your money where your mouth is."

"It doesn't matter if we drive to Belize together, nothing is going to change. Eli didn't exactly set the bar high, and you know it."

"Eli was extremely messed up for obvious reasons. He's straightened himself out." Victoria didn't know when to give up. "Luis says he's seeing a PD therapist. He even let us drag him to church one Sunday. Forgive him—you know you want to."

"Why are you siding with him?" Her stomach roiling, Gabriella smoothed her dirt-and-bloodstained shirt. "Can you come in early or not?"

"I want you to be as happy as Luis and I are. Luis says Eli's really trying and you're blowing him off." Victoria sighed. "I'm just saying my piece for a change. And yes, I will come in early."

Victoria's latest boyfriend was a gym rat buddy of Eli's, which meant his opinion wasn't exactly unbiased. "You really can't get what it's like to date a police officer." She lowered her voice, aware of the number of officers swarming around the plaza. "Every day you say good-bye like it's the last time you'll see him. Literally."

The memory of the ticking clock in the hospital waiting room filled her head, increasing in volume and velocity until the *dong-dong-dong* like a cathedral bell crowded out all rational thought.

She blinked and rubbed her temple. "Anyway, now's not the time. Just open the restaurant, please. The banana cream pie is in the walk-in. I also made apple-cranberry turnovers and double-fudge macadamia nut cookies."

"Avoid the subject all you want." Victoria's sniff was loud over the line. "Doesn't change anything. I hope Jake's okay. Call me from Laredo. And be nice. To Eli."

Gabriella disconnected.

"So what aren't you telling me?"

She turned to find Deacon hovering within inches. How much of that conversation had he heard? Heat scorched her face. "I don't know what you mean."

"Come on, Gabriella. Spill it. The CSU gal says this guy dragged himself from the Plaza to Courtside. Seems like he was looking for someone specific. That someone being you."

Gabriella shut her mouth tight and counted the benches in the plaza.

Deacon crossed his arms, his head cocked to one side, his thick, shiny raven hair spilling across his forehead. "I have hours until my deadline."

She shifted and studied the beautiful French Gothic architecture of San Fernando Cathedral.

"There has to be a reason the victim came to you before he died. What did he say to you?" Deacon stepped into her line of sight. "I'm good at reading faces, and this guy scared you."

Alberto Garza's face, misshapen with pain and horror, appeared in her mind's eye. "Yeah, he came out of the shadows at midnight, whispering my name, and he dropped dead at my feet. It would've scared you too!"

"He knew your name. He did know you. Whoa! What else?"

"No, he didn't know me; he knew Jake." Gabriella cringed and rubbed an eyebrow that seemed to have developed a tic. "Don't you dare print that!"

"Jake? Who's Jake? An old boyfriend?" Deacon stared at her like he was studying a bug under a microscope. "No, a family member. That's it. Anyone ever tell you not to play poker?"

"I'm done talking to you."

She walked away. Deacon followed.

"All I have to do is an internet search to get your family. If he's a brother or whatever, I'll find out." Deacon's declaration carried over the fountains. Dunbar and Eli cast inquiring glances her way. Deacon kept talking. "I'm coming into the restaurant tonight for some of that fabulous *carne asada*. I hope you have banana cream pie on the dessert chalkboard. Or is it strawberry rhubarb pie day?"

Ignoring his continuing commentary, Gabriella sidled past the officer who was busy trying to keep a homeless man from taking a bath in the fountains. She glanced back. Deacon had collared Dunbar and was giving the detective the third degree. Good luck with that. Dunbar would send him right to the Police Department Public Information Office.

Gabriella stopped next to Eli. He didn't look up. He studied the weapon on the ground, a frown etched on his face. Her keys were nowhere in sight. She considered knocking him to the ground and doing a search. Except he had thirty-five pounds—all muscle—on her. And he'd probably enjoy it.

Trying to deep-six her frustration, she focused on the weapon. In Texas, sporting goods stores could sell weapons as long as they ran an instant FBI background check and the buyer was a U.S. citizen with no felonies. But what would a college kid be doing with it? Domestic terrorism?

Eli squatted next to the assault rifle. Either he didn't realize she was there or he was studiously ignoring her. "Eli, what are you thinking? Why would Garza have a weapon like this?" She kept her voice down, glancing back to make sure Deacon hadn't snuck inside the yellow tape. "Do you think he could be some kind of terrorist?" The possibilities were scary.

Eli rubbed his temple with two fingers. "He could be. But it's more likely he was selling it. The cartels use college kids to act as straw buyers. They get paid to buy the guns and turn them over to facilitators who smuggle them out on the same routes used to smuggle drugs in."

Gun smuggling. Jake's area of expertise. Fear ballooned in her stomach, making the coffee she'd consumed slosh in painful waves. "Give me my keys. I have to find Jake."

"*We* will find Jake."

"Give me my keys! I'm going to Laredo . . . to his town house. Today. Now."

"You can't go alone—" Eli's cell phone rang. He held up a large hand. Those hands had propped her up when her parents decided to divorce four years ago. "Hold that thought. Don't go anywhere."

"How can I? You have my keys!" Gabriella whirled and started back to the restaurant and her car. She'd have Victoria give her a ride home to get the spare set.

"Gabs, wait. It's for you."

No one in his right mind would try to reach her through Eli. Not friends or family, certainly. Gabriella sighed and marched back. Careful not to touch him, she grabbed the phone.

"Where are you, Gabby? I've been trying to reach you forever." Her sister sounded stressed. "I've been so worried. What are you doing with Eli? He was my last option, but I figured he's a police officer. If something had happened to you . . ."

Her voice trailed off as if she were reviewing the terrible things that might have happened. Natalie didn't have to imagine the horrible accidents that might occur. She'd lived through one—just barely. Her agitation stoked hot coals of guilt in Gabriella's gut. "I'm so sorry. Hang on and I'll tell you."

She ran quickly through the events of the last seven hours, leaving out the repeated, heated discussions with Eli. A long silence followed.

When she finally spoke, Natalie's tone was tart. "I guess that explains the two ATF agents camped out in our living room."

CHAPTER 4

———

THE HOUSE SMELLED LIKE Feds. Gabriella stormed into the living room. She found a dark-haired guy in a blue suit and Ray-Bans sitting on their overstuffed sofa, along with a shorter blond man in a gray suit. Both seemed more focused on Artemis than Gabriella's precipitous entrance. She could've kissed the old, graying bulldog. He growled again, deep in his throat, his black pug-nosed face a fierce grimace. Jowls joined in with a series of vicious feline hisses from her post on the seat of the oak rocking chair. Her fat tabby body shook with suspicion. Both men squirmed.

Gabriella raised her eyebrows in a silent question to Natalie, who wheeled her chair toward the foyer. "Are you all right?"

Worry made the lines around Natalie's mouth more pronounced in a face much like Gabriella's. Her gray eyes were bright with intelligence behind the blue frames of her glasses. Instead of blonde, her long hair was auburn. "I'm fine. Everything is under control."

"Aunt Gabby, I think they want to arrest you and Mom." Ava, a miniature replica of her mother with ginger hair and an added dose of freckles, sounded surprisingly perky at the possibility. She scooted down another step from her perch on the staircase, her face pressed between the bars of the banister. "Can Eli stay with us if they do?"

"They're not going to arrest Mom—she's in a wheelchair." Cullen bounced on the step next to his younger sister. The look on his face under dark, thick curls reminiscent of his father said he was slightly more worried about the situation. "They're after Uncle Jake. Did he do something bad?"

"Hey, you two, everything is fine." Gabriella squeezed past her sister and squatted in front of them at the bottom of the stairs. "What I need right now is a monster hug and then for you two to skedaddle upstairs and play while we talk to our guests. Can you do that?"

Massive hugs ensued. Their small, wiry bodies smelled of Play-Doh and little kid sweat. Sweet. Swallowing the sudden lump in her throat, Gabriella swatted their behinds and sent them up the stairs.

She turned and squeezed Natalie's shoulders. "Introduce me to our guests."

"Meet ATF Special Agents Crawford and Morales."

Gabriella stalked across the living room to face the firing squad. She scooped up Jowls and hugged her warm body to her chest. Better to go on the offensive. "I'd like to see some identification, please."

The two men stood and made a show of displaying their badges.

The dark-haired guy was Morales. "Your sister says she hasn't seen or talked to your brother in weeks. How about you?"

Gabriella wanted answers, not more questions. "My brother works for you guys. Why don't *you* tell *me* where he is?"

"Miss Benoit, your brother left the office yesterday and never returned. He didn't report in. He's not at home. He's not answering his phone. We tried to ping it, and it appears to be turned off. His town house has been ransacked. His laptop and desktop computers are missing. We're concerned for his safety."

Gabriella sat down in the oak glider rocker that always reminded her of her mother. The two men sat across from her. Artemis waddled over and plopped down at her feet. "An ATF agent fails to report in after fieldwork and you're just now investigating?" Her pulse pounded in her ears. "You're just now telling his family?"

Blond guy, also known as Special Agent Crawford, held up a hand. His fingers were stumpy and covered with fine, pale hair. "I was just telling Mrs. Ferrari, this is a really nice house. You recently opened a restaurant, right?"

"I have a restaurant. My sister, *Dr.* Ferrari, has a psychiatric practice here at the house. What does that have to do with anything?"

"What's a house like this go for? Four, five hundred thousand?" Crawford's gaze bounced from the stone fireplace to the original Jesse Treviño paintings to the slick hardwood floors and bookshelves filled with first editions her mother collected and brought with her when they moved to San Antonio from New Orleans. "That's a lot of money for two self-employed women with no spouses."

Natalie had come into a small fortune when Paolo died, but that was none of these yokels' business. She'd used a portion of it to retro-fit their childhood home to make it accessible—as accessible as a two-story house could be. A first-floor study became Natalie's bedroom. "My parents had the house built when my dad was chief of surgery at University Hospital and my mother was a tenured professor of English Literature at UTSA. Natalie and Jake and I grew up here."

"Your parents passed and left it to you?"

"What does this have to do with Jake's disappearance?"

"Just trying to get a sense of Special Agent Benoit's family. Where might he go if he was in trouble."

"What exactly was Jake working on?"

"Where are your parents?"

The guy was a plodder. Gabriella glanced at Natalie. She shrugged and offered a thin smile. It hurt to say the words aloud, but they had nothing for which to be ashamed. "Divorced. My dad is back in New Orleans, where he's originally from. Our mother is in London, her place of birth."

With her new husband. But these guys didn't need to know that.

"Not close, are you?"

None of Morales's business. Or anyone else's. Growing up in a house filled with doctors, scientists, writers, musicians, and philosophers who engaged in wild political and philosophical arguments had woven them together in a way that had made them inseparable. Until three years ago when their mother did the unthinkable. The unforgivable. "We were. Once."

"I'll need addresses and telephone numbers."

"Where was Jake going when he left the office yesterday?"

"Special Agent Benoit was involved in a sensitive operation that we expected to come to a head last night. He told his boss he would be back in the afternoon with new information."

"He was . . . undercover . . . doing what? With whom?"

Crawford shifted in his seat. He and his partner exchanged glances. They were shifty-looking guys. The definition of *shifty* remained a mystery, but she knew it when she saw it. Crawford answered. "Not undercover. He was dealing with some informants who'd agreed to cooperate in our investigation in exchange . . . on certain terms."

"And this had to do with gun smuggling by one of the cartels?" A guess based on the weapons in the dead man's car but an educated one.

Crawford pursed fat lips and shook his head. "I didn't say that. I'm not at liberty to divulge the details of our operation. We've been on this for nearly eighteen months and we don't want—we won't—do anything to jeopardize it."

"Our brother is missing. I don't give a flying—"

The front door flew open and banged against the inside wall. Gabriella winced. Only Eli would make that kind of entrance. He strode into the house like he owned the place. He had changed out of street clothes into a charcoal-gray suit and black silk tie. That didn't make him look any less like a guy itching for a street fight. "What do they want?"

Jowls and Artemis immediately abandoned Gabriella and scampered—Jowls scampered, Artemis managed an admirable trot—toward their favorite meal ticket. Pounding on the steps said Cullen and Ava were about to do the same thing. "Eli, you're supposed to be solving a murder. I can handle this."

Crawford and Morales leaned forward. "Murder?" Morales's hand went to a pen in his pale-pink dress shirt pocket. "Who's this?"

Eli took his time hugging children and petting animals with a studied nonchalance. The pulse in his jaw gave his tension away. He turned to face the two men. "Show me yours and I'll show you mine."

Three males went through the mine-is-bigger-than-yours badge skirmish, the air heavy with posturing testosterone.

"What is your involvement with Benoit?" Morales hurled the first spear.

"Kids, why don't you go get the ice cream out of the freezer." Eli glanced at his black sports watch. "It's eleven o'clock. Close enough to lunchtime. How about banana splits? And a fudge sundae for Aunt Gabriella—she's having a really bad day. Knowing your aunt as I do, I'm thinking you've got all the fixings you need."

"There's no ice cream in this house for you." Natalie's tone was reminiscent of their mother's when her teenagers missed curfew. "I'm sure you understand."

"Understood."

Eli jerked his head toward the men. Natalie nodded. "Go on, kids, but don't make a mess."

Screeching like mini-banshees hyped up on caffeine, Ava and Cullen roared from the living room. "Eli's back! He's back."

Not back. So not back. Gabriella opened her mouth to protest. Eli shook a finger at her. Who did he think he was?

"A kid by the name of Alberto Garza died in front of Gabriella in the parking lot of her restaurant around midnight. One gunshot to the chest. Before he died, he mentioned Gabriella's brother—by name." Eli eased into the worn cream-colored, brushed-leather chair with matching ottoman where he used to sit after Natalie let him in the house on Sunday mornings. He'd pull Gabriella onto his lap when she arrived home from church so he could read the funnies to her. "I'm thinking that name means something to you two."

Morales looked at Crawford. Crawford studied the hardwood floor under his feet as if trying to decode a secret message inscribed there.

"Okay." Eli stretched his long legs and leaned back in the chair. Looking for all the world like someone about to take a much-needed nap. "Let's talk about the weapons Garza had in the trunk of his car, which we found parked at Main Plaza, the driver's-side window shot out."

"What weapons?"

"You share. I'll think about sharing."

"Look, Officer—"

"Detective."

"Detective Cavazos, this is a multiagency task force operation involving not only the U.S. Bureau of Alcohol, Tobacco, Firearms and Explosives, but the FBI and Immigration and Customs Enforcement." Morales sucked in air, his face red from the effort to spit out all those fancy names. "It is designed to take down gun smugglers who have supplied as many as thirteen thousand assault-style rifles to drug cartels in the last year. More than four thousand people have been killed by illegal weapons in Mexico in the last year alone, six hundred of them police officers. Do you get my drift? One agent, one dead college kid, cannot be allowed to compromise this operation."

Eli smiled. "I never said Garza was a college student."

Morales didn't smile back. "Be that as it may."

"Since when is the U.S. government concerned about murders of Mexican citizens in Mexico?" Gabriella joined Eli in the fray. "I would've thought you would be focused on crimes that affect U.S. citizens—that tends to be the American way."

"Oh, don't let them fool you into thinking this is some kind of altruistic effort to help our neighbor." Eli spoke before the Feds could respond. "Washington has known for years that the guns are being used by cartels that smuggle drugs into this country. Those drugs kill

American citizens. Drug dealers use these weapons to kill our law enforcement officers too. Isn't that right?"

"Again, be that as it may." Morales had a sour look on his face. "This is a top priority for the Justice Department. We will bring down this smuggling ring. No individual will stand in the way of completing the mission."

He glanced as his cohort. Crawford nodded. Morales focused on Gabriella. "We're not just looking for your brother because he's dropped out of sight."

Jowls meowed a pitiful high-pitched meow. Gabriella loosened her grip. "What do you mean?"

"Last night, Laredo authorities found one of our . . . informants shot to death on the bank of the Rio Grande a few miles from downtown Laredo." Morales's somber expression spoke volumes. "Jake Benoit's service weapon was found at the scene. Laredo PD officers believe it to be the murder weapon. They've decided your brother is a person of interest in a homicide investigation."

Jake was wanted for murder.

CHAPTER 5

———

IDIOTS. THE LAREDO PD thought Jake was a murderer. The rushing sound in Gabriella's ears made it hard to think. Natalie's cry of disbelief pierced the fog. "It's okay, Sis." Her attorney experience kicked into overdrive. "It's totally circumstantial. This dead informant was involved in gun smuggling and probably drug smuggling. If—and that's an enormous *if*—Jake killed him, it was likely in self-defense. And why would he leave his weapon at the scene? He's a law enforcement officer. He'd never willingly give up his weapon."

"Agreed. The question is, why did he leave the scene?" Morales's tone suggested he thought she might actually have the answer. "We're concerned for his well-being since he hasn't called in or returned to work."

Because he'd been forced to leave? Gabriella's stomach heaved. The image of her grinning brother shoving suitcases in the back of his SUV the day he'd moved to Houston for his first assignment with the ATF flitted through her mind. "He would never do anything to compromise his work. What do you think happened on that riverbank?"

"Honestly? We don't know." Morales rubbed bloodshot eyes. "That's one of the many reasons we need to talk to him. Miss Benoit—Gabriella—your brother is one of us. If he's in trouble, we want to help him. If he's done something he shouldn't have, we want to know why. We need to find him before Laredo PD does."

Crawford dropped a business card on the mahogany coffee table that overflowed with food magazines and restaurant supply catalogs. "If either one of you hear from your brother, please notify us immediately."

33

Both agents stood. Eli and Gabriella did the same. "If you hear from our brother, you are expected to notify *us* immediately." Gabriella stretched to her full five-ten height. She extracted a Courtside business card from her wallet. "I need to charge my cell phone, but it'll be back in service shortly. You may also call our home number or contact Detective Cavazos."

Morales plucked the card from her hand, peered at it for a second, and then handed it to Crawford, who stuffed it in his suitcoat pocket.

As soon as they were gone, Gabriella hugged Natalie. "Are you okay?"

Her sister nodded, but she held Gabriella tight an extra second or two. "When do we leave?"

"We?" Gabriella touched Natalie's forehead. Cool. Yesterday's fever had abated. "Nat, the kids need you here, and you've been sick."

"I'm fine. I'll get Marty to stay with the kids."

Martin Little, the artist and sometimes carpenter who lived next door, was the epitome of a good neighbor, and the kids loved him. "I know Marty will do it, honey, but what about your appointments? The kids aren't the only ones who need you. So do your patients."

Natalie specialized in juvenile trauma–related disorders. Her young patients relied on her, as did her own kids, to whom she'd been mother and father for two years. "I'll reschedule them. What about you? You have a restaurant to run."

"I can trust Vic to handle things for me for a few days. I've done it before. And you'll be here if she has any problems."

Natalie's silky hair fell forward, hiding her face. Her hands clenched on her lap. "I can help. Jake is my brother too. Don't underestimate my ability to help."

Two years of this. Two years of trying to get used to the idea that her sister, the one who'd been the ballerina in grade school, the one who'd made the high school soccer team, the one who dragged Gabriella from the couch to go jogging, two years of getting used to that fireball being stuck in a chair. "I absolutely know you can help, but the kids need you."

"It doesn't matter." Eli broke in finally, his face lined with empathy that softened his sculpted features. "Neither of you is going anywhere until I can go with you."

Natalie's gaze turned suspicious as it swung to Eli and back to Gabriella. "I'll check on the kids."

Gabriella tugged her phone from her purse and plugged it in while her sister wheeled toward the kitchen. Then she started up the stairs.

"Where are you going?"

She glanced down at Eli, standing at the bottom of the stairs, his hand on the intricately carved oak banister as if he was contemplating following. He wouldn't dare. "To pack—"

"Stop. Just stop." Eli took two steps toward her. She backed up, caught her Reebok on the thick rose carpet runner, and plopped down. Eli moved two steps closer. The stairs creaked under his weight. His knees—worn from years of playing basketball and running—creaked with them. "There is no reason for you to go off half-cocked."

"You heard them. I have to find Jake before Laredo PD does. I'm an attorney, and he'll need one."

"And we'll find him. I'm not letting you go down there and start turning over stones in Laredo. I know what kind of monsters live under those stones. Just give me time to follow up on a couple of things here in town."

Yeah, a 150-mile drive in that horsepower-heavy, shiny black Charger with a hemi followed by adjoining hotel rooms. So cozy. She could insist on rooms on separate floors at opposite ends of the hotel. Why? Because she was afraid the famous Cavazos charm would overcome her sense of betrayal? The sneaking suspicion weaseled its way past her defenses. Never. "You're out of your mind if you think I'm going anywhere with you."

"Go with me, and Natalie's more likely to be willing to stay here.

She won't let you go alone." Eli crossed his arms. "What's more important to you? Keeping that torch of self-righteous anger and indignation toward me blazing or finding your brother?"

Gabriella catapulted down the stairs and jabbed his chest with her finger.

"Self-righteous? *Self-righteous?*" She sputtered and stopped. He was right. Finding Jake was more important. Eli had connections to Laredo PD. He carried not one but two weapons. In a violence-prone border town like Laredo, that would be a huge plus. When she swallowed, her pride and anger made a bitter sandwich that lodged in her throat. "When can you go?"

"As it happens, Garza was from Laredo. Which makes sense if Jake knew him. The Garza family lives there. Sarge agrees the trip is necessary. Which works out well." Eli's phone trilled. He glanced at a text message. "Dunbar will track down friends here and Garza's roommate at the university. I need to hit the Discount Sporting Goods Store on south Roosevelt. After that we can go."

"Why the store?"

"The database shows that's where Garza bought guns—on six different occasions. He spread it out over a six-month period. I need to have as much information as possible before I talk to the family."

"I'm going with you."

"No. You're going to get a few hours of sleep first. You've been up for twenty-four hours straight."

"So have you."

"Try forty-eight hours, minus thirty minutes here or there." Eli's smile matched his sardonic tone. "Worried about me?"

"If you don't let me pack my bag, stick it in the trunk of your car, and leave with you right now, I'm going to Laredo without you. I'll have at least an hour's head start."

His brown eyes contemplated her with a steely gaze that made her want to drop hers. But she didn't. He growled. Did all men sound so childish when they didn't get their way? "Fine. At the store you stay in the car. The powers that be will have a fit if they think I'm allowing you to be involved in this investigation in any way."

"Why *are* you allowing it?"

"Technically, I'm not. I'm just giving you a ride so you can check on your brother." He stared up at her, his face suddenly crowded with familiar emotions. Pain danced with regret while loneliness looked on, always the wallflower. Eli whisked them away just as quickly. "It's the only way I know to keep you out of trouble."

Gabriella whirled and ran up the stairs without responding.

What could she say, really? Eli Cavazos had always been *the* trouble for her. The only question now was whether he was bigger trouble than what waited for her in Laredo.

CHAPTER 6

SO MANY CHOICES FOR murder and mayhem. The sheer number and variety of firearms stuffed into the tiny sporting goods store wedged between a hair salon and a *taquería* on Roosevelt Street was irritating. Eli wiped sweat from his forehead with the back of his sleeve, glad to be out of a blazing afternoon sun. Dozens of hunting rifles, assault rifles, and sniper rifles stood at attention on two long walls, dwarfing the other less eye-catching displays of rods and reels and hunting paraphernalia. A massive collection of handguns lay spread under glass like an enormous, deadly smorgasbord.

Waving a hand in front of his nose in an effort to fight off the odor of something acrid and unidentifiable, he strode down the narrow aisle. Gabriella nipped at his heels. She'd refused to stay in the car. The image of Alberto Garza's lax features floated in his mind's eye. Better to keep her where he could see her.

He flipped his badge open in the direction of a skinny Latino with a scar across his nose who was bellowing in Spanish on the phone. His name tag identified him as Joe Gonzalez. His free hand jabbed the air as he punctuated his points. He was upset about a delayed shipment of ammunition.

He perused the badge without interrupting his conversation. Turning his back on them, he dropped his volume until Eli could no longer hear his words. A few seconds later he laid down the phone and faced them. "What can I do for the San Antonio Police Department today?"

He made the switch to English with no discernible accent.

"Alberto Garza." Eli smoothed a computer printout and handed it to Gonzalez. "He purchased these firearms in this store."

Gonzalez shrugged and took the list of serial numbers. "Look around, Detective. We sell lots of guns in this store. Business is good."

"I'm thinking a twenty-two-year-old college student buying an FN PS90 rifle might have caught your attention."

Gonzalez picked up a soda can and sucked on it. He wiped at his mouth with the back of a hand that had black grease under its fingernails. "I don't have a lot of conversation of a personal nature with customers. I don't know whether they go to school or run pig farms or cut open brains for a living. I run the background check, I have them sign the paperwork that says they're not buying the firearm for someone else, and I collect their money. That's all the law requires. Besides I'm not the only one who works here. He could've dealt with one of the other guys."

"Why don't you look up his records? Someone also sold him an FN Five-seveN, a Barrett M107A1 long-range sniper rifle, and a Beretta M9. Sound to you like he planned to do some deer hunting?"

"If you insist." Gonzalez burped and turned to a dirty keyboard perched on a desk behind the counter. While he displayed his prowess in the hunt-and-peck style of typing, Eli watched Gabriella peruse the merchandise under the glass counters. Hunters saw sport. Some people saw self-protection. Others saw a Second Amendment right. Gabriella, as a former prosecutor, probably saw old cases.

As a police officer he saw faces. The face of a pregnant woman whose husband shot her in the chest with a .22 Smith & Wesson during a domestic dispute. The face of a teenager who killed himself playing Russian roulette with a parent's loaded .38 Special in front of his two best friends. The face of a convenience store clerk named Ralph after a guy with a 9 mil walked in and put a bullet in his head for the twenty-four dollars in the register, a carton of Marlboros, and a six-pack of Dr Pepper.

"Okay, yeah, so I remember the kid." Gonzalez looked up from the computer screen. "He said his cousin was a collector and had gotten him into guns. He put the first purchase on layaway and came in about a month later and paid cash. He came back a few weeks later and bought the FN. He seemed real excited about starting his own collection."

Eli exchanged glances with Gabriella. *Real excited.* He slapped both hands on the glass, fighting the urge to lean over, grab the guy by the neck, and squeeze him like a zit. "Garza is dead. He had three of these weapons in his trunk. You sure you don't have any ideas what he might have been doing with these guns?"

Gonzalez burped again, with less gusto. "He said he was starting a collection like his cousin's."

"Collection? One of the weapons you sold him was an engraved AR-15 assault-style rifle. I'm not a psychic, but I'm pretty sure the ATF is going to be paying you a visit in the very near future. The AR-15 showed up recently at a murder scene where three Mexican police officers were blown away in Aguascalientes."

The eloquence of Gonzalez's shrug said the story wasn't a new one, but a sheen of sweat appeared on his flaccid skin. "All right, yeah, I remember the AR-15. It was beautiful, really beautiful." Gonzalez could've been talking about a woman, the way his tone softened. "Garza came around a few times with someone else first. The other guy was doing the shopping. He was looking at AR-15s mostly. Only I couldn't sell him anything because he had a felony conviction. A few weeks later Garza came in on his own and bought the AR-15."

"What guy? Who was he?"

Gonzalez drummed his fingers on the counter, wrinkled his nose, and stared at the rifles over Eli's shoulder. "You know how many people come through this store in a day, in a week, in the last six months? He didn't buy anything. He's not in my records."

"But you remember Garza was buying for a convicted felon."

"I have no way of knowing what Garza did with the gun after

he bought it. I can't stop someone from buying a gun and then three weeks later selling it to someone else." Gonzalez took a swipe at his forehead with the back of his sleeve. "It's beyond my control—the control of any gun dealer."

"You know all the signs of a straw buyer. You could've given the ATF a heads-up." Eli pounded his fist lightly on the counter that separated him from Gonzalez. "He might still be alive if you had."

"If he got into something illegal, he has no one to blame but himself. Besides, I'm not the owner. I'm the manager. I do my job and let the Feds do theirs. If that's all, I've got inventory to do."

"Did you know Garza was the nephew of a gun seller in Laredo? Manuel Figueroa?"

"He's Manny's *familia*?" Gonzalez shrugged. "He didn't say, and I didn't ask. Manny is good people."

Good people who involved a college kid in gun smuggling.

"How do you sleep at night, knowing the assault rifles you sell kill innocent women and children, kill police officers who are outgunned and outmanned?" Eli shut his mouth. He supported the Second Amendment. People who abused it, on the other hand, were a pain in his backside.

Gonzalez snorted. "You're a cop. You know better. Guns don't kill people. People do." He turned back to the computer, the stony look on his face making it clear the conversation was more than over.

"Good luck with the Feds." Eli grabbed Gabriella's elbow and tugged her through the aisle.

Outside, he spat on the sidewalk, knowing full well it was a habit she despised.

She scooted away from him as if his aim might be bad. "What's wrong with you?"

"Guys like that get to me. He knew Garza wasn't starting a collection or going hunting with that kind of firepower. How can he even say that with a straight face? It irritates me."

"Yeah, I know. Want me to drive?" Obvious desire in her expression, Gabby eyed the Charger. She loved a fast car. Most of the time she drove like an officer involved in a high-speed chase. Fat chance she'd get her hands—sweet as they were—on his wheels. "Uh-oh."

"In your dreams." He followed her gaze. "What is he doing here?"

Deacon Alder leaned against the Charger, both thumbs punching a smartphone. He didn't seem to notice Eli's approach. "You apparently have a death wish, Alder. Do not lean on my car."

Alder looked up with exaggerated slowness. He straightened and moved an inch or two. "Oh, there you are. I was just coming in."

"What are you doing here? Are you following us?"

Gabby sounded as surprised as Eli felt. Like she hadn't encouraged the guy with the interview at the scene. Just like she'd been encouraging him with New York strip steaks, homemade onion rings, and key lime pie at the restaurant. Of all the guys to latch on to her.

"He's fishing for a story, that's what he's doing." Eli checked the beautiful midnight-black paint job on the Charger. If Alder scratched it, he'd be paying—through the nose. "He doesn't care that putting this stuff in the paper could hurt innocent people."

"I've read his stuff. He's pretty responsible." Gabby shrugged. "Besides, he doesn't have enough to write a story."

"Which is why he's here."

"You know, I am standing right here." Alder waved his phone toward the sporting goods store. "I admit it. I've been following Detective Cavazos. You'd think a cop would notice that. Maybe you're just a little distracted by your personal relationship to Gabriella. Maybe they should take you off this case. Give it to someone more objective."

The guy was actually angling to keep them apart.

"Please don't make this personal." Gabby stepped in front of Eli. He considered forcibly moving her so he could get to the jerk. "We're leaving now. Eli's giving me a ride, that's all."

"Careful. It's never good practice to lie to a reporter. You'll always be found out. I'm going in now to interview Mr. Gonzalez—yes, I know his name—my sources at the ATF know his name too." Alder inched into Gabby's space. She didn't back away. "This is the part I love about my job. Putting all the pieces together like a giant jigsaw puzzle. I'm just sorry it somehow involves you and your brother, Jake."

He already had too many pieces. Eli relaxed his fists and tried to negotiate instead of pounding the guy's face into dog meat. "Writing a story about this before we figure out who killed the victim could put a lot of people in jeopardy. The cartel doesn't mess around." Eli glanced at Gabby. "It could put innocent bystanders in danger. Doesn't that bother you?"

Alder had the grace to look uncomfortable. "There are risks, but it's my job to let the public know what's going on in their city. I'm the watchdog, so citizens can be informed and participate. That's the role of the fourth estate. That's what makes the system work."

"You just keep telling yourself that." Eli nudged Gabby toward the car. "Let's go. It's noon already. We don't have time to waste."

"Where are you headed?" Alder had the audacity to look as if he expected a straight answer. "Just out of curiosity."

"To Laredo." Gabby spoke before Eli could tell the guy to take a hike in the Sahara. "To find my brother. If you learn anything from your sources, will you call me?"

"I will. I promise." He patted her hand. "Be careful."

"She will be. It's my job to make sure." Who did this guy think he was? Obviously the connection between them had grown. Eli gritted his teeth and opened Gabby's door for her. She avoided his gaze and slid in. He shut the door and glared at Alder. "Back off, Alder. *I'm* not kidding. If somebody has to get hurt, I'd rather it be you than her."

"Same here."

He was still standing on the sidewalk when Eli glanced in his rear-view mirror and pulled from the curb. Alder didn't look so happy now.

CHAPTER 7

———

DEACON SHOVED HIS RELUCTANCE in his pocket along with his reporter's notebook. He sat in his SUV outside the Benoit house, giving himself a pep talk. Interviewing Gabriella's sister felt wrong. Gabriella was a friend, but he had no choice. The job demanded it. A job he might lose if he didn't produce a knock-'em-dead story. Rumor had it there would be another round of layoffs in the coming weeks. The newsroom was a ghost town already. Not surprising considering newspapers were dinosaurs in a digital world. Reporters were like rotary landline phones.

With law enforcement stonewalling, his only lead at this point was Jake Benoit's family. Natalie Benoit Ferrari was a respected psychologist who'd worked with children who were victims of crime. She would make a good interview in a pinch. If she came to the door.

A brutal sun beating on his back, he strode up to the house. Sweat soaked his shirt. He wiped at his face and rapped on the door of Gabriella's Spanish-style two-story adobe house with a red tile roof that matched the red roses trailing from the arches in front. A metal ramp covered with a thin black rubber tread wound its way to a wraparound porch and an arched rustic door that featured a hummingbird in a stained-glass window.

"All right. All right." Either Natalie Ferrari had a deep, gravelly voice of a smoker, or she had company. "Give me a second."

Fumbling sounds followed by latches releasing served as a preamble to the opening of the door. The man staring out at Deacon was in his late twenties. He had a military-style buzz cut, a muscled physique, an eagle tattoo on both arms, and a high-end, obviously expensive prosthesis that substituted for his right leg. "What?"

Deacon peeked over the guy's shoulder. No females in sight. He introduced himself and held out his hand. The man ignored it. "What do you want?"

"I'd like to talk to Dr. Ferrari. Is she here?"

"Why?"

This guy was annoying. "That would be between Dr. Ferrari and me."

The door started to shut.

"Marty!" A voice that sounded vaguely familiar emanated from the hallway. "Who is it?"

"It's Deacon Alder from the *Express-News*. Is that you, Dr. Ferrari? I'd like to talk to you for just a few minutes."

The woman handled her wheelchair with practiced ease. She was thin, but her arms had the muscles of a person who worked out. Deacon was too busy staring at her face to see much else. Gabriella was a pretty woman. Her sister, on the other hand, was stop-the-presses gorgeous. Auburn hair, peaches-and-cream complexion. Blue-rimmed glasses magnified gray eyes. A beautiful mouth. Belatedly, he shut his own mouth. She stared up at the man. "Marty, please don't manage me."

"He's a reporter, Nat. You don't want to talk to him."

"You're Gabriella's reporter." She smiled at Deacon. A high-wattage, blinding smile. "My sister talks about you a lot. You're the dessert fanatic."

"That's me. I've gained five pounds since I started eating at Courtside. Gabriella is wasted on those lawyers and cops. She should be cooking for presidents and kings. There'd be no more war—"

Marty's snort stopped him dead. Stupid thing to say. The guy had Afghanistan vet written all over him.

Dr. Ferrari eased her chair a little closer, a simple barrier between

Deacon and her apparent bodyguard. "I'm sorry. Deacon, this is Martin Little, our neighbor."

Deacon again offered his hand. Nothing little about this muscle-bound giant. This time Marty took it. His grip crushed a few bones. Deacon tried not to wince as he turned back to Natalie. "I'd really like to ask you a few questions about your brother."

She shook her head. "If this is about the murder victim. I'm so very sorry for his family, but I have no idea how that connects to Jake or his work. None of us do."

Deacon peeked into the interior and caught glimpses of dark wood and warm, earthy Southwest colors. A dog woofed. Cool air brushed his face. "You know, it's hotter than blue blazes out here. Do you mind if I come in?"

Bicep muscles bulging in her arms, Dr. Ferrari wheeled her chair around. "I can only give you a few minutes. The kids are upstairs deciding what to take to Marty's house while I'm gone."

"Nat—"

She frowned up at Marty. "I'll let you know when I'm ready to leave. Thanks for the offer to take care of the kids. And the pets."

His expression grim, he nodded. "Call me or send Cullen over."

Marty brushed past Deacon and disappeared through the door. He handled the prosthesis well, his gait smooth.

She was going to Laredo. Why not go with her sister? Gabriella didn't want her to go? More family dynamics. He quickly moved to the living room before she changed her mind. A bulldog raised his head, looked Deacon over, and went back to sleep. Deacon laid his mini-digital recorder on the coffee table. She glanced at it but didn't say anything. Deacon hurried to fill the awkward pause. "You can't tell me what your brother was working on?"

"I haven't talked to Jake since last week." Her hands fluttered in the air in an expressive gesture, then dropped to a book on her lap. "And when we did talk, it wasn't about work. He'd call to tell me a joke. That was his shtick—tell Gimpy Girl a joke, make her laugh, once a week, without fail. He never told—never tells the same joke twice."

"Sounds like a good guy."

"The best." An obese cat eyed the doctor's lap and then settled at her feet, obviously too heavy to make the leap. "He acts like nothing has changed." She slapped the arms of her chair. "Like I'm still me. I'm still the same person."

He'd read the articles about the car accident and the death of her husband. "You are the same person, aren't you?"

"Yes, trapped in a body that doesn't work and missing the 180 pounds that belonged to my husband, but yes, I'm the same person."

"How long has your brother been with the ATF?"

Slowly he drew her out. She told the story of a young guy who enlisted out of high school, did two tours in Afghanistan, finished college, joined the ATF, and never stopped cracking jokes.

"You think that's a defense mechanism?"

Her beautiful lips curved in a smile. "You're a smart man. Our family . . . Gabriella is the glue that has held us together through some monumentally bad . . . I'm sorry. This really doesn't have anything to do with anything, Mr. Alder—"

"Deacon."

"Please call me Natalie." She laid the book on the table that separated them. "My family history is no more tragic than the next family's. Did you get what you came for?"

Movement behind her caught his gaze.

What the—? Gun barrels . . . big ones . . . men . . . camouflage . . . At least three of them filtered into the room in seconds without making a single sound.

Deacon shot to his feet. The bulldog barked. The cat echoed the high piercing sound and burrowed under the couch. Too late, Deacon realized he'd stepped on it.

"Natalie, look out!"

Natalie didn't have a chance to turn around. The barrel of a semi-automatic weapon pressed against her neck. She froze, her pewter eyes wide, staring at him. Her hands gripped the wheelchair. She didn't seem to breathe.

Deacon started forward.

"You want the lady to get hurt, do something stupid, *señor*."

A man dressed in fatigues, a bulletproof vest, and spit-shine Army boots spoke through a black ski mask. His accent suggested a border town.

Deacon halted, hands in the air.

"*Señora*, turn around. Slowly. Gently." The gargantuan man eased the gun from her head.

Natalie obeyed. "What do you want?"

"Information."

Natalie backed her chair up and stopped at Deacon's side. Her gaze caught his. Anger overshadowed fear. The woman was Gabriella's sister in more than one way. Her fingers grabbed his. He tightened his hand around hers, offering her the only lifeline he could.

"You could've knocked on the door and asked." Her tone was crisp. "That's how civilized people ask for information. What would you like to know?"

Camouflage Man approached. His weapon bore down on them. "You are Natalie Ferrari?"

"I am."

"Where is the other sister who lives here, Ms. Benoit?"

"Not here." Natalie's voice had a breathless quality as if she'd been running. Right. Running. Glancing down at the thin, jean-clad legs in the wheelchair, Deacon considered his chances of scooping her up and diving out a window before a bullet found its way into the soft tissue of his back.

Not without her children.

"And the phone?"

"What phone?"

"Alberto Garza's cell phone."

"I don't know what you're talking about!" Natalie let go of Deacon's hand. "You're in the wrong place. My sister's not here, and there's no spare phone lying around."

The man's soft growl sent a chill revving up Deacon's spine. "You don't want to lie to me."

Natalie lifted her chin "I don't lie—"

"You're Jake Benoit's sister. Alberto Garza was his snitch. He gave his phone to your sister. She brought it here. This phone is very important to my employer." He spoke to the other men in Spanish. Deacon understood the gist of it. *Search the house.* "Cooperate and everyone will be fine. It serves no purpose to struggle and bring harm to yourself or someone else."

"If Gabriella had the phone, she wouldn't bring it here. She would give it to the police."

"It is my sincere hope that she did not. It is your only hope of getting your brother back alive."

"I'm sorry. There's no phone."

"Lay your phones on the table."

They had no choice but to comply. Natalie's sparkly purple encased phone next to Deacon's black one.

"Passwords please."

A short, fat man squatted and examined them, one by one. He shook his head at Camouflage Man.

Natalie's chair started forward. Deacon grabbed the handles and held on. He admired her guts, but if ever there was a time for restraint, it was now.

The other men rifled through magazines, opened drawers in the desk in the corner, and examined books on the shelves. All in an orderly fashion at odds with the guns and masks. In the meantime

Camouflage Man approached Natalie. Her expression didn't change. Their gazes held. He bent over. The tip of his weapon touched her cheek. "I need to know where your sister is."

"I don't know."

"You do know, and you're going to tell me."

"Mommy! Cullen took the tablet. I want the tablet. He's not giving it back!"

The high, aggravated voice preceded light steps on the stairs.

"Oh no, oh please, Ava!" Natalie revved her chair forward.

"No, no." Camouflage Man flung himself in her path. He turned toward the stairs. "What do we have here, *una chiquita*? *Qué bella*."

He met a little girl who was the spitting image of Natalie at the bottom of the steps.

She stopped, her petite face frozen with uncertainty. "Mommy?"

"Ava!" Natalie's scream said it all. Deacon darted forward. Camouflage Man whipped his weapon out so the barrel pointed at Deacon's face. "No, no, no."

Deacon stopped. His heart slammed against his rib cage. Blood pounded in his ears. The sensation like ocean waves rising and falling in his lungs made it hard to breathe. "Come on, dude. She's just a little girl."

Camouflage Man swooped the girl up with one arm. "Why don't we call this Cullen downstairs too, *m'hijita*, while *tu mama* decides whether to tell us where your *tía* is?"

CHAPTER 8

GUNSHOTS. A SHARP JERK on the seat belt jolted Gabriella from semi-nightmarish dreams that echoed with gunfire. The car had stopped. "Are we there?"

Eli eased the Charger into Park. "We're in Dilley."

Rubbing sleep from her eyes, Gabriella straightened. After a few seconds she focused on her surroundings. They weren't just in the tiny town of Dilley, a small blip on the highway between San Antonio and Laredo, they were at the Dairy Queen. Her pulse did an erratic tap dance. Her breath caught in her throat. "Oh no. No, you don't get to do this. Start the car. Now."

Eli's grin said fat chance. "I'm hungry and we never drive to Laredo without getting a Dilly Bar in Dilley. Remember, ice cream is a—"

"Food group, I know. We are *not* taking a stroll down memory lane. We're going to Laredo to find my brother. Every minute counts." She shoved her door open. A whoosh of air steamed by afternoon sun seared her face. "If you don't get this heap moving right now, I'll walk the rest of the way."

The engine revved. She slammed the door. The car ripped back, and her head banged against the headrest. "This is not a heap. The drive-through it is, then. It's almost two, and you haven't eaten today. It won't slow us down, and you don't have to enjoy it."

"Fine, but I'm not eating a Dilly Bar."

"You've become a food snob."

"Have not."

Once the hamburgers and fries were in the car, the aroma was almost more than Gabriella could bear. Not only because she hadn't eaten in more than twenty-four hours, but because it smelled of road trips she'd taken with Eli. He had a thing about Dairy Queens. He wanted to stop at one in every little town between San Antonio and Corpus or San Antonio and Laredo. She was a chef and the man she loved preferred fast food.

Used to love.

Many of those trips had been to see Jake.

"Remember that last trip to Port A?" Eli had read her mind. His voice was gravelly with contained emotion. "That time on the beach when he wanted us to bury him in the sand."

Gabriella smiled, remembering. "Then some hot babe in a bikini walked by and he felt like an idiot because we'd buried him so deep he couldn't get up."

Eli laughed, the sound brittle, like ice cracking on weighted tree branches in the winter. "We left him there for two hours. Brought him cherry limeades and half a dozen of the double-chocolate brownies you brought with you. And put sunblock on his nose so he looked like a total dork."

"He was a goofball."

"He is a goofball. Except when he's working, and then he's a consummate professional." Eli shook his head, his expression bewildered. "Where is he? He wouldn't drop out of sight without making contact with his superiors—not willingly."

"Somebody he knew, somebody he trusted, got a hold of him." Gabriella let her gaze sideswipe Eli. He seemed lost in thought. "Somebody he shouldn't have trusted."

His gaze shuttered and returned to the windshield. He'd retreated to cop world, a place where he could think about catching the bad guy. "What do you know about his partner? Bob somebody?"

"I think he might have retired, but I'm not sure. I don't know who it is now. He didn't like to talk about work." Instead, he liked to joke and pick her brain for recipes. The guy liked to cook. "He was like you in that respect."

"You left that world behind when you left the DA's office. Why would you want me to talk about work?"

"Because your work was important to you, which made it important to me." All the broken dates, the missed holidays, the sudden departures in the middle of an evening out—she understood them. She understood the nature of his work better than most. All she wanted in return was for him to open up to her. "Maybe I thought talking to me would help you deal with some of the things you saw and did. I guess we'll never know."

The words floated in the air between them.

Eli's jaw worked. His pulse jumped.

But he didn't speak.

Par for the course.

She'd been so afraid of losing Eli, she'd never really contemplated what it would be like without Jake. She stared out the window. *He's not dead. He's missing.*

"We'll find him."

Again Eli read her mind.

"I know."

"So what's going on between you and Alder?"

"None of your business." The response came automatically. Deacon was a friend. As much as a reporter and a former assistant district attorney could be friends. Sure, he saw her as a conduit to information shared by her former associates in law enforcement and often wanted to capitalize on those relationships. That was his nature. She rarely gave him anything, but he still kept coming back. He continued to eat her peach pie and engage her in heated arguments over everything from immigration to stem-cell research.

She liked sparring with him. He was uncomplicated.

People called Eli a lot of names, but uncomplicated didn't number among them.

They were both silent for the next fifty miles. Eli turned the radio off after *ranchera* and country music began to alternate with static. A horn blared. Eli swerved into the left lane. The seat belt snapped against Gabriella's chest in a painful hug. Eli muttered to himself and swerved back. "Sorry, the closer we get to Laredo, the more semis there are trying to run each other off the highway. It's probably stop and go from here to the international bridges."

He sounded exhausted. Gabriella risked a quick look at him through half-open eyelids. He needed a shave and a comb. He caught her gaze. She swiveled and pretended to be interested in the passing scenery.

It had been at least a year since she'd been to Laredo. Every time she came back to this town it looked a lot more like an industrial-manufacturing sprawl and a lot less like a lazy border town. One thing hadn't changed: the brown cloud that hovered over the city. It reminded Gabriella to smile with her mouth closed. Otherwise she'd be grinding grit between her teeth when the wind blew.

Still, it wasn't all bad. The hot sun in the window reminded her of the smell of *cabrito* grilling and vendors hawking corn on the cob and *paletas* on the street in Nuevo Laredo. Eli's mom's smiling face crowded her memories. She loved paletas. No wonder Eli was an ice cream man.

"Will you visit your parents while we're here?"

No answer.

Gabriella cocked her head and studied Eli's profile. The pulse in his jaw suggested he was gritting his teeth. "Eli?"

"This isn't a social visit. We'll check into a hotel first and then go to Jake's town house. I'd like to get to the Garza family tonight, if possible. I'll hit the local ATF office tomorrow morning, early."

And she would be with him, whether he liked it or not. She could always call a cab or rent a car. "Are you checking in with local law enforcement?"

"Sarge made a call to advise Laredo PD I'd be in their jurisdiction. He said they weren't too thrilled to have me here. The response was generally along the lines that they would be willing to share information regarding their investigation. I can ride along as an observer but not conduct my own inquiries."

They didn't know Eli, that was obvious.

Gabriella watched the urban landscape whiz by. Suddenly, she got it. A half laugh escaped her open mouth. "You haven't told your parents about us, have you?"

He glanced her way, then back at the windshield. "Actually, I did."

"How did they take it?"

"My father has been a minister for more than fifty-five years. How do you think he took it?"

The naked misery in the words almost made her forget she was the wronged party. Her hand crept out of its own volition. His gaze swung toward her, his expression bitter. "My dad claims forgiveness is there for the taking. All I have to do is ask. He doesn't seem to get that I already tried that route."

That sounded so like Pastor Xavier Emmanuel Cavazos. "You could've told him it was my fault. You didn't have to tell him the whole story."

He studied the windshield. "I could've, but it didn't seem—"

"Honorable." The sarcasm seeped out of its own accord. She studied her side of the windshield. "Sorry."

"Dunbar had some other news while you were dozing." Eli reverted to his business-as-usual tone. "Alberto Garza's roommate claims not to know anything about Alberto being involved in any gun smuggling. He had issues making rent, then suddenly was flush with money, but the roommate said he'd gotten a job working for an uncle who just happens to have a sporting goods store in Laredo. The girlfriend is apparently en route to Laredo as we speak. They didn't get a chance to interview her before she split. So the interview is mine, as well as the family and the uncle at the store."

"So we just check in and drop off our bags?"

"Yep. We'll hit Jake's place first after the hotel—see if there's any sign of him." Eli pulled into a hotel on San Bernardo Avenue about two blocks from the old international bridge. "I'll get the bags. You check in."

Eli set the parking brake without looking at her. "The rooms are reserved," he added, an odd note in the simple statement. "And paid for."

She stopped, one leg out of the car. "I can pay my own way."

The wheel under his hands seemed to greatly interest him. "Forget it. It's on me."

"Why?"

"Because if I hadn't messed up, we'd be married by now and sharing the room and the cost." He leveled his gaze on her. "Your paying is just you being penalized once again for my mess up."

His reasoning was flawless. She slid from her seat.

Eli's voice floated after her. "Besides, it's only until I convince you to take the ring back and set a date."

The words were weighted with shared memories more than a year old. The first time he popped the question had been over a meal he cooked at his apartment—grilled orange roughy served with baked potatoes, asparagus, and rocky road ice cream. He swore the choice of ice cream wasn't a Freudian slip. He went the candlelight and flowers route, complete with getting down on one knee. The ring, a vintage European-cut diamond with three sapphires on each side, belonged to his grandmother. Gabriella said yes.

A month later he started reneging on dates. He stopped picking up when she called. He waffled about setting a wedding date.

In short, despite all his protestations to the contrary, something changed.

Then came the shooting.

"Good luck with that." She grabbed her bag and took off. "You'll need it."

CHAPTER 9

SILENCE STRETCHED FOR SEVERAL seconds, then snapped.

Both hands in the air, Deacon inched forward. The semiautomatic assault rifle between him and the little girl with ginger hair and gorgeous gray eyes didn't give him much wiggle room. She struggled in Camouflage Man's grip. "Mommy!"

He swung her over his shoulder as if she weighed no more than a five-pound sack of potatoes. His ski mask rode up enough to reveal wiry gray whiskers on his chin. "*No llores, m'hijita.* I like little girls. There's no reason to cry."

"No!" Natalie shrieked. She shot forward until she was even with Deacon. "Give me my daughter back. She has nothing to do with this. What are you? Some kind of monster?"

Deacon grabbed her shoulders, afraid she'd topple forward on the living room floor, and hurled himself in front of her. "Don't hurt her. Isn't there something else you want—money maybe?"

Ava whimpered.

"Leave her alone. She's a little girl!"

One of the other intruders stomped down the stairs, dragging by his T-shirt a young boy who looked like a taller version of Ava, except for the dark, curly hair. "Found this *chiquito* at the top of the stairs."

Camouflage Man didn't even seem to register the second child. "Find it?"

"*N'ombre. Nada.*"

"Let the boy go to his mother." Camouflage Man sighed. "This isn't going well, señora."

Deacon stepped in front of her. "Because there's nothing to find, dude. Just let them go, please."

The boy darted toward Deacon. He scrambled to help him, but the look of horror on the kid's face underlined the fact that the boy had no idea who Deacon was or if he was one of the bad guys. "It's okay, go to your mom."

"To answer your question, señora, I'm not a monster." The man patted Ava's backside with a gun-laden hand. "I don't hit ladies or kill children. So, I will make you a deal."

"We don't make deals with home invaders—"

"Deacon, let him talk, please."

Natalie's imploring tone made Deacon set aside the desire to smash this guy's face. "What kind of deal?"

"Tell us where your sister is." The man dropped a kiss on Ava's head. "Now."

"Please, I don't know."

"You do know."

"Mommy!"

"She's on her way to Houston to the ATF offices. She thinks they know more than they're saying about Jake's disappearance."

"You wouldn't lie to me, would you?"

"You have my daughter."

He deposited Ava gently on her feet. "Go to your mama."

Icicles pierced Deacon's spine at the sight of the man's smile. "For your brother's sake, you better talk to your sister soon. Tell her we're on our way. We want that phone."

His unspoken words reverberated through the room. They wanted Gabriella.

Natalie threw her arms around her children and squeezed them to her body. She glared up at the intruder, anger making her cheeks dark in her pale face. "Gabriella doesn't know anything."

Camouflage Man backed away, the semiautomatic pointed at Deacon's face. *"Vámanos!"* At the door he squeezed the trigger.

Deacon whirled and threw himself over the children huddled on Natalie's lap. Bullets sprayed the bookshelves that lined the far wall. The *ping, ping* tap-danced a bizarre tune in his ears.

"Just a little motivation. You can pass that on to your sister."

They left as quietly as they'd come.

CHAPTER 10

THE DOOR TO JAKE'S two-story town house on Laredo's near north side stood ajar.

Eli's hand gripped Gabriella's elbow and tugged her back on the narrow porch. She stumbled over a ceramic *chiminea* filled with half-burned logs. "Maybe he's—"

His jaw clenched, lips tight, Eli shook his head, held a finger to his lips, and then pulled his S&W from the holster on his hip. "Stay put," he whispered.

Why did he always say that? He knew she wouldn't. "Maybe Jake's home."

She'd called her brother's number five times in the last four hours. One last time in the hotel lobby before they drove the ten minutes to the town house. And connected with voicemail five times.

Eli glared and cocked his head toward the driveway. No vehicle other than the Charger. She returned the glare and tugged her phone from her pocket. At the very least, she'd be ready to call for help.

Eli squeezed through the door, his S&W leading the way. Gabriella watched his broad back disappear from sight. Her mouth went dry. Her legs felt detached from the rest of her body. Sweat soaked the underarms of her T-shirt. She moved into the shade of a barren trellis, trying to escape a sun seeking the horizon.

He'd been shot once. Maybe the odds said it couldn't happen again. Not this soon. The uncertainty of that thought assailed her. Her experience as an attorney told her bad stuff happened to people. Repeatedly. Maybe he wouldn't survive this time. While she stood on a small, rectangular cement porch next to a broken chiminea, doing nothing but sweating.

Forget that.

Gabriella slipped through the door. In the foyer she glanced around, looking for a weapon of some kind—anything. Jake loved baseball. A bat would be good about now. Or a fireplace poker. She found nothing but a pair of navy running shoes and a coatrack weighted down by a UT sweatshirt, a faded Windbreaker, and half a dozen ball caps.

Gabriella inched forward until she could see the living room. The air whooshed from her lungs, leaving her light-headed. She bent over and stuck her hands on her knees. Purple spots pinged from side to side in her vision. Somebody appeared to have used the room as the site of a WWE championship match.

A glass coffee table had crash-landed on its side and shattered. Books and magazines were strewn across the carpet. A big-screen TV lay toppled across the couch. She forced herself to move forward. "What happened to you, Jake?" she whispered. She held her breath, somehow thinking it would help. No answer.

Hands shaking, she turned over a broken picture frame lying face-down on the typical tan apartment carpet. Her own face smiling like an idiot greeted her. She had one hand on Jake's arm. He stood next to Natalie's chair. Natalie held an oversized pair of ceremonial scissors. They were cutting the ribbon in front of the restaurant. Below the caption, the headline screamed Former ADA opens Courtside Restaurant. Jake had framed the article and hung it in his living room. Swallowing the painful lump in her throat, she propped the photo up on the only chair still upright. "Oh, Jake!"

A shriek from a nearby room echoed in seeming response. Trying to control legs that threatened to sprawl in all directions, Gabriella bolted down the hallway.

"Stay back, Gabs." Eli pointed his weapon at a woman who had both hands in the air, her back against the refrigerator. "Who are you?"

With her chestnut hair floating in feathered wisps around her face, her tawny skin, huge brown eyes, white sundress, and her silver sandals, the young woman looked like an angel in distress. Her mouth opened, closed. She nodded toward the key she held between one thumb and forefinger with nails painted a sparkly pink. "I didn't break in." Her delicate voice quivered. "I promise you I have a right to be here."

"What gives you the right?" Gabriella slipped into the room. "Tell us who you are. Where's Jake?"

"Who are you?" The woman started to lower her hands and then seemed to think better of it. "What gives *you* the right?"

Eli flashed his badge. "This gives me the right, and she's Jake's sister. That gives her the right. Your turn."

"Mirasol Mendez. My friends call me Sunny. Jake calls me Sunshine." She started to cry. "He's my fiancé, and I don't know where he is. He's just gone."

Gabriella exchanged glances with Eli. Her first thought was *no way*. Followed by: How well did she really know her brother? She knew his type. He usually went for crazy-smart, tall, sand volleyball, athletic women with nice tans and lots of running shoes and jobs that paid well. This woman—girl really—made any woman over thirty feel like an old heifer. "That doesn't explain why you're here in his house when he isn't home. You don't . . . live here, do you?"

"Of course not, my dad . . ." She licked lips slick with pink gloss, her cheeks suddenly rosy. "I'm doing the same thing you are—looking for him."

"Have a seat." Eli eased his weapon back and nodded toward a chair at the Formica table for two wedged against the wall in the miniature kitchen. Hands still half in the air, Sunny sat. "When was the last time you saw Jake?"

The young woman didn't answer for a few seconds. She glanced at Gabriella, back at Eli, her dainty lips pursed in a frown. "I've seen you both in photos. Jake has a picture of you cutting a ribbon at your restaurant in the living room." She paused, nibbling at her upper lip with tiny blindingly white teeth. "I told him."

"Told him what?"

"I know you."

Eli's bushy eyebrows quirked up. "Me? You know me?"

"Sure. Your dad's a pastor. Some friends of mine, Chuy and Rudy Figueroa—their families go to your church—"

"My father's church."

"Yeah, your father's church. I've been there for weddings and baptisms."

The discomfort on Eli's face would have been amusing if Gabriella wasn't feeling some of her own. She loved that church. She loved Eli's parents. The emotion on Eli's face gave way to something else. Distaste. "So you know the Figueroas. I've heard talk that they might be involved in some extracurricular activity, such as gun smuggling."

"People like to gossip. They're businessmen. They've got several businesses—a body repair shop, a sporting goods store, a bunch of pawn shops. I've been friends with Chuy and his brothers since I was little."

"I imagine they were excited when you started dating an ATF agent." Gabriella jumped in. Cross-examining witnesses was her forte. "So, that takes us back to the detective's question: When did you last see Jake Benoit?"

Sunny's face crumpled. "Thursday morning. I came into town. We had breakfast together. We haven't been apart more than twenty-four hours since we met in April."

"What did he say the last time you spoke? Did he tell you where he was going or when you should expect to see him again?"

Sunny sniffed and swiped a paper napkin from a stack on the table. No niceties like a napkin holder for this bachelor. She took her time drying her face. "He said he was going to be really busy at work that day, but he would call me when he got home. I told him he'd better do more than that. I wanted to see him. He laughed." She wadded up the napkin and tossed it on the table. "He said he wanted to see me too . . . He said he was addicted to me, and he would have to have a fix or he'd go crazy."

A strange analogy for a law-and-order Christian like Jake. Gabriella gripped the back of a chair. A feeling of dread wrapped itself around her throat and squeezed. "Did he talk to you about his work? Did he say where he was going?"

"We didn't talk about work. We talked about . . . We talked about a lot of things."

"Like what?" How could Jake have a girlfriend—a serious girlfriend—Gabriella knew nothing about? "Give me an example."

"My father likes Jake, but he says he's a little old for me. He says . . ." Her gaze dropped to the table. "Daddy is a retired sheriff, so he knows about law enforcement. He says Jake could get himself killed and where would I be? Jake says no one has any guarantees that they'll be around tomorrow. A person could get hit by a bus or fall off a ladder or get swooped up by a tornado."

Hoping to inhale a scent that would remind her of her brother, Gabriella breathed. Dish soap, dust, coffee grounds, and the musky smell of a damp towel couldn't conjure him up. Had he forecast his own death?

"This is interesting. Not one of you is the man who lives here."

The cool words came from beyond the kitchen door.

Gabriella whirled. Eli put one hand on his holster and grabbed her arm with the other. He slid in front of her.

A guy who looked like he should be selling insurance or real estate sauntered into the kitchen in a five-hundred-dollar suit and shiny leather loafers. He flipped out a badge. "Carlos Rincon, Laredo PD, Homicide. Either the three of you are breaking and entering, or you're harboring a fugitive. I can't wait to see which it is."

CHAPTER 11

BLANK STARES AT TWENTY paces. A detective standoff. Gabriella eased back and let Eli do his thing. He would win at that game. The silence lasted three beats before Sunny sashayed across the kitchen and shook her delicate manicured finger at the man. "Are you following me, Detective Rincon? If you are, Daddy isn't going to be very happy. No more hunting trips. No more packages of venison—"

"Nobody's following you." Rincon broke in, a patch of red creeping up his neck to his smooth-shaven cheeks. "Not LPD, at any rate. Who are your friends?"

"They're not my friends. We're just getting to know each other." She made it sound as if they were at a sorority spring social. "This is Jake's sister and her boyfriend. He's a cop from San Antonio."

Now wasn't the time to correct her. "I'm Gabriella Benoit. Do you always waltz into people's houses without knocking, Detective?"

"The door was open. Your brother is a person of interest in a homicide."

"And you were surveilling the town house. Waiting to see if Jake returned here." Eli's tone was sardonic. "To pick up clean underwear, maybe?"

Rincon smiled, showing teeth that had probably made several payments on a Mercedes for some orthodontist. "Stranger things have happened. The powers that be told me you would be in our jurisdiction, Detective Cavazos. They're under the impression you planned to check in with us and cooperate on our investigation. You're out of your jurisdiction."

"I don't need your permission to check on a good friend." Eli's words dripped ice water. "I planned to stop by later today to ask you to extend professional courtesy to a fellow detective."

"Professional courtesy doesn't extend to allowing you to mess with our murder investigation."

"Jake Benoit is a certified peace officer." Gabriella summoned her attorney persona again. Years of making closing arguments to juries came rushing back. "He has a spotless record. He's also a veteran who did two tours in Afghanistan. It's preposterous to suggest he has done anything lawless."

"Save me the speech, please. I've already heard it from his ATF buddies." Rincon held up a well-manicured hand. He glanced at Sunny, his aquiline features hard. "And from the girlfriend. Even her father swears by him."

"Sounds like a smart man." Gabriella started to move away from Eli, but his hand grasped hers and squeezed, hard. She tugged back and made her escape. "Jake has dedicated his life to service. He's never even had a speeding ticket."

"You haven't heard from Mr. Benoit—either of you?" Rincon's gaze swung back and forth between Sunny and Gabriella. "He hasn't paid you a visit in San Antonio, Miss Benoit? Or dropped in at the ranch, Miss Mendez?"

"No!" They responded simultaneously and with equal heat.

"The evidence you have against my brother is circumstantial, at best. His gun was used in a homicide. That doesn't mean he was even present when the crime occurred." Gabriella crossed her arms. "If he killed the victim, why did he leave his gun at the scene? He wouldn't. He's a smart man, very smart. Something has happened to him. He's in trouble, and you should be trying to find him to help him, not arrest him."

"Our investigation is far from over. And let me make something perfectly clear." Rincon removed his glasses and wiped the lenses with a monogrammed white handkerchief. "The Laredo police department is heading up a murder investigation. So I expect you to stay out of the way."

"We're here to talk to Jake." Eli's tone was mild, but his eyes were hard. "It's not our intent to get in the way. Jake Benoit's disappearance may be related to a homicide that occurred this morning in San Antonio. Finding him is part of my investigation."

"Right. The bottom line is this: Either of you interfere in this investigation and I'll have your rear ends thrown in jail faster than you can say Miranda rights."

"Understood." Gabriella spoke quickly to ward off the furious words about to spill from Eli's lips. "At least tell me this, what puts my brother at the scene other than the gun?"

"Since you asked so nicely." Rincon gave Eli a pointed look. "The dead man was an ATF informant used by your brother to gather information on gun smuggling. Your brother told his colleagues he would be meeting with the victim to gather some intel on a cache of weapons slated to go over the day he disappeared. I have a witness who saw a vehicle fitting the description of your brother's SUV leaving the scene."

"Who's this witness?"

"I'd prefer not to say. In the interest of the witness's safety. The life span of folks touched by this ATF operation keeps getting shorter and shorter."

Nobody seemed to feel the need to finish the rest of that sentence, so Gabriella did it for them. "And what about the life span of ATF agents? Is it getting shorter?"

CHAPTER 12

——

ALL IN A DAY'S work. Deacon slapped his laptop shut and leaned back on the Adirondack chair situated behind the porch arches of the Benoit residence. A firsthand account of a home invasion related to a murder in downtown San Antonio and—somehow—related to an ATF international gun-smuggling investigation. He'd whipped out a *Crime Beat* blog, uploaded a few photos he'd snapped of the aftermath to his Facebook page. The managing editor loved it. It would make page 1 of tomorrow's hard copy newspaper. Above the fold. Too bad he hadn't been able to snap a few photos with his phone. That would've been icing on the cake and put a lock on his position when the layoffs came. Which stank because it meant one of his friends would get the ax instead. It really stank.

The sweet scent of the honeysuckle curled around trellises to his right mingled with the roses' fragrance, calming him. *You gotta do what you gotta do, bro.* The police had documented the scene, taken statements, and left with promises that the information would go directly to Eli's sergeant. They understood the break-in was related to the murder of Alberto Garza and the disappearance of Jake Benoit.

Natalie had taken the children in the kitchen to feed them their favorite supper of chicken tenders, mac and cheese, and canned mandarin orange slices. Those choices surely would make Chef Gabriella shudder. Marty, who came running at the sound of sirens on his street, was with them. The smell of food made Deacon's stomach turn, so he retreated to the porch.

His insides wouldn't stop shaking. These thugs were after Gabriella.

They wouldn't stop until they found her. He pulled his phone from his pocket and called her again. Again, no answer. *Please God, let her be okay. And Eli, too, I suppose.*

Reporters reported the news. They didn't live it. Unless they were combat reporters.

Feeling this angry and this scared rattled him.

Time for the next story. That was his life. Moving from one story to the next.

Only he didn't see how he could move on from this one. Especially if something happened to Gabriella and her brother.

If only he could figure out how the invasion related to gun smuggling. What was on the cell phone these men were so anxious to find? What had Jake Benoit or his CI documented that was so important to those thugs? It could be texts or video or recorded conversations. The possibilities were tantalizing. Evidence someone didn't want to fall into the hands of the police. That was the real story. The next story. His editor was already salivating over the possibilities.

"How are you?"

He glanced up. Natalie pushed through the screen door and rolled her chair out onto the porch. He managed a smile. "Breathing again. You?"

"Worried about Gabriella. Thankful to be alive." She slipped off her glasses and rubbed her eyes. Without them, she appeared even younger. "Thankful no one was hurt. Saying my prayers."

Even after everything she'd been through, she still looked like a movie star. She didn't seem happy to have him on her front porch. What had he done? Besides try to ward off her attackers? His grip tightened on the laptop. "The kids?"

"Anxious to tell Aunt Gabby all about it. It won't hit them until they try to sleep tonight. We'll have some sleepless nights in our future." Her effort to be matter-of-fact failed miserably. "Did it seem strange to you that the leader was so polite?"

"Yeah. He was polite." Never had civility been so brutal and threatening. Deacon took a breath and worked to keep his face neutral. "He certainly knew how to instill fear with very little effort."

"Even when they searched the house, they were careful not to make a mess."

"He was almost grandfatherly." Deacon warded off the image of Camouflage Man with his arms around Ava. "Until he sprayed the bookshelves with a semiautomatic."

"Yes, until then." Her chuckle held bitterness. "I lied to him. When he realizes that, he'll be back."

"He put you in an untenable position. Your kids or your sister."

"I have no qualms about lying. I needed to misdirect them from Gabriella and keep the kids safe. Now I have to figure out what to do next. My children have been through so much. I won't let them be hurt."

"Kids are resilient." At least that's what he'd been told. He had no experience with children. He'd grown up in a household with older cousins. "And you're an expert in dealing with trauma and children. They're in good hands."

"You were writing a story for the paper?" She pointed to his laptop. Her tone became more clinical. "About what happened?"

A story for the paper, and the blog, and Facebook, and whatever other social media his editor deemed appropriate. Times had changed. "Yes."

"About these children and everything they went through? You're putting it in the paper for one hundred thousand people to read?"

Tiny tendrils of regret grew and tightened around his throat. Usually, he didn't mind people's distaste for his job. Reporting the news was important. But just now, making that look in her gray eyes go away seemed just as important. "Give or take, our readership is down . . . Internet news, twenty-four-hour cable, blogs. But yeah, that's what I do."

"How do you look at yourself in the mirror when you're reaping benefits from other people's tragedies?"

"I don't reap benefits. I barely make enough to pay my bills. I tell stories, stories that need to be told. People need to know what's going on in the world. How else will they make informed decisions?" He stopped. Why did he feel the need to make this woman understand what he did for a living? "Did you reach Gabriella? I tried and still no answer."

"She's not picking up. Neither is Eli." She shivered. Her gaze wandered to the yellow bells and Pride of Barbados blooming in the front yard, bright yellows and oranges amid grass already starting to go brown from the summer heat. "I hope they're . . . I hope everything is . . . okay."

"Detective Cavazos knows the ropes. As much as I dislike the guy, I figure Gabriella is pretty safe with him."

"Are you in love with my sister?"

The question hung in the thick, humid air. Deacon smoothed his hands over the laptop. At one time he'd considered it. More than once, if he was truthful. "What makes you ask that?"

"It's the way you say her name."

"We're friends, but our views on life are very different. She may be a chef now, but she has a lawyer's mind. A law-and-order view of the world." He let his gaze fall to the flowers in the yard. "Besides, I could never love a woman who doesn't like jazz."

Please God, tell me this woman likes jazz.

"She deserves a man who appreciates her."

"Yes, she does, but she's an adult, and she's made her choice—no matter what she may say." Which wasn't much, not to him anyway. She was too classy to complain about her love life to another man. "You don't like Eli either?"

"I don't dislike him. He's a flawed man fighting demons just like the rest of us. I don't like what loving him has done to my sister."

She slipped on her glasses with long, thin fingers. She had beautiful hands. "Anyway, she's in danger. She needs to know that. We should be searching for that phone."

"Don't look for anything. That's what the cops are for. You don't want to put those kids . . ." Deacon stared at her lifted hand. "We told the cops everything we know. Detective Dunbar will get in touch with Eli. You keep trying to call Gabriella."

He pulled a business card from his shirt pocket and held it out. "Call me after you talk to her."

"Why, so you can grill me for more information?"

Her tone stung. "So I know she's all right. And what the plan is to keep you and the kids safe."

"You're not staying?" Suddenly she sounded concerned. A spurt of relief flooded him. She didn't think he was so bad after all. "Where are you going?"

"I need to follow up on some things. But I'm only a phone call away. I promise." Amazing how ten minutes of shared, unmitigated terror could forge a bond between two people. "Do you have a place to go tonight?"

Natalie's face smoothed. "We'll stay here, of course."

"No, you won't." He halted. A woman in a wheelchair, little kids. These guys were cowardly, gutless monsters who hid their faces while they did their dirty work. Nothing—not even the cops—could keep them from coming back and finishing the job. "You can't stay here. You heard what they said. Don't you have family you can stay with?"

"My dad is in New Orleans. Mom is in England." Emotion seeped into her voice, but her expression didn't change. "We'll be fine. Marty is next door. Or we could always move to a hotel. One that will take a dog and a cat."

Deacon blew out air in a gusty sigh. This was crazy. They were part of his story. Story and private life stayed separate. Cardinal rule.

But he'd never been shot at with the subject of his story before. Never drowned in his story's gray eyes. "Look, my editor wants me in Laredo. I know you don't understand what I do or why I do it, but I have to do it. Maybe it can help both of us. You can get away from here. You can be close to Gabriella. You can help figure out where to search for this phone. You can be there when they find Jake."

She frowned. "What are you saying?"

"I'm saying I'll take you—all of you—to Laredo with me. My aunt and uncle live there. They have a nice, big house with several extra bedrooms. It has an excellent security system in a gated community. You'll stay with them."

The screen door opened again. This time Ava and Cullen spilled out. Each carried a big cookie—they looked like their aunt's creation.

"That's a good idea. The kids would love a road trip." Marty followed behind them. He eased the door shut while Ava climbed onto Natalie's lap and Cullen flopped into the rocker next to Deacon's chair. Marty's tone was carefully neutral. It said *don't scare the kids.* "You could use a vacation, right, kids?"

"I want to go to Disney World." Cullen spoke through a mouthful of cookie. "Or to the beach."

"We need more time to plan for that." Natalie summoned a smile for her children. "This is a spur-of-the-moment road trip. To Laredo."

"Because of the bad men?" Ava snuggled against her mother's chest. "I didn't like them. They were mean."

"Yes, they were." Natalie stroked the girl's hair. "But God protected us, and He'll keep protecting us."

"I'll take care of the house and the animals. When those beasts come back, I'll be here." The determination in Marty's voice matched the angry glitter in his jasper eyes. "Count on that, kiddo."

"Then it's settled." Clearing his throat, Deacon disentangled himself from Cullen and stood. "You'll be safe with Aunt Piper and Uncle George. And they're fun." Deacon edged toward the steps. Time to make arrangements. To balance this new twist of responsibility with his job. "They have a swimming pool in their backyard. And parrots that talk. And they like to play Twister."

"I like pools. I never met a parrot." The uncertain look disappeared from Ava's face, replaced with a shiny glow of anticipation. Kids were easy. He should have some. Ava slid from her mother's lap. "Cullen, we're going to Laredo. Let's get our suitcases. Maybe we can see *Abuelo* and *Abuelita*!"

"¿Abuelo? I thought your parents—"

"Eli's parents. My parents never come here. The kids haven't seen them in years. My husband's parents are in Italy so . . . We always thought Gabby and Eli would get married. They got attached to his parents, and we've stayed in touch."

She wheeled her chair toward Marty and touched his arm. "Are you sure?"

"I'll call my brothers in Austin." Marty fingered the smartphone in his big hand. "All three are veterans, two were Army Rangers. They'll come down to stay. We'll be ready."

A military contingent. Deacon grinned. If he decided to return to the Benoit house, Camouflage Man would get his own surprise. "I've got a few things to wrap up here, then I'll come for you. Don't go anywhere."

The sound of Natalie laughing—a bedraggled, halfhearted laugh, but still a laugh—followed him down the steps to his SUV. Her words echoed around him. "Where would we go? We'll be right here, waiting for you."

The visual forced Deacon to slow for a second. What was he getting himself into? Taking a woman in a wheelchair and two children to Laredo and involving his aunt and uncle in something dangerous? All for what? Up to this point in twenty-nine years of life the most he'd ever been responsible for was feeding the fish in his aquarium.

For the first time, standing on the sidelines wasn't enough.

CHAPTER 13

GABRIELLA EYED THE NUMBERS on the house. At eight o'clock on a Friday night quiet reigned in this neighborhood with its medium-sized, less-than-affluent houses. The cars parked in the driveways were fancier than the houses. Most of them had ornate bars on the windows and keep-out, watchdog signs on chain-link fences. Landscaping was sparse, mostly rubber trees and lantana and bougainvillea vines bursting with purple-and-hot-pink flowers. Alberto Garza's family lived on a west-side Laredo street that was surprisingly somewhere in the middle in a town that had always been starkly divided between haves and have-nots.

She spotted the house number. Her stomach flip-flopped. The Garzas already received the news. They'd had some time to digest it. Had they passed the denial and gone straight to the anger stage? Time to find out, whether she liked it or not. They might know something that would help her find Jake. "They're probably eating supper right now." She hazarded a glance at Eli. He looked as happy to be here as she was. "Maybe we should do this tomorrow. They've had a terrible day."

"We should get it over with." Eli glanced at his watch. "Tomorrow isn't going to be any better for them, and we'll have all night to think about it."

"Right."

Wherever the Garzas were in the grieving process, they weren't going through it alone. Vehicles jammed the broad half-circle cement drive in front of the pale-pink one-story stucco house. A lone white

76

Mercedes led the pack of a dozen dark-colored SUVs and pickup trucks.

Eli parked behind a long line of cars on the street. He opened Gabriella's door for her. "Are you ready for this?"

She smoothed her sleeveless blouse—already damp with perspiration—and patted her limp hair. If San Antonio was hot, it was nothing compared to Laredo. Her hands were shaking. "Yep."

A wiry, young guy dressed in black jeans and a black undershirt answered the door. His gaze traveled from Gabriella to Eli. "Who are you?" Thanks to a fat silver stud embedded in his tongue, he sounded as if he had a speech impediment.

Eli waved his badge and made the introductions. "We're very sorry to bother you at a time like this, but we really need to speak with Alberto's parents."

"They already talked to some policemen. We're making plans for my brother's funeral—for when they release his body to us. They can't even tell us when that will be. Leave us alone." The teenager's hand went to his face. The tears tattooed across his knuckles matched the ones he tried to hide on his cheeks. "My only brother is dead. My parents lost a son. We don't want to talk to you. Can't you understand that, *ese?*"

"We're very sorry for your loss." Eli's tone was soft, respectful. "We hate to intrude, but we're trying to find the people who did this to your brother."

Gabriella stepped over the threshold into the teenager's space. "Your brother came to me." She spoke to him the way she spoke to crime victims on the stand. With the greatest of empathy. "I spoke with him before he died."

The teen's eyes reddened. His jaw worked. "You're . . . the one. The police said . . . you found him?"

"He found me."

The boy's response was lost in a shuffle of feet. A man who

clutched a housecoat over a paunch of a belly with one hand and a glass in the other ambled into the foyer. "Diego, who is this?"

"*Papi*, it's the lady who found Beto."

"He found me." That fact needed to be clear. She hadn't asked for this. She hadn't gone looking for it. "He came to me."

"Let them in, Diego." Mr. Garza raised a stubby hand and waved them forward. "Come."

His gait was so unsteady, Diego had to guide him forward down a long tile hallway into a sitting room packed with at least two dozen people in all shapes and sizes. All red-eyed, tissues in hand, all staring at Gabriella and Eli. Mr. Garza jerked his bald head. "Leave us, por favor."

The room cleared. Except for two women on a stiff brocade sofa. The older one, a lovely woman with silver-streaked black hair swept back in an elegant bun, sat ramrod straight, hands clasped in her lap. The younger woman continued to sob quietly into a tissue. Diego went to her while Mr. Garza patted the other woman's shoulder. "*Mamá*, it's the lady *con la policia de San Antonio.*"

"They have come to tell us what happened to Beto?" Her enormous brown eyes, dark with mascara and eyeliner, peered up at Gabriella. They were clear and piercing. "You found my Alberto?"

"He found me."

"Oh, you were there when he died?" The younger woman's sobs increased in volume. "Did he say anything about me? I'm his girlfriend, Kristina Briones. Did he mention me?"

"I'm so sorry." The need to be truthful walked the tightrope of compassion. "He only spoke a few words. He was very injured."

Diego's arm encircled the girl. She collapsed on his shoulder.

"Why did he come to you?" Mrs. Garza's voice was dry and crackling like dead leaves underfoot in the fall. "Who are you?"

Gabriella sank onto the love seat across from the women. For some reason Mrs. Garza seemed in control of the room and the situation.

Mr. Garza stood guard, his hand on her shoulder, but Mrs. Garza clearly would do the talking. "I'm no one in particular. I own a restaurant in San Antonio. It's possible your son knew my brother."

"Who is your brother?"

Gabriella explained. Her face anxious for the first time, Mrs. Garza plucked at the lace on her black floor-length skirt. She peeked up at her husband, then back at Gabriella. "Alberto was premedicine at the university. How would he know an ATF agent?"

"That's what we're trying to determine." Eli spoke for the first time. "Mr. and Mrs. Garza, a college education is very expensive these days. Medical school, astronomical. Please take no offense, but how was he paying for it?"

"He was a good student. He received a scholarship, some grants. It wasn't enough to cover everything. It was hard, but he worked."

"Worked doing what?"

"He had a job on the campus. At the student recreation center." Mr. Garza spoke up. "He did other things. Worked for his uncle. Picked up items for his uncle's store and brought them to Laredo for him."

Eli shifted, his gaze intense. Gabriella tried to unobtrusively elbow him. He glowered at her. "What kind of items? What uncle? What store?"

Mr. Garza's eyes narrowed. The grief-stricken father gone momentarily, he set his glass on the end table with a definitive smack. "What did my son say to you, exactly, *Señorita* Benoit?"

"He knew my name and he mentioned Jake, but he died before he could tell me whatever it was he needed to tell me." Gabriella gripped her hands in her lap, trying to keep her voice level. "That's why I'm trying to find out more about your son. Anything you could tell me about his life might help. Something has happened to my brother. Your son was trying to tell me my brother needed me to do something or come to him."

"He was a good son, a good student, a responsible young man." Mrs. Garza's long nose wrinkled. Her eyebrows lifted. "Do not think otherwise. Undoubtedly, he was in the wrong place at the wrong time."

"You still haven't answered my question." Eli's tone softened. "What store? What items?"

"My brother, Manuel Figueroa, owns a sporting goods store here in Laredo." Mrs. Garza's thin lips pursed. "He also has some pawn shops and an auto repair shop. He's a good businessman who employs many people."

"And your nephews, Rudy and Chuy, work for him."

"*Sí.*" Her voice cracked. "Alberto, he is good student, good boy. He never does anything wrong. Always so good in school."

"Until he started buying weapons for someone else. What's the name of the store?"

"No. No. I don't believe it."

"Mrs. Garza, I talked to a store manager in San Antonio who sold him the guns. What's the name of your brother's store?"

"You're just trying to blame Beto for something he didn't do." Kristina straightened, sniffed, and wiped her nose. "Señorita Benoit, this Jake Benoit. He's the one in the newspaper today. The one they're looking for who murdered the man on the banks of the river and then ran away."

"Jake never ran from anything in his life." These people were grieving, but they didn't get to sully her brother's reputation either. "He's an honorable man. If we can find him, maybe we can find out who did this to your son."

Mrs. Garza looked up at her husband. His face darkened to a molten red. "No."

"Yes." Mrs. Garza turned to Kristina. "Tell them what you told me."

Kristina huddled among the members of her dead boyfriend's family. Her long hair was wet and matted to her neck. "Alberto texted me Thursday afternoon. He said he was in trouble and he had to leave town." She chewed her bottom lip. "He said he'd gotten mixed up in something bad, but it was a mistake. A big mistake. He kept saying he was sorry, sorry, sorry."

"What kind of trouble? Sorry for what?" Gabriella grappled with the need for restraint, the need for more information, and the desire to escape this room with air so heavy with grief it threatened to crush her. This was one of the many reasons she chose to leave the legal profession. "What did he get mixed up in?"

"He said they'd found out."

"Who found out what?"

"Everybody, apparently." Her brittle laugh cracked and fell around her. "Your brother knew Beto had been buying weapons in San Antonio for . . . for someone here in Laredo."

"He was a straw buyer." They already knew this. It didn't help. "Who was he buying for?"

Kristina went on as if she hadn't heard. "He needed the money. He couldn't make rent. He was ashamed to tell his parents. He knew they would want him to come home and go to school here in Laredo. So he asked his uncle for advice about getting a job. Mr. Figueroa said he could use his help, running errands. Money problem solved."

"So the task force ID'd him as a buyer and sent Jake to bring him in." Eli leaned against the wall next to the door, his arms crossed.

"Except the ATF wanted him to stay in play, that's what they called it. They wanted to get the guy here in Laredo who was selling to the cartel."

The cartel. Bad guys to cross. Very bad guys. "So his connection found out he was informing?"

Kristina shrugged, her lips quivering. Tears trickled down her bronze cheeks. "I think so. He said he was going to San Antonio. He wouldn't be able to contact me for a while but not to worry. He was going to talk to a lawyer he could trust."

Gabriella exchanged glances with Eli. She was the lawyer. How did Beto know about her? Jake would never reveal family information to a CI. Not intentionally. "What did he say about the lawyer?"

"Only that he thought he could trust her. He said he wouldn't have a phone for a while. When he could, he'd call me. Only he never did." Her anguish a palpable presence in the room, she dropped her head into her hands and sobbed.

Gabriella fought the urge to do the same. Jake had used a college kid to get inside a gun-smuggling ring. Somehow the kid found out about her and came looking for her. Now he was dead, and Jake was missing. What happened to Beto's phone? So many missing pieces and no way to fill them in.

"One more time." Eli stood. "The name of the store here in Laredo. And the address."

This time, Mr. Garza didn't hesitate.

They were almost to the car when Kristina called Gabriella's name, forcing her to halt. The desire to be free of the haunting grief of this family froze her hand to the car handle. She ducked her head, breathed, and turned.

"Please, miss, I need to know." Kristina stumbled down the uneven sidewalk and through the gate. She touched Gabriella's arm. Her fingers were icy. "I didn't want to ask in front of Beto's mama. Did he . . . did he suffer?"

The lump in Gabriella's throat choked her. She squeezed the girl's hand. "He slipped away." It was true. Here one second, gone the next. "He was very brave. He found me and tried to give me a message. It was an honorable thing to do."

"He was a good guy." Kristina hiccuped a sob. "He didn't deserve this." She tugged a pen from her back pocket and turned Gabriella's hand over where she wrote a telephone number on her palm. The pen pressed into her flesh. "Promise me you'll call me when you find who did this. I want to be there to spit in his face. I want him to suffer like Beto suffered."

Gabriella cradled her hand against her chest. "We'll do our very best to find who did this. I promise."

Kristina nodded and backed away. "I hope your brother is still alive."

"Thank you."

Shoulders slumped, she turned and trudged back into the house.

Gabriella turned to see Eli watching her across the hood of the car. He smiled at her. "What are you looking at?"

"You have such a good heart."

"Shut up and get in. We have to find Jake and catch a murderer. Time's wasting."

Still smiling, Eli did as he was told.

CHAPTER 14

———

"GABS! GABBY! YOUR PHONE is buzzing."

Gabriella jerked awake. Eli's fingers touched her cheek, withdrew. In her foggy state of exhaustion, she almost raised her hand to bring it back. So much had happened today. Alberto Garza's family. Sunny Mendez. Kristina Briones. Too much to process. Still, it didn't matter. All that mattered was figuring out how to find Jake. She slid upright in the Charger's leather seat and pushed her hair from her face.

The phone. Jake. News.

Natalie. Her heart jerked in a painful hiccup. She should've called Natalie. She'd be worried. Gabriella rooted through makeup, gum, mints, keys, billfold. Finally, her hand closed around the phone.

Her sister's voice was low and hoarse. Gabriella could barely hear her. "What's the matter, Nat? Are the kids keeping you awake? Tell them I said to get in bed and stay there."

"You're in danger."

"What? What are you talking about? Where are the kids?"

"The kids are in the back of the van, asleep. They're fine. Listen to me. Why haven't you been answering your phone?"

"It was dead and I had to charge it. Then I left it in the car while we interviewed Alberto Garza's family. I'm sorry. Are you okay . . . Did you say back of the van? Why are you in the van?"

"It doesn't matter. Thugs—"

"Back of the van?" The sound of air rushing and static mixed with faint music registered. Natalie wasn't at home. She was driving. Gabriella glanced at her watch. Nine twenty on a Friday night.

"You shouldn't be driving and talking on the phone at the same time. Where are you going?"

"It's hands-free, as you know, and I'm perfectly capable of driving and talking at the same time. Even at night." The snap in Natalie's tone sounded like the old Natalie. The one who married a surgeon ten years her senior, had two children, and still managed to earn a PhD in clinical psychology before she turned twenty-seven. "Deacon is with me."

"Deacon?" Gabriella wrestled her own volume back down. "Deacon Alder, the reporter, is in your van?"

"Yes. He was at the house interviewing me when those thugs broke in."

"Interviewing you? What thugs? What happened?"

The Charger swerved and halted at the curb in a hard brake that knocked Gabriella against her seat belt. Eli's features were set in a grim, stony frown. "What's going on?"

She held up one finger and focused on listening to Natalie's rapid-paced, jerky rendition of a story her tone said even she couldn't believe.

"They wanted a cell phone?"

"A cell phone. But I'm more worried about their preoccupation with you. They seemed to think Alberto Garza told you something before he died. What, I don't know."

"What happened?"

"We didn't have it. They searched the house. Then they left."

"What aren't you telling me?"

"Ava came downstairs in the middle of it. I had to tell them where you were or the man would hurt her."

Gabriella's throat constricted. Her lungs no longer took in air. She gripped the door handle with her free hand. Her fingernails bit into the flesh of her palm. "Is she . . . Did they . . . ?"

"What?" Eli released his seat belt as if preparing to spring into action. "What's going on?"

"She's okay. Everybody's okay. But I lied. I told them you went to Houston. They threatened to come back if they didn't find you."

The shaking of her arms and hands made it hard for Gabriella to keep the phone on her ear. "So they just turned the place upside down and left?"

"They fired a few shots." Natalie's voice dropped to a whisper. "They said it was a warning for you."

Jake, what did you get us into? Gabriella pushed her door open and stumbled from the car. Eli followed. A streetlight lit up a bus stop bench. She grabbed the back of it. Only the fact that her stomach was empty kept her from hurling. She drew a shaky breath. "So that's why you're in the van."

"Yes. Marty and his brothers are watching the house. They're taking care of Jowls. The kids insisted Artemis come too."

Marty had three brothers, all vets. He'd shared his family history at one of many neighborhood block parties. "Where are you going?"

"To Laredo."

"You're what? No, no, no, it's no better here. You're safer in San Antonio." Maybe. Not at the house. "Deacon, what are you thinking letting her come to Laredo? Have you lost your mind?"

"Priestess of Pie, how goes it?" Deacon's attempt to sound jaunty came out more like a knock-knock joke at a funeral. "Have you learned anything about your brother's whereabouts?"

"Nothing I plan to share with you. This seems a little far to go to get a story. Even for you."

"This isn't about a story." The exhaustion in his voice had been replaced with a steely anger. "You need police protection. Real protection. Not just Eli and his ego. The ATF needs to find Jake before the bad guys do."

The painful hiccup was back. "What are you talking about?"

"Those guys weren't playing around. I've never experienced anything like this in my life."

Going from reporting about crime to being the victim of a crime. It had to be a new perspective for Deacon. Not one anyone should experience. "Are you all right?"

"Yeah, just slightly freaked out."

"Why are you coming to Laredo? This town is more volatile than an IED."

"I may be saving their lives." The earlier spurt of anger had been replaced with a tired irritation. "You can thank me later."

Panic fueled the anger that blew through Gabriella at the thought of anyone trying to hurt Natalie and the kids. Coupled with not knowing where Jake was or if he was even alive. It was too much. *God, it's too much. Why is this happening?*

She settled onto the bench, legs suddenly weak. Eli's shadow hovered over her. He put both hands on her shoulders. She grabbed his fingers and hung on.

"Who's on it? Who's investigating?"

"Homicide, ATF, the same crew that has the Garza murder."

"Where are you going, exactly?"

"To my aunt and uncle's house. They raised me. You can trust them. They live off Del Mar Boulevard in a very nice gated community. Good security." Deacon's sigh blew across the line. "Look, they'll be safe there. I promise. I wouldn't be bringing them to Laredo if I didn't think it was for the best. I promise."

Something about his tone produced a lump in Gabriella's throat. She tried to speak, cleared her throat, and waited a second. Tried again. "I want to see them. Eli will want to interview all of you."

"It'll be too late tonight. We just left the SA city limits. We'll rendezvous tomorrow when we can. In the meantime, be safe."

"What about the story?"

Deacon's laugh was more of a snort. "I filed what I had. Which isn't all that much. I had to do it to keep my job. But right now, keeping Natalie and the kids safe comes first."

This was a huge concession from a hard-core journalist. "You're okay."

"I consider that high praise from you." A soft chuckle trailed off. "Take care of yourself, Miss Queen of Pie."

"You too." Gabriella disconnected, sucked in a long breath, and slid away from Eli's touch. "We need someone to go through Alberto Garza's possessions again. His apartment, everything."

Eli sank onto the bus bench next to her. "Tell me what's happening."

Gabriella smoothed the smartphone's cover, the facsimile of an old library card, against her jeans and breathed. Eli took it from her and laid it on the bench between them. "Start talking."

She told Natalie's story, beginning to end, without stopping. Eli rolled an unlit cigarette between his thumb and forefinger while watching cars go by. His posture was so relaxed, he might have actually been waiting for a bus, but the grit of his jaw and the pulse that jumped there said differently.

"So. They're coming. A lady in a wheelchair. A reporter who doesn't know a Glock from a water gun, and two little, defenseless kids." Eli craned his head from side to side and rubbed his neck. "I'm surprised they didn't bring Artemis."

"They did. The kids refused to leave him."

"Well, you never know when you'll need a trained guard dog."

The image of Artemis's pug face and his massive rotund body standing guard over anyone made Gabriella chuckle. The chuckle turned into an out-and-out laugh. After a second, Eli joined in with a belly laugh she hadn't heard in a long time. They both howled. A couple walking by, hands linked, stared and walked faster.

"Sorry, I don't know what's so funny." Gabriella swallowed another giggle. "Hysteria mixed with exhaustion."

"Yeah, or maybe I'm just that funny." Eli snorted. "Sorry, it's not really that funny."

They both sighed.

"We need to get you to Alder's aunt and uncle." Eli stood as if he intended to go now. "You can stay with Natalie and the kids."

"In your dreams. We need to find that cell phone and we need to find Jake."

"Do you have a raisin for a brain? They're looking for you. I need to keep you under wraps."

"All the more reason I shouldn't stay with Natalie. It puts her and the kids in danger. I won't do it. Not with Jake still missing. Maybe dead."

The stare down lasted several seconds.

Eli plopped on the bench. "So they're searching for a cell phone. I imagine Dunbar has already gone through Garza's stuff with a fine-tooth comb." He toyed with his wristwatch, his expression thoughtful. "And the Feds too. I'm sure there's nothing left at that apartment that hasn't been dissected."

"What about here? Maybe he gave it to the girlfriend. Or hid it at his house."

"He was meeting your brother. If it contained evidence, he would've had it with him."

"The Mitsubishi?"

"They didn't find it in the car. That's why these thugs are after you. He told you something they don't want you to tell me. They think you have the phone."

"What's on it that's worth killing for?"

"Depends on what Garza knew. Who the gun buyer was. Who the facilitator is. The location of the safe house where the guns go before being transported. The transportation operation. Recorded conversations. Videos. Who knows? Obviously we've got major players involved here or the Feds wouldn't be pursuing this. Jake wouldn't have been involved if it was small potatoes. It still goes back to the guns." Eli held out a hand. "For now, you're going back to the hotel. You've had it."

"What about you?" She stared at his hand. It had been warm and sure on her shoulder only a few seconds ago. "You've had it too."

He glanced at his watch. "The gun store is closed by now. Maybe I can get in touch with Jake's partner."

"If you're going to see Teeter, I'm going too. Where you go, I go."

"Not so I've noticed."

She stood and brushed past him. "Whose fault is that?"

Eli vaulted from his seat and opened her door with a flourish. He waited until she slid past him into the seat, then leaned in, his face close to hers. "I know you like to tell people it was all my fault, querida, but you and I both know there was more to it than that. You left me long before you decided I cheated on you."

She closed her eyes so she wouldn't have to see the pain etched on his face. He might be right. A series of unfortunate events . . . her parents' divorce, Paolo's death and Natalie's injuries, and then a suspect in a homicide shot Eli. The odds of getting hurt multiplied with every new devastating event.

Had she been looking for a reason to leave before she got hurt? If she had, she'd left far too late.

CHAPTER 15

IF HER FRIENDS HAD used Gabriella's name in the same sentence with *hotel* and *Eli* before this evening, she would've laughed them out of the house. Yet, here she was. Standing outside her hotel room door, Eli looking over her shoulder. Using the overhead corridor light to illuminate the black hole that was her purse, Gabriella fished out her hotel key card and swiped it. The red light stayed red. "Oh, please."

She tried again. Nothing. She closed her eyes and leaned her forehead against the door. Her legs would give out any second, and she'd be a crumpled heap on the dirty hotel carpet in front of Eli. Her whole body ached to lie down. Five or six hours of sleep and she'd be good to go another forty-eight or until they found Jake. She swiped yet again. Same infernal red light stared at her, unblinking, standing between her and her bed.

Eli tugged the card from her hand and swiped. The light changed to a bright, cheery green. He pushed the door ajar and handed her the key card. "Get some sleep."

She stuck the offending card in her pocket. Tomorrow, she'd ask management for a new, more reliable one. "Tomorrow we find Jake. Sunday, we go to your dad's church before we head back to San Antonio."

They would find Jake. No other alternative existed. Then they would all go to church together and thank God for His goodness and His mercy and His grace. Then she would get back to Courtside where she could experiment with a new recipe, create soufflés, and knead bread dough until her shoulders ached.

Eli's bloodshot gaze held hers for a second before it dropped. He ducked his head so long locks of his dark hair hid his eyes. She almost missed the shake of his head.

"Your dad finds out you've been in town and you didn't come to church, he'll kick your behind all the way to Monterrey." She could hear the fire-and-brimstone sermon as clearly as if Xavier Cavazos stood in the corridor with them. "Besides, with everything that's happened, it would be good to hear your father's words of wisdom, don't you think? Maybe he can explain why stuff like this keeps happening."

No explanation existed. Other than the evil that worked so hard to permeate the world. As long as it had a foothold, people like Jake and Eli would never lack for employment.

"Some other church, but not his . . ." Eli blew out air. "I'd be surprised if he let a sinner like me soil the carpet of his sanctuary, but I wouldn't mind sitting next to you at a service. Maybe some of your goodness and faith will rub off on me."

A mental snapshot of them sitting together on the pew made her throat tighten. Going to church with Eli had once been a dream of hers. "Everyone who enters a church is a sinner, including me. You said yourself your father believes in forgiveness. You have to face him sooner or later."

"You don't know anything about my dad and me." He moved away from her and turned to face the guardrail overlooking a full parking lot. "Besides, it's not his forgiveness I need."

Choosing to ignore the last statement, she left the door open and went to stand next to him. "Because you've always refused to talk to me about him. I'm the last one you talk to about how you feel. You wouldn't talk to me about your work. You wouldn't talk to me about how you felt after you got shot. You go off and lick your wounds in some dark corner and leave me feeling like a bystander."

"Oh yeah, men love talking about *feelings*." He glanced at her. She held his gaze, willing him to let her in, just once. He ducked his head, as usual. She thought he would chicken out, as usual. Then his mouth opened. "He made me memorize the Ten Commandments and recite them before I could sit down to eat supper."

"You could've learned those a whole lot better."

Gabriella's acidic tone earned her a small chuckle. "I remembered them fine."

"Your dad was worried about your eternal soul."

"I needed a dad who was worried about his son—all of him, not just his soul. When I became a police officer, I thought that would show him . . . show him I'm good."

"You are good."

"No, I've done things . . . things you don't know about." He straightened and pulled the ever-present cigarette from behind his ear. "And then I messed up things with you. My dad saw that coming a mile away—150 miles away, actually."

"Why can't you tell me?" The million-dollar question. "Is it worth it, you not giving me any explanation?"

"Tell you?"

"Don't play dumb with me."

"There are things I've done that I'm not proud of. Things that happened before we even knew each other." His jaw worked. "I'm trying to come to grips with them. Figure out how to make my life work. I thought I should do that first."

Her throat ached with the effort to hold back tears. She swallowed and prayed she could get the words out without crying. His refusal to let her in never ceased to hurt. "Did it ever occur to you that I should be a part of that effort?"

The words were a bare whisper.

"I wanted you to be. I still want that." His bass grew hoarse. "I just needed time to figure things out. You exploded before I could."

The creaking of his apartment door sounded in her ears just as it had that night when she'd gone to tell him she wanted to try again. She'd missed their counseling session for the third time, and he wasn't returning her calls. Everything had changed after he was shot. The missed lunch dates. The sudden disappearance for the weekend. Hanging up his phone when she walked into the room. She was afraid of what the future held, but more afraid of living without him. She planned to tell him she wasn't ready to give up.

The door opened. Instead of Eli, there stood a woman in a black silk robe. She looked as if she'd just stepped off the catwalk in Madrid. "Can I help you?" She had a gorgeous accent to match bronze skin and eyes the color of *café con leche*.

"I know, and I'm sorry. But some things can't be undone or unseen. And you won't explain yourself." Gabriella snatched the cigarette from his fingers, snapped it in two, tossed it on the cement, and ground it under her heel. "Stop tempting yourself. These things will kill you."

"I knew you still cared about me." He went back to studying the parking lot. "If you knew the whole story, you'd be even less inclined to forgive me."

"Trust me."

"Like you trust me?"

"I was there. I saw her. In your line of business and my old job, that's considered clear and convincing evidence."

"You saw a woman in my apartment. Did you see me with her?"

"She was in a robe."

"Circumstantial."

"Eli."

"Trust me." He stepped into her space. The words hung in the air between them, vibrating with everything unspoken. Lights sparked and crackled around her.

She inhaled his scent and felt his touch even though his fisted hands hung at his sides. "You don't make it easy."

"I'm working on it. Give me time. Is that too much to ask?"

The same old stalemate.

"Time is running out. I want kids. I want a family."

His body jerked as if she'd slapped him. He ducked his head. "Life is complicated. Give me a chance to figure it out."

His pain permeated down to her marrow. "I don't know if I can."

Eli went back to memorizing the parking lot below them. Gabriella let out her breath, only just then realizing she'd been holding it.

"So, I need to go see Sunny tomorrow after we see Natalie and the kiddos. Meet Sunny's dad. I have the feeling she wasn't telling us everything. Maybe she knows something about what Jake was doing. Maybe she was searching for the cell phone when we busted in on her." His tone had reverted to Eli the Cop. "We have to figure out who Alberto Garza was buying for. That's the key. The person Jake was going to take down after he got Garza in custody. If Sunny Mendez was really Jake's girlfriend, then maybe that's her family's only involvement."

Gabriella leaned against the railing. The muscles in her legs quivered. "Maybe. But it's all we've got at this point. It's got to be a lead. The more time that passes, the more I'm sure—"

His knuckles were white on the railing. "I know."

"If Jake was bringing in the guy, he didn't do it alone. The ATF doesn't work that way."

He let go of the railing and propped himself up on his forearms, his head down. "Have you ever met your brother's partner?"

Gabriella wracked her brain. "Teeter? I don't think so. I've heard his name, that's it. It turns out there's so much about my own brother that I don't know. We used to be so close. How did that happen?"

"Did it ever occur to you that we're a lot alike in some ways? After your parents divorced, you got quieter. More self-contained. Paolo died. Natalie ended up in a wheelchair. You got quieter still." Eli took a breath. He'd just strung together more sentences than she'd ever heard him complete on a subject not related to his work. "Then you broke up with me. Maybe Jake didn't want to add salt to your wounds with his happy news."

"That's ludicrous." Gabriella paused. Not really. And the carefully chosen words signified Eli had given her emotional state over the years considerable thought. "But thank you for trying."

"I have my own experience with siblings."

Eli rarely talked about the fabulous four as he called his older siblings. Most of what she knew had come from his mother, Virginia, or Christmas cards sent from faraway places. His oldest brother was career Air Force. Another served as a missionary in Africa. One held a post as a physician with the World Health Organization. His lone sister taught school in inner-city Dallas.

Only Eli lived close to home and aging parents who always seemed to be trying to hide their disappointment at his choices. The child with the most unresolved issues would be the one who would care for those parents in their old age.

None of that could be solved tonight. "Larry Teeter might know more about my brother than I do."

He faced her again. This time, his hand really did touch her face. A deliberate gesture. One finger traced her jawline. She froze. Her skin burned white hot. He brushed her bangs back from her eyes. "Only about what was going on recently. Jake's still your little brother. When we find him, you can chew him out about not keeping in touch. And things will be different."

The question implicit in the words hung in the air between them. Despite a split second of hesitation, she edged away from his touch. "Good night, Eli."

His hand dropped. His gaze enveloped her. "Do you ever wonder why you're thirty-four and I'm the closest you've ever come to getting married?"

She edged toward the door. "Apparently, I had good reason to be hesitant."

"Your parents aren't a good example of how marriage works."

"Examples don't matter. Your parents have been married sixty years and you still—"

"We'll do it better."

"Who is she to you?"

He shook his head.

Gabriella grabbed the door handle and slipped inside her room. "As always, it was good talking to you, Eli."

He remained at the railing, his back to her. "Tomorrow will be a long day. Get some sleep."

Fat chance of that now.

She closed the door and double locked it. Was she locking herself in or Eli out? The question ran laps in her head long after she slipped under the sheets and closed her eyes.

CHAPTER 16

THE WHOLE "ARE WE there yet?" thing wasn't a joke. Kids really did ask that question over and over again on road trips. Cullen and Ava had taken turns interspersing that question with two dozen other ones. Was that a cow by the side of the road? Did cows drink milk? How did airplanes fly? Where was Aunt Gabriella? Would Uncle Jake be in Laredo? Did Deacon's uncle have dogs? Cats? A playscape? Natalie answered every question with a patience that seemed to come from an unending well.

Finally, they finished their third snack of animal crackers and apple juice and nodded off. The hiss of air streaming from the AC combined with the steady beat of the wind against the Toyota Sienna soothed Deacon's frazzled nerves. He could almost fall asleep now that he had accepted that Natalie could, in fact, drive with the help of a computerized system that allowed her to do everything with her hands.

Her presence, on the other hand, kept him awake. In the enclosed space she smelled wonderful—like roses. And she was good at small talk, good at drawing him out. She didn't seem to mind the steady stream of 18-wheelers that passed the van like it was standing still. The way their speed and bulk made the van sway in their wake. She didn't even mind when the only radio stations left were in Spanish or played country music.

"Stop looking at me like that."

"What? I'm not looking at you." Deacon forced his gaze back to the passenger-side window. Nothing but darkness. It didn't matter.

He'd made this drowsiness-inducing trip down 1-35 South hundreds of times. Just a bunch of mesquite and prickly pear cacti dotted the scenery with an occasional ranch gate that led to an unseen sprawling ranch house. "Why would I look at you? I've seen a woman drive before. It isn't pretty."

"You flinch every time a semi passes us."

"I do not."

"I'm a good driver. Maybe even a better one than I was before the accident." She patted the controls that allowed her to drive with her hands. "This baby has all the bells and whistles. It's an AEVIT system."

"I know. You told me. You're doing great."

"Thank you. I'm glad you approve." Her tone was dry. "Gabriella sounded exhausted."

"And determined, as usual. She might be a chef now, but she's still tough as any prosecutor I've ever known."

"You knew her when she still practiced?"

"I covered a couple of her cases right after I started at the *Express-News*, right before she quit and opened the restaurant. She had cross-examination down to an art form, and her opening and closing arguments were perfection. Students should study them in law school classes."

"You stayed in touch because her ability to argue impressed you?"

Over the years, they'd parried over her cooking on numerous occasions. She had a sharp, analytical mind and she was well informed about world issues and politics. "And I liked her tiramisu."

"You liked *her*."

"Like I said before, not like that."

Natalie's gaze meandered his way. She sought something. He gave her his best you-can-trust-me look. Which probably made him look more like SpongeBob SquarePants. She focused on the road. "You're sure your aunt and uncle won't mind a dog?"

"Aunt Piper says Cleo, their cat, will love the company." A little white lie. Aunt Piper was being nice. She was like that. "Cleo is short for Cleopatra, Queen of the Cats."

"How long did you live with Piper and George?"

"About ten years."

"A long time." The compassion in her face made her that much more beautiful. "And your parents? You don't have to tell me if you don't want to."

"They died in a small plane crash when I was eight."

"I'm sorry."

"It was a long time ago."

Silence for sixty seconds filled with Artemis's snuffling snores mingled with Ava's more ladylike little-girl snores. "I know how it feels to lose people suddenly and tragically. Your life is divided into before and after."

"I was blessed to have family who took me in and loved me." His early memories were filled with swimming lessons and T-ball and birthday parties, but the later ones were just as good. George and Piper Seville had stepped in with hugs and kisses and the same firm discipline as his parents. "They raised me like their own. They never missed a beat."

"Very blessed."

Deacon glanced over his shoulder. Cullen and Ava both slumbered, their heads back against booster seats. He settled back in his seat. "It must be hard for the kiddos. Losing their dad, moving into their aunt's house. Adjusting to you . . . your . . ."

"The biggest challenges aren't the ones you expect." She rescued him. "Like my bedroom being downstairs and theirs upstairs. They take their baths and then come cuddle with me downstairs. We read stories and then they go upstairs and put themselves to bed."

Not having kids of his own had Deacon at a disadvantage. "Kids don't usually do that?"

"I don't tuck them in." Her voice quivered ever so slightly. "I miss that. Gabriella and I talked about buying another house, one more suited to our situation, but we love this house and it's familiar to the kids. They're fine with it. Kids mature faster in these circumstances, faster than you want them to . . ."

Silence prevailed for a few miles.

"Paolo was larger than life. Funny. Sarcastic. Passionate about being a surgeon. Passionate about everything." She spoke as if there had been no pause. Her left hand touched the lever mounted on the car door. It allowed her to accelerate and brake. Her right hand fingered the mini steering wheel mounted in front of the console. "At least that's the way I remember him now."

"Now?"

"Some people talk about memories fading. For me, it's not like that. I think sometimes that my memories get shinier with age, more sparkly with time. Paolo's picture is clearer in my mind than the photos on the fireplace mantel. He was seven feet tall, pure brawn. Antonio Banderas gorgeous." She chuckled. "When really he was five eleven in his boots, cute in a sort of nerdy way—"

"Us guys really like being called short and nerdy."

"But he was so charismatic. Romantic. He loved the big flourish and the small touches. I never knew what would be next. A week in Hawaii or a single rose on my pillow."

Hard shoes to fill. "You miss him."

"I have a full life. My practice. The kids. Trying to keep Gabby in line."

"That would be a full-time job. Especially with Eli in and out of the picture."

"Eli's Eli. He has a good heart. At least I thought he did until he did what he did." Silence filled the van with white noise from the radio. "I never thought he would do something like that."

"It boggles the mind why anyone would do that to your sister."

"No woman deserves it."

"Gabriella doesn't talk about it."

"Of course not. It reminds her too much of what happened with my parents. She still hasn't forgiven them for being human. For having their own lives. My dad is of French-Creole descent. We have pirates in our family tree. He loves the ocean and sailing and the French Quarter. His idea of fun is a crawfish boil, a Cajun band, and an occasional icy-cold beer."

"Sounds fun."

"My mom is your stereotypical British subject."

"Ah."

"Yeah. A severe case of opposites attract."

"Until they don't."

"Exactly. Their split was awful and bloody and full of histrionics—on my dad's side. My mom slipped away all prim and proper, but I know she tried. She tried so hard. She was tired and homesick. She never really liked South Texas with its mesquite and heat and droughts. She couldn't do it anymore." Natalie sighed. "I don't know why I'm telling you all this. I haven't talked about it in a few years. Gabby refuses to engage in any rehashes. I miss my mom and dad, but I don't begrudge them their lives now. Life is short and hard."

"The divorce doesn't bother you?"

"Of course it does. I prayed that they would get back together. Then I left the struggle at God's feet. It's not something I can control. He'll take it from there."

The lights of Laredo twinkled in the distance. Deacon had seen them hundreds of times over the years. Tonight, with a sensitive, intelligent woman at the wheel, they looked different. Brighter. Beckoning. "You've been through so much. Yet you still believe and trust."

No response for several miles. She glanced his way. "After the accident, I considered all the possible ways for a paraplegic to kill herself."

Deacon breathed a prayer of thanksgiving that she hadn't chosen that way out. "Why didn't you?"

"Ava and Cullen. Gabby. Jake. My parents. I had many reasons to live. Only selfish reasons for choosing not to. It took time, but counting my blessings over and over again allowed me to start to believe that living was better than dying."

"I'm glad you decided to live."

She didn't look his way again, but she did smile. "Me too. Every day is living proof that God is working for my good. The first thing I did after rehab was learn to drive and buy this vehicle. I loved taking road trips before. I love taking them now."

"I wish it were under better circumstances." He groped for words that didn't sound like a corny come-on. "I always liked the beach."

"Me too."

Quiet filled with promise lasted until the next exit.

"This is our exit. Take a left onto Del Mar Boulevard."

She followed his directions, but she kept glancing in the rearview mirror. "You'll think I'm paranoid."

He perused his side mirror. Headlights behind them. Not unusual. "If anyone has the right to be paranoid, we do."

"There's a pickup truck behind us. It passed us a while back. Then slowed down. So I passed it." Her tone was dispassionate. Like a doctor's recounting of symptoms before delivering an unwelcome diagnosis. "It's been hanging back behind us since then."

"For how long?"

"I don't know. I first noticed it around Dilley. Then I didn't see it again for a while. Then it was back."

Eighty miles and some change. "Probably nothing."

"Probably."

What were the odds? The thugs after Gabriella were smart. Follow sister number one to find sister number two. Had they led these monsters right to Gabriella? To the place he'd promised them would be a safe house? "You know what? Let's take a right up here on McPherson Road."

"Is that the way to your house?"

"No, but I feel like a cruise down memory lane in my old hometown. I haven't been here in ages."

"Right." She snorted. "You won't see much in the dark."

"Yeah. I said right on McPherson."

She followed his instructions. A surprising amount of traffic hummed on the streets of Laredo, considering the hour. "Okay, now turn left here at Calton Road."

"Where are we going?"

"Just cruising, like I said." He swiveled in his seat and stared through the back windows. It was tough to see anything but headlights blinding him. He faced front and tried to relax against the leather seat. "Is the truck still there?"

She glanced in the rearview mirror and her side mirror. "When I stopped at the stop sign back there, I could still see it. Are you planning to spirit us away on an airplane? I see airport signs."

"No, although it doesn't sound like a bad idea." His stomach clenched. Too many cups of coffee and not enough food in the last twelve hours. Adrenaline pulsed through him. "Right on Maher Road." He glanced back again. "Do you see the truck?"

"I think so, but they're backing off."

"I bet they are."

"Ah-ha."

"What?"

Natalie shook her finger at him. "I also see signs for the Laredo Police Department Headquarters."

"Yep. It'll be on our right in a few blocks. I used to go there all the time to pick up copies of reports and interview officers. Like I said, memory lane."

"Nice view of the airport." She eased the van into the parking lot and pulled into a van-accessible space. "Nice building."

A few smaller airplanes were parked on the tarmac across the road. "Fairly new. A lot of the city offices have transitioned to this area from downtown."

"You could be a tour guide."

His chuckle sounded weak in his ears. An older model Ram or Toyota Tundra rolled past the entrance to the parking lot and kept going south on Maher Road.

"You're a very smart guy." Natalie turned off the van. Silence prevailed. She sighed, leaned back in her seat, and closed her eyes. "Are we going in?"

"We could get a police escort to my uncle's."

"Because that would be flying under the radar."

"I know. It was just a thought."

"Are we spending the night here?"

"I don't think the police would take kindly to us camping out in their parking lot." As much as he wouldn't mind spending the night this close to a beautiful woman with her two children and a snoring bulldog as chaperones. "Let's give it a few minutes and we'll reverse our steps."

"Are we there yet?"

Deacon jumped and turned. Cullen yawned and stretched. "Are we there yet? I want milk. I need to brush my teeth. Is Aunt Gabby here? What time is it?"

Natalie laughed. Deacon joined her. The hysterical laughter of two people on the run.

CHAPTER 17

PEOPLE WHO LIVE IN subdivisions with gates fool themselves. Gates only keep honest people out. Eli kept that thought to himself as he pulled through the gates into the neighborhood where Deacon Alder's aunt and uncle lived in one of the older subdivisions on Laredo's north side. Decidedly elegant in an upper-middle-class way. The streets were lined with palm trees—not native to this part of Texas—and the houses were mostly two-story white adobe with red tile roofs. A long way from his parents' simple wood home on the south side with its wraparound porch and tiny front yard full of esperanza, Pride of Barbados, and lantana in purple, red, and pink.

Gabby had been silent and distant during the short ride from the hotel. If she slept anything like he did, they both should've forgone the cost of two hotel rooms and spent the night watching movies on pay-per-view. One prickly look from her and he'd dropped any attempt at conversation. Three cups of coffee, and his eyes were still gritty and his mouth dry.

The GPS lady announced their arrival at Piper and George Seville's house in a voice far too chipper for so early in the morning.

"Nice." Gabby unbuckled her seat belt but made no attempt to get out. "I wonder what his uncle does for a living."

"I always thought Alder was from up north." When he gave it much thought, which wasn't often. "He sounds like it when he talks."

"I don't know. He doesn't talk about himself much. He graduated from UT Austin. Parents are dead. That's about all I know." She clutched her purse to her chest and pushed the door open. Then she leaned back as if she'd changed her mind. "All the conversations we've had are always about politics or religion or something happening at the courthouse. It's never personal, at least on his side. He always asks about Natalie and the kids, but when I venture into his territory, he changes the subject."

Talking about a man who so obviously planned to take his spot in Gabby's life did nothing for Eli's frame of mind. "Maybe he has something to hide."

"Or maybe he's a private person." She shot him a dark look. "You should relate to that."

He did. Talking about his problems was as much fun as a prostate exam. But not talking about them had served to cause even more pain. He closed his eyes. The words were on the tip of his tongue. Would his revelation cement the cavernous break in their relationship, or bring them back together? It was a terrible chance to take.

He breathed and eighty-sixed the thought. "I don't relate to anything about a reporter who does nothing but snoop around and try to make the PD look bad in his blogs."

"Sometimes the PD doesn't need any help in that department."

"Whose side are you on?"

"Jake's side." She slid from the car, turned, and stared back at him. "Can you call a truce with Deacon until this is over, please? He's taking care of Nat and the kids. I owe him for that. So give him a break, okay? Let's get their stories and then get to the gun store as soon as it opens."

"Okay."

Frowning, she tucked her windblown hair behind her ear. "Promise?"

"Scout's honor."

"You were never a scout."

And his honor had been called into question. Mercifully, she didn't point out that salient fact. "You take Natalie and the kids. I'll interview Alder."

"He has a first name." She didn't seem convinced.

"I'll take Deacon."

"I'll be listening with one ear."

"You can trust me."

She didn't deign to respond to that laughable comment.

Deacon and Artemis met them at the door. Gabby scooped up the bulldog, who covered her with slippery kisses in response to her steady stream of doggy-love. They followed Deacon into a breakfast nook with lemon walls and white curtains that covered a bay window. It was bigger than Eli's dining room. Nat and the kids sat eating enormous plates of eggs, bacon, toast, and fresh fruit.

Deacon introduced them to his aunt as Pip. She was a tiny lady dressed in a turquoise embroidered Mexican dress like the ones Eli's mom favored. Her feet were bare. Her gray hair hung to her waist. Silver bangle bracelets adorned her age-spot-marked arms and turquoise-and-silver hoops hung from her earlobes. Not the look he expected from someone living in a half-a-million-dollar home.

"Deacon's the only one who calls me Pip as in pipsqueak. It's Piper. You look hungry." Her words were hard to hear over a steady stream of chatter from two gray parrots in matching roomy cages that took up one wall of the nook. Instead of shaking their hands, she hugged them both and planted kisses on their cheeks as if greeting family. "George is cleaning the pool. It doesn't need it, but he's like that. The children are going swimming in a bit. I have fresh oatmeal, eggs, turkey bacon, pineapple, mango, cantaloupe, strawberries, and papaya. Coffee, iced tea, fresh-squeezed orange juice, or chocolate milk."

"Nothing for me, thanks."

"I'll have coffee, please." Gabby swooped down on the kids and covered them in kisses. Ava returned the favor while Cullen pretended to slide under his chair to escape her "girl cooties."

Ava then hurled herself at Eli and landed a hug around his knees.

He lifted her up by the waist until she looked down at him, giggling and breathless. "Hey, beautiful. Are you doing okay?"

"Bad men shot at us."

"I know, but you're safe now, and I'm going to catch the bad guys and put them in jail."

He deposited her on the chair next to her brother and leaned close to both kids. "You understand that, right? Everything will be fine."

"They have parrots. They're African Grays. They talk." Cullen popped up and scooted to the cages. "This is Fidencio. And the other one is Fidencio Two. George says it's easier if they all have the same names. Say hello!"

Eli obliged. The birds' gray plumage had a gorgeous scalloped pattern. Their tails were maroon and their intelligent eyes a sharp orange. They responded by repeating their names and then his. Cullen clapped. "George says they're very smart. They know what they're saying."

"Obviously, Cullen is smitten." Natalie smiled and motioned for her son to sit. "Give Uncle Eli and Aunt Gabriella a chance to breathe, son."

"They have a cat named Cleopatra, the Queen of Cats, but she's hiding from Artemis."

"Enough, son."

"Are you gonna find Uncle Jake?" Ava slipped her small hand into Eli's and leaned against his side, a small, light, fragile weight. "I miss him."

"Me too." He squeezed her hand. "That's the plan."

The clock was ticking. He turned to Deacon, who remained standing in the doorway, his expression distant. "Can we sit somewhere and talk about yesterday?"

Deacon jerked his head toward the sliding glass doors. "It's still cool enough that we can sit by the pool."

Cool was a relative term in Laredo. At eight o'clock in the morning, humid air billowed on a southerly breeze that did nothing to dry sweat. Eli followed him out to a patio that encircled a beautiful tile-edged, peanut-shaped pool with a stone waterfall at one end. The lush landscaping suggested a gardener with a green thumb and an irrigation system. A tall, muscular man clad in a baggy neon-orange swimsuit and flip-flops dropped a net into the well-watered grass and padded toward them. He had a full head of silver hair. The hair on his chest matched. After the introductions that included a warm, firm handshake and a sharp head-to-toe appraisal, George left them to their discussion.

"What does your uncle do for a living?" Eli settled into a patio chair more comfortable than anything in his living room. "He's done all right for himself."

"Import-export. Something to do with sunglasses." Deacon set his coffee on the glass table that separated them. "He's mostly retired now. Two of my cousins took over the business."

"You're sure Natalie and the kids are safe here?"

"I wouldn't have brought them here if I weren't." He ran his hand through already messy black hair. The guy needed a comb. A wrinkled shirt and dark circles under his eyes suggested he, too, had spent a sleepless night thinking about topics like this one. "George had the best possible security system installed when they built the house. It's monitored."

"Gabby and Natalie have a security system."

"But they only turn it on at night."

"If something were to happen to them—any of them—it would break her."

"I know."

Deacon said it as if he knew Gabby intimately, better than Eli. That wasn't possible. No one knew her better than he did. He gritted his teeth and stared at the lapping, crystal-clear water in the pool. The clean scent of chlorine filtered through the air. To be that clean. The water would feel good, but it couldn't wash away his mistakes.

"She deserves better than you."

The gauntlet thrown down. "You don't think I know that."

"So let her go."

"It's none of your business."

"You're so full of yourself you can't see what you're doing to her. If you really cared about Gabriella, you'd let go. You've been haunting her for six months. If you were anyone but a cop, it'd be called stalking."

"Let's stick to the subject at hand. What happened yesterday?"

"Her mother cheated on her father with a mediocre poet and they divorced. Her understanding of love and faithfulness was destroyed. But she decided to trust you. You cheated on her and threw her love away. How do you think she'll ever trust again?"

He hurled the stones with unerring accuracy. This reporter thought he had all his facts, and he knew how to string them together in a succinct story. Fake news. Still, the bruises hurt. Eli groped for self-control, never his strong point. He'd promised Gabby. "What happened yesterday?"

Deacon's recitation was equally succinct. If the sequence of events affected him, it didn't show.

"Polite, huh?"

"In a murderous sort of way."

Bees buzzed the yellow rosebushes that crowded the stone fence that surrounded the backyard, giving the Sevilles some semblance of privacy for their swims.

"One other thing. We think they followed us to Laredo."

"You're kidding me."

Deacon related the details regarding the last leg of their trip. "We stayed in the PD parking lot for about forty-five minutes. No one followed us here."

"You didn't notice someone was following you before? Do you have canned peas for brains?"

"I get that I'm not a cop like you. I don't have catlike reflexes and carry cannon-sized guns, but I care about these women." Deacon stopped. He gritted his teeth. His jaw throbbed. "I don't have any experience with this stuff, but I got them here, and they're safe, so back off."

He was right. As much as it pained Eli to admit it. "Sorry."

"I worked at the paper here after I graduated from UT. It's been a few years, but I still have friends in the media and contacts in law enforcement." Deacon's tone shifted from fierce self-defender to a reporter on the hunt. "I'll start hitting them up."

"For your story?" Eli poured sarcasm over his words like kerosene on a fire. "You claim to care about them, but all you care about is the story."

"I can help find Jake. And end up with a good story when it's all said and done." Deacon's scowl pinned Eli to the chair. "I can multitask by doing my job and making sure my friends don't get hurt."

Unlike some people hung in the air between them.

"I don't need another civilian meddling in this investigation."

"And you don't tell me what to do. I only told you out of courtesy. This is between Gabriella and me."

"There's nothing between you and Gabriella."

"You're right. I'm glad you can finally concede that. But now that I've met her sister and the kids, I have more skin in the game."

Sudden heat crept across Deacon's face. Natalie was a smart, beautiful lady. They were caught up in a volatile situation. His reaction wasn't surprising. But still dangerous. "You're a reporter, not a cop, just remember that."

"Believe me, ten minutes with thugs armed with assault rifles taught me my place."

"So these sources you have. Tell me about them."

"Chris Matthews is a reporter at the *Laredo Morning-Times*. His house has been firebombed. That's how close to the truth he's traveled. Everyone knows there's widespread corruption in law enforcement here. His fiancée works at one of the TV stations. He can tell me what the latest word is and tap their sources."

"What about law enforcement? Do you know homicide detective Carlos Rincon?"

Deacon shook his head. "But I can put out some feelers with my folks. If he's dirty, it's likely somebody knows."

"But nobody does anything about it?" It was a rhetorical question. Laredo was a different world. A border town that was more Mexico than it was United States. Cartel violence had nearly destroyed it. Tourism disappeared in the late nineties. Businesses went belly-up. Poverty, always rampant, grew incrementally. It was the Wild West all over again. "See what you can find out, but be careful."

"Worried about me?"

"Not particularly. But for some reason Gabby cares about you and Natalie chose to come here with you." The words stuck in his throat. He might as well accept this fact now. "So don't give them something else to worry about, or worse, grieve."

"Do you think he's still alive?"

The question that haunted Eli every second of every minute. "It seems unlikely."

Deacon glanced over his shoulder at the house. "Don't tell her that."

"She was a lawyer and prosecutor in the DA's office. She's no stranger to these scenarios."

"She's hanging on to hope."

"Which means so will you and me."

On that, at least, they could agree.

Surveillance equipment would be nice at that moment. Gabriella eyed the sliding glass doors. Nothing about Eli's and Deacon's body language told her how the conversation was going.

"We can always shove them into the pool if they get into a fist-fight over you." Natalie sipped her iced tea and smiled. She seemed more relaxed now that she had poured out the story of yesterday's home invasion to Gabriella. "That would wash some of that testosterone off."

"May the best man win." George stuck a pod in the Keurig and made himself a cup of coffee. The aroma wafted through the breakfast nook, its medicinal effect immediate. "The pen may be mightier than the sword, but I'm still concerned that the gentleman with the gun has the upper hand over my nephew."

"There will be no fistfights." Gabriella offered the mandate with a sliver of hope. "Or guns. They're grown men."

Piper, who was clearing dishes from the table, snorted.

Natalie's grin widened.

It was good to see her smile, if only for a second.

"If they have any sense at all, they'll keep the conversation on what happened yesterday and how to find Jake." Gabriella picked up her coffee cup and then returned it to the table. Her stomach already burned from too much caffeine. "Which is what we need to do. Is there anything else you can tell me about the men who broke in? You didn't see any faces? No identifying marks?"

"They were covered head to toe." Natalie's smile disappeared. "The man in charge was older. His ski mask shifted once, and I saw a gray beard. Other than that, they were almost . . . well behaved, if you can say that about people holding you at gunpoint in your own house."

"We need to find that phone."

"Did Eli talk to the CSU folks?"

"Yes. Nothing. Dunbar is working on the warrant for the phone records. We may be able to find out something that way. At least what phone calls he made and to whom." Her gaze went to the patio doors again. Eli stood and walked to the pool. He seemed to be contemplating the water. "But it takes time, and we don't have time. We need to get going."

She went to Natalie and bent over for a hug. Her sister smelled of Estée Lauder. She inhaled and closed her eyes, reassured by the familiar scent, then she straightened. "We'll get him back."

"I know. Where are you going now?"

"To the gun store owned by Alberto Garza's uncle."

"Please stay here with us." Natalie grabbed her hand. "They're after you."

"All the more reason to find Jake and put an end to this."

"Let the cops do it. Let Eli do it."

"You know I can't do that, Sis."

Eli came through the door first. Neither the look on his face or Deacon's told her anything about how the conversation had fared. "Are you ready?"

She nodded.

"I'll call you later with whatever I find out." Deacon directed the statement to Eli, who nodded. "You do the same?"

"You got it."

Wonders would never cease. The tone of cooperation bordered on something from the peace talks in times of war. "Where are you going?"

"I'll explain later." Eli bolted past her. "The gun store probably opens at nine. Let's head out."

"I have contacts at City Hall." George trotted into the breakfast nook. He'd changed into a pale-green guayabera, loose-fitting white linen pants, and boat shoes. "I'll snoop around there and take some of my buddies out for coffee."

"Thank you." Gabriella shook her finger at Eli. He sighed. "We can use your help. All of you. But the most important thing is that you be careful. We don't know who we can trust. We don't know who has Jake."

"Well then, let's find out." Deacon led the charge to the door. "We'll rendezvous back here tonight."

It was quite the ragtag team of investigators. Somehow, it seemed hopeful.

CHAPTER 18

ELI HUMMED "STREETS OF Laredo" as he perused Zaragoza Street. The National Sporting Goods store was sandwiched between a duty-free establishment and a pawn shop at the corner of Flores and Zaragoza in the heart of downtown Laredo. The old Spanish land grant grid of streets hugged the Texas-Mexico border not far from where I-35 South ended in the old international bridge. A black pickup truck sat in front of the pawn shop. Across the way was San Agustín Plaza. Beyond the patch of green stood the front door to stately white San Augustine Church, which held court with a graceful bell tower and clock.

For a Saturday morning, downtown Laredo wasn't exactly teeming with shoppers. Violence in its sister city of Nuevo Laredo, only three blocks from Eli's current location, had seen to that. Still, cars were parked at meters on the plaza. Folks shared cement park benches under live oak trees that provided scant shade. Trash swirled in the hot wind in front of the drab storefronts with faded signs in Spanish painted on aging brick. An elderly couple exited the duty-free store, their arms loaded with brown paper bags. The air smelled of dead fish and cigarettes. Both made Eli's gut burn. He dug into his pocket for his roll of Tums and came up empty. He'd eaten them all the previous day.

The thought of those intruders in Gabby's house didn't help. Terrorizing a woman in a wheelchair and two fatherless children. His chest hurt with the desire to destroy them.

Gabby wiggled on the seat next to him. She hugged her purse to her chest. "Are they open?"

"Sign says nine o'clock."

She nodded and turned her head to stare out the passenger window. Eli contemplated his strategy for this encounter. They were in hostile territory now. The chances that the Figueroa family was fronting for the cartel were extremely good. Kristina Briones's story hadn't left much doubt what Jake had been up to before his disappearance.

Garza had incriminating evidence. The cartel thugs thought he'd told Gabby what that evidence was. Given her his phone. Even if she didn't know anything, they thought she did. Keeping her safe was paramount.

Eli tightened his hands on the wheel. The chances of getting Jake back alive dwindled to nothing. How Laredo PD and Sunny Mendez figured into the story was way beyond his reach—for now. "I want you to stay in the car."

"No." Gabby's head popped back up. She sounded like a small child being denied a treat. "Not happening."

"I'm not kidding. Do not get out of the car. No matter what." He double-checked his weapon, even though he knew it was loaded. "If it looks like trouble, I need you someplace where you can call for help."

Her face set in determined lines, Gabby opened her door. "I need to be where I can see what's happening. I'm not letting you go in there alone."

"You're not armed."

"You have a backup piece. Give it to me."

She'd spent enough time with him at the shooting range to handle a weapon, but that meant nothing when confronted with armed, living, moving assailants. He had enough to worry about without dodging accidental friendly fire. "No."

It was a standoff, but he had the guns and the upper hand. Eli slid from the car and walked toward the store. A dark late-model luxury car roared around the corner, its motor revved, muffler popping.

The window rolled down.

A long barrel extended beyond the tint.

Eli went for his weapon.

Bullets exploded around him in the erratic, maniacal *rat-tat-tat* of an automatic weapon.

He hurled himself to the sidewalk. The cement scraped his nose. Gravel and rocks scratched his face. Trash stank around him.

The seconds ballooned until they seemed to last for years. *God, don't let them take Gabby. I know I don't deserve any favors. I'm not worth the air I waste. Save Gabby. Save Gabby.*

The screeching of rubber on asphalt faded into the distance, the shots with it.

Eli rolled to his feet and pounded after the vehicle, trying to get a fix on the license plate. The car had none. He got off one shot, then common sense told him the car and its occupants were far beyond the reach of a simple S&W.

He whirled. "Gabs!"

His heart pelted against his ribs so hard, he had trouble forming the syllables. Maybe this was what a heart attack felt like. *"¿Querida?"*

The black pickup truck—Ram or Tundra—parked in front of the pawn shop started to move. Tires squealed, the motor revved, and the truck bounced forward. Straight at him.

Eli dove toward the sidewalk—again.

He rolled and blasted a shot at the moving target. He got a glimpse of a dark-haired driver. A man. Maybe. Then it was gone.

He lay on his back, not breathing. The sun burned his face. Sweat trickled into his hair and tickled his ears. "Gabs? Gabriella!"

No answer.

Eli rolled over and propped himself up on his hands and knees, fear a blade pressed against his throat.

She sprawled, not moving, facedown in the dirty strip of sparse grass between the sidewalk and the curb. The Charger's bullet hole–pocked door stood open, shielding her from the street. He crawled to his feet and stumbled toward her.

Her head lifted. "That's it. That *is* it!"

He recognized the tone and the wild, fierce look in her eyes. It hit people that way sometimes. Shock, disbelief, anger rolled into a vicious, consuming desire to pound someone into the ground. "It's all right, *corazón,* they're gone." He knelt and pulled her into his arms. "I'm not going to let anyone hurt you. It's okay."

For once she didn't fight him. She huddled close, her forehead resting on his shoulder, her heart pounding against his chest. He inhaled the clean smell of her favorite natural store shampoo. His hand rested in her fine, silky blonde hair. His fingers tightened around the soft strands.

Images bombarded him. Gabby slipping a pie into the oven, her cheeks red from its heat, laughing as she shut the door and turned to harass him about something. Gabby wrapped in a blanket, lying on the rug, Artemis snoring at her feet, as she studied the flames in the living room fireplace. Gabby dodging him on the basketball court, tossing in a perfect hook shot, then turning to land a kiss on his lips out of sheer exuberance.

The enormity of what he'd lost confounded him. How to get it back. Get her back.

Her hands came up, palms flat on his chest. Her eyes were closed, her breathing ragged. He didn't move, afraid the slightest gesture would send her reeling back. In six months she hadn't let him get this close. Now fear drove her into his arms. She knew he was good for this. Protection. He couldn't be trusted with anything else but this.

Finally, she raised her head and let out a long breath. "It's not okay. Somebody just tried to kill us."

Forcing himself to focus on what he did know how to do, Eli stared at the empty street. "They tried to kill you, mi amor. They know you're here."

The creaking sound of a door opening made him turn.

He rose and pulled Gabby up with him. He stepped in front of her, hand on his holster.

A young guy dressed in black jeans and a black shirt with a button-down collar and long sleeves sauntered from the sporting goods store. He smiled. "*Hijo,* you must've really made someone mad."

CHAPTER 19

————

THE GUY LOOKED A lot like Alberto Garza, only alive. Eli extracted his badge from his belt loop and held it up. Dressed-all-in-black peered at the credentials and shrugged. Eli edged closer. "You know those people?"

"Sorry, I didn't get a look. Liked the sound of their artillery, though." His amused smile revealed perfect, sparkly white teeth. "Sounded like they might be collectors."

Collectors. Collectors used a gun show loophole in the law to sell their so-called private collection of firearms without having to run an instant background check or even giving a receipt. "What makes you say that?"

"They didn't stop by my store. Guess they just came from a gun show."

The guy was yanking his chain and enjoying it. "How 'bout we go inside and wait for the police." Eli lifted his phone to his ear. Detective Rincon probably wasn't on duty on a Saturday. Maybe Rincon had called in a favor to get a cop from out of town off his back.

The Johnny Cash wannabe feigned disinterest until the call was complete. Then he crossed his arms, his lips twisted in a defiant smile under a wimpy mustache. "You do your cop business out here. We're closed. Death in the family." He headed toward the door.

Eli drew his weapon. Getting shot at rattled a man's nerves. Worse, Gabby had been in harm's way. He should've locked her in the Sevilles' house with Natalie and the kids. That would be next on his list. Getting her safe. "I don't think so. We talk in there, or we talk out here. What's your name?"

"*¡Cálmate!*" The guy raised his hands in mock surrender and jerked his head toward the door. "Chuy Figueroa, at your service."

A row of AR-15 rifles glistening in the fluorescent lights greeted them at the door. Gabby's fingers slid between Eli's. Startled, he peered at her face. She looked gray with exhaustion. "Do you need to sit?"

"I'm fine. That couldn't have been random." She kept her voice just above a whisper. "Who were they, and how did they know we were here?"

"We've talked to half a dozen people since we got here. I don't trust anyone at this point." Eli ran down the list mentally. "Take your pick."

"And what about the pickup truck? Do you think it was the same one that followed Natalie and Deacon here from San Antonio?"

"It seems likely. The question is, which one of the people we talked to sent them after us?"

Alberto Garza's younger brother's insolent expression throughout the interview of his family and the way he'd hovered over the girl-friend of his dead brother had triggered more alarms in Eli's head.

The father, on the other hand, had looked scared. Of what?

Eli zeroed in on Figueroa. "Where's your father?"

"In Mexico on a business trip. He'll be back in time for Beto's funeral."

Consorting with the enemy, or hiding out until the situation cooled off? Eli counted to ten, slowly. "So, your dad hooked Alberto up with someone who wanted him to buy guns for him. Who was it?"

Chuy lit a cigarette and sucked on it, taking his time. "I don't know what Beto was up to. He went to the store in San Antonio whining that he needed a job, he needed money fast. My dad took pity on him and offered him a gig doing deliveries, kind of like a courier."

Ignoring Gabby's disgusted look, Eli stepped into the plume of smoke and inhaled. Secondhand smoke was better than no smoke at all. "Buying and delivering guns."

Figueroa glanced at a sleek, expensive-looking wristwatch. It seemed he had somewhere to be. "He did whatever my dad asked him to do. We're completely legit here. I need to close up. I have to help my *tío* make the arrangements. Beto wasn't my best buddy, but he was family."

"When was the last time you saw him?"

"Let me check my calendar." Figueroa's smirk deserved a whop upside the head. Eli counted to ten again. The smart aleck gazed into space. "Thursday? Maybe. Thursday afternoon? Something like that."

Right about the time Jake was meeting another informant at the river. And then disappearing. "What was he—?"

The bell over the door dinged as it opened. Rincon walked in, looking all spiffy and clean shaven. The guy must lead a double life as a stockbroker. "And we all know how into family members you are, Figueroa." He slid one finger down the barrel of a rifle like he was checking for dust. "Especially the dead ones."

"It's like a convention of cops in here. I haven't seen so many police around here since the *policía* were on trial at the federal court-house." His grin got wider. "Who important got murdered? I know you aren't here about my cousin. SA is outside your jurisdiction."

"Shut up and I'll tell you."

"You didn't just tell me to—"

"Shut up? Yes, I did. These folks are visitors from out of town. We don't like it when tourists get shot at. It's bad for business." Rincon tapped on the glass case with two manicured fingernails. "They're asking questions about a missing ATF agent who is connected to a family member of yours. Maybe your folks aren't happy about that. Maybe you know something about the situation."

"N'ombre."

"Like you'd tell me."

"You're the one asking the stupid questions."

Rincon inclined his head toward the door. "Detective Cavazos, Miss Benoit, let's talk outside."

Rincon's questions only took a few minutes. Eli gave him a bare bones recitation. Not that he could remember much about the shooter's car. Black or dark-blue, four-door, BMW, maybe. Gabriella hadn't seen a thing.

"So whose face did you get in?" Rincon leaned against the storefront, one manicured finger rubbing a spot on his temple.

Eli ran down the list, including the visit to the sporting goods store in San Antonio and the armed intruders who'd broken into Gabby's home. Rincon pursed his lips in a frown. "It sounds like you'd do well to stay out of this. Keep your friend under wraps until we finish our investigation."

"Are you getting anywhere?"

He shifted and straightened, obviously hearing the challenge in Eli's question. "We're making progress."

"What's the ATF saying?"

"Nothing. The ATF is looking for a missing agent. We're looking for him as a murder suspect. Those goals don't exactly mix. They're trying to stay ahead of us." Rincon stopped. His gaze went to Gabby. "However . . . that is one place where you might be able to stick your nose and I wouldn't mind a bit."

"What do you mean?" Her face brightened. She was itching for a fight, that was obvious. "I'll do anything . . . anything to find my brother and make sure he's okay."

"You're the agent's family. You have a right to know what's going on. Get in the ATF's face and stay in their face until someone tells you something."

"Didn't LPD have involvement in the task force trying to stop gun smuggling?"

"We did, but now that we're investigating this murder—"

"They know you'll use the information to find Jake and put him in jail." Her voice strengthened. Anger could do that, buoy a person up when nothing else could. "You want to string my brother up for a murder he didn't commit."

"Find him, and he'll have the opportunity to tell his side of the story. We don't have all the facts, and I'm a fair man. You get some information that will help us find your brother and bring him in, and I'll make sure he gets a fair shake."

"I'm an attorney, Detective, don't try to snow me. I find my brother, rest assured, I'll be protecting his rights."

Rincon didn't seem fazed by Gabby's attitude. "Understood. But I can keep him alive."

"What do you mean?"

"If he's mixed up in something involving one of the cartels, his life is in danger if he isn't already—"

Eli jerked his head at Rincon. The detective followed him to a safe distance from Gabby. "Who in the ATF will talk to us? Any ideas?"

Rincon's eyebrows popped up. "She's his sister. Doesn't she know who he's tight with?"

"She's had a lot on her plate for the last few years."

"I looked into her . . ." Rincon wrinkled his nose as if an odor disagreed with him. "And you."

"So you know what she's been through. She has a sister in a wheelchair and two kids living in her house now." Eli worked at his game face. "And an ex-boyfriend who wants her back and won't leave her alone."

Rincon's gaze strayed toward Gabby, who stood, arms crossed, staring out at the street. "I can see why you don't want to give her up. We haven't been able to get any cooperation from the ATF. You might try a guy named Larry Teeter. He's a newbie. He was assigned with Benoit. He seemed pretty upset about his partner's situation. He didn't tell me much, but I bet he'd spill it all to a family member."

Nothing new there. "Thanks."

"I scratch your back; you scratch mine."

Not exactly. Not if it meant helping Rincon put Jake in jail. "Sure. Right. If we find out anything pertinent, we'll let you know."

CHAPTER 20

———

WOMEN WERE GOD'S WAY of driving men crazy. Eli slapped his sweaty hand to his aching side and huffed as he tried to keep up with Larry Teeter. That and jogging. Gabby refused to consider returning to the Sevilles'. She argued that Teeter would be more likely to open up to Jake's terrified, sad sister—and Teeter claimed the only time he could talk was during his "run." Only seriously deranged people ran in South Texas on an August afternoon. Ninety-five degrees with 100 percent humidity. A person could cut a slice of air with a bread knife.

Eli's lungs threatened to explode. He hadn't jogged since before the shooting. Teeter had set aside an hour to jog—for stress relief he said—before a family commitment that couldn't be missed.

Even by a guy whose partner had been missing for two days.

His route from an apartment complex through a city park and past half a dozen store parking lots filled with cars seemed never ending. And they still had to run back. Eli couldn't decide if the pain in his side was from the scar tissue or sheer laziness. "Do you mind slowing it down a little?"

Teeter glanced back. Sweat rolled down his obsidian skin. "What's the matter? City cops got it so cushy they can't keep up anymore?"

Gabby ran in place for a few seconds. She had given up jogging after she opened the restaurant, but she still punished herself regularly on a treadmill in her office. This pace was a piece of cake for her.

"Look, can we just grab a bench or something and talk? It'll only take a few minutes."

Teeter's arms pumped. He leapt over a broken beer bottle in the middle of the sidewalk. "I promised myself this run. I need it. If I don't run five miles a day, my middle starts to spread."

Eli gritted his teeth and wiped sweat from his eyes. Teeter's middle didn't look like it needed any work. In fact, he looked like he spent more than his share of time with the weights at the gym. Eli sucked in air and tried not to gasp. Only pride kept him from puking. "Fine. How well did you know Jake?"

"They stuck us together about six months ago." Instead of stopping at a yellow light, Teeter picked up the pace, forcing them to cross on the red. "His partner retired, and they didn't want him flying solo on this operation."

"When was the last time you saw Jake?" Gabby didn't even pant when she spoke.

"Thursday morning. We briefed the boss on our plan of action. We spent about thirty or forty minutes on it."

"You said 'our' plan of action. Why was he out in the field on his own after that? You didn't deploy together?"

"He said he had a personal matter to take care of. He was supposed to meet me at our informant's apartment that afternoon at 3:00. I got there about 2:50, 2:55." Teeter's breathing was light, regular. "The apartment was in shambles. The guy was nowhere to be found. Jake either never showed up, or he'd already come and gone."

Gabby stopped and ran in place at a restaurant with outdoor tables that lined the street. Eli willed her to stay there. He needed water. And a chair to sit in. Eli hated jock wannabes. If there weren't witnesses, he'd be tempted to shoot them both. "What was the personal appointment—did Jake tell you?"

Teeter tugged a water bottle from the belt around his narrow waist and sprayed his face. The enormous biceps in his arm flexed. "He had a meeting with his fiancée and the minister."

"The minister?" Gabby stopped running in place and stretched both arms over her head. She actually looked better than she had thirty minutes earlier. "He had a fiancée, and he was meeting with a minister?"

"Yeah, Reverend Cavazos." Teeter's white teeth flashed in a smile for a second. He cocked his head toward the sidewalk. "Gotta keep moving, guys. I understand your father was going to marry Jake and the woman he'd been dating. At least he called it dating."

Gabby took off after him. Eli followed suit. No wonder Jake hadn't mentioned it to her. Talk about courting trouble—having the father of his sister's ex-fiancé marry him. Not a promising start. Or maybe Jake saw it as a chance to get the two of them together, if not in the same room, the same church. "Sunny Mendez. Jake asked my father to marry them?"

"He didn't tell me he had a girlfriend, let alone that he was getting married." She missed a step and almost fell on the curb. She righted herself before Eli could reach her. "If I find him, I'm going to kill him myself."

"Easy." Eli picked up his pace despite legs that felt like pudding. "We don't know the whole story."

"Don't easy me! My brother was thinking about marriage and hadn't bothered to tell me! Or introduce the woman to his family."

"Sorry." The more stressed Teeter got, the faster he seemed to run. "I'm just repeating what he told me. He wasn't the most forthcoming guy in the world, and I really hadn't been working with him very long."

"Tell us about the operation." Eli panted. This amount of exercise couldn't be good for a guy. "Does Sunny Mendez have anything to do with it?"

Teeter sped up some more. "I don't know."

"An ATF agent is missing, maybe—" Eli halted in the middle of the sidewalk. "Stop. Enough. Just stop. Jake's missing. Your operation is in complete chaos. What can it hurt to tell us what you know? If

we find him, we can ask him what happened and get this all straightened out."

Teeter slammed to a halt and turned. It took several yards for
Gabby to realize she was alone. Her face red with exertion, or more
likely fury, she whirled and jogged back.

Teeter wiped at his face with a towel tied to his fanny pack.
"Sunny Mendez likes to party. Laredo has its version of a party circuit
for folks who have lots of money and time on their hands. There's not
a lot to do here, if you haven't noticed. Jake went with her to some of
these soirees."

"Jake and a party girl." Gabby ran her hands through her sweat-
soaked hair. "That's not my brother."

"Some of the best parties are hosted by a guy named Luke Donovan.
They call him LD."

"I assume you're going somewhere with this."

A man dressed in homeless couture staggered between them,
bringing with him the stench of stale beer and urine. Teeter paused
until the guy stumbled past. "Donovan considers himself Laredo roy-
alty. He's a transplant from New Jersey who made his money in the
import-export business. He's a decorated Vietnam vet who decided
to reinvent himself in a border town after returning from the war.
Clothing, jewelry, high-end crystal, art, primitive furniture. He built
himself a mansion north of town with two pools, a bowling alley,
movie theater, and a dance floor. He gives lavish parties."

"The only law broken there is the one of good taste."

"He's living beyond his means. We've been going over his finan-
cials with a fine-tooth comb."

"And Alberto Garza had something on him?"

"We don't know. The guy they found dead on the riverbank
was Donovan's godson. Colby Langston. He was a college student at
TAMU here in town. His phone was missing, and his apartment had
been ransacked. Laptop and desktop missing."

Like Jake and Beto Garza. Someone was erasing all electronic evidence collected by these three men.

"How was Langston related to Garza?"

"He was another straw buyer. Same facilitator."

"Who?"

"That's what we intended to find out. We were going to meet Langston to get some evidence from him and bring him into protective custody. Same with Garza. We had two witnesses who said they had something on the facilitator. We figured we could shut down the whole operation, cut off the supply to Nuevo Laredo. Now the informants are both dead, Jake is missing, Laredo PD is trying to pin a murder on him, and whatever they had on the facilitator is gone."

"What did they have?"

"Langston wouldn't say. He wanted to talk immunity first. The kid was a budding lawyer."

Eli moved closer to the storefront. He jerked his head. No reason to block the sidewalk.

Gabby didn't seem to notice. She started jogging in place again. "Does it strike you as odd that right when you're about to blow the operation wide open, your informants are killed and your partner goes missing?"

"It does." Teeter leaned over and put both hands on his knees. He heaved a breath. "My gut feeling is that somebody tipped off the facilitator."

"You're talking about somebody on the task force?" A serious accusation—one that could deep-six Teeter's career. "Do you have proof of that?"

"Nothing solid. Which is why I haven't spread it around. But I'm keeping my eyes and ears open. There's a fortune to be made in gun smuggling, just like drug smuggling. Way more than someone in law enforcement makes."

"Be careful who you say that to. Maybe Donovan paid someone

off for inside information." Gabby's tone had softened. She, too, could see where this train of thought could get Teeter. "On the other hand if he is tied to the cartel, he wouldn't want Jake around."

"He also wouldn't want to appear concerned about it. Jake said he shook his hand, offered him a glass of champagne, and gave him a tour of the place. He even suggested Jake might consider a position as his bodyguard. A lot more money in it, to quote the man."

Maybe the reason Jake hadn't said anything about his alleged girlfriend was that she was part of his plan. "So Sunny was Jake's ticket in. He was using her?"

"At first, I think so." Teeter's gaze bounced to Eli. "But he got sucked in."

Teeter sounded as if he'd had some experience with love. Eli could relate. "Is it possible that Donovan has Jake stowed away in that mansion?"

"It's possible or in one of his warehouse properties, but we don't have enough evidence—any evidence now—for a warrant for either one." Teeter must've noted Gabby's fierce response to this statement. "We're working on it. I've told you what I can, but you guys need to stand down. We'll finish this operation, one way or another."

His last words hung in the air. *With or without Jake.*

Her expression hard, Gabby cocked her head. "What do you think of Rincon?"

Teeter shrugged. "Too much of a dandy for my taste."

"He has expensive tastes."

"Do I think he's on the take?" Teeter wrinkled his nose. "With Jake missing and Rincon on the warpath to charge him with murder, I'm not discounting him or anyone else for that matter."

"What about the witness who supposedly saw Jake drive away from the river Thursday?"

"An old guy fishing at Dos Laredos Park."

"Nothing to do with the meeting?"

"Nope. He described the vehicle, but he couldn't describe the driver. He wears bifocals."

"Name?"

"Thomas Benavides. I'll text you an address, but the guy doesn't know anything."

Sometimes it depended on who asked the questions.

"Anybody could've been driving that car." Gabby's sharp tone said she was forcing herself to see the entire situation from Jake's perspective. And she didn't like it. "Time isn't on our side. I want my brother back."

"Me too. If you think I don't feel responsible for not being there for my partner, you're crazy. We'll get the people who did this." Teeter glanced at his smartwatch. "My sister is having a gender reveal party in half an hour. I told her I wouldn't miss it." His voice turned hoarse. He paused and stared out at the park across the street. A park filled with kids playing soccer and moms with strollers. "When stuff like this happens—like with Jake—you realize nothing's more important than family. I'm taking an hour to be with them, and then I'll be back at the office."

He stepped into Gabby's space. "We're on this."

Eli caught Gabby's gaze. He shook his head. *Let the man go.* "We want the same things. Go be with your family."

"They understand what the deal is."

"Keep us in the loop."

Without answering, he swiveled and began jogging back toward his apartment complex.

"Let's go." She took off after him.

"Gabs, wait. Where are we going?"

She glanced back but kept moving, forcing Eli to keep up.

"To talk to your dad. Sunny never mentioned she was supposed to meet Jake at the church that day. We have to find out if they showed up, if your dad talked to Jake that day. That way when we talk to

Sunny this afternoon, we can confront her about her lie of omission. We need to know why she didn't tell us about that meeting."

"Gabs, stop running."

"No, what—?"

"He'll be getting ready for tomorrow's services. He'll be at the church and the door will be locked."

A walk replaced the running in place. "Right."

Saturdays were sacrosanct for Xavier Cavazos. A day of preparation and prayer.

"We're not that far from the witness's neighborhood. Let's pay him a visit." Like it or not, a visit to the Cavazos homestead was now on their list, but Eli had no intention of entering the inner sanctum of his father's church during that visit. "Then I'll talk to Sunny, give her a chance to explain. *Then* we'll stop by the house. We'll see if what she tells us matches what my dad knows."

"What do you mean, *I'll* talk to Sunny? You mean *we*."

"You're not going."

"Why?"

"The bad guys are looking for you. We just got shot at. We don't know what Sunny Mendez's involvement in this is. You're not walking into an ambush."

Gabby picked up her pace again. She wasn't even breathing hard. "I'm going. It's not up to you."

"No. Not when we don't know who we can trust. Let me do this one." Eli grabbed her arm and headed in the opposite direction of Teeter's run. This traipsing around in the open was over. "You're in danger, and you're not walking into any more danger. Not on my watch."

"You're not the boss of me."

He jerked to a stop and got in her face. "You have a death wish? Don't do this to Natalie. She may have lost a brother already. You know that even if you don't want to face it. You want to help? Take care of your sister and those kids. Be smart. Use your head."

She backed up a step. The anger drained from her face. "You get one stop without me. Mendez's ranch. After that, I'm all in. You got that?"

"I got that."

A temporary truce.

CHAPTER 21

THOMAS BENAVIDES' HOUSE WAS the mirror image of those found in Laredo's sister city across the border. Tiny, shotgun style, a pale-turquoise paint peeling from the sun-drenched wooden walls, it sat between pink-and-yellow houses. Gabriella beat Eli through the wooden fence gate and up the steps to the concrete front porch. The windows were covered with wrought-iron bars. Wind chimes and bird feeders hung from both post oak trees in the front yard. The neighborhood was six blocks from the border and about three from Dos Laredos Park. The front door stood open. A screen door kept out mosquitoes and flies. The voices of Spanish language *telenovela* actors drifted through open windows. She knocked. The screen door rattled. No one responded. She rapped again. Nothing.

The exquisite smell of meat cooking on a mesquite barbecue pit reached Gabriella's nose. They hadn't stopped to eat. Her mouth watered and her stomach rumbled. "Backyard?"

Eli nodded. He tromped down the steps and led the way through neatly trimmed, if sparse, grass to the backyard. An elderly wizened man with a white stubbled chin and a bald brown head stood at an enormous barbecue pit—the kind made from a black barrel and often pulled by a pickup truck to a family *pachanga* at a local park. At first impression it seemed that Yoda lived in Laredo. He wore a white T-shirt and baggy black pants. A German shepherd as grizzled as his owner unfurled from his spot in the grass. A low growl hummed in his throat.

Spatula in hand, the man turned. He was about Gabriella's height and weighed no more than she did. His dark eyes widened. The spatula dropped. Both hands popped up, palms flat. *"No vi nada."*

The dog's growl turned into a bark.

"Chico, *cállate!*"

The barking ceased, but the dog stood at attention beside his owner.

"I'm sorry. We didn't mean to scare you." Gabriella frowned at Eli. He eased back a few steps. She introduced herself. "Do you speak English?"

He nodded. A matching woman pushed through the back door. She had a can of Coors in one hand and a tortilla basket in the other. She was every bit as wizened as her husband, but her eyes were brilliant blue and her hair silver. She wore a flowered housedress and flip-flops. She halted without speaking.

"Your wife, Señor Benavides?"

He nodded. He still hadn't moved.

"I'm looking for my brother. You may have seen him."

He shook his head vigorously.

"Can we sit down for a minute?" Gabriella pointed to the picnic table, from the looks of it also homemade. "We just want to ask a couple of questions, and then we'll leave you to your lunch."

"You like *cerveza?*" The woman held up the can. "Beer?"

"No, but *gracias.*"

His face grim, Mr. Benavides nodded, but he picked up the spatula and went back to the fajitas on the grill. His wife settled the beer on the table. Her flip-flops smacking on the cement patio, she disappeared into the house.

"You told the police you saw an SUV leaving the riverbank on Thursday afternoon."

"I didn't see anyone."

Gabriella dug a photo from her purse. She approached him with great care. The dog's growl reverberated. Mr. Benavides shook his finger at him. "Enough, Chico, or I'll make you go inside."

Chico dropped his wiry body into the grass and laid his head on his paws, but his gaze never left Gabriella. She extended the photo of Jake, Natalie, the kids, and herself in front of the Christmas tree. They were being silly. Natalie had stuck her fingers up in rabbit ears behind Jake's head. Jake stuck his tongue out. The kids both had their mouths open. Gabriella's eyes were closed. "That's my brother."

Mr. Benavides didn't take her offering, but he studied the photo with obvious care. He shook his head and began flipping the fajitas. The pungent aroma of green pepper, onions, and jalapeños grilling mixed with that of the beef. "I can't help you."

"He's missing. I'm afraid for him. What if he were your son? Wouldn't you want someone to step forward and tell you what they saw?"

His lips pressed together in a thin line.

"Do you have children?"

A quick, hard nod.

"Can you imagine how my parents must feel?"

Another nod.

"Please, I'm begging you."

"The man was *un rubio, un guero*."

Blond. Light skinned. A gringo.

"What kind of car?"

"Black Chevy SUV."

Jake's latest vehicle. "Was he driving?"

Mr. Benavides shook his head. "They stuck a black hood over his head."

"What did they look like?

"*Ejército*. Army uniforms." He shuddered. "Big guns."

"Did you hear shots fired?"

He nodded and stabbed the meat with a grill fork. He moved pieces to a foil-lined pan.

"Did they see you?"

"No."

"Then why are you so afraid?" Eli spoke for the first time. In Spanish. This set off a tidal wave of Tex-Mex. Gabriella's Spanish wasn't bad, but in his excitement Mr. Benavides spoke so rapidly she could only make out about half of it, mostly the English words that cropped up.

He was fishing. He heard shots and crept through the trees until he reached an opening. When he realized what was happening, he stayed out of sight. He waited until they were gone to approach the man's body facedown in the mud. Dead.

One of the policemen came back later and told him to keep his mouth shut. Not to talk to anyone.

"Detective Rincon?"

Mr. Benavides shook his head. "I don't know his name. He never said. He came after dark. After we sleep. Pulled me out here. Spoke in my ear. Left in dark."

"You're sure he was a policeman, not ATF?"

Mr. Benavides crossed his heart with an index finger gnarled with age and arthritis. "If police don't protect you, who will?"

Who indeed?

"We won't tell anyone we've talked to you." Gabriella stuck the photo in her purse. "You don't have to worry."

"I don't worry. My wife worry enough for both of us." He speared several succulent-looking fajitas, dropped them in a corn tortilla, and added a generous dollop of *pico de gallo*. "You take taco with you. You go."

"That's kind of you, but it's not necessary. Enjoy your lunch."

His sad gaze said there was little chance of that. "I hope you find your brother. You go now."

They left him standing in the middle of his yard, staring at the taco as if he didn't know what to do with it.

CHAPTER 22

COUNTRY LIVING HAD A certain appeal to a city cop. The well-graded gravel road on the Mendez ranch circled in a wide arc in front of a stone and wood ranch-style house of mammoth proportions. A tan Suburban sat off to one side next to a smaller SUV and a black Lexus. Eli contemplated the porch dotted with white wooden rocking chairs. At first glance, perfectly idyllic. An auburn Labrador retriever bounded down the steps, tail wagging, bark friendly. For a retired sheriff, Mr. Mendez was doing mighty well for himself. Ranching in the broiling heat and rain-bereft, mesquite-and-nopal country surrounding Laredo couldn't be much more lucrative than law enforcement.

Eli let his gaze range to the outbuildings. A red barn bigger than his parents' home, a few smaller structures. Two ATVs. A chicken coop and a bunch of chickens. Picture perfect.

As much as he needed Gabby to be safe, Eli missed her company and her sharp mind. And he would appreciate her woman's perspective. She'd been too angry at him—at the situation—to speak during the drive back to George and Piper's house. Other than to remind him she expected a full report in no more than three hours.

She expected him to return safely.

At least that meant she cared what happened to him.

He turned off the engine and stared at the house. Gabby's take on Sunny Mendez, given to him the previous evening, ran through his mind. *"She's looking for a way out of all this. Daddy's a traditional father of Mexican American descent. In his culture, sons and daughters live at home until married. Sunny wants her own life. So she latches on to a guy she knows Daddy will like—law enforcement. Figures he'll fight it less. Turns on all the charm and reels Jake in like a salmon to its spawning grounds."*

She got all that from ten minutes in a room full of cops.

"You're not the only one who studies people. Chefs are like bartenders. We're people persons."

Gabby was not, nor had ever been, a people person. She was as prickly as a crowded pin cushion on the outside, but soft as a feather-bed on the inside. It took a long time to get to know her, but once she latched on to a person, she held on. Unless someone did something stupid, like break her heart.

"Stop living in the past. Do better." That's what his shrink said. That's what his friends said. That's what his pastor-slash-father said. That was hard to do when the past showed up at your door with a living, breathing reminder of a man's mistakes, his sins.

He shoved open the door, hopped out, and slammed it. The re-triever approached, tail beating the air. Not a guard dog. He held out his fingers. The dog sniffed. His mouth went wide in what could only be described as a smile. Eli patted his head. The dog woofed in a *follow-me-fashion* and led Eli to the primitive wood door with a stained-glass window of a hummingbird. He knocked and waited.

Nothing.

More knocking.

Sunny opened the door. The sleepy look on her face disappeared, replaced by hope. "Did you find him?" She glanced over Eli's shoul-der. "Is Jake with you?"

"No, I'm sorry."

The dog barked once and ducked between them. "I was so hope-ful." She knelt and hugged the dog. "Honey misses Jake too. She doesn't take to most strangers, but she's a very good judge of charac-ter. That's why she liked him and she likes you."

Eli petted Honey some more and took the moment to study Jake's alleged fiancée. It was possible she looked even more angelic in her pink sundress and bare feet than she had Friday night. When she finally stood and shook hands with him, hers felt like a small velvet bag of fragile bones. "Can you tell me anything? Any little bit of progress? I'm so worried about him I can't sleep. I can't eat."

"I'm sorry. We talked to Larry Teeter this morning. He said the ATF had nothing new." Eli watched her face. Her expression didn't change at the mention of Teeter's name. "You knew Jake's partner, right? Larry Teeter."

A thin vertical line formed between her eyebrows as she thought. She shrugged. "I think I met him once, maybe. So, he didn't know anything else? Are they looking for Jake?"

"Those guys couldn't find their umbrellas in a rainstorm." A man the size of a professional football player stood in the doorway. With a bushy silver beard and a silver ponytail that escaped a black cowboy hat, a black leather vest, plaid Western-style shirt, and blue jeans creased down the front, he looked like a cross between John the Baptist and John Wayne. The rifle in his hands did nothing to soften that impression. "Who's our guest, Mirasol?"

Her pensive face transformed by a smile, Sunny straightened. "Daddy, this is Detective Eli Cavazos. Remember, I told you about him."

"You didn't tell me you invited him out to the house." His tone registered on the friendly scale but held a note of interrogatory. "And Jake's sister. She didn't come?"

Interesting question. "She's gone back to San Antonio to be with family while they wait for word."

The lie came easily. Mendez was an unknown quantity. Sunny's trustworthiness remained to be quantified. No sense taking any chances.

"I'm sure it's a difficult time for her." Mendez held out his free hand as if to shake. Eli inclined his head toward the firearm. A long, slow smile followed. "Just getting ready to shoot me some javelina, Detective. No need to be so tense."

"I tend to be wary of armed men."

"Sorry." He laid the rifle on a long, narrow table that ran the length of the tiled foyer under a gold-framed mirror. "Maybe you'd like to join me. We'll have a late lunch. Then we can all go together. Sunny is quite a shot."

Sunny's petite nose wrinkled. "It's too hot, Daddy. Don't make Detective Cavazos tramp around in the dirt with all the mosquitoes and rattlesnakes. That's no way to treat a guest."

"I suppose you're right, *mi hija*." Mendez dropped a kiss on his daughter's head. His hand caressed her hair. "We should feed him first. Go tell Leo to prepare food."

No sign of discord here. In fact, they seemed the picture of a loving father and daughter. The doting quotient made Eli's sweet tooth ache. The primary goal was to interrogate her. Not to spend an afternoon shooting wild hogs. "Lunch would be great and it would give us a chance to chat before we go busting animals for pork chops."

Mendez patted his rifle, as if to soothe hurt feelings that its services wouldn't be needed right away, after all. "Sunny'll get the cook started on lunch. We can have a drink, eat, and then I'll see what kind of shot an SAPD officer is away from his natural habitat. How about a Corona and a shot of Jose Cuervo while lunch is prepared?"

"Iced tea or water would be great." Eli made a show of looking at his watch. It was one o'clock. "I've got a lot of stops today."

"Fine, that's fine. I'm sure my daughter will reappear any minute." Mendez waved him toward the hallway. "You'll have to forgive her. She's been beside herself since her young man disappeared."

"Nothing to forgive. I'm hoping she'll remember something that will help us figure out where he is."

"She's been interrogated by half a dozen people already." Mendez moved ahead, his stride that of a much younger man. "It hasn't helped find Jake Benoit. And it's made her a wreck."

"I'm sure you can imagine how difficult this is for the family. You can see what it's doing to your daughter—and she's only known Jake, what, a few months?"

They moved into an enormous living room overpowered by the largest stone fireplace and mantel Eli had ever seen. "Four months." Mendez's tone was mild. "I'm going to look for my daughter."

A smile carved on his craggy face, he strode from the room, his ostrich-skin cowboy boots clicking on the rose tile.

The minutes stretched until it seemed Eli's presence had been forgotten. Finally, Mendez returned, Sunny behind him with a tray laden with glasses and a pitcher of lemonade. "I'm sorry it took so long. I wanted to make the lemonade fresh."

They sat. The next thirty minutes were excruciating in their politeness. Mendez expertly steered the conversation away from Jake and Sunny's relationship while Sunny seemed to listen to his stories with rapt attention as if she'd never heard them before.

Every time Eli moved toward that topic, Mendez came up with a new story about his days in law enforcement or Laredo politics. He played the "do you remember so and so" game well. Most of the big names Eli did remember, but he'd done a good job of blocking them out.

Finally, lunch was served in an airy dining room that featured a half-dozen floor-to-ceiling windows with filmy white, lacy curtains. A feast had been laid out on a vast pine table that seated twelve. Much more than sandwiches. Venison steaks, Caesar salads, cottage fries, fresh fruit, apple pie. Eli couldn't remember the last time he'd eaten a meal that didn't come out of a bag or a box—not since Gabby broke up with him. He turned down a second and third offer of a beer.

"How did you meet Jake, Sunny?"

Sunny picked up her glass, moved it to the other side of her plate without drinking. "I ran into him at a party at a friend's house. I did her decorating, so she invited me to the unveiling, so to speak." She traced the condensation on her glass, her gaze flitting to her father and back to the glass. "I didn't know Jake was an agent then. I just saw him and thought he was . . ."

Jake had that power over women, no doubt. Eli had watched women catch sight of him for the first time. They did a double take—every time. Sort of the same thing Gabriella had elicited in Eli for the first time five years ago when she was still an assistant DA. She had those same blue eyes, fair skin, and fine bone structure her brother did. But her hair was blonde, his auburn like Natalie's. Eli had testified in a case she was prosecuting. Even in her dark-blue suit and high heels, she'd exuded charisma.

Eli forced himself to focus on Jake's love life, not his own miserable mistakes. "So you introduced yourself? It was love at first sight?"

"My friend introduced me." Her gaze found her father and then skipped back to the salad she was picking at with her fork. She had yet to take an actual bite of food. "Jake was nice, really polite, but not much of a talker. I did all the talking at first. It's a wonder he didn't run the other direction. But he didn't. He asked me for my number instead."

"How did you find out he was ATF?"

"He told me the first time we met for coffee. He was like that. He took things slowly. I liked that about him."

Her father dropped his napkin on his plate and stood. "Since you aren't interested in hunting things that bleed, we could do some target practice instead. I have my own shooting range."

"Thanks for the offer, but I don't have time for target practice with Jake missing." Eli tried to sound apologetic. "Sunny, you said the day Jake went missing you were waiting for a phone call from him, but it never came. Why didn't you mention that you had an appointment with my . . . with Reverend Cavazos for marriage counseling?"

Sunny glanced at her father. His bushy eyebrows rose and fell. She sighed. "It was supposed to be our secret. We'd only known each other a short time, and I knew people would find it hard to believe."

"Ah, to be young and in love." Mendez's chuckle sounded genuine. "They hardly know each other and they want to get married. Can you imagine, Detective?"

"I've known Jake a while. He tends to have that effect on people." Eli scooted his chair back and dropped his napkin on the table. "When a person knocks your socks off like that, there's no going back, is there?"

"I think he was as surprised as I was. It was like we got on a nonstop flight and we couldn't get off." Sunny sniffed and wiped at her face with her napkin. "He's the one who suggested we see Reverend Cavazos. It was his idea. Then he didn't even show up."

Her father sighed. "I'm sorry, *m'jita*. I know that must've hurt. Maybe he was able to disembark from that nonstop flight, after all."

"Did you object to your daughter dating Jake?"

"He seemed like a good man, but to be honest, I had mixed feelings." Mendez took a long swallow of his Tecate. His expression somber, he settled the bottle on the table with a thump. "I love my daughter. You know as well as I do the badge is a double-edged sword. A man might know how to defend himself and his loved ones, but on the other hand, he's constantly called upon to risk his life. And occasionally, the lives of those he loves."

Eli couldn't argue with that. It seemed unlikely that he would have the opportunity to speak to Sunny alone. Mendez had years of experience in law enforcement. He knew all the players in this part of the country. Time to change tactics. "What's your take on the situation here in Laredo in regard to gun smuggling?"

Mendez's face relaxed. "Same as the rest of the border towns between here and California. It's thriving."

"What do you think of the Feds' efforts to stop the flow of guns into Mexico?"

"I think they're in a tiny tugboat on the open ocean in the middle of a tsunami."

Nice metaphor. "You haven't heard anything specific about the players in this region?"

"A man hears a lot of rumors." He covered his mouth and burped. "Not ones he cares to repeat. We have four international bridges. Border Patrol agents are spread thin. Bringing in National Guardsmen who can't actually patrol can't even be called a bandage. The wall can't go up fast enough as far as I'm concerned."

"Did you and Jake have any conversations about his job?"

"Very little."

"He didn't pick your brains?"

"He listened to my stories when he came to pick up Mirasol. He had good manners."

Mendez should've been a gold mine of information. Jake wouldn't want to divulge any aspect of his operation, but Sunny's father might have provided some tiny piece of the puzzle. "Do you know Luke Donovan?"

Sunny knocked over her glass of tea. It soaked the tablecloth and ran onto the tile floor. She jumped from her chair. "I'm so sorry."

"Get Lourdes to clean it up." Mendez shook his head. His daughter darted from the room. "Sometimes she has the social graces of a goat, but who can blame her? A girl needs her mother."

Sunny was an adult. Treating her like a child didn't change that. "If I may ask, where is her mother?"

"You were asking me about Luke. I know him. We occasionally socialize. The man throws a good pachanga."

Changing the subject was Mendez's way of telling him his personal life was not Eli's business. "You stay in touch with your friends in law enforcement. I figure you would've heard any noise about him."

"I may have heard chatter here and there. He spends a lot of money for a man who should be ready to retire." Mendez glanced toward the doorway. "It seems my daughter has lost herself again."

"What do you know about Donovan's business?"

Mendez selected a toothpick from a delicate ceramic bowl on the table. He rolled it between thick finger and thumb. "Import-export of nice furniture, jewelry, fancy crystal. I'm sure he does well, just not that well."

"Do you think he might be in business with the cartel?"

Mendez's gaze meandered toward the view afforded by the enormous window—open fields as far as Eli could see. "Ask yourself how he can afford the big house, the fancy cars, the trips to Europe."

"I am."

"Why ask me?"

"I'm told you have your finger on the pulse of this town."

"Donovan and I don't move in the same circles. Other than our service in Vietnam, we have nothing in common. I'm not interested in the gossip of old biddies. I'm old and as retired as a man with a family ranch can be." Mendez stood. "I enjoy a smoke after lunch. Care to join me? Lourdes knows to bring my coffee to the study."

A smoke sounded good. Eli glanced down the hallway as they walked away from the dining room. No sign of Sunny. Had the demise of her tea glass been an accident brought on by the mention of Donovan's name, or a ploy for leaving the room to get out of discussing him? Either way, she was gone.

The study turned out to be a gun room. No books. Instead, a display of weapons that ranged from pistols to what looked like a submachine gun of the Bonnie-and-Clyde variety covered three walls. The hair stood up on Eli's neck. Serious firepower. His hand went to his hip to the touchstone provided by his own weapon. "Nice. This is an impressive collection. What is it? World War II?"

"Good eye." Mendez went through the ritual of snipping the cigar with a V-cutter and lighting it with a match. The fragrance billowed through the room as he puffed. "Sure you don't want one? They're Davidoff Nicaraguan. All Nicaraguan tobacco. Very smooth. Full bodied."

He talked about cigars the way he did guns and his daughter. His most important possessions.

"Thanks. I'll pass." Eli sucked in the smoke. The scent of savory wood with a touch of spice—cinnamon maybe—filled his nostrils. He wasn't technically smoking, but he could still get a hit of nicotine. "Tell me about the guns. Are they legal? Can they be used?"

Mendez laughed. "Spoken like a true LEO." He went to the first display. "This is an M1 Carbine designed by David Williams, the only major gun designer to be a former convict. It's fairly common but representative of rifles used during WWII."

His hand caressed the barrel and moved on to a second rifle. "This M1 Garand was a workhorse. General George Patton called it 'the greatest battle implement ever devised,' and it was at the time. Soldiers could load an eight-round en-bloc chip into the rifle and have a semiautomatic."

"Now we're dealing with AK-47s and hundreds of rounds a minute."

"Times have changed."

"What about this one?" Eli pointed to the wicked-looking gangster rifle.

"That's the Thompson machine gun, better known as a Tommy Gun. The first rifle to be labeled as a submachine gun. Even before World War II it was favored by gangsters during Prohibition. One expert calls it the gun that made the twenties roar. Thompsons were used in the St. Valentine's Day Massacre."

He went on and on, sharing tidbits about his favorite pistols, rifles, and bayonets.

"Impressive." Eli managed to get a word in edgewise after about ten minutes. Texans and their guns. Everyone and his mother owned them. Not only owned them, but loved them like family members. "So do they work?"

"Yes. I wouldn't have a weapon in the house that didn't." Smoke streamed through Mendez's nostrils. He rolled the cigar around the edge of a marble ashtray to loosen the ashes. "What's the point?"

"What's the value of your collection, if I can ask?"

He shrugged. "It's insured at half a mil."

"Wow. Aren't you afraid someone will steal it?"

"Not in the least." Mendez guffawed as if Eli had told him a joke. "One of the advantages of having weapons and knowing how to use them in a hold-your-ground state. You come on my property to take my stuff, you can expect a welcoming committee."

Eli had no desire to discuss with Mendez the finer points of Texas's penal code when it came to the use of deadly force and trespassers. He cocked his head toward the gun safe that stood guard on the fourth wall. "I guess you have guns even more valuable than these?"

"These are historical. Meant for display." Mendez waved the cigar toward the safe. "The meat and potatoes of the firearms in my possession don't need to be displayed."

"Could it be that some of them aren't quite . . . legal?"

"I would never." His tone said he would and did.

Eli's phone vibrated. Again. He glanced at the screen. A dozen texts, all from Gabby. "I'd better get going." He shook Mendez's hand. "Thank you for your time, Mr. Mendez."

"Andy. Any time. Come out after this is over. We'll do some hunting. There's a big-game ranch not far from here if javelina aren't your thing."

He wasn't inclined to shoot lions or zebras either. "Thanks for the invitation."

A minute later the front door closed behind Eli. He heaved a deep breath for the first time in an hour and a half. Like many Texans, the man liked his guns. Which kept a cop on his toes. Eli used the remote to unlock the Charger and strode toward it. A few feet from the bumper, a hiss sounded. He glanced around. Sunny stuck her head out from the open window of the Lexus. "Wait for me at the front gate."

He nodded and took off. Ten minutes later Sunny joined him. She slipped into the passenger seat and settled into the leather with a sigh. "Why did you bring up LD? The party where I met Jake was at LD's."

What was Jake doing there? Scooping out a potential suspect? "I heard he might have switched from imports to exports."

"You think he might have Jake?" Sunny removed her oversized sunglasses. Her eyes were wide with undisguised curiosity. "Why haven't you gone after him? Why are you out here talking to me?"

"According to Larry Teeter, there's not enough evidence. Did you see or hear anything at Donovan's parties that would help?"

Her gaze on the car's bug-splattered windshield, she chewed her lower lip. "Once, I heard a couple of LD's employees talking about taking him somewhere after the guests left. It was already two in the morning. The bars were closed."

"A friend's house?"

"No. A meeting at one of his warehouses."

"That's all you heard?"

"One of the guys turned and saw me walking toward them. They moved the conversation into one of the other rooms."

"What's the layout of the house?"

Sunny used a DQ napkin to sketch the layout. "It's huge. Makes our place look like a guesthouse. At least a dozen bedrooms, all with their own bathrooms. A study, a gaming room, a movie theater, a kitchen twice the size of ours, two dining rooms—"

"Security?"

"Big guns. All around the house, inside the house."

"Basement?"

"In Laredo? I doubt it."

"You don't know what warehouse they were talking about?"

"Nope."

"Are you sure?"

"If I knew, I'd tell you. I want Jake back." Her voice broke. "Do you think he's dead?"

"We won't stop until we find out."

She sniffed and nodded. "I have to go. Daddy will be looking for me."

"Can I ask some personal questions?"

"Sure."

"Where's your mother?"

"She was a lot younger than Daddy. She left when my brothers and I were little. She was tired of being alone all the time while he was off saving the world. At least that's what he says."

"How old are you?"

"Twenty-five."

"Do you work?"

"What does this have to do with anything?"

"I'm trying to understand your relationship with Jake."

"You can't understand why a guy like him would be interested in a woman like me." For a second the angel-child persona slipped. Her clipped words matched the hard look on her face. "Not very smart. Still living with her daddy."

"I think you're very smart." Smart enough to know she had a sweet deal living in her father's house, bills paid, driving a car he provided. "Do you work?"

"I told you. I decorate people's houses. I have a degree in interior design. LD's wife gave me a break when I came back from A&M. Then she recommended me to others. My father's very traditional. You're of Mexican descent. You know what I mean."

"I do." Eli's father was different. He encouraged his children to fly the coop. To trust in God's plan. "That's why you didn't tell him you and Jake wanted to get married?"

"Jake's not Catholic."

"That didn't bother you?"

"Jake and I talked about it. He knew I had questions. That's why he wanted to meet with your dad."

So many balls in the air for Jake. Love, faith, his job. Somehow he'd dropped one. Life was complicated for most people, but even more so for law enforcement. Eli belonged to the same club.

"You want to know what Jake saw in me? Do you like my perfume?"

A light, clean scent of fresh flowers that wafted through the car the second she got in. "Sure."

"It's Elizabeth Arden. I buy it at Walmart. Jake liked me because I'm not what I look like. He says I'm a mystery he wants to solve."

"What *are* you like?"

"You'll never know."

Thank the Lord. "You better go. Daddy will wonder where you are."

"You don't approve of me, do you?" Her tone said she found that fact amusing. "You like people to think you're the rebellious preacher's kid, but you're really as uptight as your father."

She had no idea. "I'd advise you not to poke the tiger. Or to judge. I try not to."

"But judgment is written all over your face." She slipped from the car, then bent to peer through the window. "Be careful, Mr. Detective."

She was gone before he could ask her why.

He started the car and let it idle. The wind blew dust across the rocky road that led to the highway. A tumbleweed rolled across the road and came to rest against a magnificent Spanish Dagger. He wasn't one to judge. He had his own sins for which he would answer. He pulled his wallet from his pocket and plucked the photograph from its hiding place. Whatever Jake had done with Sunny, it only made him human. Eli could understand in a way few could. God willing, he would have the chance to tell Jake that. He returned the photo to his wallet and tucked it away. Finding Jake came first and foremost.

Sunny Mendez wasn't telling him everything she knew. She claimed to be head over heels for Jake. She'd gone after an ATF agent. She obviously liked a challenge. She'd come out here, risking her father's ire, to nudge Eli toward Luke Donovan, her alleged friend. She was by no means the obedient daughter. Andy Mendez, the doting father, knew more than he was saying as well.

Next step was to find out more about Luke Donovan's real estate holdings and his finances. They might hold the key to Jake's whereabouts. And somewhere along the line, the key to Sunny Mendez.

Larry Teeter, another man who knew more than he was saying. The ATF could get information Eli couldn't. He punched in the special agent's number.

Voicemail.

CHAPTER 23

——

WATCHED PHONES NEVER TEXTED. Or something like that. Gabriella glanced at her phone. Three o'clock. Where was he? She scooped it up and thumbed another text.

Where R U?

Nothing. She tossed the phone on the massive oak dining room table. The sound of the kids screaming and laughing in the pool wafted through the sliding glass doors behind her. Piper's melodic laugh mingled with their high, sweet giggles. That they could be so carefree after the home invasion was a testament to their resilience. Gabriella wanted that. She wanted to jump in the pool, play Marco Polo, and dunk her nephew without a care in the world. If kids knew what adulting was like, they wouldn't be in such a hurry to grow up.

Here she sat, waiting, like a ridiculous damsel in distress. Eli had driven her here with no consideration for her opinion of the situation. He'd dragged her from the car and pushed her through the door.

Big, stupid ox.

Big, caring, stupid ox who was risking his life for her family.

She stared at the gun that lay next to her laptop. The last thing he'd done before leaving her at the door was to hand her his backup piece. Fully loaded. "Keep it close. It won't do you any good hidden in the bathroom or under a pillow."

"But the kids—"

"Keep it on you."

She accepted it, which meant accepting the situation. Her presence could put Natalie and the kids in danger. She ran her fingers over the barrel. Smooth and cold. Until fired. Then hot and deadly.

She grabbed her phone again.

Answer me.

Where R U?

Talk to me.

Nothing. The urge to hurl the phone across the room grappled with the knowledge that she was being childish.

What about Deacon? No word from him either. Two men out there saving the world without her. This stank.

She switched to her thread with Deacon.

Where R U?

Check in, please.

What R YR sources saying?

Once again silence.

Men stank.

"You keep texting him, you'll ruin his concentration." Natalie maneuvered into the room and past the dining room table. Artemis followed behind, her rotund shadow. She held out a glass of iced tea. "You know he has a rhythm to everything he does. You'll ruin his vibe."

"Actually, I was texting Deacon. But now that you mentioned it, Eli should've let me go with him. I shouldn't be here, putting you guys in danger. I just want to make sure he's okay." The ache started in her temple and worked its way down to the vicinity of her heart. Not Eli. Not him too. "He should be back by now. How long does it take to interview an alleged girlfriend and her father?"

"We're safe here. He had to drive out to the ranch and back. It takes time. And finesse. You're worried because you still care about him and you know finesse is not really in his toolbox."

"I'm worried because he's risking his life to find Jake." She settled the glass on a coaster next to her laptop. She had resigned herself to always caring about Eli. That didn't mean she trusted him. Time for a change of subject. "I've been looking at social media. These millennials. They leave their pages wide open to the public."

"They know if you're on social media, you can expect the whole world to know your business." Natalie stretched her arms over her head and craned her neck. "That's why my children won't have access to social media until they're thirty. I'm not sure they'll even have cell phones."

"Good luck with that." Gabriella angled the screen so Natalie could see it. "They had Facebook pages, but they didn't post much."

"That's because Facebook is for old people. Did you try Instagram or Snapchat?"

"Snapchat, their photos disappear. With Instagram it's just photos. Mostly selfies. Hashtag good food. Hashtag handsome dude. Hashtag romantic night. Gag me with a spoon. There are pictures of Kristina Briones with Beto. Beto with his cousins. Lots of red plastic cups. Lots of stupid, drunk grins and gang signs. Why do girls stick their tongues out when they do selfies with friends?"

"What about Jake and Sunny?"

"He's an ATF agent."

"He has a personal life."

She searched Jake Benoit. Nothing. Mirasol "Sunny" Mendez. The angel face appeared first on the list. She clicked. Photos of Sunny and Jake. At a restaurant. Eating steak. Outside the church. At a Tejano concert. At BorderFest at the Civic Center in front of the rattlesnake pit. Lots of hashtag romance stuff. "I wonder if he knew she posted these photos."

"I'm betting he didn't. What a great way for someone to keep track of him." Natalie leaned in for a closer look. A little tracking device called Sunny Mendez. "She's a looker, but not his type."

"That's what I said. He always went for the athletic marathon runner with legs up to her waist and a permanent tan. What does this little girl have that ensnared him?"

"I didn't meet her. You did. But you know as well as I do, we don't get to pick the people we fall in love with." The sadness that etched her face was a shard of glass twisting in Gabriella's chest just below her rib cage. Natalie had lost her one true love and Gabriella was to blame. "It'll break my heart if our little brother finally found someone and she turned out to be a snake in the grass."

"We don't know that for sure, but either way, he deserves so much better."

"As much as he pretended not to be devastated over Mom and Dad, he was."

"We all were."

"I called them both last night."

Gabriella slapped the laptop closed. Blood pounded in her ears. She busied her hands checking her phone for texts. Nothing. "Why?"

"They're our parents."

"They dropped out of our lives when they divorced. When was the last time they saw Ava and Cullen? When was the last time they called you?"

Artemis, ever the mediator, whined and tried to climb Natalie's pale-blue capris. She leaned over and tugged him into her lap. "At Christmas."

"There you go. My point exactly."

"They'll fly in as soon as they can. It's hard with her being overseas and his surgery schedule."

"You're kidding."

"You think because they stopped loving each other, they stopped loving us, but they didn't. They were beside themselves over Jake's disappearance." Natalie's hands scrubbed between Artemis's ears. The old bulldog panted. His massive head swiveled to convey his disapproval at Gabriella. "They want to be close. We need them to be here if anything—"

"We'll find him alive and they'll turn around and go home."

"They committed the supreme sin of choosing to have lives of their own. Of choosing to be happy. They recognize that life is short and sometimes things don't work out the way we want them to. We both know that. Look at me."

"Why are you taking their side?"

"Because I'm sick and tired of being sick and tired. My Paolo is gone. My kids need their grandparents. They need their family. I need them. You need them too. So get over it."

"You've obviously given this a lot of thought. Why didn't you say something before?"

"Because you needed to work through some things first." Natalie scooted around the table and laid her hand on Gabriella's. "You're making progress. By coming here with Eli, you're learning to trust again. To forgive. To forgive him and yourself."

"When are you planning to move on?"

"Pardon me?"

Gabriella couldn't pretend to know what it was like to lose a wonderful, sweet, funny, handsome husband like Paolo, but her sister was equally wonderful, funny, sweet, and good looking. She deserved another chance at love.

Natalie tapped on the wheelchair's arm. "I'm doing enough just to keep my practice going and take care of my kids."

"Don't use them as an excuse. You know how many people in this world use wheelchairs and are happily married, working, doing good. And parenting."

Natalie's gaze dropped. "So what do you think of Deacon?"

"Deacon? Deacon!" Not an entirely unexpected development, given the intensity of the event that had thrown them together. Whether the feelings would be sustained was another matter. But it broke the ice for Natalie, allowed her to at least think about the possibility. "Hallelujah, that's what I think."

"It's just a question."

"I know, but it's a good question. He's a decent guy, funny, smart. But a reporter, that counts against him in Eli's book, but—" Gabriella's phone chirped. A text. "When this is all over with, we'll return to this topic."

The text was from Deacon. His ears must've been burning.

Be out front in 5. Slowing down to 60. Be ready to hop in.

How did he know she was back at the house?

What is going on?

Meeting Eli & sources. Be ready.

So Eli and Deacon had been in communication. Neither had bothered to keep her in the loop. She jumped up so quickly, her chair flew back and teetered. She grabbed the laptop and the gun.

Natalie's gasp made her stop.

"I know. Eli gave it to me."

"I don't want it around the kids."

"I know."

"Stay here."

"I have to go."

"I know. Be careful."

Gabriella paused long enough to hug Natalie. Then she ran back into the fray.

Where she belonged.

CHAPTER 24

SELF-COMBUSTION APPEARED TO BE a distinct possibility. Deacon kept his gaze on the street in front of him. Gabriella radiated irritation. He hadn't been the one to dump her at the house. Thank God that had been Eli's job. She would never have let Deacon get away with it.

He shut the vent to stave off the fumes from a dilapidated VW van with orange Tamaulipas tags that puttered ten miles under the speed limit in front of them. Might as well flip the switch and let her explode. Then they could get back to doing something constructive. "How's it going back there?"

What he really wanted to ask was, *How's Natalie doing?*

"Where have you been? Where's Eli?" Gabriella twisted in her seat to face him. Her seat belt snapped. She growled. Literally. Like a feral cat. "Where are we going, and how do you know he's meeting us there? Have you two been talking?"

And leaving her out. That's what she really meant to say. "We've been texting. He's on his way back from the Mendez ranch."

"He texted you but not me." Her voice rose an octave.

"We were working."

"What happened out there?"

"He says he got some more information on Luke Donovan. Andy and Sunny Mendez seemed legit. He'll get into the details when he gets here."

"We're supposed to be a team." She snorted. "You two are

chauvinistic men masquerading as feminists. Jake's my brother. And Eli is my . . . He's someone . . . He's my friend."

The crux of the matter. This was about fear for both the men in her life.

"Eli's fine. And believe me, he doesn't underestimate your abilities. He's keeping you off the front lines because you really are in danger. They're not after him or me. They're after you. You can work behind the scenes and still be effective. Together, we'll find Jake."

He couldn't promise Jake would be alive when they did, but they would find him. Gabriella and Natalie would have closure, however painful.

Closure was a stupid word.

"We'll see about that." She said the words quietly, but they were undergirded with a steely determination. "What did you find out?"

"I have a friend who's a reporter at the *Morning-Times*. Crime beat." An SUV ran the red light. Deacon laid on the brakes and the horn at the same time. "I'd forgotten how bad the drivers are here."

"Deacon!"

"He's been working on a story about corruption in local law enforcement for a couple of years. He's—"

"Years? He hasn't been able to break the story? What reporter stays in Laredo for years? Is he any good?"

"All great questions, if you'll let me finish. Yes, he's an excellent reporter. He's engaged to a local woman, a TV reporter. Her elderly parents are here so she stays; therefore he stays. Anyway, this story is a tough nut to crack. He received death threats after an interview with the chief of police in which he asked questions about gun smuggling. No one will talk on the record about it. They'd rather not get gunned down in the street or have a pipe bomb explode in their mailbox. His boss isn't eager to publish something that can't be corroborated by the federal law enforcement agencies, and they aren't talking. I don't blame him."

"How well do you know this guy? Will our investigation end up on the front page tomorrow?"

"I've known Chris since I worked at the paper years ago. He'll want first dibs, but he can be trusted with an embargo. He has more information than we do, so you need to trust him."

"So what does he say about the ATF and Rincon?"

"Chris didn't want to talk on the phone. That's why we're going to the Sunshine Lounge. We're meeting him there."

"The Sunshine Lounge. That sounds promising."

"Hey, it's a landmark among journalists who work here." The smells were most vivid in his memory. Cigarette smoke, stale beer, and the *antojitos* they served—little bowls of beans and Fritos. The feel of the chalk silky on his fingertips, lining up the shot, watching the female reporters whisper and jockey for position. They looked so different in jeans and T-shirts compared to their reporter suits during the day. "It's also a hotbed of gossip. You can find out all kinds of things about stories-in-progress and law enforcement. It's owned by three cops—which makes it a semi-safe place to drink—"

"There's no such thing."

"I mean there won't be a shoot-out as the result of a disputed shot." He amended the statement. Gabriella had every reason to feel the way she did about alcohol, but not everyone who drank ended up with his car wrapped around a tree. Or in a wheelchair. "How's Natalie doing?"

"Who's asking? The reporter or the friend?"

Gabriella's tart tone didn't bode well, but Natalie was an adult and so was he. "The guy who brought her down here to keep her and her children safe."

"You went through a terrifying experience with her, so it seems like you really know her, but you don't."

"I'm not an idiot. I know that." Maybe a little bit of an idiot. Or a closet romantic. "I just want an opportunity to get to know her. You're her sister, not her mother."

Bad move. Gabriella's mother was a sore subject. Not that she ever talked about her. Gabriella's dogged silence on the subject spoke volumes.

"Now isn't a good time. There's too much emotion and too much adrenaline." As usual she wouldn't be drawn into the mother subject. "It's in the day-to-day, ordinary life that you figure out stuff like that."

"You think I can't handle her being in a wheelchair?" Her lack of confidence in him—and in Natalie—was crushing. "Do you really think I'm that shallow?"

"No." She wiggled in her seat. "I'm sorry. I don't. But this is my sister we're talking about. She's been through so much. The kids have been through so much. I don't want her to get hurt."

"You'd rather she not try at all? What happens when you and Eli finally get married?"

"We're not getting married."

"You are. Stop messing around and get it over with."

"Oh, shut up."

"You shut up."

Gabriella might just be the sister he never had. Or sister-in-law. A guy could dream. "Let's find Jake. Then we'll duke it out."

"Fine."

"Fine."

The Sunshine Lounge was anything but. Gabriella shut the door of the silver Infiniti Deacon borrowed from his aunt Piper and stared up at the grungy, squat building painted a drab gray color. A pink-and-green-neon Tecate sign with a palm tree and garish orange sun provided the only splashes of color. Two small windows on either side of the door had been covered with black paper. A few desiccated weeds decorated strips of dirt that served as a front yard for the establishment. A half a dozen parking spaces were full. The grim building matched her mood.

She glanced over the car's roof at Deacon. "Why does your friend want to meet here?"

"Because no one will think twice about an old colleague looking him up and asking to get together at the Sunshine Lounge for old times' sake."

"Y'all spent a lot of time here, I take it." She stepped over a splotch on the asphalt that looked like vomit and headed for the cloudy fingerprint-smeared glass door. "Back in the day when you were young and a partier."

"I'm still young, thank you very much. Every Thursday night, like clockwork, we played pool, gossiped, flirted, and drank large quantities of cheap beer. I was one of the few journalists who called Laredo home." He pushed the door open and held it for Gabriella. "Everyone else was a long way from home. We were like family to each other. We took turns having parties at different apartments, playing cards, and watching movies."

"You *are* too young to have good old days." Squinting in the sudden darkness, she waited for her eyes to adjust before moving forward. "Sounds like not much has changed, though."

"The news business is a small one in the bigger scheme of things. The same people I knew here are in San Antonio now, with a few exceptions, like this one."

He led the way between a series of scarred pool tables with green felt covers. The joint was hopping on a late Saturday afternoon. An old Jason Aldean song, "When She Says Baby," wafted from tinny speakers. Considering the bar's dive appearance, the crowd was surprisingly diverse. Several guys Gabriella pegged as off-duty cops had a lively game near the front door. The way they stood between the tables, facing the door, was the first tip-off. The not-quite-at-ease posture. The gazes that hugged her outline and then dismissed her as no visible threat. One in particular made eye contact. She held his gaze. He shrugged and went back to his game. She continued her own assessment of threats.

Deacon zeroed in on a table near the back. In the dim overhead lighting—not conducive to a decent game of pool—stood a tall, balding man who vigorously chalked his cue. He was almost as skinny as his stick. He greeted Deacon like a long-lost friend and comrade in arms. He made the introductions. Chris eyed her with a healthy mixture of curiosity and wariness.

"So you want to pick my brain." He gave the chalk another twist on his stick and laid it on the table. "Like I told Deacon, it's tit for tat. I've been trying to break a story on gun smuggling for years. This sounds like the best shot I'll ever have."

"Deacon tells me you haven't been able to break it on your own." Gabriella eyed the door. No Eli. She slipped onto the stool across from him. "I realize it's like working in a war zone down here, but surely there's still a few of the good guys left who appreciate the role of the fourth estate."

"Sure, and like me, they'd prefer to stay alive." Chris tapped the far side pocket and took his shot. The yellow solid dropped from sight. Not bad. "I live for the story, but I'd rather not die for it."

"What's different now?"

"From what Deacon has told me, which granted isn't a lot, this may be the opportunity to take them out of circulation for good and break a story of national significance that could save my job."

Deacon's constant anxiety over his job was universal in the newspaper business, which had been on its death bed for years, and not news to Gabriella. The stakes were high for journalists who loved their profession. "Take who?"

A waitress dressed in shorts only slightly longer than panties and a hot-pink tank top approached the table with her order pad on a small tray. "What can I get you?"

"Would you like a beer? That's basically all they have here." Chris approached the table, grabbed his longneck, and nodded at the waitress to bring him another. "But on the upside, it's happy hour."

Happy until someone drove drunk and killed someone or ended up in jail for a DUI. "No, thanks."

"Bring the lady a club soda with a twist of lime," Deacon broke in. He knew her story. He'd seen the results in Natalie. "I'll have a Coke, lots of ice, please."

The waitress trotted away in high-top pink Converse tennis shoes. "Now answer my question. Take who out of circulation?"

Chris handed Deacon a pool stick. "You and me buddy, like old times."

"I'll bury you like old times. You break."

Chris did as he was told. Nice break, but no balls sank. "It's all yours, friend." He sauntered back to the table. "The cops who are being paid by organized crime to look the other way."

Finally. "Do you know that for a fact?"

Chris glanced around. He chewed on his lip for a few seconds. Toby Keith's foot-stomping, fist-shaking "Courtesy of the Red, White & Blue" pounded the air around them. Finally, he tugged a dark navy backpack from the floor and plopped it on the table. "I want your word. I get first dibs on the story when these guys go down."

"I'm not in charge of this investigation, but whatever I can do, I'll do."

"Your brother obviously thought Luke Donovan was the key. He and his partner both."

Nothing new there.

Chris pulled a brown folder from the backpack and opened it. He proceeded to lay out a series of photos and shove them one by one across the table at Gabriella. "The family resemblance is strong. There's no doubt you and Jake Benoit are related."

It was night and the car's windows were tinted, but Chris was right. Jake sat in the passenger seat of the black SUV. He held a camera with a long lens in his right hand.

"How'd you get this? Where was it taken?"

A bell dinged. She glanced up.

Eli. *Thank You, God. Thank You. I don't deserve Your help, but I thank You for being so gracious. Even if I'm an unforgiving, unforgetting, merciless sinner.*

Eli surveyed the scene with that same neutral cop stare he always used in unfamiliar territory. His face was sun-reddened and his shirt collar damp with sweat. He looked windblown and dusty. And rugged in blue jeans that molded to his muscled frame. Every woman in the place stared. From the waitress to the woman hanging on her boyfriend. Deacon waved. Eli stalked toward them.

"Remember, we're here to play pool." Gabriella brushed past Deacon and made a beeline for Eli. "Where have you been? Why didn't you answer my texts?" Just managing to keep her voice down, she planted herself in his path. "You could be dead and I wouldn't even know it. What's wrong with you?"

"I missed you too." He bent over so his lips were close to her ear as he pulled her into a hug. His scent of cologne and man sweat enveloped her. The anger dissipated in a wave of sudden heat brought on by his whispered words and his breath on her cheek. "Everything is fine. I'm fine."

She broke away, whirled, and marched back to the table. "This is Deacon's friend Chris. He's about to tell us how he obtained photos of Jake taking photos."

Chris propelled the yellow solid ball into a corner pocket with an elegant stroke. "Nice to meet you."

"Same here." Eli's mocking chuckle followed her. "Nice place, Deacon."

"Glad you like it. It's owned by cops. Makes it safe yet dangerous. You never know which around here."

Or whom to trust. Just like in life.

The four of them squeezed around the table, heads together. "I'd been trying for months to get someone from the ATF to talk to me. All I got was the party line. Word was going around at the courthouse and the federal building and the police station. Something big was up. I heard your brother was one of the agents involved."

"How?"

"I've been here ten years." Chris shrugged. "I'm not bragging. I have a network of sources built up over the years. Guys I can buy a drink or a steak. Court reporters and administrative assistants who like to feel like they're in the know. A cup of coffee from Starbucks. Some Dunkin' Donuts. They like to talk. Cops sick of the status quo love a gripe session over a few beers when someone else is buying. People who just like the idea of being that 'unnamed source.'"

"Okay, so what happened?"

"Your brother wouldn't talk to me. He wasn't interested in beer or steak or being an unnamed source. Totally a 'talk to the PIO' straight shooter. So was his partner. So my photog and I decided to follow them."

"You surveilled two ATF agents?" Eli's grin showed he appreciated his new acquaintance's perseverance, even if he wouldn't want it directed at him. "That's probably against the law."

"I doubt it." Chris grinned back. "At least not if we don't get caught. It went on for a while. Days. Nights. Finally, we got lucky. We followed them to a warehouse district off Mann Road on the northwest side." He stabbed at the top photo. "That's where he was the night this was taken. They were surveilling a piece of industrial property we found out later is owned by none other than Luke Donovan."

"He's in the import-export business." Deacon's raised eyebrows matched his sarcastic tone. "Donovan has warehouses. So what?"

The waitress reappeared with Chris's beer, Deacon's Coke, and the club soda. Deacon slid the folder over the photos. A Dr Pepper for

Eli, even as he gazed longingly at the beer. The waitress trotted away. He turned back to the photos.

Gabriella shuffled the photos. She laid one of three men carrying automatic weapons on top. "Who needs men with artillery to guard warehouses filled with furniture and clothes?"

"The same is true at LD's mansion, according to Sunny Mendez." Eli tapped on the table with one finger. "Lots of guys with guns. She says he has security up the wazoo. Big guns, as she described them. On the perimeter of the property as well as at the house."

Gabriella turned to Chris. "Were you able to confront Jake or Teeter with the photos? What did they say?"

"Your brother disappeared before we had a chance. Teeter isn't talking to us."

"And there's this." Chris tugged a photo from the bottom of the stack with two fingers. He handled it like it was dusted with anthrax. "What's our friendly neighborhood homicide detective doing there?"

Detective Carlos Rincon stood, arms crossed, talking to a man Gabriella didn't recognize.

"Hot-diggity-dog!" Deacon pumped his fist. "Now we're talking."

"Rincon is in on it."

"Then he knows where Jake is." White-hot anger surged through Gabriella. The bar's walls shimmered. "Jake could be there, right now. We have to go."

Deacon grabbed her arm. "Hear the rest of the story."

Chris shook his head. "After Jake disappeared, that's the first place we went. The guards were gone. Apparently they go where LD goes. We managed to look through some windows. Lots of boxes. Nothing seemed out of place. At least not from the outside. No cars. No activity of any kind."

"Then we confront Rincon."

"If we do that, we'll never find Jake." Eli slid his arm around her.

She stilled. "We're better off to follow him. Let him lead us to the gun-smuggling operation. That will get us to Jake."

"It will take too long—"

"I searched Webb County tax assessor-collector records." Chris's voice dropped to just above a whisper as he pushed a computer-generated Google map toward them. "LD bought an eleven-acre industrial park five years ago not far from this property. No one would question it as a move to expand his holdings."

"It's an ideal location." Gabriella studied the map. At its widest spot—no more than half a mile—the property hugged the U.S.-Mexico border. "A gun smuggler needs a way to get the guns into Mexico."

"Exactly." Deacon traced the border with one finger. "Typically, though, the guns are disassembled and smuggled across, hidden in any number of creative ways."

"Laredo has four international bridges. The import-export business is worth more than five hundred billion dollars. About twelve thousand commercial trucks cross the bridges each day," Chris added. "Then there's the railroads and air travel. The Port of Laredo is the number one inland port on the U.S.-Mexico border. It's the perfect place to smuggle guns. They don't call it the Gateway City for nothing."

"By the same token, with terrorism on the rise and the tension between our government and Mexico over border security and illegal immigration, it has to be more difficult to smuggle anything." Gabriella shuffled the photos and touched the river. The property was located directly on the Rio Grande. A few dozen feet separated Donovan's property from Mexico. "It doesn't matter what it's for—whether it's bootleg counterfeit purses, drugs, people, or guns, they come over this border in either direction."

"And now we've got the wall in some places."

"And the National Guard."

"The National Guard is purely for show," Deacon scoffed. "It's not like they're actually posted on the border. They're consulting and strategizing. Whatever that means. They're not legally allowed to patrol the border."

"Window dressing." Chris nodded. "Political razzle-dazzle. ICE has its hands full dealing with the fallout from the way families were being ripped apart when they get caught crossing. The media and social service agencies are swarming all over the border, watching their every move as they try to reunite families and house them. Border Patrol is stretched to a breaking point."

"Maybe. It's a mess, but we need all the help we can get stemming the tide." Eli rubbed already red eyes. "It still seems unlikely those guns are going over the same way immigrants are coming this way."

"We should leave the discussion of these moral issues for another time." As much as she agreed with Chris, they couldn't afford to get bogged down in problems they couldn't solve any place except at their respective voting booths. Jake needed their help. "While agencies are dealing with other critical issues, is the cartel taking advantage of the holes left in border security?"

"A few weeks ago the HIDTA folks seized twenty-one assault rifles, something like a thousand rounds of ammunition, armor carriers, and a bunch of camouflage suits." Chris took his cue from Gabriella's tone. "In broad daylight. In a parking lot in downtown Laredo."

She ran the acronym through her mental card catalog. Nope. "Explain."

"High Intensity Drug Trafficking Areas. The Feds work with local LEOs to stop drugs coming in, includes Homeland Security, Laredo PD, Webb County SO, Zapata County SO. The crossover to guns is obvious. They confiscated almost six thousand guns in '17. But the point is, it's rampant, and there will never be enough officers to stop the flow."

"Obviously the cartel agrees." Looking contemplative, Deacon sipped his soda and sighed. "They need the firepower."

"Sure. The cases coming before the U.S. District Court here prove that," Chris conceded. "But it's like sticking a thumb in a flooding dike. The sentences are three or four years in federal prison. Like a nice hotel for some of these guys."

Gabriella felt rather than saw the approach of someone. She glanced up. One of the men she'd pegged as a cop ambled their direction. He wore a black Garth Brooks T-shirt, jeans, and heavy-duty black work boots. At second glance he was younger than she initially thought. Late thirties. Good teeth. Full head of black hair. Five-o'clock shadow. He held a Corona in one hand, a pool cue in the other.

She nudged Eli. He looked up. His big hands slid the photos back under the folder. He straightened. "Hey."

"You look familiar." The man gestured with his beer. "I know I've seen you somewhere before. Back in the day."

Eli shrugged and took a sip of soda. "Maybe."

"Did you go to Cigarroa High School?"

"Many moons ago."

"Kyle Sullivan." He set the beer on their table and extended his hand. "WCSO, I oversee tactical."

Webb County Sheriff's Office. He looked like an LEO. Gabriella simply had the wrong agency.

"Eli Cavazos, homicide, SAPD."

"You played football, right?"

"And baseball and basketball."

"That's right. All-around jock. I was on the varsity football team when you made JV as a freshman. Everybody thought you were the wonder boy."

"It was a long time ago."

"The good old days. Touchdowns and cheerleaders."

Sullivan's gaze shifted to the others at the table. Eli didn't rush to fill the silence.

"So what brings you to town?" He picked up his beer but didn't drink. "Besides hanging out in this skanky dive bar with these rabble-rousers."

Miranda Lambert's "Gunpowder & Lead" beat a strangely comforting rhythm on Gabriella's shoulders. She shivered.

"How are you doing, Kyle?" Chris saluted the cop with one finger. "It's homecoming night. You probably weren't around when my buddy Deacon was a reporter here." More introductions. "Kyle is one of the owners of this dive bar. That's why he can call it skanky and we can't."

"Not if you want to keep coming here." Sullivan nodded at the table. "Looks like you're talking shop."

"Actually we're celebrating." Deacon slapped Chris on the back. "My friend and his woman have finally set a date. You remember Lydia Martinez, the reporter at KLDO? They're tying the knot next month."

Sullivan whistled. "Nice. So you're pulling the trigger, Matthews?"

Strange choice of words for a sheriff's deputy. Chris didn't blink. "She told me to make up my mind. Do the deed or hit the road."

"Enjoy your freedom now." Sullivan upended his bottle and drained it. "Once you tie the noose—I mean knot—it's all downhill. If I can do anything for you while you're in town, Cavazos, let me know." He started away, then stopped and turned back. "Your parents still out there on the south side?"

"Sure."

"They must be getting up in years. Did your dad retire?"

"No."

"Probably should. You know, enjoy life a little while he still can." He slithered away.

Eli's eyes were black holes. He straightened. Gabriella wrapped her arm around his. "Stay."

"He knows something—"

"He's fishing." Gabriella hung on to his arm—for his sake, not her own—and turned back to their companions. "Nice save, Deacon."

"Sullivan's a jerk. He's probably PO'd. He's made the moves on Lydia more than once. He makes a move on every female reporter on the crime beat here. And he's married."

"It's a common phenomenon, from what I hear." Eli's arm jerked. Gabriella let go. "What now?"

"We need to retrace Alberto Garza's steps." Eli ran his thumb over the glossy photo paper. "If we can believe Chuy Figueroa, Garza visited the store Thursday afternoon. He called his girlfriend and said he was scared. That he'd gotten into something bad. He told her he'd call when it was over. He parks his car at Main Plaza around midnight on Thursday night. Gets shot. Stumbles to the restaurant and dies at Gabs' feet. Why park at the plaza? Why come looking for Gabby?"

"My guess is he saw his buddy get executed. Either he was there and escaped or he was close enough to see what happened. If he knew they had Jake, he had to get out and find a safe place to hide." Chris shrugged and picked up his cue. "The part with Gabriella goes back to Jake Benoit. We won't know until we find him."

"Rincon asked Chuy for security camera footage at the store." Eli paused, seeming to feign interest in Chris's pool prowess. He banked a shot that sank a stripe. "He's not likely to share, but I saw cameras at the pawn shop. Maybe they would."

"We could ask Teeter to go after it," Gabriella offered. They were grasping at straws. "He said he was sure someone on the task force was a mole. We should share our intel on Rincon. He can work it from the inside."

"I have his cell phone number." Eli pulled his phone from the back pocket of his jeans. "He'll know what Rincon knew about the meeting between the CIs and Jake."

The Bon Jovi song "Bed of Roses" began to play. "That's me." Chris scooped up his phone from the table and turned his back. A minute later he whirled, one hand up like a stop sign. "Never mind."

"What do you mean, never mind?" Eli had his phone to his ear. "I'm calling him right now."

"He won't answer. That was my source at the PD. A dispatcher." Chris tucked the phone into his back pocket. "Teeter's dead."

CHAPTER 25

——

NOT JUST DEAD. MURDERED. Eli parked his Charger next to Chris's Honda CR-V in the Webb County medical examiner's office parking lot and turned off the engine. According to the reporter's source, Larry Teeter had been killed in a public execution in a Laredo mall parking lot. The ride over had been mostly silent, with Gabby staring out her window while Eli endeavored to keep up with Matthews, who drove his own car. Deacon followed behind the Charger.

The medical examiner's building had been constructed after Eli left Laredo. Beyond the airport on Highway 59 past Casa Blanca Lake got him to the general vicinity. Matthews did the rest. Her face white and taut with emotion, Gabby seemed lost in thought. She probably wondered, as he did, how a man so bulging with muscle and so healthy, could be lying on a morgue slab only a few hours later.

"Are you ready for this?"

She turned and faced him. Her eyes were bloodshot. Lack of sleep or emotion. Or both. "Did we do this?"

"They likely were watching him anyway."

"Then he talked to us and they killed him?"

"Or the mole in the task force thought he was getting too close to the truth and shut him up." He shoved open his door. "I don't suppose you'll stay here and let me find out."

"In your dreams."

"You'll be the one with the nightmares."

"I'll just add it to my collection."

178

Something else they shared. Other people collected state plates. Law enforcement folks collected nightmares. "I know."

Matthews had his backpack over one shoulder as he led the way up the sidewalk and knocked on the door. Deacon crowded him. The two were practically salivating at the thought of a story, even as they endeavored to show proper respect for the dead agent.

"The ME is closed to the public, but this murder will bring out the reporters." Matthews dropped his keys into a pocket on the backpack and withdrew his phone. "Plus the investigating officers, his family, if he has any. I've got a colleague and a photographer at the scene. They'll let us know what's going on there. Someone will let us in."

"Did they say if the body had been transported here?"

"No, my source did. The cops are still cleaning up the scene, but I figure you don't want to be late to this party. You'll learn more here."

"It's not a party." Gabby's voice cracked. She turned and stared at Highway 59 in the distance. Cars raced by, their drivers oblivious to the tragedies over which a doctor presided at this tan, one-story, fake-adobe building. "It's not a party."

"I know. Sorry. Newsroom speak."

Like cop speak.

Another sharp rap and a young Hispanic man in dark-blue scrubs shoved the door open. "How is it possible you got here this quick? Like vultures attacking roadkill."

"Love you too, Mike. You remember Deacon Alder from back in the day?" Matthews cocked his head toward Eli and Gabby. "Mike is an autopsy technician. Mike, this is Homicide Detective Eli Cavazos and an interested citizen. They have questions for Cady."

"That's Dr. McGee to you, and she's getting ready to start an autopsy. The Feds and the local LEOs want a quick turnaround on this."

"I'd like to see the body." Gabby spoke up. The quiver in her voice was gone.

Mike held the door open and they all traipsed into a reception area. "Are you family? The deceased's girlfriend is already here."

Pain hit Eli in the gut. Teeter had been loved. That someone would never be the same. "Was she there when it happened?"

"Just came out of a movie."

"The deceased had a name." Red spots shone on Gabby's cheeks. Anger would bring her through this. "Special Agent Larry Teeter was my brother's partner."

"Then I guess you'll want to talk to his boss." Mike jerked his thumb at Deacon and Matthews. "You two aren't getting in, no way, just so you know. I'll talk to Dr. McGee about you two." The thumb pointed at Eli and Gabby. "Wait here." He swiveled and disappeared through a set of double doors.

She brushed past Eli and pushed through the doors after their guide.

"Gabs!"

She didn't listen. Eli followed her in. Footsteps behind him said Deacon and Matthews didn't follow directions any better than Gabby.

The closer they got to the autopsy suite, the stronger the smell. The one Eli associated with every case he'd investigated since becoming a detective. Rubbing alcohol and disinfectant mixed with blood and raw meat. The odor of violent death.

A lean man in an ill-fitting gray suit stood next to a wood bench where a black woman, with deep-red stains on her red blouse and white shorts, sat sobbing. Her keening bounced off the walls and reverberated in Eli's ears. A sound that he'd heard hundreds of times. A sound that punctuated dreams filled with gunshots and sirens and pounding footsteps through dark alleys and backyards and the smell of blood. A tall, gangly woman in a white coat over blue scrubs shook her head and patted the woman's shoulder.

As they approached the words *home* and *you shouldn't be here* wafted toward them.

"Dr. McGee, I told them to wait outside." Mike whirled and planted himself between Gabby and the doctor. "She's not family and he's from the San Antonio Police Department. And we got reporters already. They all want to talk to you."

"Ease up, Michael." Dr. McGee craned her neck to see over her anxious technician. She had an East Texas twang and the leathery skin of someone who liked to spend her free time outdoors. "None of you should be here. This is a private moment. You can make an appointment to come back Monday."

Gabriella ducked past the doctor and accosted the gray suit man. "Are you Larry Teeter's boss?"

"Who are you?" Her guest had no discernible accent, but tethered emotion colored his words. "What are you doing here? A colleague of mine is lying in there—"

"I know. Larry Teeter. He was my brother's partner. Jake Benoit." Her voice shook so slightly only someone like Eli would hear it. "What happened to Special Agent Teeter? Did you find Jake?"

"I'm Special Agent in Charge Chuck Jensen." He shoved his fisted hands into his pants pockets. "I'm sorry. We haven't found Jake."

"Do you know my Larry?" The sobbing woman held up both shaking hands. "They shot him. They put him down like a dog."

Her hands went to her face. Her entire body shook as she bent over, cradling her head in her hands, begging for peace. "Oh, God, Oh, God, Oh, God."

Dr. McGee moved toward Matthews, who was furiously scribbling in a notebook. "Out, out, out." She made shooing motions with hands big enough to palm a basketball. "No reporters. Don't make me call your boss and complain, Chris. Wait in the lobby. Someone will make a statement later. You know the drill."

Their expressions like that of wistful little boys, they backtracked until they disappeared through the double doors. Mike marched behind them as if to make sure they didn't try to mount another offensive.

"Did you know my Larry?"

For a second Eli considered joining the reporters in their retreat. He faced the woman on the bench. Her anguish was like a torch that burned through his body, searing every muscle, every tissue. He swallowed against the lump in his throat. "I met him, once. Ma'am, I'm so sorry."

Words that meant nothing. No words could erase the memory this woman would carry with her for the rest of her life. Time would dull the edges only slightly. Not even sleep would allow her to escape. She'd joined the nightmare collectors club.

Gabby eased onto the bench and wrapped her arm around the woman's shoulders. "What's your name?"

"Tiffany Lockhart."

"I'm Gabriella Benoit."

Together, they rocked. One woman cried. The other consoled without words.

Eli stepped closer to Jensen and Dr. McGee and introduced himself. "What exactly happened to Special Agent Teeter? We just talked to him this morning. We were trying to get information on Ms. Benoit's brother, Jake."

Jensen rubbed his temples below thinning gray hair with both hands. His Adam's apple bobbed. His gaze traveled to the glass window that separated them from the autopsy suite where Teeter would suffer more indignities. "We all know this comes with the territory." His hands fisted. "Teeter was a good man. Decent. On his way to becoming a good agent."

"It's tough. I know." Eli waited, giving him room to collect himself. No man liked to be caught with his emotional pants down. "I've been where you're standing."

Jensen turned to Dr. McGee. He cocked his head. Together, they moved away from Teeter's girlfriend and Gabby and into the autopsy suite.

"I did a cursory exam at the scene. I'd just begun the prelim when Agent Jensen and Ms. Lockhart arrived." Snapping on gloves, she moved to the table where Teeter's body lay. His eyes were closed and his mouth slack, those solid muscles now flaccid. She pointed to numerous bullet holes in his chest and abdomen. "He was hit fourteen times in the right bicep, chest, and abdomen. Three more times in the right outer thigh, once in the calf just below his right knee."

"Overkill."

"Two shots penetrated the heart. He would've been dead within seconds." Her gloved hand touched the dead man's shoulder as if to apologize for her blunt explanation. "They dropped him in his tracks."

"What kind of weapon?"

"I haven't extracted the bullets yet. I understand that witnesses described semiautomatic or automatic gunfire."

Eli turned to Jensen. "No one else was hit?"

"No. Ms. Lockhart was less than a foot away. She hit the asphalt and he fell on top of her, whether to protect her or because he was dying, we can't really know."

"Nothing from the witnesses?"

"People are scared silent." Jensen's gaze hardened as he stared at Teeter's body. "The movie just let out. Forty or fifty people streaming out, mixing with Sunday afternoon shoppers. No place else to go in Laredo. The PD is doing interviews, but everyone says the same thing. It happened so fast. Black four-door sedan. Dark tinted windows. Window comes down, Hispanic man. A few seconds, *boom, boom, boom,* pandemonium. Everyone scatters, hides, hits the deck. Car speeds away. Same story over and over again. Slight variations. Dark-blue or black car. Black guy. Hispanic guy. Black bandana over his mouth. Sunglasses, no sunglasses."

"Typical witness statements. Who's handling the investigation for LPD?"

"Detective Rincon."

"Doesn't that guy ever take a night off?"

"I know. They called him in, rightly assuming this is related to Operation Talon."

Operation Talon. The operation had a name. "How much do you know about him?"

Jensen glanced at Dr. McGee. She smiled. "I'm ready to get started. Are you gentlemen planning to assist or observe?"

"I'd rather not watch you cut up a friend." Jensen headed for the door. "I know you don't work for me, Doctor, but I'd appreciate a courtesy copy of your report as soon as possible."

"Happy to oblige."

Back in the hallway, Jensen motioned toward the door. "I need a cigarette."

"The reporters are out there."

"They probably know more than I do, but I can't share with them."

"Is there a back door?"

Jensen led the way through a long hallway and out to a back area dotted with a few mesquite trees and nopales. He lit his cigarette and took a long drag. His hands shook. He offered the pack to Eli. With a silent apology to Gabby, Eli took it.

"This is so far off the record you'd have to travel around the world before I'd repeat it. I'll deny saying it."

"I just want to find Jake." Eli caressed the cigarette, took the light Jensen offered, and inhaled. The first lungful burned all the way down. "I'm not interested in horning in on your investigation."

"Jake insisted Rincon was in on the gun-smuggling operation."

If Jake was right, the cop was pretending to hunt Jake down to charge him with murder, when in fact he'd known all along where Jake was. Or that Jake was dead.

"But he couldn't prove it?"

"He said he was getting close. He said we'd be able to drop the hammer on the whole thing within a few days. Then his CI was murdered.

He disappeared and Alberto Garza was killed in San Antonio. Rincon is part of the interagency task force created to stop the flow of guns over the border."

"What made him think Rincon was the mole?"

"Something Andy Mendez told him. He didn't go into specifics, but he said the old guy had hinted that we should be careful with Rincon. Garza was scared out of his mind. He said he knew too much. They would never let him live if they found out he was a CI."

"Who is they?"

"Jake said he'd have all the pieces as soon as he brought Garza in. Garza refused to talk about it on the phone. He wanted protection in exchange for whatever he had. Same as the other CI."

"Chuy Figueroa said Garza came by the store Thursday afternoon. He was running an errand for his uncle. That night he shows up in San Antonio and gets shot near Gabby's restaurant. He dies." Eli ran the timeline through its paces for the millionth time. "Have you tried to reconstruct where he was in between? Rincon claims he's trying to get security videos from the sporting goods store. Has he told you anything?"

"We just got warrants for the cameras at the adjoining pawn shop. My guys are looking at the video now."

A time-consuming chore. Time they didn't have. "Rincon's determination to find Jake and charge him with murder is all show. If he's in on it, he knows where Jake is. If Jake is alive, he's going through hell."

"He's a tough son of gun." Jensen rubbed his clean-shaven face. "Even if Rincon pretends to bring him in, he'll end up on a slab in McGee's morgue before he gets to the courthouse."

"We'll find him before that happens."

"I'll find him. He's my agent. You have no jurisdiction here."

Eli took one more puff and ground the cigarette under his sneaker. "That woman sitting in there with Tiffany Lockhart is all the jurisdiction I need."

"And I'm telling you both to stand down. I don't need any more people getting in my way. If Rincon sees you with me, he'll know something is up. The ATF won't buddy up to a homicide detective from another jurisdiction on something like this. It's a huge red flag."

"Understood. We'll do our own thing."

"You'll get yourself killed."

"Not your problem."

Jensen used the end of his lit cigarette to light another one. He puffed and coughed. "Tiffany said they saw some Marvel Comics flick. They could've used a super hero. I'd like to be one today."

"I know that feeling."

———

Seconds so agonizing they hurt crept by. Gabriella offered Tiffany another tissue. She crushed it to her face and dropped it on a growing pile on the bench. The sound of an electric saw escaped from the room behind them. Tiffany bowed her head and sobbed. "It's my fault. All my fault."

"There's no way this is your fault." The woman was in shock. "Larry was an ATF special agent. This had to do with his job."

"I insisted he spend some time with me after Megan and Jeff's gender reveal." Her voice broke. "They're having a boy. Larry wanted to go back to work. I put my foot down. Spend just a couple of hours with me or forget the whole thing."

"I'm sure he wanted to spend time with you. He was caught between his job and the people he loved."

"And I made it worse. I made him choose. If we hadn't gone to the movies, he wouldn't have been in that parking lot—"

"It didn't matter where he was. It's likely they were following him."

More heart-wrenching sobs.

"You shouldn't be here." Gabriella rubbed Tiffany's back. "Do you have family who can come get you?"

"My brother is on his way. He was in surgery. He's a trauma surgeon." She took a long, shuddering breath. "I don't want to leave Larry. I can't leave him here."

"It's horrible. I know." It could be Jake in there, but it wasn't. To be thankful was bizarre and selfish, but human. "It will take time, a lot of time, to begin to process this. You can't do it here, in this place."

"I'll never process this. Never." Tiffany's voice broke. "We were planning to get married. Do you get that? You can't imagine what it's like. Did your boyfriend get gunned down after seeing a movie?"

Gabriella could imagine. Her boyfriend had survived. Their relationship hadn't. Both were at fault. Her inability to cope with the thought that it could happen again. His impenetrable hard shell around his thoughts and feelings. His inability to be faithful and to be truthful. PTSD or his true nature? She'd been too scared to find out. "I've seen enough to know that learning to put one foot in front of the other takes time and prayer and more time."

"I'm too angry to pray." She crumpled up another tissue and threw it at the wall. "What's the point? Will God raise him from the dead?"

Anger, pure and powerful, and a corrosive acid that could destroy everything good in its path. "Can I try?"

"Please." She sobbed and buried her head in her hands. "Please."

Gabriella hugged Tiffany and bowed her head. *Give me words, God. I know I've been selfish and unforgiving. I'm sorry. This isn't about me.*

"God, we don't understand. We can't. We're humans." She whispered the words close to Tiffany's ear. The woman shuddered. "I lift Tiffany up to You. Let her know You are here. That this has meaning. That our lives have meaning. Somehow, help her to see a bigger picture. Don't let anger and hate in our hearts rule her. Get her through the next few minutes, hours, and days."

Tiffany's sobs grew. "Jesus. Jesus." Her cries for relief reverberated in the hall. "Sweet Jesus!" She stopped rocking. The sobs subsided.

Gabriella opened her eyes.

"Thank you." Tiffany straightened. "I'm not sure I can believe in a God who lets this happen."

"I know." Gabriella wiped her own nose. "But I can't imagine going through this stuff without Him, either."

"Why, I don't understand why."

"Me neither."

"Your brother is missing."

"Two days now."

"Larry talked about him some." She shredded a tissue, then another. "Which is surprising. He didn't talk about work much."

"What did he say?"

"That your brother took chances and broke rules." Her gaze shifted from the tissue to Gabriella. Her bloodshot eyes held a universe filled with pain. "Larry was new at this and he was a straight shooter. A planner. A guy who liked to follow the playbook."

"He didn't like Jake, then?"

"No, he did. That's what was surprising. He said he was a good guy who wanted to stop the bad guys, no matter what it took. He was willing to sacrifice everything. Larry respected that."

"What about after Jake's disappearance? Did he say anything about it?"

"He was worried. He didn't say much, but it was obvious." She ran her hand through umber-dyed hair in the latest Beyoncé style. "He was tense all the time. He couldn't sleep. He doubled his runs."

Just this morning, he'd run like the devil chased him. "What did he say?"

"That he was afraid Jake had gotten in over his head. That he might have trusted the wrong person and that he was probably dead."

"The wrong person? Nothing specific?"

"He said in more than one way. He seemed really concerned about your brother's girlfriend. Sunny something. I thought that was weird. I mean, why did he care about Jake's personal life? He said he thought they were moving too fast. We've only known each other eight months, and we were planning to get married in September. He said that was different. I agreed." Tiffany gave a halfhearted chuckle. "Because I knew what I wanted, and I wanted him. I wanted to have babies. We would've made beautiful babies. I told him my biological clock was ticking. He laughed at me and said we had plenty of time for that."

Plenty of time. Until time ran out. Gabriella's biological clock banged louder than Big Ben these days.

Jake was younger. Sunny, even younger. No biological clock banging there. What was the rush? Jake was in over his head with Andy Mendez's daughter. Why couldn't he see that? Or could he? Was he using Sunny, or did he really care about her as much as she seemed to care about him?

Tiffany didn't seem to notice Gabriella's turmoil. "Larry told me to be sure to turn my security system on every night and not to open my door to anyone. Not even local police. To call him if anyone showed up at my door wanting to question me."

She touched the spatter of dried blood on her shorts. "He said if anything happened to him, to leave town and not come back."

"That sounds like good advice."

"I have a job here. I'm a nurse. I have family here."

"What did you see today?"

"I saw the man I love gunned down." Tiffany's anger crackled like lightning and consumed the oxygen in the air between them. "He was laughing about how much popcorn I'd eaten and then he was dead."

"We want to find my brother, but we also want to find the men who did this and make them pay. You can help."

She closed her eyes. Her long fingers with polished, blunt-cut nails went to her temples. She rubbed. "It's a blur. My heart stopped beating. I couldn't think. I couldn't breathe. My legs gave out. I was falling. The car was black with tinted windows. The window rolled down on the front passenger side. A Hispanic man leaned out. I saw spurts of fire and heard *bang, bang, bang* over and over again. People were screaming. Then I was on the ground and Larry was on top of me. His blood was everywhere. His eyes were open. But he didn't see me."

"What kind of car?"

"I don't know cars. I don't know guns either. Like a machine gun. Big and ugly."

"Thank you." Tiffany would relive this scene over and over again for months and years to come. "Every little bit helps."

The double doors banged open. A burly black man in surgical scrubs raced toward them. "Tif, are you okay?"

She rose and fell into his arms.

"Sis, Sis, are you hurt?" He held her out. "Is that your blood?"

"It's Larry's."

"You poor baby. Let's get you home. Mama's waiting." He looked over his sister's shoulder at Gabriella. "I'm taking her home."

Home was where Tiffany needed to be. With time, she might become a whole person again. Eventually. The two leaned in to each other as they stumbled down the hall, big brother's arm around little sister. The beginning of a long road toward healing.

Gabriella's aching throat closed. *Jake, where are you?*

Eli strode in from the opposite direction. "It's about Rincon."

She cleared her throat and swallowed. "It's about Sunny Mendez."

He shrugged. "Both. Powwow back at the house."

She stood. Her legs wobbled like wet noodles. "You and Deacon and Chris."

"Yep."

Gabriella sniffed. "Why do you smell like smoke?"

Eli didn't answer. His phone chirped like a cricket. He held the door for her and then let it slam behind him. He tugged the phone from his pocket. His face turned stony. "Looks like we have lunch plans tomorrow."

"What? We have no lunch plans until we find—"

"My mom says Tía Naomi saw us downtown and told Pops."

"Ah. Is he spitting fire?"

Eli held the door of the Charger for her. "It just says don't be late."

"We were headed to see him anyway."

"Yeah, but now he's mad. That doesn't help."

"I didn't know your mother could text." She slid in and gazed up at him. Dread creased his face. At thirty-four he still looked like a recalcitrant child. "Does she tweet?"

"She even does FaceTime with her grandchildren." He punctuated the statement by shutting the door in her face.

A person could see symbolism everywhere if she tried.

CHAPTER 26

———

IT WAS ABOUT WHO you knew. Gabriella's father used to say that. Maybe he still did. Gabriella squeezed onto the couch next to Eli. Watching him collaborate with his sworn enemies—the media—only served to heighten her sense of a world turned on its side.

George saved a spot on the love seat for Piper. Natalie planted her chair next to him. Chris took the overstuffed chair. A cup of coffee in one hand, Deacon stood. The ragtag team kept growing. Sniffing shoes and nuzzling ankles, Artemis made the rounds. Cullen and Ava's chatter in the next room where they watched a Disney movie provided background music.

"I had coffee with the chamber of commerce president and the director of the economic development foundation." His forehead wrinkled, George pursed generous lips. "They both waxed eloquent on the state of affairs in this city. Law enforcement has done wonders in bringing peace to the streets of our fair city and bringing an end to the bloodshed of the nineties. What's more, citizens like Andy Mendez and Luke Donovan have bolstered the city's reputation as a place where it's lucrative and safe to do business. They wish we had a dozen more of each."

"Not to mention, what both men give to charity." Piper made the rounds with a platter of brownies. The smell made Gabriella's mouth water. She grabbed one and handed another to Eli. Piper smiled and placed the platter on the glass-top coffee table. She sank onto the love seat next to her husband. "They set a great example in that regard.

And Luke's adult sons and daughters—all four of them—returned to town after college to continue in the family business. One of them is on the city council."

"I simply don't believe Luke Donovan or Andy Mendez is involved in anything illegal." George hurled his two cents' worth into a fray that had lasted twenty minutes thus far. "We've socialized with Donovan for years. We're in the same business. We attend the same church, for crying out loud."

"Were in the same business." Deacon looked like he wanted to pace, but the room didn't allow for that. "You're retired."

"For a year. That doesn't mean I'm dead. I keep my finger on the pulse of my business. I keep my eye on your cousins to make sure they don't run the business into the ground."

"Georgie!" Piper patted her husband's knee. "Your uncle is right, Deacon. We've been to many social events at Luke's house. I know his wife, Cecilia. They've been to dinner parties here."

People who led double lives. Like Rincon. "People aren't always what they seem." Gabriella tread lightly. They had agreed in advance not to mention the detective's alleged involvement. "When was the last time you were in their home?"

"A month or so." Frowning, George scratched his silver beard. "The Fourth of July celebration, I think."

"But we have an invitation to his annual end-of-summer fling." Piper offered this statement like a surprise birthday gift. "We hadn't thought we'd go because we have guests."

Summer in Laredo didn't end until October. "When is it?"

"Tonight." Piper glanced at the slim silver watch that hung loose around her thin wrist. "It starts at nine—about an hour from now."

"Perfect." George set his cup on the coffee table. With a glare at her husband, Piper slid a coaster under it. "We'll go, schmooze, and take a look around. Maybe there's an arsenal somewhere in the house, maybe your brother is being held there—"

Piper clapped her hands. Her bangle bracelets tinkled. "I've always wanted to go undercover—"

"No, no, no!" Deacon shook his head so hard, he spilled coffee on the slick Saltillo tile. He grabbed a tissue from the box on the table and knelt to wipe it up. "That's not happening. If this guy is a gun smuggler, he's a ruthless, amoral criminal who already had at least four people killed." He glanced at Gabriella. "Sorry."

"Don't be." Jake's death loomed on her periphery every second of every minute. "Deacon's right. We're not putting anyone else in danger."

"I don't believe it's up to either one of you." George stood and held out his hand to his wife. "We've been attending these soirees for years without a single hiccup. The man is charismatic, generous, and quite the comedian. We'll tell Cecilia we're thinking of moving into their neighborhood and ask for a grand tour."

A killer masquerading as a good citizen.

"You will not." Deacon moved to the doorway as if to bar their exit. "You're crazy. Back me up on this, Eli."

His expression cut from granite, Eli leaned forward, elbows on knees, fingers laced. For a second he seemed to be praying. "We would park nearby and keep the house under surveillance the whole time. We'd be right there. If something looks out of whack you text us or just get out of Dodge. It's a chance to have someone on the inside. Someone they'd never suspect."

"I'll bring the camera's telephoto lens." Chris stood as if to leave immediately. "The more eyes the better."

"They'll spot us if there are too many of us." Eli shook his head. "You get your photographer and take another swing by the warehouses. But don't go in. Just do a drive-by to see if there's any activity."

"I don't like this." Deacon managed to pace the length of tile between the back of the furniture and the big-screen TV that hung on the far wall. "This is more than they bargained for. This was supposed to be a safe house, nothing more."

"It is a safe house." Natalie wheeled her chair toward him. "For the kids. I truly appreciate everything you and George and Piper are doing. So does everyone. We know what a risk you're taking. Thank you. Eli knows what he's doing. You can count on him."

She touched Deacon's clenched fist. It relaxed. So did his face.

George and Piper slipped from the room to change.

"I didn't bargain for this." Deacon sank onto the love seat. Natalie moved her chair so she sat as close as possible to him. "I would never have brought y'all here if I thought it would involve my aunt and uncle in the actual investigation. They're civilians. They're elderly."

"I heard that," Piper called from the stairs. "I am not senile yet and my hearing is excellent."

Deacon studied his hands. "Promise me nothing will happen to them."

"We'll be right there every step of the way." Gabriella elbowed Eli. "And you will be, too, Deacon."

"I never realized what cops went through until that scene at the house. I felt so helpless . . . so impotent. They held all the cards. They could've killed a child in front of me. Or Natalie." Deacon raised his head and stared at Eli. "Now it's my aunt and uncle. They're like my parents. Give me a gun."

"Have you ever shot a gun?" Gabriella beat Eli to the obvious question. "Ever even handled one?"

"I'm a Texan. Of course I have." He grimaced and ducked his head again. "Junior ROTC in high school. I may have gotten kicked out."

"You got kicked out of ROTC?" Eli smirked. "I didn't know that was possible."

"Shot the instructor in the foot. Accidentally." His woebegone expression kept Gabriella from laughing. "Anyway, I have shot a gun. And if you don't give me one, I'm betting Uncle George will. He has one in a gun safe in the master bedroom. I've seen him clean it."

"In an operation like this, I need to be able to focus on the bad guys." Eli's tone was surprisingly gentle. "I can't be worrying about whether you shoot yourself in the foot or me in the back."

"Nobody is going to shoot anybody," Natalie interceded. "This is surveillance. An observe and report situation. George and Piper are attending a party. While they're there, they'll take a look around. Nothing more. Nothing less. Deacon won't need a gun, and Eli won't have to use his. Everybody clear?"

When Natalie used her mother-slash-doctor voice, no one dared disagree.

"Crystal clear." Deacon stood and squeezed past her chair. "But you should ask George to give you the combination to the gun safe."

"I'll think about it." Natalie's gaze followed him to the staircase. "Where are you going?"

"To change."

Deacon wore khaki pants and a blue short-sleeve cotton shirt with a button-down collar. "Into what?"

"I assume we want to wear black. I have sweats and a T-shirt. No black shoes, but gray should be okay, shouldn't it?"

"Civilians," Eli grumbled. "It's too hot for sweats. Somebody sees you dressed like that, don't you suppose they'll think it's odd?"

"What then?"

"Jeans are fine. A lightweight, dark-colored T-shirt." He sighed. "Next you'll want to synchronize our watches."

"Should we?" Natalie giggled. "Just kidding. Get moving. Piper and George will be ready any minute."

Dressed maybe, but ready? Gabriella studied Eli's face. He had the same thought she did. No one was ready for this.

CHAPTER 27

———

DAYLIGHT RECONNAISSANCE PROVIDED THE usual challenges. Eli pulled the Charger into a parking spot on the street a block from the gated entrance to the Donovan mansion after getting as close as he dared for a quick look. His parents' home on the south side would likely fit in the living room of the Spanish-style home. Its elegant sprawl took up half a city block. His brief perusal encompassed terra-cotta roof tiles, curves and arches, balconies, textured stucco, and lots of ornamental wrought-iron work and rustic wood.

He'd learned long ago not to judge people by the trappings. George and Piper were perfect examples. Kind, generous souls who lived clean, law-abiding lives. They had earned the right to live well through hard work and financial decisions. They'd certainly looked the part of Laredo's upper crust when they waltzed from their home. Piper in her sleeveless white sequined dress that showed off still-shapely legs and George in his white slacks and emerald-green guayabera. They looked more like a couple about to elope than two people who might be walking into a suspected gun-smuggling criminal's lair.

Lair. A dime-store detective novel word if Eli ever heard one.

"We're too far away." Gabby tapped on the passenger window. "We can't see a thing from here."

"We can watch to see if we recognize anybody who goes in." Eli itched for another cigarette. That was the problem. One led to two and so on. "As soon as it gets dark, we'll reconnoiter."

She didn't respond. The drive to Laredo's far north side to where the country-club set lived had been noisy with unspoken words. She refused to stay at the house, and if he didn't let her go with him, she would go with Deacon, who had insisted he take surveillance on the back side of the Donovan property. From there he would be able to see the patio, swimming pool and cabana, maid's quarters, guest-house, tennis courts, and what Sunny had described as an oversized detached garage-slash-workshop sitting well away from the house.

"What do you suppose a place like that goes for?"

"A million-plus." Gabby didn't look at him. "It's an older home, but the landscaping is gorgeous and immaculate. It's at least six-thousand square feet, and if the inside is anything like the outside, it's a dream home. Not to mention the size of the property. It's four or five lots."

They'd never talked much about architecture. Gabby lived in the home her parents built when she was a child. Eli had an under-furnished apartment downtown. "Your dream home?"

"No way. Too many bathrooms to clean."

Eli laughed. "You can afford the house; you can afford the maid."

"I don't feel comfortable letting someone else clean my toilets."

"You never had a cleaning lady growing up?"

"My mom thought chores were character building. We split the house. Jake and I got bedrooms and bathrooms. Natalie got kitchen, living room, and dining room."

"She was the favorite?"

"Always."

They both laughed this time. The laugh of two exhausted, semi-hysterical people.

"Do you think he's still alive?"

The question quivered with barely contained emotion. Gabby wanted so badly to be tough. But she was a bundle of fear inside. As much as he would never let her know, they had that in common. So why did he find it so hard to let her in? To let anyone in? She'd earned the right. He took a breath. "I did something I haven't done in a long time last night."

Her startled gaze caught his. "What?"

"I prayed."

"I'm so—"

"Don't get all mushy on me."

"I won't. I promise." But she smiled that silly smile women get when they think they've won a point. "How did it feel?"

"Like He might drop a boulder for my having the audacity to come crawling back to Him after all I've done."

"But He didn't."

"Nope. He seemed okay with it."

"What do we do now?"

Did she mean about them or about the stakeout? Easier to stick to work. "We stay put until dark. Then I'll scope it out. If Donovan goes inside, George and Piper will see him. They can keep an eye on him."

She sighed. "Okay, but I'm going with you."

"Did you forget they're hunting for you? They want to do to you whatever they've done to Jake. Be smart, Gabs—"

"Don't Gabs me."

More loud silence.

His phone dinged. A text from Dunbar. Not good news. "They looked through Garza's phone records. They didn't find anything that helps." No big, fat clues that would lead them to the bad guy and end this nightmare. "He made calls to his girlfriend, his mom, his uncle, and to your brother. That's it. Nothing significant."

"It would've been too easy if he'd called Donovan, I suppose."

"Yep. The stuff of *NCIS* or *Criminal Minds*."

She chuckled, then groaned. "Why haven't we heard from George and Piper? Maybe it was a bad idea to send them in."

"They're the perfect undercover couple for the job. No one will suspect them." *Please God, let me be right.* "They don't want to stand around texting at a party."

As if to prove him wrong, the cricket chirped. He grabbed his phone and unlocked it.

Usual people. Usual food. Usual small talk.

Are u able to look around?

Cecilia gave us grand tour. Nothing unusual except awful abstract art.

Where r u?

Bathroom

Is there basement?

No.

Security?

Tons.

Is Rincon there?

No. moving to patio/pool area for better look.

be careful.

Roger that.

George was enjoying his role far too much.

The minutes ticked by. A steady stream of shiny, freshly washed BMWs, Mercedes, and Jaguars crawled by. The sun apparently decided to prolong the day. It refused to sink in its proper trajectory. Gabby kept peeking at her watch.

Finally.

"Text Deacon. Tell him we're taking the south end. He's got the north side."

"Yes, sir."

She did as she was told. A few seconds later Deacon texted back. "He says the back side has the same wall, only higher. He's headed in to get a closer look."

"Just look. Nothing stupid."

"I'll tell him."

Night-vision binoculars around his neck, Eli slid from the car. Gabby, who was in charge of the flashlight, did the same. He touched the holster on his hip under a Windbreaker he didn't need in this August heat. "Stay behind me."

"Yes, sir."

"Gabriella."

The use of her full name would deliver the message. He strode along the sidewalk until it turned into neatly mowed zoysia grass that fringed the low, faux-adobe wall that ran the length of Donovan's property. Avoiding the manned gate, Eli slipped into the darkness at the far end. Gabby's steps were light behind him.

He peeked over the wall. A decorative fountain welcomed guests to the steps, which featured hand-painted tiles and curved wrought-iron railings that led to a series of arches supported by creamy beige columns.

Faint music floated on the sticky night air. Saxophones and trumpets? At least it wasn't mariachis.

"I want to see what's in the garage." Gabby's voice was silky cool. "And the guesthouse."

"We wait until the party's over."

"That could be hours."

"Welcome to my life."

"Why are we standing out here now?"

"We need to know where the security is headquartered. To watch their movements. What's the security for? Are they guarding any of the outbuildings? You don't just hop a wall and barrel into an occupied property."

"Good observation."

It took a second to register. Gabby hadn't uttered those words. A man's voice.

Eli whipped his gun from his holster and whirled.

Moonlight cast a sliver over Carlos Rincon's face. He held his weapon in a shooter's stance. "Not so fast, Detective SAPD."

CHAPTER 28

"IT'S DÉJÀ VU ALL over again." Eli kept his voice down. He inched closer to Gabby. She didn't move. Every ounce of her being focused on Rincon. His figure was silhouetted against the moonlight, but he appeared to wear black pants or jeans and a black guayabera. A black baseball cap covered his head. "You need to quit sneaking up on us."

"What are you doing here?"

"I could ask you the same question." Eli eased in front of Gabby. "Are you a guest, or moonlighting as a member of Donovan's security detail?"

"Stop moving. I don't have to explain myself to you." Rincon's weapon didn't waver. His voice was low, cool, every syllable like chipped ice. "I'm not the one out of my jurisdiction, sneaking around in the dark outside a private citizen's home."

"Where's Jake? What have you done with him?" Gabby pushed past Eli. Her tone was equally icy, controlled. A very dangerous thing—for Rincon. "If you've hurt him, I promise you I'll rip you to shreds myself."

"Señorita, I promise you we're all on the same side here."

"That's not what I heard." Eli grabbed Gabby's arm and tried to drag her back. She dug her heels in. "I heard you went over to the dark side. You're in up to your dirty eyebrows. You and Donovan both."

"You heard wrong." Outrage soaked Rincon's words, but he still managed to keep his voice down to a hoarse whisper. "I don't know who you've been talking to, but I don't have Benoit. I'm not on the take. I'm trying to find your brother and bring him to justice."

"So why are you standing there holding a gun on us?"

"Because it's become impossible to know who to trust anymore. The good guys and the bad guys are indistinguishable."

"Ain't that the truth?"

"Don't believe him, Eli. He's scum. He's got Jake. He may have killed him."

"I swear on the Bible I do not." Rincon lifted the weapon toward the sky. His other arm came up in the standard *I-surrender* pose. "I don't work for or with Donovan. I'm out here doing the same thing you are."

"What's that?"

"Investigating the disappearance of an ATF agent who is a person of interest in a homicide."

"So you're following us."

"What are you doing outside the home of a prominent Laredo businessman?"

"Put your weapon away and we'll talk."

Rincon acquiesced.

Eli did the same.

"Eli—"

"It's easier to talk this way." He eased into Gabby's space and tugged her back. "We're not exactly in a safe place. It's time to huddle up. Let's give him a chance to explain."

Eli squatted. Rincon ducked down next to him. Gabby crossed her arms. Her expression was lost in the dark night. A second ticked by, then another, and another. Finally, she knelt, but she left a large piece of real estate between herself and Rincon. "We have photos of you talking to Donovan at an industrial park he bought a few years ago. Why?" She produced her best assistant DA voice. "In the middle of the night. No other law enforcement in sight."

"Stinkin' ATF. Always slinking around." Rincon lifted his ball cap and resettled it. "I interviewed Donovan as part of Operation

Talon. You know the details of the operation, I assume, after talking to Jensen."

"You met him in the late evening in an isolated industrial park."

"He insisted. He didn't want anyone to know he was under investigation. It's not good for a man's reputation. He wanted to show me he had nothing illicit going on in those warehouses."

"All he had to do was clean up the place before you got there."

"I walked through his entire operation. I saw nothing to indicate a cover-up."

"Why all the heavy artillery then?"

"The man's paranoid. Probably with good reason." Rincon's hand rested on his weapon. "People with his assets get snatched all the time. Kidnapped. They disappear into some hole across the border. Their families cough up millions of dollars. Sometimes they get their loved ones back. Sometimes they don't. Donovan isn't taking any chances."

A reasonable, well-thought-out explanation. The guy had an answer for anything.

"Are you buying this?" Gabby obviously wasn't convinced. "They've rehearsed this."

"Why?"

"To get us to relax our guards."

"Be assured, I don't want you to relax your guard." Rincon heaved a sigh. "I don't want to be responsible for your deaths. I'm warning you. You're barking up the wrong tree. It's not Donovan. If we find Jake, we find out who the facilitator is. I'm sure of it. You won't find Jake here or anywhere near Donovan's properties."

"Are you following us?" Gabby's frustration beat like tom-toms in Eli's ears. If not Donovan, who? "If you really want to find Jake, following us won't get the job done."

"You forget I still have a murder to solve. And the prime suspect is your brother. I have every reason to believe following you could get me closer to him. What did Sunny Mendez tell you?"

"She said to check out Luke Donovan."

"If she really thinks it will help you find Jake, she's sadly mistaken." Rincon groaned. "Donovan appears to be clean."

"What do you think of Mendez?"

"I've known Andy since I came out of the academy." Rincon's voice dropped even lower. "He's a hero in these parts. People still remember him as a paragon of the law. They name their kids after him."

A good leader and a loving father. Every lead turned into a dead end.

"In the meantime, Jake has been missing forty-eight hours now." Desperation married exhaustion in Gabby's voice. She needed sleep. He would get her to sleep—at least for a few hours—before they headed to his parents' house if he had to handcuff her. "We have to find him."

"I'm aware." Rincon shoved his glasses up his nose. "I have a murder to solve and now an ATF agent has been gunned down on my turf. It's a war zone."

Eli stopped himself from pointing out the obvious. Laredo had been a war zone for years.

Eli's phone buzzed. Glad he'd placed it on vibrate, he pulled it from his Windbreaker pocket and hazarded a glance.

A text from Deacon.

Little hiccup here. Caught trespassing. PD called.

Eli held it out to Rincon. "It's for you."

CHAPTER 29

———

ALL-NIGHTERS WERE FOR COLLEGE kids. Deacon shut the front door with only a squeak. Darkness still reigned, but dawn would make an appearance in the next hour. He didn't bother to turn on a light. He knew this house like the back of his hand. Plenty of all-nighters back in the day. With any luck everyone would still be sleeping. He didn't feel like explaining himself.

Rubbing his gritty eyes with one grimy fist, Deacon squinted at the lit security panel and punched in the code. Every muscle and bone in his body ached. Riding in the back seat of a cop car, hands in cuffs, had not been a stellar moment in his career. In the past he might have considered it a badge of honor to be nabbed while working a story. But in this case it only proved to Eli that Deacon couldn't be trusted with the nuts and bolts of a surveillance operation. He'd committed a major tactical error.

Now he needed an attorney to fight trespassing and breaking-and-entering charges. Donovan wasn't backing down, despite Rincon's attempt to smooth the man's feathers. At least the discussion had given Eli and Gabriella time to bail.

Poor choice of words. Trespassing might be a misdemeanor but breaking and entering was not. Given his spotless record and career, the night magistrate had set a low bail.

This jailbird needed sleep. He swiveled to head toward the stairs.

"Stop. Don't move or I'll shoot you."

Natalie sat in the foyer. She held a gun with both hands. Artemis stood at her side. A low growl hummed in his throat.

"It's me. Deacon." Guns drawn twice in one night. At least this was a relatively small one. "I'm gonna turn on the light, okay?" He flipped the hall switch.

"Deacon. You scared me!" Natalie let the gun sink into her lap. "I'm so glad you're okay. Gabriella told me what happened."

She wore a silky blue housecoat. Her bare feet looked small on the wheelchair footrests. Her manicured toenails were pink. Deacon managed to gather his wits. "Uncle George actually gave you his gun? He wouldn't give it to me."

"Gabby gave me Eli's backup weapon before y'all left for the party."

"I'm sorry it's come to that."

"Me too."

"Are my aunt and uncle okay?" He hadn't been able to see much in the spotlights in Donovan's backyard. With any luck they'd slipped away before anyone realized their nephew had been caught trespassing on their host's property. "They were probably irritated that their nephew was the one person in the surveillance team who managed to get himself arrested."

"They were worried about you even though Eli and Gabriella assured them you would be fine. It took them forever to settle down. They hashed and rehashed everything they saw and heard at the party, none of which was germane to my brother's disappearance."

She wheeled around. Artemis leading the way, the three of them paraded into the kitchen. "Do you want coffee or iced tea?"

"The last thing I need is caffeine." The postadrenaline jitters had left his hands shaking and his head throbbing. He sank onto the closest chair. Artemis trudged over to the rug by the sliding glass doors where he curled up next to a sleek black-and-white cat stretched out full length. "Cleo finally made an appearance."

"And Artemis made a friend. Your aunt says that never happens with Cleopatra, Queen of the Cats."

"Nope. She's very picky about her friends. Why are you still up?"

"Under normal circumstances I don't sleep much. Even less here." Her voice had a breathy quality. Despite her words, she sounded tired. "I'm a creature of habit. I have trouble settling down when I'm away from home."

Her hands fluttered.

To cope with her life.

"I'm sorry this is so hard."

"Every hour that passes is another hour my brother is somewhere being subjected to something horrible." This time, her voice quivered. She cleared her throat. "I try not to imagine what's happening to him. Or his body broken and dumped in the Rio Grande—"

"You can't do that to yourself."

"If anybody knows that, I do. It's a case of doctor heal thyself." Her chuckle was dry. "Do you want to talk about what happened out there?"

Better than imagining what had happened to Jake in the last two days. "I miscalculated."

"Eli says you jumped the gun and put yourself and everyone in more danger."

Sounded like Eli. But this time the guy was right. "I guess they got back all right?"

"They're sleeping. At least I hope they are. Gabby didn't say much, but she's disappointed at how things turned out. Nothing on Donovan. Rincon isn't in on it. A big, fat dead end, she called it."

"It's a sad state of affairs when we're sorry a cop isn't on the take."

"I didn't mean it that way."

"I feel like such an idiot."

"You're doing the best you can. You're a reporter, not a law enforcement officer." She moved her chair closer. "How about a glass of milk? Piper has chocolate syrup."

He reached for her hand. To his amazement, she let him hold it.

Her fingers were warm and soft. He leaned forward and kissed her palm. She sighed. He let himself peek at her face. Pain mixed with sadness. "Sorry. I'm delirious with fatigue."

"I'm not sorry." She leaned in.

She smelled like roses. He met her halfway.

Deacon had experienced a few first kisses, but none like this. Her lips met his and it felt as if they'd kissed a hundred times, maybe a million. They knew each other inside and out. Every hurt, every joy, every uncertainty. Without one spoken word.

She backed away. Literally moved the chair back. Beating a hasty retreat.

"Wow."

"Wow, indeed." She laughed. This time the notes held warmth. "We may win the award for world's worst timing."

"It feels like great timing to me."

"I'm a psychologist. I know all about what happens to people thrown together in times of upheaval and terrific stress."

"You don't believe in love at first sight?"

"I do. I fell in love with Paolo from one breath to the next."

Of course. This wasn't her first rodeo. Deacon stared at the table, then the darkened window behind her, then the covered cages where Fidencio I and II slept. "When I walked into your house on Thursday, I took that breath. Before the upheaval. Before the terrifying ordeal."

"Deacon."

"Like the old umpire said, 'I just calls 'em like I sees 'em.' If you don't feel it, that's a different story. Just say so and I'll back off."

"You're the first man I've kissed since . . . since Paolo." Her hands gripped the wheelchair arms. Her knuckles were white. "But I'm a very different person than I once was."

"You look beautiful from where I sit."

"Thank you." Her grip loosened. "You're sweet. Can we leave this conversation for a different time?"

"As long as you promise there will be a conversation."

Smiling, she nodded. "Tell me what happened out there."

"I just knew I could scale that wall like a commando and slip over to the garage for a peek in the window. The music would cover any noise. People were talking and laughing. They were eating and drinking. No one was looking."

"Why not wait until the party ended?"

"Because then the security boobs would be doing their rounds at the outlying buildings and on the perimeter. During the party they were all up around the house." It seemed like a good theory at the time. "Besides, I had this whole special ops thing going on. I guess I've watched too many movies."

"Did you have time to see anything inside the buildings?"

"Two matching gray C-Class Mercedes Benzes, a red Jaguar XE, and a silver Ram pickup."

"Cars."

"A Shopsmith, a workbench, and a bunch of woodworking tools. It looks like he's building some kind of picnic table."

"Totally sinister."

"Yep, who'd a thunk it?" He cradled his throbbing head in his hands for two beats. "Absolutely nothing worth the risk I took. He had nothing to hide at the house. Now he knows we're on to him."

"Detective Rincon swears he's clean."

"We believe Rincon?"

"Eli believes him. He told Eli he'd get you out on bail."

"The night magistrate did that."

"There is no night magistrate."

"Ah."

"You should go to bed."

"You should go to bed."

Neither of them moved.

"How would you feel about me picking you up?" Not wanting to spook her, he remained seated even though every muscle tensed for action.

"Are you planning to sweep me off my feet, so to speak?"

"As a psychologist, you must know of the healing properties of a good hug."

"I do."

"So?"

Her porcelain cheeks turned rosy. She nodded. "I could use a hug myself."

He stood and slid his arms under her. She didn't weigh much more than a child. He eased into the chair and let her body settle against him. Her arms slid around his neck. He leaned his forehead against her shoulder and breathed. "You smell so good."

"You, not so much." She giggled, but her arms didn't loosen. "It was warm out there this evening, wasn't it?"

"I'm so sorry." He jerked back. "I must stink to high heaven. I wasn't thinking."

"I don't mind." She grinned. "You smell manly."

"A thousand pardons." He allowed himself thirty seconds of hug, then rose and lowered Natalie back into her chair. "Next time, I promise to be freshly showered and shaved."

"I'll look forward to it."

"You should sleep."

She backed her chair away from the table. "I think I might be able to now. Kisses and hugs are great medicine."

The hugs and kisses were a prescription for more insomnia in Deacon's book. "If you need more, let me know. I'm always available."

She disappeared through the kitchen door.

Serious highs and lows all in the same evening. Jail and kissing the woman of his dreams.

He would never sleep now. Deacon went to the kitchen counter and searched for the old-fashioned coffeepot his aunt kept in the cabinet. A single cup from a Keurig would not be enough to greet the new day.

CHAPTER 30

———

SUNDAY MORNINGS SHOULD BE for church followed by a leisurely lunch. That world didn't exist while Jake was still missing. The clock banged in Gabriella's head. Eli refused to let her attend a service at his father's church. Instead, they ate Piper's pancakes and rehashed the rehash on everything they knew about Operation Talon until it was late enough to visit Eli's parents.

The reporters were headed to a hastily called unusual Sunday news conference regarding Teeter's murder. They would report back. And plumb the internet for nuggets of gold about Sunny Mendez, Luke Donovan, Alberto Garza's family—anything that might give them a clue that led to the next step.

Eli's father had met Sunny. He knew Alberto Garza and his cousins. He would know Andy Mendez and Luke Donovan. He was a keen judge of character. Any light he could shed on Sunny Mendez's relationship with Jake had the potential to be helpful. And it was something they could do on a Sunday morning when everything was closed.

The small, white house with its front porch swing and planter boxes of flowers hadn't changed in the past few years. Even after more than a year, it felt like coming home—to Eli's home. Thankful to get out of the blazing noon sun, Gabriella stepped through the door Eli held for her. He hadn't lived here for more than fifteen years, yet he still had the key to his parents' house. He led the way down the hallway to the kitchen. "Mama, Mama!"

Virginia Cavazos trotted from the kitchen, fingers covered with roped veins and age spots curled around a dish towel. She looked as gorgeous at eighty-five as she had when Gabriella had met her four years earlier. The joy at seeing her youngest son suffused her face. "*M'ijo.* You're here. And Gabriella. Come. Sit. I have *pollo con calabaza* on the stove. Fresh tortillas. *¿Cómo te vas, m'ijo, cómo te vas?*" She hugged Eli's middle and then stepped back, her look appraising. "You need a haircut."

Eli's face darkened. His gaze darted toward Gabriella and back to his mother. "The lady who cuts my hair took a leave of absence."

Ignoring the sudden flash on the feel of his wiry hair in her fingers, Gabriella accepted the hug Virginia offered and found herself wrapped in the scent of White Shoulders and motherly love. "It is good to see you, Señora Virginia." After a few awkward moments, they'd settled on Virginia, when Gabriella couldn't bring herself to call this kind, soft pillow-shaped, large-lapped woman mother. "How are you? It's been . . . so long."

Virginia's sad smile hung in the air between Gabriella and Eli. He shifted, his gaze on his shoes. He ducked his head. "I need to see Pops. Is he around?"

"*Papí* is still at the church." Virginia said it as if Eli should know better. And he should. Sunday was a workday for pastors. Even Gabriella, a relative newcomer member of the family, knew that Xavier, in particular, worked at the church every day, always there for choir practice, youth group meetings, the food pantry, trustee meetings, and more. Not to mention doing some marriage counseling. Especially not to mention. "Go talk to him and then walk him home. The four of us, we'll sit down and eat together. It will be ready in thirty minutes. Do not be late."

Eli didn't move from his spot in the doorway. He ran a hand through already ruffled hair. His mother gave him a look. He ducked his head again. "Sí, Mamá."

The second he disappeared down the hallway, Virginia had

Gabriella's hand, tugging her into a chair. She bustled around the kitchen, pouring iced tea and placing sugar and fresh lemon slices on the table. Neither of them spoke until she was seated across the long pine table. "How are you, really?"

Gabriella swallowed. "I'm fine."

Virginia shook her head. "*Mentirosa*. Eli is *un idiota*. I know this. *Idiota*." She sighed, tears in her faded brown eyes. "But, he is also a good man. Of my boys, he has the kindest, most gentle heart. It is scarred, yes, and flawed, but he has a good heart."

Eli was Virginia's youngest, and it was obvious she doted on him, as did everyone, except Xavier, perhaps. Gabriella searched for words that wouldn't alienate the nicest mother she'd ever met. "It's not enough. What he did . . . You can't imagine how he hurt me."

"I can imagine. Neither Xavier nor I am perfect. We've been married more than sixty-five years. Much time to inflict hurt." Her face a mask of undisguised pain, Virginia's wrinkled hands smoothed the flowered place mat on the table. "No, being good isn't enough. We all fall short. We make terrible mistakes. But when someone we love does this, we forgive them. Just as God forgives us. Haven't you ever done something terrible, something awful, and been forgiven?"

An acute pain in her chest made it impossible for Gabriella to answer. She could only nod as the air whooshed from the small kitchen, collapsing the walls around her, allowing the memories to flood in.

The December evening was cold. She decided to serve linguini with a bottle of Pinot Grigio. It was Paolo's thirty-fifth birthday, and Gabriella wanted to make him a meal from his country. They gorged on linguini with clam sauce, bruschetta, salad, and tiramisu. His face flushed, his eyes shining, he insisted they open a second bottle of wine. In the mood to celebrate, Gabriella obliged. She'd personally filled his glass—twice. Three hours later, he wrapped his Jaguar around a heritage oak, killing himself and paralyzing Natalie.

Gabriella gulped her tea, trying to wash away the sour taste in her mouth and the stone in her throat that threatened to choke her. Next Virginia would be saying the Bible said to forgive. Jesus said to forgive. Natalie seemed to have forgiven.

So, why couldn't Gabriella forgive Eli? Unlike her, he hadn't killed anyone. She could pray for others. Like Tiffany Lockhart. But Eli? She held him to a higher standard. She needed to repent and be forgiven as much as he did—more.

———

Eli walked the dirt road slowly, kicking at stones, avoiding ruts, ignoring the desire to turn and run like a little boy trying to escape his punishment. He forced himself to look ahead, down the road. His father sat at a picnic table shaded by a chinaberry tree in the church's side yard. He appeared to have shrunk, his wizened body a mere shell of the one Eli remembered from his childhood. He had a Bible open in front of him, yellow tablet filled with scribbles next to it. "Pops, it's too hot to be sitting outside."

At the sound of Eli's voice, he looked up. His joy was muted but still there. By the grace of God, still there. "Elijah." He took off his thick black-rimmed glasses and laid them aside in a deliberate motion. He was the only one in the world who called Eli by his given name. The name of a prophet who was taken up to heaven in a chariot of fire. "How are you, *m'ijo*?"

Eli strode through brown grass brittle with drought and dropped onto the bench across from his father. He gazed out at wild olive and Montezuma cypress trees with boughs sagging in the hot, dry breeze. "You were going to marry Jake Benoit?"

"So this is business, not a social call." Pops replaced his glasses and fixed Eli with a stare magnified by the lenses. He was famous for that stare.

"A little of both."

Pops picked up his Bible and smoothed the worn leather cover with fingers knotted by arthritis. "I was considering it, but I had not made a decision. Jacob asked me to see him and his fiancée for some marriage counseling. They had an appointment Thursday, but they did not keep it. So it seems doubtful that I would marry them."

"Did Jake call you to reschedule?"

"No. Why do you want to know this?"

"He's Gabby's brother. She didn't even know he was getting married."

"Then Gabriella should speak with her brother. How is it that you came to know about this?"

"Have you met his fiancée?"

"Sí, Mirasol Mendez. A silly young girl, perhaps too immature for marriage, but I hadn't made that determination yet."

"You know that she's a friend of Chuy Figueroa . . . and his cousin, Alberto."

"*Claro que sí.* His family attends our church here. I baptized his sister and she married here. *¿Por qué?*"

Our church. He always said that. Our church. As if Eli still dragged his feet behind him every Sunday morning when they'd trudged on the dusty road to the church at the crack of dawn. Eli had swept the sidewalk and checked the pews again—as if some slovenly elf had come in during the night and dropped bubblegum wrappers on the floor of the sanctuary while they slept. It seemed like a very long time ago. Eli studied the dirt road, still not paved, still filling the air with choking dust.

This church was only a few hundred yards from the Rio Grande. A few hundred yards from another country where warring cartels waged bloody battles over drugs and guns. Somehow, it had never touched his family. Now it might.

"There's a chance . . . a chance that they're not good men. That they are involved in something illegal."

His father smoothed the pages of his notebook. "Not good men? Your tía Naomi called. She told your mother she had seen you here downtown. With Gabriella. She assumed we knew." His tone was only faintly condemning and hurt.

"Gabby's at the house now, with Mamá. And I'm here now, Pops."

"You have reconciled?"

"No. She's here because her brother is in trouble. The men I mentioned may have something to do with that trouble."

His father wouldn't be distracted. "She is a good woman. She loves you. You love her."

"I'm well aware of that."

She loved him, but she didn't trust him—for good reason. He didn't deserve her trust. Somehow, he had to earn it back. But to do that, he had to find a way to tell her the truth about his past. And their future.

"Are you trying to reconcile? Have you begged forgiveness? Have you sought counseling?"

Each question pierced Eli's skin like nails to a cross. The truth that gnawed at him every time he looked at her. Would she understand? Would she want to help carry his complicated burdens? "I'm trying," he whispered. "She is very hurt."

His father smacked him on the shoulder with the notebook, his strength surprising. "Try harder." He stood. "We must go eat. I can't answer questions on an empty stomach."

During the walk home, they talked of other things. News of his siblings. Family matters. Whether the Astros or the Rangers were a better team this year. At the lunch table, Eli tried again to extract the information gently, but his father wasn't having any of that. He focused on Gabby, drilling her with questions about her restaurant, Natalie, and the kids between praise for Mamá's cooking. "You should serve pollo con calabaza in your restaurant, Gabriella. Your customers will want the recipe."

"I might make it my Thursday night special, but these law enforcement types are more into beef than chicken and squash." Gabriella smiled. She never hid the fact she loved his parents, sometimes more than she loved Eli. "I admit to pilfering Virginia's recipe for *pastel de tres leches*. It's a best seller with Mexican hot chocolate on cold winter days."

Tres leches cake was also one of Eli's favorites.

"Pops, Alberto attended youth group at the church." Eli handed the basket of homemade corn tortillas to Gabby. Her smile didn't waver. Eli forced himself to smile in return. "According to his girlfriend, he was recruited to act as a straw buyer by his uncle Manny Figueroa. He then recruited other members of the group. They're college students. They need money. It's easy. They're easy targets."

"I catch anyone doing this in my church, I will kick their behinds all the way across the river myself." Xavier laid his napkin on his plate, still laden with food. "These boys went to our youth group, vacation Bible school, and they played kickball in the church parking lot. It's hard for me to reconcile them as hoodlums."

They would always be Pops' sheep. If they didn't stay on the straight and narrow, he had failed in his job. He would want to bring them back into the fold. "Beto was trying to make amends when he was killed. He was working with Gabby's brother to bring down the operation."

"God bless his soul. I'll go see his parents tomorrow afternoon."

"Do you think you'll be asked to perform his funeral?" Virginia tugged the napkin from his plate and nudged it toward him. "You have to eat."

"His parents didn't attend our church. I suspect Father Oliver from Sacred Heart got that call." He once again covered his plate with the napkin. This time he stood. "I must get back to the church. The trustees are meeting to discuss repairs. The youth have their Bible study. Life goes on despite all the ways of a fallen world."

"Pops, wait."

"You have eaten nothing." Virginia picked up his plate. "You'll be hungry later. I'll keep it warm for you."

She cast a warning glance at Eli. He subsided. No one made Xavier Cavazos talk if he chose not to do so.

A bang told them the front door had closed. "He hasn't been eating. You give him indigestion with this third degree of yours." Virginia scowled at Eli. "A strong wind and he blows away."

"Is something wrong?" Fear crawled through Eli. He stood and went to the kitchen window to stare out. "Is he sick? Has he been to the doctor?"

"You know him."

Eli did. A team of oxen couldn't drag Pops through a doctor's door. A tradition Eli carried on.

Something else to worry about.

"Your dad hasn't lost his touch." Gabriella pushed against the porch's wooden floor with her *chancla*. Swinging created a tiny breeze in the sweltering South Texas air. The afternoon temperatures blistered the ground. Crickets mused in the distance. A mourning dove cooed from its perch in a fragrant eucalyptus tree in the front yard. It could almost be a simple Sunday afternoon. Almost. "He's got to be in his eighties, and he's still the best preacher I know."

"Eighty-six." His back to her, Eli stuck both hands on the porch railing. "Mamá is bringing out the homemade ice cream in a few minutes. She wants to know if you want chocolate syrup or butterscotch topping."

"He chewed you out, didn't he?"

He turned to face her. "When I got shot, I lost you."

Gabriella stabbed her foot against the floor and brought the swing to an abrupt halt. "Are you trying to blame your infidelity on me?"

"No. Whatever you think I did is on me. But it's like you suddenly realized that this law enforcement thing is for real. Up until then you understood the concept that I could get shot, I could die, but it was just an abstract concept. Until it happened. You withdrew into the restaurant. You were never around. You even stopped showing up for the counseling sessions."

"Once, okay, twice, but a pipe broke and the kitchen was flooded. I had—"

"A broken pipe was more important than fixing our relationship? We were engaged to be married." He crossed his arms over his chest and leaned against the railing. His face deserved a place on Mount Rushmore. "You left me, not the other way around."

"That's bull." He was right. He was so right. Sitting there at the hospital, waiting for a surgeon to tell her whether Eli had lived or died, she'd come to a horrifying realization. If he died, her world would die with him. The restaurant, the house, the animals—everything would be a gray void where he'd once been. "And if you felt that way, you could've said something instead of cheating on me."

"Right." He wore the masculine man-of-few-words like a crown. "You bailed."

"No. No!"

"You know, I've seen a few cops get shot over the years. Their wives and girlfriends always cling to them, so relieved they're still alive, that they're afraid to let them out of their sights." He walked over to the swing and plopped down next to her. She inhaled his musky scent of bitterness. "You . . . I had to order *carnitas* to see you. Even then you barely came out from behind the kitchen doors."

"You're exaggerating." Not really. She couldn't explain it. The terrible icy fear that encased her every time she'd looked into the fathoms deep of his eyes and thought about how close he'd come to death. She'd lost her parents to divorce, almost lost her sister. Then Eli. Her instinct had been to run, to save herself, to leave him before he left her. In the end she'd been right. He hadn't died; he'd just found someone else. "I was trying to run a restaurant. Alone."

"I was the one alone. I don't do alone very well these days." He took her hand in his and rubbed his thumb across her knuckles. The hair on her arms stood up. "You, on the other hand, seem to do it very well. I'm trying, Gabs. Can't you see that?"

"I do see it. I know how hard it is for you. I'm trying to decide if it's too little too late." She couldn't fight the image of his fingers touching another woman's skin. "Are you still . . . Do you still . . . ? I've heard you still see her."

His hand dropped. "You really want to go there?"

"I want the truth."

He laughed, a bitter, grating sound. "I tried telling you the truth before. All it got me was a lonely apartment."

Gabriella tucked her hands under her thighs. "I'm an attorney. I know how to do background checks, and I know people who will do them for me. She runs an escort service. How could you get involved with a call girl? You're a police officer. How could you?"

"If you'll park your high horse for a minute, I'll tell you. I met her when I worked vice, long before I met you. Long before we got engaged. We're not involved. We see each other . . . as friends."

For some reason she'd allowed herself to hope against all rational thought, that it was just a big misunderstanding. Her throat was scratchy, her tongue swollen. The words stuck on her lips. "How much do you pay her for her company?"

His fist smacked against the swing's wooden arm. The swing vibrated as he shoved himself to his feet and stomped down the steps. He whirled, hands fisted. "You have no idea who or what Lily is to me."

Gabriella shot from the swing, marched down the steps, and halted within inches. "And you wonder why I can't take you back."

The woman's name was Liliana Chacon. She came from a family of drug dealers and extortionists and shadowy mafia-like figures. And he called her Lily. That should've been somebody short and a little chubby, who liked soccer and grape Fanta. Not a woman who looked as if she'd just walked off the set of a Victoria's Secret commercial.

Tears would've been a relief, but none came. They'd dried up six months earlier.

"Not everything is about you." He dug car keys from his jeans pocket. "Tell Mamá I went to the store. I want a root beer float."

Cigarettes, more likely. He wanted to escape. To walk away as usual.

A man in dirty gray work pants and a dirty wife-beater pelted down the road toward them. "The church's on fire." Panting, he slammed to a halt behind the Charger. His gaze swung wildly from Eli to Gabriella. "They firebombed the church."

CHAPTER 31

———

SIRENS SCREAMED.

God, no. Pops.

Eli took off like a gangbanger running from the cops. Running for his life. Running for every regret and every hurt and every disappointment. He outdistanced Johnnie, the gardener-slash-custodian, even though the other man was younger and more agile.

The block to the church seemed to stretch until it became miles. His sight dimmed. His legs turned to rubber. He stumbled over curbs, rocks, and weeds.

Fire trucks and ambulances screeched to a halt in front of the building. Firefighters emerged. Hoses unrolled. Voices shouted.

Smoke and flames billowed from the broken double doors that led to the sanctuary. Eli slammed to a halt. "Pops? Pops!" The yell came out a croak.

He bolted toward the doors.

A firefighter grabbed his arm. "Whoa, whoa."

"My dad's in there."

Three firefighters in full gear raced past him.

"We've got this." The firefighter gave him a gentle shove. "We'll get him out."

Eli fought him off and lunged for the door.

The guy wrestled him back. "Stop, stop."

The doors burst open. Gray-and-black smoke billowed. The stench of burning wood, rubber, and plastic assailed him, along with intense heat.

Eli stumbled back.

Two firefighters emerged, Pops' limp body propped up between them. His head lolled. His glasses had disappeared. Burns, holes, and black soot stained his white shirt, once crisp and starched. Blotchy burns on his chest and arms showed through.

His legs dragged behind him.

"Papí! Papí?"

"Get the EMTs over here!" The firefighters lowered Pops onto the water-sodden grass. "He's breathing. We're going back in."

They disappeared back into the smoke and flames that consumed a place central to Eli's life his entire childhood. Even now as an adult, his backup plan, his go-to place. The place where he could always find his father. And his Father.

He fell to his knees. *God, please, don't take him. I have so much to tell him. So many secrets I've kept from him. He can't go yet.*

Ugly red blisters pocked Pops' face under soot and water.

"Papí, I'm so sorry." Eli touched the sparse, rumpled gray hair on his father's head. He looked so vulnerable. So hurt. "This is my fault."

Pops groaned. His eyelids fluttered, then closed again.

"Out of the way, sir." EMTs lugging a gurney barreled down on him. "Let us get a look."

They knelt and began to work on him. Fighting to breathe, Eli stumbled back. A hand touched his back. He turned. Horror in her eyes, Gabby stared up at him. His mother, both hands to her mouth, sank to her knees next to Pops. "Xavier? Xavier!"

"Please stay back, ma'am." The EMT glanced up, then went back to setting up an IV. "Are you his wife?"

She nodded.

"Does he have any medical issues we need to know about?"

"High blood pressure. High cholesterol." Mamá took Pops' hand and kissed it. "He had a slight heart attack three months ago."

"Mamá!"

She shook her head. "Not now, m'ijo. How is he? Is it bad?"

"He has numerous burns. Smoke inhalation. Shock. We'll get him intubated, start oxygen in the ambulance. We need to transport."

The EMTs gently hoisted him onto the gurney and rolled him away. Mamá trotted alongside.

"Where are you taking him?" Eli moved after them. He didn't want this to be the last time he saw Pops. Not like this.

"The medical center on Saunders Road."

"I'm going with you." Tears running down her wrinkled face, Mamá looked back, but her hand stayed on Pops' shoulder. "You stay here, Hijo, find out what happened. Who did this? You find them."

She was right. He would find out and they would pay.

He released Gabby's hand. "Go back to the house. Get Mamá's car and her purse. Go to the hospital. Keep me posted. I'll get there as fast as I can."

"It'll be okay." Her gaze held his. "He'll be okay."

"Don't let anyone close to her. Watch your back."

"They'll wait to see if we got the message before they try again."

"All the same, be safe."

"You too."

As soon as the ambulance pulled away, he surveyed the scene. The firefighters had the blaze under control. Thick smoke continued to roll from broken stained-glass windows. Water poured from the open doors to the narthex. The smell of burning drywall, rubber, and plastic permeated the air. Sirens screaming, ambulances continued to race from the parking lot.

Media units rolled in. The vultures had arrived. So much for the news conference. The media from out of town would get a two-for-one. They would dance in the streets over this one. He perused the arriving vehicles. Deacon rolled from his aunt's Infiniti. Chris Matthews's Honda screeched to a halt next to a CBS Southwest satellite truck.

All hands on deck for a story that now involved Eli's father.

Crime scene tape sagged and danced in the breeze along the edges of the parking lot. Uniformed officers held back the media, and the rubberneckers crowded behind it.

Deacon waved both arms. He cupped his hands around his mouth. "Eli, over here."

Eli shook his head and turned his back.

His phone chirped. Deacon. "I can't talk to you right now."

"Is your dad all right?"

"He was inside. They took him to the hospital. Gabs is with him."

"I'm so sorry, man."

"I gotta go."

"What do you know?"

"Later." He disconnected. Blood pulsed in his ears. Wind blew a fine, cooling spray of water from the hoses across his face. He took a deep breath and let it out. Time to be a cop, not a son.

He jogged over to a police officer talking to a firefighter. Both held radios in their hands as they stood outside a ladder truck. The officer's name tag read Jose Gomez. "Any fatalities? How many injured?"

"Who are you?"

Eli explained and flashed his badge.

"Most of the damage is in the sanctuary. It's virtually destroyed." Gomez shook his head. "By the grace of God, so to speak, most of the occupants were in the education wing in a meeting."

The firefighter took over. "Smoke inhalation, shock, some burns that are still being assessed. Eight injured, but none severely. Except your father. He must've been in the foyer when the incident occurred."

Education wing was a grandiose name for a few meeting rooms down the hall from the sanctuary. Hitting the sanctuary had been intentional. Not to keep injuries low, but for symbolic purposes. Hit where it hurt most. A house of God. His father's house. "We need to—"

"You need to stand down." Gomez bristled. "You may be a San

Antonio cop, but you're out of your jurisdiction and this is personal to you. Let the Feds do their thing."

Eli didn't contradict him. It wasn't worth his breath. He would do what he had to do. "Who's coming?"

"ATF, ICE. HSI, FBI, all of them have been notified. It's about to be alphabet soup here."

"They're worried it's an act of domestic terrorism?"

"Or a hate crime. Firebombing a church usually is."

Not in this case. In this case it was a warning to back off. "What do the witnesses say?"

"The only people outside were a couple of kids arriving for a youth meeting and the gardener. He was so excited it was hard to make heads or tails out of it."

"I'll talk to him."

"Not officially, you won't. You know him?"

"His dad worked here for thirty years, until he retired last year. Johnnie used to come with him when we were kids."

They'd played cops and robbers, war, and every other game that had nothing to do with what went on in church.

"Apparently, he was mowing out front when a dark-blue or black Beamer pulled up in the handicapped parking space closest to the building. A guy wearing a black bandana over his mouth and nose ran up to the door. He tossed in a couple of Molotov cocktails and ran out. Came and went in a matter of seconds. Arson is on the scene now."

"Molotov cocktails. Old school."

The first notes of Aretha Franklin's "Respect" emanated from his phone. Gabs. His choices had been either that or "Chain of Fools." Eli excused himself and walked toward the building, away from the inquiring eyes of the media, now jammed into the parking lot.

"He's a tough old bird." She spoke without preamble. "They upped the fluids, started him on antibiotics and oxygen, and dressed his wounds. His windpipe is swelling. They'll keep him intubated and start medications to fight the swelling and treat the damage to his lungs. The doctor said they'll keep him under observation for at least forty-eight hours. It takes that long for the burns to fully develop so they can tell how bad they are. And the swelling could get worse. His blood pressure is through the roof. It also looks like he hit his head when he fell, and he has a couple of broken fingers."

Gabby knew better than to sugarcoat the news for him. Eli took a moment to digest the litany of injuries and their consequences. "Is he conscious?"

"He was in and out, but they gave him painkillers." Her tone uncertain, she paused for a second. "I didn't know if you'd want me questioning him, but I gave him a notebook and a pen. I asked him if he saw anything. He wrote down that he was walking out of his office. He didn't see the perpetrator."

"Good. We don't need him to be a witness they think can identify someone."

"He's out now. Your mom's sitting with him."

"How is she?"

"Alternating between praying and comforting everyone else."

"I can't believe he had a heart attack, and she didn't bother to tell me."

"Knowing them, they didn't want to worry their kids."

"Now I'll worry about what else is going on that they haven't told us." Eli drew a long breath. This wasn't the time for this. "I'll be there as soon as I can."

"What have you learned?"

Eli gave her a quick summation.

"Cowards. Hurting an eighty-six-year-old preacher. Those people get a one-way ticket to hell." Her words needed no response. Anybody with a moral bone in his body would feel the same way. "Have you told them anything?"

"No. I don't know who to trust." He let his own frustration seep through the statement. "Rincon may not be on the take, but Teeter was convinced someone was."

Her silence told him she agreed. "We're back to square one. If Donovan isn't the facilitator, who is?" The million-dollar question. "Get Jensen involved."

"How do you know we can trust *him*?"

"We have to trust one person down here." Her breathing was light and rapid. He could almost hear the wheels turning in her finely tuned brain. "What about Deacon and Chris Matthews?"

"I meant who carries a gun and knows how to use it."

"They know the players. They know their way around. Use them as guides, if nothing else."

"They're both here. All the media outlets that came to town for the news conference are here instead. I'll talk to Deacon when I can."

A series of black SUVs with tinted windows rolled up to the crime scene tape. A window rolled down. A second later the patrol officer moved the tape and the cars filed in.

"I gotta go. The cavalry's here."

"Don't step on toes and don't do anything without me."

She could not be allowed to participate in what came next. A bunch of cartel-backed thugs were gunning for her. "Meet me at the house. We'll regroup and go from there."

CHAPTER 32

——

HOSPITALS WERE TREACHEROUS PLACES. Hope and despair, living and dying, miracles and agony, lived side by side in these sterile rooms. What's behind door number one? Would door number two yield better results? Taking a deep, cleansing breath, Gabriella ducked past the curtain drawn around Xavier's bed and forced a smile.

Virginia's face was placid. She sat as close to her husband's bed as possible. She kept rearranging his sheets and patting his hand in the spot where no dressings clung and no IVs were connected. Her voice murmured in a continuous singsong of prayer mixed with encouraging words of affection. *"You'll be fine, Dios te ama. You're fine. By the grace of God, you're here. You're fine. I love you,* mi amor. *Sleep. Sleep."*

"How is he?"

Virginia looked up. Her eyes were clear and her smile quick. "Peaceful, finally. He was fighting the tube until they sedated him. I talked to Naomi. She'll go to the house to pick up another Bible for him before she comes up here. It'll soothe him when he does wake up. I imagine the one he had burned. He's had that Bible since before we were married." Virginia sighed, but her tone held no sadness. "He has at least twenty others, every translation, various languages, and it can be replaced a hundred times over. He can't."

"And you?" Gabriella offered the coffee. "How are you managing?"

"God is good. In everything He works for our good. My Xavier will be around to compliment my cooking and remind me to turn off the stove for many years to come." She stood. "He'll sleep for a while. I need to stretch my legs."

Gabriella joined her, glad for the silence after the horrific noise of fire trucks, ambulances, ER drama, and the terrifying realization that Xavier had been in the crosshairs of criminals who would stop at nothing to protect their lucrative gun-smuggling operation.

"You and Eli know who did this." For the first time Virginia's voice had an edge. "This is about your brother."

Declarative sentences. Not questions.

"We're working on it."

"Eli will bring these people to justice."

Again, her voice held no doubt.

He would. Whether it would be in time to save Jake remained agonizingly unknown. They had to figure this out. Now. Before any more innocent people were hurt or killed. "He's working on it right now."

Virginia stopped at the windows at the end of the hallway. They overlooked the parking lot that surrounded the building in a never-ending circle. In the distance a small, obviously man-made pond sparkled in the late-afternoon sun under U.S. and Mexican flags flapping in the wind.

"He needs you."

Virginia's expression told Gabriella the woman wasn't talking about the investigation. "Eli is a one-man band. He's never needed anyone."

"There's something I want to tell you." Virginia set the coffee cup on the ledge. She seemed to contemplate the view with its blue sky and merciless sun. "I've wanted to tell you for a long time. I've never shared this with anyone, least of all Elijah."

The use of Eli's full name spoke of the importance of this admission.

"If you haven't told Eli, are you sure you want to tell me?"

"When you've heard my story, you'll understand why I'm telling you first." She motioned toward a bench that would afford them a view of that sky with a lone cumulus cloud floating in the distance.

"I'd rather you allow me to tell Elijah when Xavier is well enough to give his approval."

It didn't matter what the story was. It belonged to Virginia and, apparently, Xavier. Gabriella joined Virginia on the bench. "Of course."

"When I was fifty years old, I still worked at the church as the secretary, receptionist, and jill-of-all-trades." She plucked at mud and bits of weeds that marred the knees of her tan capris. "I spent almost as much time there as Xavier did. With the ladies' potlucks and the craft group and working on the bulletin and the newsletter. I filled up my days, yet I was restless. The kids were in school. They had their own activities. I joined a Thursday night Bible study, mostly to fill time when Xavier was working. He was always working, but how can a wife complain when her husband is working for the Lord?"

Her voice faltered over the last few words. They both had worked for the Lord. Far more than Gabriella had done. In recent years, she'd let teaching fourth-grade Sunday school and helping with the food pantry fall by the wayside, replaced by excuses and the restaurant. "A good and faithful servant."

Virginia snorted and shook her head. "If only it were so. A member of our church, a lay leader, taught the study of Acts. It was in the spring, after my birthday."

Somehow those words had importance to her. Thirty had been a big birthday for Gabriella. At that time she'd been embarking on a new relationship and opening a restaurant. Big plans. Fifty was another benchmark birthday that lacked luster now as the future seemed to hold no promise of either.

"He was a good teacher. Passionate. He had a deep voice that mesmerized when he read the Scripture. He brought the stories alive." Virginia bowed her head. "I found myself staying after. I told myself it was to tidy the room and make sure the door was locked, but it was to talk to him."

"He was tall and dark haired with gorgeous dark eyes and a

kindness about him that touched me. No rough edges. No critical eye. No tedious discussion of minute detail."

Gabriella wiggled. She fixed her gaze on the blue sky. More cumulus clouds had gathered with the earlier one. They covered the sun.

"Xavier taught his own class on Thursday nights. Often they went out for coffee after. Sometimes he met with the AA folks and prayed with them. He never returned home before ten or eleven o'clock—"

"Are you sure you want to tell me this?" Heat burned Gabriella's cheeks. *God, whisk me away from here, to any place but here. She's Eli's mother.* "It sounds very personal."

"Believe me. It's something I would rather not share, but God calls us to witness, to help others on their journeys. I'm praying you'll learn from my mistakes, even as you forgive them."

"Believe me. I would never judge—"

"I had an affair with this man."

"Virginia—"

"It didn't last long. I was overcome with guilt, and so was he. It was as if the fire was quenched the second we realized what we'd done. He left the church immediately. I struggled with whether to tell Xavier. I prayed and I prayed. Then I got my answer." Her voice broke.

The silence in the pause strummed in Gabriella's ears. Virginia's pain kept time with her shame. "Virginia, please."

"I was pregnant. Fifty years old and pregnant. I knew it was possible, but it seemed so improbable. A change-of-life baby."

"Eli."

"Yes. Xavier isn't Eli's father."

Sunny Mendez had said Eli looked nothing like Xavier. But that was often the case. A throwback to another generation. Maybe he looked like Virginia's father. Or her brothers. It hadn't meant anything. But now it did. "What did you do?"

"The only thing I could. I went to Xavier and confessed I'd broken my vows. I begged forgiveness. He cried with me. He ministered to me like the pastor he is. He never once threw my sin in my face. He reminded me that every child is a gift from God, no matter the timing or the genesis.

"He is a good man." Virginia's aim was unerring, true, and the quiver of the arrow as it passed through skin directly into Gabriella's heart hurt her ears. She'd done nothing but throw Eli's conduct in his face. She'd allowed it to come between her and the man she claimed to love. "Eli could never understand why Xavier set the standards so high for him. But it was because he does the same for himself.

"Eli is younger than his brothers and sister. He doesn't remember that Xavier was just as demanding and strict with them. He was the last one at the table as he grew up, so it felt directed at him. It was. Xavier loves him. Eli is his son in every way that counts. He would never visit the sin of the mother on her child."

"He's an incredible man. A great husband and father."

"He would tell you himself he only does what God expects him to do. Jesus died for our sins. God's grace and mercy are never ending." Virginia clasped Gabriella's hand in hers. It was warm, and her skin like soft crepe paper. "Let he who is without sin cast the first stone. I know what you think Elijah did. He says no, but regardless, you risk losing so much by not forgiving him. Your soul is filled with bitterness. You are made less by your unforgiveness. In God's eyes, you fall short. Elijah loves you. You love him. Life is like a spring breeze. It rustles the leaves in the trees. Then it's still. It's gone."

"I don't know why it's so hard for me to forgive him."

"Because your mother cheated on your father and you still haven't forgiven her."

An observation so sharp it drew blood. No amount of time softened the pain every time the memories broke through Gabriella's emotional blockade. How could her mom do that to a man as kind, smart, funny, and handsome as her dad? The question she'd hurled at her mom the day it all came out. She shoved the memories back in their box. "Eli told you?"

"It's his theory."

Gabriella couldn't contain a bitter laugh. "He would try to make this about me."

"No, he wants to understand. He's never tried this hard with another woman, but he believes you are worth it." Virginia's hand tightened on Gabriella's. "And I know he is worth it."

"Why are you telling me this?"

"I wonder if I would have been as forgiving if the situation had been reversed." Virginia shook her head. "Would I have been as forgiving as Xavier? Or would I be like you?"

"So self-righteous, you mean?"

"Elijah has flaws, but he is not a liar. If he won't tell you what happened, then find out." The intensity in her voice grew. She withdrew her hand and shook her finger at Gabriella, like a mother chastising her child. "You were once a lawyer. Gather evidence. Make your case. Why haven't you investigated? Are you afraid of the truth?"

The swish of silk and scent of Liliana's Christian Dior assailed Gabriella—a memory she would rather forget. Circumstantial evidence. She stood. "So Naomi is on her way?"

"And Martha is driving down from Dallas. You've never met Eli's sister. She reminds me of you. Headstrong. Independent."

"Like Eli, you mean."

"I must get back to Xavier." Bones creaking, she hoisted herself from the bench and held out her arms.

Gabriella walked into the loving, forgiving hug. "Thank you," she whispered.

"Go find your brother."

Gabriella started walking, then broke into a trot. By the time she reached the parking lot, she was running.

CHAPTER 33

NOTHING LIKE THE PUBLIC execution of a young law enforcement officer to lure media to a backwater border town. Add a church firebombing, and Laredo became the place to be. Deacon squeezed into a spot next to the Associated Press border correspondent, a stringer for CBS Southwest, and a Univision Spanish language TV reporter.

The stench of sodden, burnt wood and rubber hung in the air. The church's belfry tower still stood as a sentry amid the blackened ruins of the sanctuary. The half-burnt pages of hymnals and pew Bibles fluttered on the ground. The queasiness that had dogged him in the car as he drove to the scene returned.

"This stinks. Literally and figuratively." Chris squeezed in next to him. "Is Eli's dad okay?"

"At the hospital. Eli said he'd get back to me."

"He's still talking to a jailbird?"

"Very funny." Word traveled fast. "How did you find out about it?"

"I have my sources in the jail." Chris shrugged. "And while you were hobnobbing with the Saturday night drunks, I was mining my sources. I have news on our earlier discussion."

Deacon had filled them in via text on the developments regarding Luke Donovan and Detective Rincon. "Not here." Deacon caught the inquisitive gaze of the AP reporter. "Later."

They were caught in the children's game ring-around-the-rosy. Going round and round and falling down, never getting anywhere. He'd never met Jake Benoit. At this rate he never would. And they couldn't go back to their lives in San Antonio until they solved the case. Gabriella's life was in danger. And with her, Natalie and the children.

"Right after this—"

Laredo Fire Chief Enrique "Ricky" Ramirez strode toward the crime scene tape. An entourage of officers in uniform, the Laredo police chief, and several men in black suits followed. Including Chuck Jensen. Eli was nowhere in sight. A gold mine of sources. Photographers, who'd been shooting the scene for b-roll, jostled each other to get cameras back to their tripods.

"Here we go," Chris muttered. "Life in the fast lane."

The murmuring died away. Cameras clicked. Flashes flared. Reporters tugged at digital recorders.

"I'll go first. Then you'll hear from my law enforcement colleagues." Ramirez raised his voice to be heard over cars passing on the street, a train whistle in the distance, and a flock of grackles that had taken up residence in live oak trees nearby, like an audience ready to heckle the headliners. "The fire spread quickly. The building is a total loss. Estimated value is two hundred thousand dollars. Eight people were injured. Their names are not being released due to HIPPA. However, we can tell you that five were male and two were female. The oldest was eighty-six and the youngest sixteen. Three remain hospitalized, one in serious condition. Five were treated and released. By the grace of God. If this had happened during the service this morning . . ." His Adam's apple bobbed. He paused and cleared his throat. "The arson team is on the scene. The investigation is just beginning. They have a lot of work to do. Everything is preliminary at this point."

"But you're sure it's arson?" A petite TV reporter from the ABC affiliate beat the rest of them to the question. "What sparked the flame?"

"There's no doubt it was arson. We have a witness who saw the perpetrator jump from a vehicle, open the front door, and hurl two Molotov cocktails into the church's foyer."

"Do you think this is related to the death of Special Agent Larry Teeter yesterday?" Deacon didn't bother to raise his hand. This wasn't a typical news conference. They were standing very close to sacred ground. "Who is the witness? Can he describe the bomber? What about the car?"

"Witness statements are still being taken. It is way too early to speculate about motives or connections. The witness says the perpetrator wore a black scarf over his mouth and nose. The car was a dark-blue or black Beamer." Ramirez wiped sweat from his forehead with his sleeve. His face turned ruddy in the glaring sun. "This could involve any number of scenarios. We'll look at the possibility of a hate crime, a domestic terrorist attack, or it could be domestic violence. We saw that at the Sutherland Springs church shooting. As I said, it's far too early to say. We have the ATF, ICE, Homeland Security Investigations, and the FBI working with us and their tremendous resources available to us. The good folks of Laredo can rest assured that we'll get to the bottom of this. Attacks on our places of worship won't be tolerated."

Ramirez glanced around and nodded at Jensen. "The ATF special agent in charge will address questions about yesterday's incident as was the original topic of the scheduled news conference."

Blotting his grim face with a tissue, Jensen stepped forward. The collar of his white shirt was dark with sweat. He cleared his throat. He tugged at his tie. "First, we want to assure the public that we will apprehend the monsters who cut down our colleague and friend Special Agent Larry Teeter yesterday. Because this homicide occurred in their jurisdiction, Laredo police department is working jointly with us on this homicide investigation."

"ICE, the FBI, and Homeland Security are also involved due to the nature of the incident and the timing of this event here today. As Chief Ramirez stated, we can't rule out any scenario involving domestic terrorism or a hate crime."

"Do you really believe that?" Chris raised his hand. "Doesn't it seem more likely that this was a warning from the gun smugglers you're investigating in Operation Talon?"

Jensen's face darkened. "We're not leaping to any conclusions. Methodical and thorough investigation is necessary to determine if there are any connections. However, as Chief Ramirez stated, we do have a description of the vehicle—a dark-blue or black BMW—from both incidents. In both cases the actors had black bandanas over their faces."

"So they are both related to your investigation?"

"That's one avenue that's being explored. The question becomes how are they connected? What does this small church have to do with our investigation?"

The running commentary in Deacon's head didn't help. Neither did the constant roller coaster of emotions that ran roughshod through his brain every time Natalie's face appeared in his mind's eye. Which was every five seconds. *Come on, come on, focus. Do the job.*

He'd never had this problem before. He wasn't sure he liked it. Get the story, make the deadline, sleep, get up, and do it again. Keep the only job he'd ever wanted. Now his priorities were all cattywampus.

"Is it possible the connection is Jake Benoit? Is there an update on your efforts to find your missing agent?"

"Again, we don't intend to speculate, and we'd ask you to restrain yourselves as well." Jensen's tone was cool and clipped. "We'd like to spare the families as much pain as possible in this difficult situation."

"Has any progress been made in finding Benoit?" Deacon kept up the pressure. *Give us something new, something concrete.* "Do you think he's still alive?"

"Special Agent Benoit has family awaiting his safe return. Again, I'd ask you not to speculate in your stories." Jensen's jaw bulged. He gritted his teeth. "Benoit is under my command. I assure you we're doing everything we can and we will continue to do so."

"With the murder of Special Agent Teeter and the firebombing of the church, aren't you stretched thin?"

Jensen ignored the question and plowed forward. "We're asking you to broadcast our tip line number periodically for the foreseeable future. We've interviewed more than fifty witnesses to the execution of Special Agent Teeter. We have sketches of the driver of the car—granted we don't really have a face, but it's a start—and a variety of descriptions of the car. Those are being distributed to you as I speak."

However, the link between the cases remained a mystery. What did Teeter's death have to do with the desecration of a small, non-denominational church that had been a part of the fabric of its neighborhood for more than fifty years? Eli might know. Whether he would share remained to be seen.

"Are you any closer to determining who the facilitator is behind the gun-smuggling ring pouring thousands of guns into Mexico? Reports show the biggest percentage of guns recovered in Mexico come across the Texas–Mexico border. Are you any closer to plugging those holes?"

His gaze on his notes, the ATF agent paused. His steely glance came up and zeroed in on Deacon. "Again, I caution the media against speculating publicly. We urge you not to inflame the situation and perhaps damage our chances of finding the people who murdered our agent in cold blood in a very public manner. As well as our missing agent."

Not a confirmation. Not an answer at all.

"A manner often used by the cartels to send a message," Chris followed up.

Jensen backed away. The other feebs took turns talking about vague, nonspecifics regarding firebombings of churches, hate crimes, and domestic terrorism.

When was no answer an answer?

CHAPTER 34

———

A STRONG WORK ETHIC could be in short supply in a town where violence and a small-town culture intermingled like clothes in a washing machine. Not so when it came to the church's gardener-slash-custodian. Eli found his old playmate Johnnie Lufkin behind the church, scythe in hand, chopping at weeds around trees in a long yard that ran into a winding alley. Not wanting to startle the man, he called out.

Scythe at the ready, Johnnie whirled.

"It's me, Eli."

Johnnie stared for a long moment, perhaps recalling as Eli did, long ago memories of the sweltering, endless summer afternoons of his childhood. By fourth or fifth grade, Eli's life as a star athlete in training took over. Their paths seldom crossed after that. "What you want?"

"To know what you saw."

Johnnie lowered the scythe and went back to work. "I didn't see nothing."

"That's not what you told the officers."

"You talked to them, you know what I saw and didn't see. No faces. Just a gangbanger out to mess up a church." Muttering curses, he swung the implement harder. It whistled as it slashed through the dandelions and crabgrass. "They hurt a good man."

"I know you care about my dad, so I want to ask you to help me find who did this and make them pay."

This, Johnnie understood. He stopped working. "You find them; I kill them. How about that?" He grinned. "We make a team."

"It sounds like a good plan, only I'm not allowed to do that." Still, it was worthy of consideration. "We throw them in jail to rot for the rest of their lives. That's a fate worse than death."

Johnnie frowned, but he nodded. "The bomber was a big guy. Tall. Lots of muscle. He ran fast, like a young guy. I didn't see his face, but the guy in the car—I could tell he was old."

"How?"

"His hands on the wheel were wrinkled. He has old man hands."

An old man. Not a lot of help, but Johnnie was trying.

"Did either of them say anything? Was there anything about their voices that caught your attention?"

On TV they always had an identifying tattoo or scar. Something that allowed an immediate and undeniable ID. In real life that didn't happen so much.

"The guy didn't say anything." Johnnie went back to work. "He just laughed."

"Did he see you?"

"No. I ducked behind the bushes." His gaze dropped to his dirty work boots. "After he drove off, I ran to the doors. I went inside, but the fire and the smoke were bad. I couldn't see anything. I called for Mr. Xavier, but he didn't answer. I called 911 and I came for Miss Virginia."

"You did good. Very good." Eli pulled a business card from his wallet and handed it to Johnnie. "I want you to go home. Get cleaned up. Hug your wife and your kids. Stay there until someone calls you to come back. If you remember anything else, call me. You need anything, call me. My cell phone is on the back."

He handled the card as if it were fragile. His head bobbed. "I can do that. I'll think hard. I'll call you if I hear anything or see anything."

"I don't want you messing in this. Do you understand?"

Johnnie jerked his head toward the sodden burnt remnants of a building where they had played together as children. "This is my job, my whole life. What do I do now?"

"You do this, Johnnie." Eli swallowed against the stupid knot that lodged in his throat. "We'll need to haul off the debris first. You know my pops. He'll want to rebuild as soon as possible. He'll expect you to be ready to go to work."

Eli needed to get back to see if the news conference had ended. He turned to go, then stopped. "Thanks for calling for help. Thanks for coming for me. You got help here quick. That's really important."

"God bless you."

"Thanks. I hope so."

Thinking about Johnnie's words, Eli stewed as he walked around the church. The guy laughed. Step one, find the guy. Step two, stuff his tongue into his lungs. Step three, lock him up for a hundred years.

The news conference had ended. Jensen looked green around the gills as he strode away from the gaggle of reporters restrained only by the crime scene tape strung across the church parking lot. Mud and wet grass squelching under his Nikes, Eli followed. Better to hit Jensen now while his defenses were low.

"Hey. Nice job." Eli slid in next to the ATF agent in charge and matched his stride. He seemed headed for a cluster of Laredo PD officers. "What aren't you telling them?"

"Thanks. It's the same car, same driver. Descriptions match." Jensen tugged a pack of cigarettes from his pocket and held it out to Eli. Not wanting to seem unappreciative, Eli accepted it as well as the offer of a BIC. He lit his cigarette and tried to return the lighter. A steady stream of smoke spiraling from his nostrils, Jensen shook his head. "Keep it. I've got dozens. This isn't a hate crime or an act of terrorism. We know it. They know it."

Eli tucked the lighter in his polo pocket. Now all he needed was the pack of cigarettes to go with it. "What about the Colby Langston autopsy?"

"Nothing except the bullets came from Jake's gun."

"And Garza?"

"Beretta. He bled to death. Signs of struggle. They won't have toxicology reports for a few weeks, but the ME suggested he may have been using prescription drugs."

To take the edge off his stress? A perk from his employer?

"What about the security camera footage?" Eli inhaled. The scent of tobacco pinged every pleasure center in his brain. His shoulders relaxed. If being with Gabby meant giving up alcohol, nicotine was his drug of choice. "Anything there?"

One of the other Feds yelled Jensen's name. He took another drag, dropped the cigarette, and grounded it into the mud under his foot. "They're still culling through it, but it does show Garza walking into the plaza after he leaves the store. He stands around by the gazebo for a few minutes like he's waiting for someone. Then he takes off in the Mitsubishi. Gotta go."

No way he would choose a location close to the gun store and out in the open to meet with Jake. So what was he doing there? No way Figueroa would share any knowledge he had of the purpose of that visit.

Eli took one last drag from the cigarette. Who was he to judge? Thankful Gabby couldn't see him at this moment, he stubbed it out on the sidewalk and headed the two blocks back to the house.

Getting away from the destruction eased the tension in Eli's shoulders. The sun beat down on him. Sweat dripped from his hair and trickled down his neck. It didn't matter. Pops lived. Gabriella lived. The church could be rebuilt, but it would never be that place where he picked up stray bulletins from the pews or swept the narthex under his father's critical gaze.

He would find the psychos who did this and obliterate them from the earth.

Sorry, God.

In front of his parents' house, he tapped the remote and slid into the Charger. The leather burned his fingers. He hit the button, rolled down the windows, and turned the AC on high. "Respect" floated from his phone. Rubbing his burning eyes with his free hand, he answered. "Is he all right?"

"He's still sleeping. Your mom is with him."

"You're supposed to be with them. Where are you?"

"She told me I could leave. Your tía Naomi is on the way and so is your sister. I'm at Piper's. You said you'd meet me here."

"You need to be on guard. They won't." Gabby would be safe at the hospital. She needed to be safe. The drive-by, Teeter's death, the firebombing. She had to be safe. "I want you there."

"What did you find out?"

Eli related his conversation with the arson investigator and Jensen.

"I'll take a walk around the plaza."

"I'll do that."

"You need to see your father and check in with your mom."

"She'll understand. You can't be out there on your own."

"It's broad daylight. I won't go near the sporting goods store. I'm in your mom's car. No one will even know."

The drive-by had occurred in broad daylight. "Like that makes any difference."

"I'm going."

Definitive statement. End of discussion. She loved to remind him that he wasn't the boss of her. "In and out. If anything looks the least bit wonky, don't get out of the car."

"I've got this."

"Call me as soon as you're done. We'll meet back at the house after I stop at the hospital."

She disconnected.

The desire for another cigarette inundated him. He tugged the lighter from his pocket and played with it for a second. A quick trip to a convenience store and then he would head to the hospital.

A tap struck the passenger-side window. Startled, he reached for his weapon. Deacon's head popped into view. "Open up."

"Are you following me? That's a good way to get shot."

He unlocked the doors and Deacon slid in. He didn't look happy. "That was a waste of time. They're placating the media with little dribbles of information, most of which we already have."

"I talked to Jensen. He says if Rincon isn't in on it, another cop is. He's not ready to concede that Donovan isn't a player."

"With all their resources—"

The ringtone for unknown callers filled the car. The number didn't ring a bell. "Cavazos."

"We need to talk." The urgent whisper made Sunny's voice almost unrecognizable. "I have some information I think might help find Jake."

"If you know something, you need to tell me right now."

Deacon edged closer. His eyebrows rose and fell. *Who is it?* he mouthed.

Eli held up his index finger.

"Not over the phone. You told me I could call you if I thought of anything."

Deacon leaned in as if trying to hear both ends of the conversation. Eli swiveled toward his door. "Why are you whispering?"

"My dad doesn't want me to get involved."

"Where are you?"

"Not here. I'll meet you in a safe place."

"Where?"

She reeled off an address. "It's southwest of town, in the county. I told my dad I was going to get a pedicure, so I don't have a lot of time. Don't keep me waiting."

"Why call me? Why not LPD?"

"You said to call you. I did. I'm trusting you to keep your mouth shut. Nobody can know. They'll kill me if they find out I called you."

"Who'll kill you?"

She disconnected.

Eli swallowed a string of expletives. He dropped the phone on the seat and pounded on the wheel. It could be something or nothing. Sunny was a big, fat question mark. She could be a little girl who wanted attention, or she might actually have something useful. The only way to find out was to be at her beck and call.

"What is it?" Deacon's exasperated tone penetrated Eli's irritation. "Stop hyperventilating and tell me what she said."

"Can you get on the internet here?"

"I can if I make my phone a hot spot."

"Do it." Eli shared the gist of the conversation and repeated the directions she'd spewed at him. "See what you can find out about this address."

Deacon applied himself to his laptop. The car filled with the silence broken only by the hum of the engine and the AC.

"The property is owned by a company called STAR Trucking of South Texas."

"Does that help us?"

"The paper trail is crazy. It's ridiculous. From there it goes to Texas Trails Company, which has a headquarters in Houston. None of the names of the principals ring a bell. This will take some time to unravel."

"Get out."

"What?"

"Get out of the car."

His phone rang again. Gabs. Eli ignored it.

"No way, Jose. This is the biggest story of my career." Deacon hugged the laptop to his chest. "You're a big guy, but not big enough to haul my carcass out of this car, and that's what it will take. You're not getting rid of me."

"It may be absolutely nothing. This girl has too much time on her hands, and she's itching to get out from under her dad's thumb. Get out."

"Make me."

"Are you still in high school?"

"I'm not getting out of this car."

"Respect" interrupted a conversation spiraling out of control. Gabs again.

"Aren't you going to answer that?"

Eli shook his head. "I'm definitely not taking her."

"She'll kill you." The portrait of a rebellious teenager, Deacon rolled his eyes. Next he would stick out his tongue. "Besides you need me to keep working the real estate records. I'll deep dive while you drive. I can call some folks, redeem some favors."

"Fine."

"Whatever."

Eli pulled away from the curb and headed for Saunders Road. Despite the shimmering August heat, hell had frozen over. The fact that he was in a car with a reporter whom he'd despised with great passion for the better part of three years provided all the evidence he needed that the world had turned inside out.

Deacon spent the next ten minutes on the phone, apparently talking to Chris Matthews. Like a good boy, he didn't tell Chris what he was up to, just asked him to do some record checking at his end. From the sound of Deacon's voice, Chris wasn't too happy about not being given all the details. Twenty minutes later, they pulled through the gate of an industrial park that looked as decrepit as the one owned by Luke Donovan.

Deacon glanced up from his computer screen. "Do you see her?"

"Shut up and keep working."

"It looks like Texas Trails Company is a subsidiary of a holding company called Purple Heart Express."

"That's a strange name."

"Yeah, but it doesn't stop there." Deacon's rapid-fire keystrokes were impressive in that he only used two fingers and his thumbs. "This is ridiculous. I need more time."

"We don't have more time. We're here, but I don't see Sunny." He let his gaze rake the dozen or more long, rectangular, ramshackle warehouses. They were mostly tin structures with flat roofs and wooden loading docks. The place seemed deserted. "Come on, Sunny. Where are you?"

Deacon looked up. "Maybe she decided to go with the pedicure instead."

Maybe. What did she know about Jake's disappearance? Who was threatening her?

"I'll take a look around." Eli put the Charger in Park and turned off the engine. "You stay here."

"No way, dude." Deacon's phone rang. He snagged it and thrust it to his ear. "I gotta call you back."

Eli shoved open his door and got out. Deacon did the same. They reached the front of the car at the same time.

The jolt that knocked him from his feet came out of nowhere.

CHAPTER 35

———

THE TINY POCKET OF trees and grass in the middle of a city founded by Don Tómas Sanchez in 1755 had the grandiose title of San Agustín Plaza. The minutes stretched as Gabriella sat in Virginia's ancient Ford Explorer. Nothing seemed out of the ordinary. Just people enjoying a stroll through the outlet stores a few blocks away stopped in the plaza to buy raspas, roasted corn, or a cold soda.

She adjusted the sun visor, then fiddled with her sunglasses. Now or never. With one last glance toward the sporting goods store, closed this Sunday afternoon, she slipped from the SUV and trotted across the uneven red brick street. Like most of the plazas, this one had four sidewalks situated like spokes from the four corners of the park. A statue of Mexican General Ignacio Zaragoza stood guard on one spoke, the plaque proclaiming they would preserve freedom or die trying, while a statue of San Agustín welcomed all who entered from the other side. In the center stood a small gazebo of concrete blocks and wrought-iron railings surrounded by a circle of well-manicured bushes.

A young couple snuggled on one bench while a *turista* with a backpack used his camera to snap photos of his wife on the gazebo. Letting her fingers trail across the bushes, Gabriella ignored the signs that read *NO PISAR EL CESPED* and walked across the grass to a filthy water fountain on the right. Not in a million years would she drink from its spigot. Still, she bent over and let the water run. Nothing on the ground behind it.

The turistas vacated the gazebo. Phone in hand as if she intended to take a selfie, Gabriella bounded up the steps with all the enthusiasm of a visitor. The floor appeared newly swept. The Laredo Parks and Recreation folks were far too efficient.

"*¿Qué haces?*"

Startled, she turned. A bearded man in dirty overalls and holey sneakers stared up at her. He was missing his two front teeth. She forced a smile. *"No hablo español muy bien."*

"Where are you going? Lost?" He held out one dirty hand. "I be guide?"

"I don't need a guide." She contemplated his attempt at an ingratiating smile. "Do you live around here, señor?"

"Juan Garcia. I live around." He grasped the railing and hauled himself up the remaining steps. His gait wobbled. "I show you where shops are?"

The Spanish equivalent of John Smith.

The rank odor of unwashed body, tobacco, and urine wafted over Gabriella. Given temperatures hovered near one hundred and the man obviously didn't have access to facilities, she couldn't blame him. "Do you spend a lot of time here at the plaza?"

He nodded.

"Were you here Thursday afternoon?"

"I here every day."

And likely every night. "A friend of mine was here." She described Beto Garza. "He lost his phone. He asked me to try to find it for him."

A satisfied look on his face, Juan nodded. "I seen him. He see me."

"Did you see his phone?"

Juan shrugged and held out his hand.

Gabriella dug a ten-dollar bill from her bag and held it out.

Juan reached for it. She snatched it back. "What did you see?"

"He give me twenty to leave it. Said someone would come for it and if it not here, someone would die."

Gabriella pawed through her wallet for another ten. "Where?"

Juan stuffed the bills into his pocket and pointed a greasy finger toward the ground. He grinned.

"Show me."

Stifling the urge to pinch her nose, she followed him down the steps. He took a sharp right and pointed once again. The dirt at the base of the gazebo had been disturbed. She glanced around.

"I look out."

Trusting a homeless man with her safety called into question her sanity, but what choice was there at this moment? She dropped to her knees and dug around. Sweat rolled down her forehead and dripped into her eyes. Her heart pounded as if she'd just run the fifty-yard dash. If someone caught her doing this, Eli would never let her forget it.

Her fingers touched plastic. She groped in the dirt. A Ziploc baggie. A smartphone.

She scooped it up, dragged her Reebok across the dirt, and turned.

Her homeless man had disappeared. Chuy Figueroa and a man she hadn't seen before sauntered across the street from the pawn shop. Closed didn't mean they weren't in the store.

She tucked the phone in her back pocket and hopped over the four steps in one jump.

Chuy's pace picked up. So did his companion's.

Gabriella whirled and picked the sidewalk spoke that would take her to Virginia's SUV. An elderly woman hobbled along using a rollator. She had a sack of groceries sitting on the pad in the middle. A chubby lady in an embroidered Mexican dress pushed a stroller and held hands with a toddler.

This was not the place for a shoot-out. Not that Gabriella had a weapon.

She dodged the rollator woman and picked up her pace. Unable to help herself, she glanced back. They were gaining on her.

She broke into a trot, passed stroller family, and dashed to the SUV.

Thank You, God, for remote entry. Two seconds later, she was in the car, key in the ignition.

Start, start, start.

Whining engine. She twisted the wheel and peeled out of the parking space.

Chuy, who had stopped at the end of the spoke, waved and blew her a kiss. *See you soon* was written all over the gangbanger's face.

CHAPTER 36

———

ELI LURCHED. FIERY PAIN ripped through his muscles from head to foot.

Tick-tick-tick resounded in his ears. A vaguely familiar sound. His mind searched while his body jerked and flailed. Police academy. Taser. Fifty thousand volts.

A heavyweight boxer punched him in the back over and over again. His arms and legs jerked and then stiffened. Control of his body belonged to someone else.

He resented that fact deeply.

That somebody would pay.

He fell flat on his face. He opened his mouth to scream obscenities and inhaled a mouthful of dirt. The smell of earth stuck in his nose. His pulse pounded.

His spine crunched. Air whooshed from his lungs. Yellow-and-purple lights danced in the periphery of his vision.

The attacker jerked Eli's arms back so hard they left their sockets. His mind screamed at his body. *Move. Move.* Nothing. Something hard tightened around his wrists. Too tight. More pain, but tolerable. Two sharp pricks. The removal of the metal prongs.

The guy—considering the weight, surely it was a guy—grabbed his legs. The same deal. Legs tied together. Zip ties?

Think. Think. He raised his head and peered behind him. More shiny black boots. Camouflage pants tucked in neatly.

His gun.

His captor ripped it from the holster. The *click-click* meant he checked to see if the magazine was loaded. Of course it was. Pressure on the back of his head could only be the barrel.

Eli closed his eyes. *Sweet Gabriella, te amo. Forgive me. Te amo.*

"You'll be fine, *mi amigo.*"

A melodic voice, deep, rich. He opened his eyes and peered up. Army boots polished to a high sheen. The stock of a semiautomatic of some kind. A big hand touched his shoulder. "Don't fight it. Struggling will only make it worse."

"Where's Sunny Mendez? What did you do to her?"

At least his voice worked again.

"Don't worry. I don't hurt young girls." Chuckling, Camouflage Man leaned past him and tugged at his pocket. His phone appeared in the periphery of Eli's vision, then disappeared again. A jingling sound followed. His keys went the way of his phone. "Especially that one."

What did that mean?

"Cooperate, m'ijo, and you'll be fine. I promise."

"I'm not your son—"

"It'll be fine."

A black hood appeared in front of him.

"No, don't—"

Darkness prevailed.

Feeling returned to his arms and legs. More pain. Pure anger followed. He struggled. The elephant on his back didn't move. His lungs couldn't suck in air. No air, no oxygen. He would suffocate. *Gabs, I'm sorry. Mamá, Pops, I'm sorry.*

The weight released. He gasped.

His arms jerked back. He stifled a scream of pain. His body lifted.

His feet were on the ground. Two people, one on each side, dragged him.

"Deacon? Deacon!"

The hood muffled the words. One of his captors jabbed him in the back. "Save your breath. He's fine."

Eli's feet lifted from the ground again. He was airborne. This time, he slammed facedown on hard metal.

A second later, something thudded next to him. A warm body brushed against him. A shoulder or a hip. "Deacon?"

A muffled moan.

Deacon. Still alive. At least they were in this together. That thought provided additional evidence that hell had frozen over. Deacon was a pain in the behind, but he had a decent mind. He wouldn't keel over at the first sign of trouble. He'd proven that.

Together, they would figure this out. They would heap a world of hurt on these guys.

A slamming sound. Doors closing.

An engine growled. Shifting gears grumbled. An SUV or a van. He sucked in air through his nose. The only smell was his own sour breath and the mustiness of the hood itself. *Think, think.*

Eli shimmied onto his side and began to work the zip ties that held his hands clasped behind his back. They didn't budge.

The vehicle bounced. His head banged on the floor. He swore. *Sorry, God. I could use some help here.*

Be still and know that I am God.

Really, God? I never doubted that.

He relaxed against the warm metal and closed his eyes. Sweat rolled down his face and wet his upper lip. Heat shimmered around him. Locked inside a metal box with no AC. His throat ached for water.

The truck stopped.

Short ride.

Breathe in and out, in and out. If their captors intended to kill them, why not do it at the industrial park? "Deacon. Come on, Deacon. I need to know you're okay."

The words reverberated inside the hood. How much could Deacon hear through the one he likely wore?

"This is all your fault." Muffled but intelligible.

"Why is that? You insisted on coming."

"What did they hit us with?"

"Tasers."

"Remind me to stay home next time."

There wouldn't be a next time. "You got it."

"Can you see anything?"

"Nothing."

Squeaking. A rush of air cooled his damp body. Doors opened.

Someone grabbed his ankles. His head banged on the floor as they pulled his body out. Feet swinging in the air. Then on the ground.

"Up and at 'em, mi amigo."

Camouflage Man's voice.

"Easy, guys, easy." Wry amusement laced Deacon's words. The guy had guts. "Treat me well and you'll receive an excellent tip. I promise."

"There's a wiseacre in every crowd."

An *oomph* by a gasp suggested Deacon might now regret his little joke.

More dragging by the arms. This routine would get old fast. "What do you want?"

"Quiet."

Thudding footsteps. Another door. More half-drag, half-walk. Something sharp dug into his wrists. Suddenly, they were free. His shoulders relaxed. Blood rushed to his arms. He breathed. *Snip. Snap.* His legs were free. Too bad they felt like wet noodles.

They moved again. Creaking under his feet gave the impression of a metal platform of some kind. It moved. His knees buckled. His captor swore and grabbed him.

The sensation of moving down. Like an elevator only open. Humid air wafted across his face. Gears grinding. A squeak. Another. An abrupt stop.

More walking-slash-dragging. Voices called to each other in

Spanish. Orders flew in curt tones. They were talking about a ship-ment. *Box them up. Movement tonight. Everything has to be ready.*

Eli memorized the words. If he could get loose, get to a phone, they could ping his location and nab these guys in the act of shipping guns. Where and to whom remained beyond his reach. He struggled. The cool metal of a barrel touched his neck. "You've been so good, amigo, don't screw it up now."

A kindly voice. Grandfatherly. Deacon and Natalie had described their home invader as almost grandfatherly. Until he sprayed the bookshelves with an AK-47.

He held his breath. The barrel receded.

Eli breathed.

An almost gentle push set him flying forward. His arms and legs flailed. Once again, he landed flat on his face, the wind knocked from his lungs. This time the surface felt softer. More like dirt. Even so, his nose hurt. This was getting old.

Thump. Thud. Deacon's words were a little less colorful than Eli's. Didn't the guy ever cuss?

The creak of a metal door clanging shut.

Gasping for air, Eli scrambled to his knees and tugged at the hood. His fingers were all thumbs. "Come on." The hood gave. He shoved it over his head.

Still dark. Completely and utterly dark.

His nose burned. He wiped at it. Warm liquid. Blood. "Deacon, are you there?"

"I'm here."

"Did they get your phone?"

"Yep. And my laptop. My editor will be so PO'd that I didn't file a story today."

"I'll write you a note. Can you get the hood off and stand up?"

"I am. I am." Shuffling and growling. "What the heck. I can't see a thing. Where are we?"

"Good question." Eli settled back on his knees. Maybe his eyes would adjust. "Give it a minute."

The seconds ticked by. He closed his eyes and opened them. Opaque darkness.

A moan broke the silence.

"Are you all right?"

"Yeah. You?"

"I'll live."

"Then who's moaning?"

Eli strained to see in the darkness. Nothing. The sound emanated from the far reaches of the darkness. "Hey, who is it? Is someone there?"

Another moan.

Eli waved his hands in the air. Nothing. He stretched his arms to their full reach. Nothing but stinking darkness. He edged forward, hands in front of him. His nose didn't need another collision. Nothing.

His fingers touched a firm surface. He ran his fingers over it. Smooth, solid, but soft. Ignoring the pain that radiated through both nostrils, he sniffed. Dirt, mustiness, cool but humid. An enclosed space.

"Whoever it is, are you hurt? Where are you? I'll come to you."

"Water. Water, please." A ragged, breathless whisper.

Another prisoner. How long had he been in this dungeon? "Sorry, dude. I wish I had some. I'm coming to you."

He patted his shirt pockets. Empty. His fingers slid into his jean pockets.

The BIC.

Eli swallowed a hysterical laugh. *See, Gabs, I took up smoking again for a reason.* He wrapped his hand around the lighter and pulled it out. It took two tries to light it. The smell of butane intensified the desire for nicotine. At the same time it steadied him. His miniscule torch in a sea of night remained lit.

Not much to see. Deacon entered his space. "I never thought I'd thank God for a smoker."

"Shut up." Eli held up the lighter higher. "Hey, buddy, talk to me."

"Over here."

Ahead of him to the left. Eli edged toward it.

A figure huddled in the corner, back against the wall, barely discernible in the flickering flame. Eli squatted. The battered, bruised face lifted.

"Jake?"

CHAPTER 37

——

"I'M GONNA HUNT HIM down and then I'm gonna kill him," Gabriella muttered as she cut one-third cup of shortening into the mixture of flour, sugar, baking powder, and salt she'd tossed together in a bowl on Piper's pristine kitchen island. The oven was preheating and the strawberries sliced and glistening with sugar. When in doubt, cook, had always been her motto. "And then I'll kill him again."

"And then I'll kill him again."

Fidencio I—or was it II?—bobbed his head and squawked in agreement.

"Fidencio, hush."

"Fidencio, hush."

"You'll argue with anyone, even a bird, won't you?"

Gabriella swiveled. Natalie maneuvered her chair past the kitchen table and stopped on the other side of the island. Her fair skin was pink from being outside in the sun watching Ava and Cullen do cannonballs into the pool under Piper's supervision. "What are you making?"

"Piper had some strawberries that needed to be used. I decided to whip up some strawberry shortcakes."

"Jake's favorite."

"I figure there will be leftovers." Gabriella's throat closed. She concentrated on gently stirring in three-fourths cup of milk, just enough to blend it. "Eli happens to like them too."

"Have you talked to Vic?"

"Just got off the phone with her. Business as usual. She's worried about us, but she's a trooper. She'll make sure I don't have to worry about the restaurant."

"Eli will call when he calls." Natalie snatched a strawberry and popped it in her mouth. "Yum. And just so you know, that's not appropriate talk for a Christian woman."

"He did it on purpose. He had no intention of coming back." Eli was an overbearing, sexist, macho man. Careful not to take her frustration out on the dough, Gabriella smoothed it into a ball on a floured, cloth-covered board and began to knead it. Baking was the best therapy. "And just so you know, God understands. He knows I'm not some sissy wallflower."

"He shared information. He agreed to you going downtown on your own." Natalie still sounded disbelieving. "That's huge."

"Huge." Fidencio agreed.

"Hush, Fidencio." Natalie and Gabriella shushed the bird in unison.

Natalie's gaze went to the phone on the table. Using a pair of Piper's gardening gloves, Gabriella had removed it from the baggie. So far, she'd been unable to come up with a password to open it. Baking usually cleared her brain, but so far, nothing usable had occurred to her. "Deacon hasn't called either."

"When was the last time you heard from him?"

"Before the news conference."

"Try calling him."

"I did. Twice. It went to voicemail." Gabriella concentrated on rolling the dough into a half-inch thickness. This was ridiculous. Baking while Eli searched for her brother. Her brother, his friend.

She used a floured three-inch cutter on the dough and laid the cakes on an ungreased cookie sheet. The oven beeped. Ready. "In you go." She slid the pan into the oven, set the timer, and washed her hands.

Feeling only slightly calmer, she scooped up her phone and scrolled through her texts until she found one from Chris Matthews with his number. She punched it in and seconds later he picked up.

No, he didn't know where Deacon was. Or Eli. They parted after the news conference, so Chris could head back to the newsroom to file his story. "He wanted to talk to Eli to see what the next move was. Then he would file his story." Chris's voice became muffled. "Sorry, I'm at work. My editor had a question about my story. Then he walked off down the block. I assumed he was going to find Eli at his dad's house. Piper's car was still at the church."

"And that was it? He didn't let you know what was next?"

"He did call me about half an hour later from Eli's car." Chris sounded distracted. "He wanted me to dig up anything I could on a property outside the city limits in southwest Webb County. Another warehouse property. Why? What's going on?"

"Give me the location of the warehouse." Gabriella made writing motions to Natalie, who buzzed over to the table, picked up a flowered grocery-list tablet, and handed it to Gabriella, along with a pencil used down to a nub. Belatedly Gabriella added a "please."

"Got it. Did you find out anything?"

"Yeah, sure did. The principal behind the shell company that Deacon had traced the ownership to was none other than Andy Mendez."

Mr. Law-and-Order. Father of the Year, Vietnam vet, rancher. Had he added something new and unexpected to his resume? "What does a rancher need with warehouses?"

"Good question. One I plan to ask him after I finish here and drive up to the ranch."

"Did Deacon say how he obtained the address or why he needed information on it to start with?"

"Nope. I called him back with the info about fifteen minutes later. He didn't even say thanks. He said he'd call *me* back. Gotta go. Boom. He hung up on me."

"Where was he?"

"I got the impression he and Eli were headed to this property, but I don't know that for a fact." More muffled words directed to an unseen colleague. "Look, I gotta go. My editor is having a hissy fit."

"Chris, wait. Don't go to Mendez's. Not yet."

"Yeah, right. We're on to something here. Your brother and Larry Teeter had the wrong warehouses. It's obvious."

"Which means Andy Mendez isn't who he pretends to be. Going out there now could be—is dangerous. Let me talk to Eli first. Find out where they are and how they found out about the address. I'll call you back. You'll have more information to approach Mendez with."

A beat of silence. "I'll give you two hours."

"Thanks—"

He hung up.

"Stinking reporters."

"Stinking reporters."

Both Fidencios agreed. Gabriella ignored their chorus. Better to save her breath. She also ignored Natalie's questions while she tried Eli again. No answer. Then Deacon. Again, no answer.

"This is not good." She related her conversation with Chris to Natalie while checking on her shortcakes. Starting to puff. "I don't like the way this feels. I don't like it, Nat."

"Me neither." Natalie rolled her chair into Gabriella's path. "We need to get into this phone. Think. Do you know his birthday?"

"Nope. I know his age."

"What about his girlfriend's?"

"Seventeen."

"We could try 1722 or 2217."

"After so many tries, we'll get locked out." Gabriella chewed her bottom lip. "If you're a teenager in love, don't you think you know everything about your boyfriend, including how to get into his phone?"

"Naturally. Especially because you want to check to see who he's texting." Natalie nodded. "Puppy love 101."

Gabriella scrolled through the numbers on her phone. She'd added

Kristina's number to her contacts Friday night from the smudged numerals scrawled on her hand in ink. She touched the number. After several rings, Kristina's high voice answered. "Who is this?"

Interesting salutation. Gabriella identified herself and explained the situation. "You said you wanted to help find who did this to Beto. Tell me you know his passcode for his phone."

"Of course I know what it is and I'll give it to you." Kristina began to sob. "But I want his phone. I'm working on a collage of photos for the memorial services. He has photos on there that I don't have."

"I can't give you the phone yet, but I'll work on getting it to you when this is over." Depending on what was on it, the phone might be evidence in a trial. "If it's possible, but you know it might not be."

"I know." She sniffed and the sound of nose blowing filled the air. "It's my birthday: 0322. He said no way he'd forget it if he had to use it all the time to get into his phone."

"He was a smart guy."

More sobs. "Call me when you know what happened. Promise."

"I promise."

Gabriella hung up and tapped in the number. Voilà. A selfie of Kristina and Beto outside a bar on San Antonio's River Walk stared up at her. "We're in."

The video turned out to be audio only. The phone camera appeared to be pointed at a tile floor. At one point a dog's face appeared. Big orange snout, sad brown eyes. Music played in the background. Norteña. Two voices, maybe three.

"Turn it up." Natalie crowded closer. "Can you see anything?"

A coffee table. A semiautomatic weapon of some sort. The dog again. He woofed this time.

Someone told him to shut up in Spanish.

Voices discussing a delivery.

"Why is this guy with you?"

"He'll start making the deliveries next week."

"You sure?"

"Manny uses him."

"No need to come up to the house. Text. Drop your package at the gate."

"Understood."

"When do we ship?"

"They move everything on Sunday."

"Ready."

"Yes."

Not exactly stimulating conversation. Gabriella hit pause and inhaled the lovely fragrance of baking cake. *Just breathe.*

Natalie sat back in her chair. "That was totally anticlimactic. What are they so worried about? You can't see any faces."

"You can hear them talking about making a shipment Sunday night. Obviously guns. I don't recognize anything about the location, but one of the voices is vaguely familiar."

"Which one?"

"The guy who says Manny uses him and asks when the shipment is."

"From where?"

"I don't know." Eyes closed, she leaned forward, hit Play again, closed her eyes, and inhaled that mouthwatering scent of cake again. A few seconds later she opened them. "It's not someone I know well, but it's familiar."

"We need to call someone about this. Turn it over. Maybe someone from the task force will recognize the voices."

"Jensen from the ATF. Maybe even Rincon. We need reinforcements. We're not like our idiotic men friends who think they can go charging in like superheroes." Gabriella's phone dinged. She rushed to unlock it. "Speaking of idiots. A text from Eli. Thank God."

U hv something we want. We hv something U want.

The attached photo showed a body sprawled facedown on the ground. A black hood covered the prone figure's face.

Gabriella's stomach roiled and pitched. What was Eli wearing when they left for his parents' house four hundred years ago—earlier in the day? A blue button-down, collared shirt and dark-blue jeans. Nikes. She studied the photo. Blue shirt. Jeans. Nikes.

Her hands shook. She gritted her teeth and typed with thumbs that seemed to swell.

Who is this? Where's Eli?

Don't Y recognize him? A smiley face emoji followed.

"What is it?" Her neck craning, Natalie crowded closer. "What's he saying?"

"The text isn't from him." Cold chills shimmied up Gabriella's spine. A heat wave followed. Her lungs shriveled up. Her vision darkened. *Breathe. Breathe. God, oh, God, please.*

She tried to type. Her fingers refused to cooperate. *Stupid typos. Stupid autocorrect. Breathe.*

What did you do to him?

Nothing that can't be undone. Yet.

Another photo appeared. Jake's bruised, battered face. Purple-and-black circles surrounded closed eyes. Blood encrusted his swollen, cracked lips.

Gabriella's heart hurt. Every part of her body ached as if his wounds had been inflicted on her muscles and bones. "Oh, Jake."

Natalie tugged the phone from Gabriella's fingers. "What have they done to him?"

Gabriella grabbed it back and started typing.

What do y want?

U. U and the video. Come Alone.

The urge to hurl blew through Gabriella.

"No way." Natalie grabbed at the phone. "No, no, you can't. We'll call the police."

Holding it high over her head, Gabriella danced away from her sister. "One way or the other, I have to go."

"Tell them you already shared what you know with law enforcement."

"Then they'd have no reason to keep our guys alive. Besides, they know that's not true. They must think that whatever was on that video will expose their operation. The ATF hasn't descended on them."

"You can't go out there alone."

"They'll kill them."

"Look at the photos." Natalie's tone had retreated to cool, clinical, but her warm hand gripped Gabriella's arm. "Are you sure it hasn't happened already? And what about Deacon? Chris said they were together."

The urge to vomit grew. Bitter acid burned Gabriella's throat. She swallowed, then started typing.

Where's Deacon Alder?

Reporter is fine.

Prove it. I want to talk to them.

No.

Two photos followed. One of Eli—again from behind—supported between two men in camouflage and ski masks. One of a man in a white polo shirt and khaki pants. Deacon's standard reporter attire—also between two men wearing camouflage and masks. Eli's and Deacon's hands were zip-tied behind them.

When & where?

1 hr. directions to follow.

just y. no cops or they're dead. tick tock.

"We need help." Natalie backed away. "Do you have Jensen's number?"

"They said to come alone."

"But you're not an idiot, unlike Eli and Deacon, who apparently walked into a trap."

"There must've been a reason." Gabriella stared at the phone. The directions were complicated. Thank God for GPS. "Eli has more than ten years of experience as a police officer. He's not an idiot."

"But he does think he's Superman."

Sometimes. "Chris should be able to give me Jensen—"

The oven timer dinged. Gabriella jumped. So did Natalie.

Gabriella grabbed hot pads and opened the oven door. Her jumbled thoughts righted themselves as she tugged the pan from the oven and set it on trivets. The cakes were perfect golden oblongs waiting to be sliced and smothered in strawberries and whip cream. Simple pleasures. One she loved sharing with family, with loved ones.

God, help me. Help me make the right decisions. Walk me through this. Protect Eli, Jake, and Deacon. Turn away the evildoers. We need You.

The patio door slid open. Squealing and laughing, Ava and Cullen tumbled through the door, followed by Piper. The sun had turned their skin golden brown, their cheeks pink. Ava's hair was a mass of damp curls. She danced across the tile and threw herself on Natalie's lap. "We're starving!" Her tone suggested they hadn't eaten in days. "Piper's making enchiladas for supper. I love enchiladas. Don't you love enchiladas, Mama? We're gonna feed the Fidencios and teach them to sing Gabriella and Eli sitting in a tree, k-i-s-s-i-n-g!"

The two kids chortled and danced around the room.

"What smells so good? Is it cake? I love cake." His towel around his shoulders like a cape, Cullen darted around the room, thrusting with one hand like a Jedi with his saber. "Can we have cake and ice cream too?"

Piper paused inside the door. Her gaze went from Natalie to Gabriella. "Have you heard from Eli or Deacon?"

Gabriella shook her head. "I have to go out in a bit."

"We have to go out." Natalie hugged Ava. "Baby, you two run along and change first. You're dripping on the tile. Be careful you don't fall."

"Can we play on the tablet?"

"After supper. Go."

Still chattering, the two traipsed from the room.

"Will you watch them for me?" Natalie made her appeal to Piper without looking at Gabriella. "It's imperative that I go."

"They've already lost their father. Don't do this to them." Gabriella swallowed hot tears. She'd been holding them back for years, it seemed. *Get a grip. Get a grip.* "I can't take that risk."

"I know you think you're responsible for us." Natalie moved closer. "You're not."

Piper made a move toward the kitchen. "Maybe I should—"

"It's okay, stay, Piper." Natalie held up her hand. Her fierce gaze returned to Gabriella. "Paolo was a grown man. I begged him for his keys. He kept saying he was fine. He was like that. Stubborn. Macho. He made the choice. He swerved to miss a stray dog in the street. He would've done that regardless of whether he'd been drinking. He chose to drink and to drive. And I let him. I could blame myself, but I don't. We were all grown-ups. I may have lost Jake already. I'm not sitting by while you go. I won't. Let's do this together. The clock is ticking."

Natalie's impassioned speech encompassed the most words she'd ever spoken about Paolo's death. So many lives changed. Gabriella wasn't in charge. She never had been. "I'm calling Chris."

Three minutes to get the numbers she needed from a reporter who insisted he wanted first rights to the story.

She let Jensen's number ring until it went to voicemail and left a message. "Call me back as soon as you get this message. Please. I have to be at the location in fifty minutes."

Rincon picked up on the second ring. She explained as succinctly as possible. A long pause.

"Detective? We don't have a lot of—"

"It'll take about twenty minutes to get to that location. It's in the county. I'll notify WCSO and the other agencies."

"I'm supposed to come alone."

"We'll remain out of sight."

"Their plan may be to shoot me on sight."

"Not until they get the video."

"It's not a video. It's audio of three men talking about a gun ship-ment. You can't even tell where it is."

"You found it."

"I don't have time to explain."

"They're banking on you valuing three lives too much to turn it over to the police. Tell them it's in a safe place. Text them and tell them you want to see all three men alive and standing before you hand over anything."

"Got it."

"I'm scoping out the location . . . Let's meet five miles up the road. I'll text you the location. Rendezvous in twenty minutes."

"We're on our way."

"We?"

"My sister is driving."

"We don't need to involve another civilian."

Gabriella hung up.

CHAPTER 38

——

THE LIGHTER FLICKERED AND went out. The oppressive dark returned. The image was engraved on the insides of Eli's eyelids. He shook it and tried again. A steady flame reignited. He breathed in the smell of dirt and human waste. "Jake?"

No answer. Eli squatted and touched the man's bare arm. His skin felt clammy and his breathing was uneven.

"Did he pass out?" Deacon knelt next to Eli. "It looks like they used him for a punching bag."

"Jake? Come on, Jake." Eli shook his arm. "Stay with me, buddy." Jake's long, muscle-bound body twitched. His eyes opened.

"Seriously? I have a dream and you're in it? It couldn't be Sunny? Or even Gabby and Nat?"

"Sorry, you're stuck with me, and I'm no dream." Now wasn't a good time to mention Sunny's role in their sudden appearance. Especially since Eli didn't know if she'd been used to get to him and was now dead. Or maybe, she'd been in on it.

He held the puny light closer. Jake's thick auburn hair was matted with dirt, blood, and sweat. Both eyes were black. Bruises decorated his cheeks. Blood had dried under his nose. His lips were cracked. "You look a little rough."

"All in a day's work." Jake coughed. His arms tightened around his waist. "Who's your friend?"

Eli made the introductions.

"You brought a reporter? Now I know I'm dreaming."

"It wasn't my idea."

"Are y'all here to save the day?"

"Sorry."

"You're prisoners too?"

"Yep."

"How long've you been down here?"

"Down?"

"It's a room adjacent to a tunnel."

A tunnel. It made perfect sense. Drug cartels had been building tunnels to transport their wares into the United States for decades, mostly in California and Arizona. Tunnels were a way around—or rather under—the border wall erected in some areas as well as increased Border Patrol agents, and the addition of the National Guard. "You've been missing for three days. What happened? Who did this to you?"

"Three days? Is that all? I figured it'd been at least a month. How much fuel do you have in that lighter?" Jake leaned his head against the wall and closed his eyes. "You should save it."

Eli slid around so his back was to the wall as well. Deacon positioned himself on the other side and gave a thumbs-up. Eli let up on the lever. Darkness returned.

"What happened? How'd they get you?"

Putting off the inevitable only made sense. Maybe Jake's story would help fill in the blanks about Sunny's role in this mess. "You first."

"I didn't see a thing. I was supposed to meet Colby. He said he had information for me, but he couldn't talk to me on the phone. They'd kill him if they knew he was talking to me."

Sounded so familiar.

"When I got to the meeting place on the river, I didn't see him, so I started to text him. Next thing I'm flat on my stomach, stiff as a board. I feel like someone is using a pitchfork to remove my insides."

Again, so familiar. "Tasered."

"Guys in camo were on top of me. I didn't recognize any of them.

They already had Colby. They wanted one of us to cough up an audio recording on a phone."

"He didn't have it."

"I figure Beto must have had it. He didn't show, or if he did, he saw what was happening and bailed before they could see him. They put a gun to Colby's head. He held out for as long as he could." All emotion drained from Jake's voice, but his breathing sounded louder. "Then they put the gun to my head. He gave Beto up. As soon as he did, they blew Colby away."

"How did they get on to them?"

"I told my boss and my partner. The core group on the task force had been getting updates. That included Laredo PD, ICE, FBI, and Homeland."

Jensen, Teeter, Rincon. Did that mean one of them was in on it? Or one of the other players. Not Teeter. His death proved that. Eli's head pounded. His nose ached. The darkness pressed in on him. Like being underwater. Now wasn't the time to tell Jake about his partner's death. "What happened next?"

"They threw a hood over my head and threw me in the back of van of some kind." A spasm of coughing left his voice rough and breathless. "Next thing I knew I was inside a warehouse. They had a little welcoming committee for me."

"What's on the recording?"

"Hard evidence of who the facilitator is. At first, as newbie straw buyers, they never saw the top echelon, only the middlemen. But Beto was connected."

"Through his uncle?"

"Yeah. But his uncle isn't the facilitator. Just another middle man. Last week, Beto was assigned to make a delivery. He took Colby with him. One of them recorded the conversation."

"Audio, not video?"

"That's what he said."

Had the story grown into a video, or did the thugs have their wires crossed? Did it matter?

"They thought you could tell them where the recording was, so they tried to beat it out of you?"

"Yep. Problem was, I didn't know where Beto was. I didn't even know which one of them had done the recording until Colby said Beto was the one with the phone. They were forced into cooperating in order to stay out of jail, but they were more afraid of the bad guys than they were of the ATF."

"Alberto Garza is dead."

"How?"

Eli filled in the details. "How did Beto know about Gabby? Did you send him to her?"

"Of course not. It's stupid. I felt for the guy. He was scared spitless. He needed money for college. He didn't want to ask his parents, so he got mixed up in gun smuggling and didn't know how to get out—"

"What does this have to do with—"

"I'm getting there. He needed a place to crash for one night. He didn't want his parents to know, to be endangered. I let him stay with me. One night."

"Rookie move. You got emotionally involved."

"Don't tell me you've never done it."

If he only knew. Eli's hand went to his jeans pocket. They'd taken his wallet. It contained the only photo he had of Samuel.

His son.

His secret.

He was a father. Would he get the chance to be a dad? Would he even be good at it? Would he be half the dad his own father had been—continued to be?

Eli would do everything he could to get out of this alive. For the chance to find out and for Samuel. His son had the right to know his father. He focused on Jake. "I still don't understand."

"You remember that article that was in the business section of the *Express-News* when Gabby opened the restaurant? They made a big deal about her being a former ADA turned chef. An attorney who was catering to the law enforcement crowd. Me and Natalie and Gabby and the kids were in the photo cutting the ribbon. I framed it. It was on the wall in my living room. Beto asked me about it. He said Gabby was pretty."

Fury burned through Eli. He tamped it down. Now wasn't the time for recriminations. "The article told him exactly where to find her. At least he was trying to be stealthy about it. He parked at Main Plaza, but they were following him and shot him there. I figure they thought he was dead and took off. He dragged himself two blocks to the restaurant to try to get help."

Jake cleared his throat. "If they touch a hair on her head—"

"I'm way ahead of you." Eli snorted at the ridiculousness of his own words. "At least I was."

"Me too." Deacon's chuckle was more of a growl.

Silence hovered for a beat. They were in here and Gabriella was out there. And Natalie and the kids. *Please, God, keep them safe. I need You to do what I can't do. I can admit I'm not in control anymore. You are.*

God must be so amused to see his baby steps toward a closer relationship. And Gabby would be so happy. If Eli had a chance to tell her. *And God, if You could, get us out of here alive.*

"So Beto's dead. Gabby doesn't have the recording." Jake's frustration soaked the words. "Where is it?"

"There was some security camera footage from a pawn shop next to the sporting goods store that showed Garza going into the plaza across the street. Gabs was checking it out. Maybe he hid his phone there."

"You let her go by herself?"

"I didn't let her do anything. You know your sister."

"Sorry."

"If our buddies upstairs think the video is still out there, it may be what's keeping you alive. An ATF agent could be used as leverage."

"I hated using college kids like undercover agents." Jake shifted. A half moan floated on the air. "They didn't have the training or the guts. They were scared out of their minds."

"They called the shots when they decided to buy guns and sell them to pay for their college education."

"I know, but they were stupid kids trying to make their life better." Raspy breathing filled the space for a few seconds. "Around here, the options are limited. Join the military—always an honorable choice—is the one most kids take. If they survive they can get a college education or a job skill out of it. Or they bail out of high school and turn to the dark side, like drugs or gangs."

"You didn't create the situation."

"No, but I took advantage of it."

"Guys, this is very interesting." A *thump, thump* suggested Deacon was having trouble sitting still, even in total darkness. "If I had my laptop, I'd be in seventh heaven, but right now, what we really need is to get out of here."

"Agreed." Jake's voice flagged again. He breathed. "How did you end up down here with me? I assume you were coming to get me."

"Not exactly." Eli gritted his teeth. Might as well get it over with. "Sunny called me. She said she had some information she thought might help find you. We were supposed to meet her . . ."

"So you know about Sunny." Scraping sounds made it clear Jake was attempting to rise. "Did something happen to her?"

"Easy, easy." Eli fumbled in the dark. His hand connected with Jake's arm. "No point in getting riled up. We don't know where she is." He summarized the activities of the past three days as quickly as possible.

"I see."

Not really. None of them did.

"I've had plenty of time to assess our current digs—no pun intended. By the way, the facilities are on the other side of the room to our right in the corner." Jake seemed determined to move on without further comment about his relationship with Sunny. "Last time they took me up for a punching bag session, I eyeballed the situation. The door is padlocked from the outside. Even if we get out. We're in a tunnel and we have to make our way to the platform lift a few dozen yards to the right and get ourselves back up into the warehouse without being seen."

"This thing has a lift?"

"A lift run on a generator. The tunnel floor is probably seventy, eighty feet down from the warehouse floor. The entrance is made of cinderblocks. The floor at the beginning is lined with wood. They've got ventilation. Lighting. There are rails to the left with carts on them. I assume they use those to transport the weapons."

"Where does it go?" Deacon the reporter surfaced again. "Any idea how long it is?"

"Some place in Nuevo Laredo. It could be a warehouse district, or it could be a residence that sits close to the border." Jake's shoulder touched Eli's. He was listing to one side. "How long? No idea. It was before my time, but ICE found one used for drug smuggling in San Diego that was more than two thousand feet long."

Deacon whistled. "That's like seven football fields."

"Yeah and it went from warehouses in the industrial district to somebody's kitchen in Tijuana."

"Which was convenient if they worked up a hunger moving their drugs." Eli remembered the case. U.S. agencies had filled tunnels with concrete to keep drug smugglers from using them again. However, Mexico couldn't afford the concrete, so they filled theirs with trash. The drug cartels had reopened some of them. "They didn't drag us very far, so we're close to the lift. How bad are you hurt?"

"Some busted ribs, a couple of broken fingers. My nose. Bruised kidneys, maybe."

A reporter and a wounded ATF agent. No weapons.

"What's the plan?" Deacon's eagerness made him sound very young. "I know you, Eli. You've got a plan."

"This isn't the movies." Eli hoisted himself to his feet and stretched cramped legs. "Do they feed you? Give you water?"

"Every now and then they throw in a plastic bag containing a peanut butter sandwich and a bottle of water."

A fitness and sports nut, Jake had always been on the lean side. Now he looked emaciated, and for good reason. "Have they done it recently?"

"I don't know if it was today or yesterday. It seems like it was fairly recent. If—when—I get out of here, I'm never eating peanut butter again."

"If they don't drag us out of here and shoot us before then, that's our shot."

"Lovely choice of words." Deacon groaned. "That's it?"

"We wait. Unless you have a better idea."

Deacon sniffed. "I'm working on it. I can handle myself."

"With what? Your pen and your rapier wit?"

"I'll have you know I've taken some karate in my time."

"When?"

"High school. Same time I did Junior ROTC."

"And that ended so well."

"I learn from my mistakes. I'll come up with a plan, you watch."

"I'm sure you'll come up with something right out of Marvel Comics."

"Okay, boys, no bickering. I'm closing my eyes for a minute." Jake's voice faded. "Let me know when the fun starts."

Torture and three days in darkness hadn't broken Jake's spirit.

Whether he could leave his underground prison under his own speed was another question.

Eli leaned his head back and closed his eyes, but his body hummed with the desire to do something, anything. He put both hands back, flat on the wall, and began to edge through the darkness.

"What's that sound?" Did slight panic tinge Deacon's question? "What are you doing?"

"Exploring."

"Funny man."

"What's the matter?"

"Did I mention I've been known to have claustrophobia?"

A reporter, and he had claustrophobia. But then he did have that Junior ROTC experience. "Anything I can do to help?"

"Keep talking. You can even keep insulting me. It takes my mind off my surroundings."

"You're giving me permission to insult you?" Eli's left hand touched air and then the indentation of the corner. He made the turn. His shoes shuffled in the dirt. The tunnel might have ventilation, but the air in this room was fetid. His lungs clamored for a deep, cleansing breath of fresh air. His hand touched the metal outline of the door. He searched for a knob or a lever. Nothing but a hole where a knob would have been.

He patted the entire door down. Hinges attached to a wood frame. How tight? His fingers fumbled. No way to get a hold on the door's edges. He flicked the lighter for a few seconds.

The door swung open. He stumbled back. A flashlight blinded him. He flung his arm over his face and worked to regain his balance. A chance. Now.

He lunged.

Something cold and hard smacked him in the face with a jolt that sent him spiraling back.

A second later his head connected with the dirt floor.

"Don't be stupid, mi amigo." The same melodic voice as before. "Time to take a walk."

"I'm not leaving without them."

"Don't worry, the three amigos ride again." The man motioned with his AK-47. "Time to take a hike."

CHAPTER 39

FIFTEEN MINUTES. AND COUNTING. All those years of pinging targets at the shooting range with Eli came down to a scant few minutes. Gabriella cradled Eli's Sig Sauer in her lap. She checked again to make sure the magazine was fully loaded. Fear-induced adrenaline made her hands shake.

Fifteen rounds.

Not a lot, all things considered.

Despite a steady stream of AC-cooled air, sweat rolled down her forehead. Her eyes burned. She wiped at it with her sleeve. The sun, just beginning its trajectory in the west, beat on the windshield and blinded her. Her head throbbed. As much as this needed to be over, it might be better to keep driving and driving. Never reach the end and the struggle that waited at the other end of the road.

Eli. Jake. Deacon. And now Natalie. Lives counting on her. *Jesus, I can't do this alone. I can't control this. I can't control everything. I've tried to do it on my own. I can't. I need You. Keep them safe. Cover them with Your protection. Please Lord, I'm laying this at Your feet.*

She repeated the words to the erratic beating of her heart.

The van rocked. Her stomach rocked with it. She tightened her grip on the pistol with one hand and grabbed the overhead handle with the other. Natalie's grim expression didn't waver. They turned left, then right. Tires squealed. Brakes screeched. Asphalt gave way to gravel. A plume of dust spiraled behind them.

"Time?"

"Fourteen minutes."

The van shot forward.

"We should see Rincon any second."

"I know."

Natalie's phone rang. Bluetooth picked it up. Their mother's photo popped up on the stereo console. "Natalie."

"Mom, now's not a good time."

"Are you driving and talking on the mobile—?"

"It's Bluetooth. Hands-free. I can't talk right now."

"I wanted to let you know we're still working on getting there. Our flight out of Heathrow was canceled due to weather. We can't get another until tomorrow night." Mom's upper-crust London accent sounded almost warm. "Your dad and I spoke, but he was on his mobile. I lost him when he got on the lift at the airport in New Orleans. I think he said his flight gets into San Antonio tomorrow morning. He wants you to call him with any updates ASAP."

Mom and Dad had spoken. Cataclysmic event followed cataclysmic event for the Benoit family.

"We need an address and directions for this Seville family. We'll rent a car in San Antonio and drive to Laredo when we arrive." Their mom's new husband sounded equally warm. For a guy who broke up a family. "Just give it to us and we won't keep you."

"Or we can call Gabriella," Mom offered. "I just don't know if she'll answer."

"I'm right here, Mom." Gabriella heaved a breath. Their voices sounded so good, so concerned. They were living this nightmare from afar. Her parents didn't need to know the details. They hit a deep rut. The van rocked. Gabriella's shoulder banged against the door. "We'll call you back as soon as we can."

"Don't be that way—"

Natalie terminated the call.

"She'll think I did that."

"Let's deal with one thing at a time. There's Rincon."

The detective stood in front of a dense thicket of live oak, mesquite, and huisache trees cloaked by prickly pear, cactus, and catclaw. A silver Ram pickup was parked off the road, half hidden by the trees. "Where's the backup?"

Hands on his zipper, a lone man sauntered from behind the trees. Kyle Sullivan.

"What's he doing here?" Hair prickled on Gabriella's neck. Her hands were slick with sweat around the Sig Sauer. "We met him at the bar. He knew Eli from high school. He's from the Webb County sheriff's office. He oversees SWAT."

"I hope they're right behind him." Hitting the button to roll down her window, Natalie pulled off the road. She left the engine running. "Make this quick."

As if Gabriella needed a reminder.

She popped from the van. "Where are your guys?"

"WCSO's SWAT is on the way. The warehouses are in their jurisdiction. This is Sergeant Kyle Sullivan. He oversees their tactical unit."

"We've met. What's the plan?"

Sullivan shoved a Texas Rangers cap back on his head. His dark eyes pierced her. "You have the video?"

Swatting away buzzing flies the size of her big toe, Gabriella nodded.

"Let's see it."

"We don't have time. It's just voices talking about a shipment."

"No faces?" Sullivan's voice held a strange note Gabriella couldn't identify. "What shipment?"

"This may be our last chance to hear it." Rincon held out his hand.

Ignoring it, Gabriella produced the phone and accessed the video.

A few seconds in, Rincon swore and whirled toward Sullivan. "You and—"

"Sorry, bud." Sullivan snatched his weapon from his hip holster.

He slugged Rincon in the head with the butt of his gun. The detective went down like a boulder.

Blood trickling from his forehead, he sprawled between them in drought-starved brown weeds.

Frozen, Gabriella stared into the barrel of a Sig Sauer 9 mil. The buzz of crickets so loud earlier disappeared into a strange silence. Eli's backup weapon lay on the van seat. "It's you."

"I'm just the inside man. A cog in the machine. I'll take that." He held out his free hand.

"I'm not giving you the phone. Not until Jake and the others are free. That was the deal."

"Give it to me or I'll kill you."

"If I hand it over, you'll kill me."

He raised the gun and pointed it at her head.

"You should know I emailed a copy of the video to an anonymous person with instructions. If we don't come back in two hours, he'll forward it to the ATF, the DEA, the U.S. attorney, and the Laredo police."

"It seems we have a standoff here." His amused sneer deserved a mouth full of steel-toed boot. "Fine. Hang on to the phone. We'll see what the jefe has to say about your plan. We'll go see him together."

A whirring sound. The van's sliding doors opening. Natalie. Gabriella whirled. "No, Natalie, don't!"

Sullivan grabbed Gabriella's arm and jerked her closer. The warm metal of the barrel pressed into her temple. "Tell your sister to hang tight. We'll need her to drive."

"Natalie, get out of here! Go!"

His hand tightened. "Don't be stupid, Natalie." His voice held a hint of amusement. Two women, one a paraplegic. "I'll kill her slowly, a bullet here, a bullet there, a bullet everywhere."

Only the faintest line on her forehead betrayed Natalie's anxiety. "Do what he says, Gabby." The sliding door shut.

Every muscle in Gabriella's body protested. Sullivan released her arm. He motioned with the gun. His service weapon. The irony would be wasted on him. "Time isn't on your side. If we don't show up, you know what they'll do to your buddies, don't you?"

She knelt next to Rincon and did as she was told. The detective moaned.

At least he wasn't dead. If SWAT showed up soon enough . . . Her mind pounded on the walls of a locked room, trying to find a way out.

Sullivan dragged her to her feet. He shoved her forward. "They're expecting us."

"Who's they?" She tumbled forward a few steps, then caught herself. "If you're the lowly middleman, who's the top dog?"

"It'll be a surprise. Don't you like surprises?"

God, is this the plan? Help me. Please. "Not particularly."

"Allow me." He tugged open the van door. The gun butted her back between her shoulder blades. "Red, you're a babe. Even more than your sister. Too bad about the legs. Open the sliding door."

Natalie pushed the button.

"Get in."

Like dancers who'd performed their choreographed routines a hundred times, Gabriella went first, into the front seat, and her captor squeezed onto the ramp next to Natalie's wheelchair. His gun remained inches from her head.

Eli's Sig Sauer no longer lay on her seat.

"Red, toss your phone out the window."

Gabriella exchanged glances with Natalie. She shrugged. She did as she was told.

"Tick tock." Sullivan tapped his weapon on Natalie's shoulder. "I'm sure you realize that I won't hesitate to shoot your sister. Pull back onto the road and continue west. We're almost there."

"How did you get involved in this?" Natalie utilized her soft, conversational Dr. Ferrari tone, the one she adopted with her adolescent patients. "What made you cross the line from police officer to criminal?"

"Fifteen years with the sheriff's office doesn't mean squat when you're paying child support to two ex-wives and your girlfriend has expensive tastes in jewelry and likes beaches in faraway places."

"Money."

"Isn't it always about money?"

Greed. Lust. Revenge. It was never about anything good. "You orchestrated the firebombing of Reverend Cavazos's church."

"It's unfortunate that you and your boyfriend didn't take the hint I dropped at the bar when I mentioned the reverend." Sullivan's laugh made the hair stand up on Gabriella's arms. "You kept on digging. Kept on asking questions. The whole point of the exercise was to get the video and move on. Beto and Colby were out of the way. If you'd given us the video when we asked for it nicely, you'd have your brother back and this would be over."

"Nicely? Once we'd seen the video—or heard it in this case— there was no going back. We're not idiots."

"Don't let him bait you." Natalie used her doctor's voice again. "You have the video now. Return Jake and our friends to us. Everyone wins."

"Honey, I played a lot of sports in my life. It's only the YMCA that tells kids everyone is a winner. In real life there are winners and there are losers. I intend to be a winner. Which makes you the losers."

"You don't have to do this."

"You watch too many movies." Sullivan grunted. "Turn left here."

In front of them a ten-foot-tall black chain-link fence with razor ribbon wire on top surrounded a series of dilapidated warehouses with corrugated metal roofs as far as the eye could see. A double-pane moving gate had been left open far enough for a single vehicle to enter.

Natalie stopped the van. Gabriella glanced her way. Natalie raised her eyebrows. Her fingers tapped on the miniature wheel. Gabriella managed a minute nod. Whatever Natalie had in mind, it was better than going peacefully. Sullivan had Beto's phone. The facilitator had no reason to keep them alive.

"Go on in. They left the gate open just for you."

"Who's in charge?" Natalie started forward again. "No reason not to tell us. They'll kill us anyway."

"It's such a shame too. Such beautiful women." Sullivan sounded truly regretful. "I would argue for keeping you around for a while. The bodies are piling up. Perhaps we can ship you across the Rio Grande. My compadres have nice homes where we could get to know each other better. I'd love to see what you look like without the glasses, Red."

Gabriella's skin crawled. Her stomach bucked. The phrase *better off dead* pulsed in her head.

The van jerked forward. Gabriella's head banged against the headrest. They hurtled through the gate.

"Hey, slow down!" Sullivan's weapon disappeared from her peripheral vision. A string of curse words followed. "Stop."

Natalie's fingers worked the levers on her door. "Your wish is my command."

They slammed to a halt for a split second. Gabriella's seat belt bit into her chest. Pain sliced through her rib cage. Her neck popped.

The van shot backward. It rocked. Tires squealed. Banging said Natalie's wheelchair had toppled from its rig.

Cursing suggested where it had landed.

"You're crazy." Sullivan spewed more invectives. "I'll kill you."

The van rolled. Gabriella grappled for a hold. Her hands grasped air. Air bags deployed. A second later they deflated. She choked on hazy air filled with talcum powder and the scent of gunshot.

Her face banged against the door. Like body surfing in a metal box instead of ocean waves.

Glass shattered. Time passed.

Gabriella opened her eyes. The van rested upright and head-on into a semitrailer parked in front of a warehouse loading dock. Ignoring excruciating pain in her neck, she swiveled. Sullivan slumped against the sliding door. Natalie's wheelchair lay on top of him. His eyes were closed. Blood trickled from his nose.

"Natalie? Natalie!"

Her sister grunted. "To think I was sober for this one."

"Are you okay?"

"I think my arm is broken. My head feels like someone stepped on it. I lost my glasses. You?"

"I'm okay." Adrenaline pulsed so hard her heart had catapulted into her throat. Fear held her body captive against the seat. "Where's the gun?"

Her voice sounded so calm it had to be someone else's.

"Under my right thigh. At least it was."

The safety glass in the windshield had fractured into a million tiny, spidered pieces. Gabriella tried to sit forward. Her seat belt stuck. "Can you see anything?"

"A blurry blob mostly." With one arm clasped against her chest, Natalie used her other hand to shove her hair from her face. Bruises had already begun to bloom on her fair skin. "People are coming. Whoever they are, they're coming."

Her tone reminded Gabriella of the I Spy game they had played as kids on long road trips. "Guns?"

"Big ones."

One stinking Sig Sauer wouldn't be enough. Gabriella twisted in her seat. No sign of Sullivan's matching weapon. She worked the seat belt clasp. "My seat belt is stuck. Yours?"

"I'm working on it. It's undone."

"Dump yourself out. Hide behind the trailer."

"I'm not leaving you."

"I'm right behind you. I need to get Sullivan's gun."

"Then get it."

Gabriella fumbled with the buckle. "Come on, come on."

Seconds ticked by.

Her fingers felt like blocks of wood. She tensed, waiting for shots to finish shattering the windshield.

The belt gave.

She climbed into the back and shoved the wheelchair away from Sullivan. No gun. Her lungs refused to work. Her muscles moved like molasses.

Breathe. Breathe.

One of Sullivan's legs crumpled at an unnatural angle. *Ouch.*

Swallowing against vomit, she slid two fingers in between his waist and the seat. Working by feel, she found Beto's phone and tugged it out. He didn't move. The phone went into her back pocket.

Now the gun.

She shoved him aside and searched the ramp with both hands. Nothing.

Panting, she peered into the crevices around the ramp. There. A sliver of metal. She reached for it.

Sullivan's arm shot out. His hand grabbed her wrist.

Gabriella slammed her free fist into his face. His head popped back.

A filthy river of invectives flowed over her. His grip tightened. Sullivan had more strength, but Gabriella had more fear. And more reasons to live.

Jake and Eli and Deacon and Natalie.

She gouged his face with her fingernails.

He jerked back. This time he let go.

She scooped up the gun and slid away. Sullivan tried to follow. A scream of pain reverberated inside the van.

That leg must hurt. She should feel for him. She couldn't.

Natalie had her door open. Gabriella hauled herself between the seats. "Go, go!"

Natalie slid out, legs first in an elegant move marred only by the pain-filled grunt that followed. Her upper body fell forward. She caught herself with her good arm and lowered herself to the ground on one side.

Her glasses were in the foot well. Gabriella stuck the gun in the waistband of her jeans and grabbed the glasses. She dove over Natalie onto the hard-packed dirt beyond, rolled, and came up on her knees.

Grabbing her sister under the arms, Gabriella dragged her behind the enormous tires toward the back of the trailer. It was parked next to two or three more. All were butt-end against loading docks with the typical sliding doors that looked as if they hadn't been opened in years. Window dressing. To get behind their semi, she would have to shimmy onto the dock and try the doors until she found one she could open. Exposed all the while.

"Are we having fun yet?" Natalie panted. Her cheeks were red. Blood dripped from her bottom lip. "Is there a way out?"

Gabriella handed her the glasses. The bows were askew and one lens cracked. "Do you still have the Sig?"

Natalie slid them on her nose. "Better than nothing." She tugged the gun from her capris' waistband. "It's been a while, but I assume it's like riding a bike."

Not like riding a bike. Neither of them had ever aimed at a live target while under fire.

Gabriella checked Sullivan's weapon. A standard issue law enforcement Sig Sauer P320 9 mil, with an extended magazine that held 21 rounds.

Not much against what were sure to be AK-47s that held thirty rounds. Still, better than nothing. Her back to the dock, Gabriella edged forward until she could peer around the carnage of two vehicles. Half a dozen men in camouflage approached with a variety of weapons. Big ones, as Natalie so eloquently summarized them.

Behind them, approached another cluster of people. More guys in camo. More guns. And a woman. Slender. Chestnut hair pulled into a ponytail that bobbed. Sandals exchanged for black cowboy boots. The long-standing question of Sunny Mendez's role in this fiasco had now been answered.

The AR-10 she carried was taller than she was.

Someone shouted.

Sullivan responded. The bad guys now knew Gabriella and Natalie were on the run. So to speak.

"Do you see Eli or Deacon or Jake?" Natalie rolled onto her belly and propped herself up on her good arm. She laid the gun in the dirt long enough to pull herself up next to Gabriella. One look and the Sig returned to her hand. "Who's the woman?"

"That would be Jake's fiancée."

CHAPTER 40

——

A LONG WALK OFF a short cliff. The fact that their captors didn't bother with the hoods signaled their intent. Keenly aware of the firepower at his back, Eli stepped off the hydraulic lift and raised his arm to his eyes to block the sun that shone through open doors that would take them from a cavernous warehouse with a cement floor and corrugated metal walls.

A dozen or more men packed weapons into large wooden boxes. Busy-bee workers. Handling dozens of assault rifles, hundreds of rounds of ammunition, belt-fed magazines, armor carriers, and camouflage suits. Christmas in August for the cartel.

Beyond them stood several more in a tight cluster, talking and smoking cigarettes. The desire for one hit of nicotine flooded Eli. One man stood a head taller than the others. He wore his long silver hair in a ponytail that hung from under a gray cowboy hat.

A hundred mental red flags appeared like poppies in a field.

"*Hermano.*" The captor with the melodic voice and perfect manners called out. "*Aquí estamos.*"

Cigar in hand, the man turned.

Andy Mendez. "Ah, our guests."

Eli cleared his throat and spat. "So it's you."

Without warning Jake came to life. He jerked loose from Deacon's hold and tottered forward. "What did you do to her? How could a father involve his daughter in something like this?"

Mendez guffawed and slapped the man standing closest to him

on the back. "You can bring a man out of the tunnel and have him still be in the dark."

Jake staggered past Eli. Camo Man grabbed his arm and held him there. "Where do you think you're going, amigo?"

"Where is she?"

"You think I dragged my daughter into this?" Smoke trailing behind him, Mendez swaggered across the cement floor in black cowboy boots. "Getting with you was her idea. She saw you at the church and she came home to tell me all about how friendly you were—to her and to her friend Beto. I wasn't in favor of messing with an ATF agent, but it turned into an asset until that idiot Sullivan jumped the gun and grabbed you at the river. *M'jita* had you wrapped around her little finger. And now, she's outside getting ready to bring in your sister."

Gabriella wouldn't make the same mistake. *Please God, don't let her make the same mistake.* They needed to get outside now. Find a way to warn her off. Eli slid closer to Jake. "Let it go."

"Who is this guy?" Deacon shoved forward. "Can I at least get a name?"

"Meet Andy Mendez, former Webb County sheriff, Vietnam veteran, and cattle rancher."

"Of course it is." Deacon groaned. "My kingdom for a laptop."

"You must be the reporter." An amused look on his craggy face, Mendez puffed on his cigar and let the smoke filter through his nostrils in a steady stream. "Sorry. We have other fish to fry."

He motioned to Camouflage Man. "I see you've met my older brother Pedro."

Pedro bowed. "I apologize for the circumstances. We really don't have time to chat." He nudged Eli with the AK-47. "We're on a schedule here."

"By all means, we've sheep to slaughter. Let's get it over with."

"Hey, I'm in no hurry." Deacon dug in his heels. "I'm happy to talk it over."

"Move." Pedro nudged him with the rifle barrel.

Deacon held up his hands. "No worries."

Mendez chuckled again. "I'll walk with you."

Like most megalomaniacs, the man appreciated an audience. Eli quickened his steps. "Being a cattle baron wasn't enough for you after all those years in law enforcement? Too staid?"

"Do you know what the droughts in the last ten years have done to cattle ranchers?" Mendez spared no sarcasm in the words. "During the last one, I couldn't buy hay for my herd. I had to sell off two-thirds of it."

"So this is about money?"

"It's not like my pension is sufficient for my lifestyle. Or that of my daughter." He wrinkled his nose as if something smelled bad. "But it's more than that. You're too young to remember the Vietnam War. I served my country in that hellhole for two tours of duty. I don't even have a medal to show for it. When I came back, skinny college students who smelled of pot and danced naked at Woodstock spat on me."

Eli hadn't served, but his brother was career Air Force. He understood in some small way. "Two wrongs don't make a right."

"No, but it surely makes you feel better."

A man burst through the open doors. A flood of Spanish followed. Bottom line, the van they were expecting had arrived. It crashed into a semi and rolled over. The women were loose. Everyone moved at once. Mendez grabbed an AK-47 lying on a nearby bin and lumbered out the door.

Pedro's nudge became a shove. "Help your friend. Move, move, move."

Van. Women. Gabriella and Natalie had arrived.

If they got out of here alive, he would lock them both in a room for life.

Eli grabbed Jake's arm on one side. Deacon grabbed the other.

They hustled through the doors into a brutal setting sun. Jake recoiled. His legs buckled. "We've gotcha. Just stay with us."

"I'm okay. I can do it."

But he couldn't. Physical abuse plus three days and nights in the dark worked against him.

"What's going on?" Deacon wrapped his arm around Jake. "What was the guy saying?"

Either Pedro and the others were too preoccupied by this turn of events to intervene, or it didn't matter if the prisoners fraternized now. They wouldn't be around much longer. "He said the people they were expecting showed up in a van. The van crashed. Kyle Sullivan is out there. He's hurt. The two women are holding out."

"The two women." Deacon shifted so Jake's arm went over his shoulder. He leaned into the man's weight. "Gabriella and Natalie."

"That's my guess."

"What is wrong with them?"

Eli couldn't wait to demand an answer to that question. All these years he'd spent keeping Gabby at arm's length because of some stupid macho man facade. All he wanted now was to talk to her, to tell her everything he was thinking and feeling. To talk until he couldn't talk anymore.

Pedro and the other guards herded them out into an open swath of dirt and gravel in front of several worse-for-wear warehouses. The mangled van and the immovable object that was a semitrailer couldn't be missed.

Guns drawn, half a dozen of Mendez's men stood at attention several yards from it.

Deacon whispered something that sounded like "Lord have mercy."

"They'll want the video first," Eli whispered. "They can still negotiate."

Gabriella was intelligent. She could think on her feet. *God, please. Take me. Leave her.*

Mendez stood, massive legs akimbo, next to Sunny, who cradled her AR-10 like it was her baby. "Come on out, ladies." Andy's voice boomed in the quiet countryside. "Some friends of yours are here. Isn't that what you came for? Your brother? Your friends?"

The minute they came out, they would be sitting ducks for Andy's sharpshooters. Eli shifted Jake's weight toward Deacon. The reporter raised his eyebrows.

Eli nodded.

"We'll even see if we can salvage your chair for you, Dr. Ferrari." Mendez smoothed his hand across the butt of the assault rifle. "Come on out. You give us what we want. We'll give you what you want."

When the earth turned to ashes.

"Don't do it, Gabs!" Eli flung his elbow into the guard's gut on his left. The force knocked the man on his keister. "Get out. It's a trap!"

Pedro whirled. Eli smashed into him. They hit the ground together. Eli had the semiautomatic. Then he didn't. Shots blistered the air all around him.

———

Eli was alive. His voice died away, but he was out there. Alive. Automatic gunfire splattered the semi before Gabriella had a chance to respond.

Her heart rattling her chest, she popped up and fired back. One. Two. Three. Pain etching her face, Natalie hoisted herself up on her bad arm and did the same.

"Eli's out there." Panting, her face contorted in pain, Natalie hunkered down. "That means Jake and Deacon could be too. What if we hit one of them?"

"Don't."

"Are they advancing on us?"

Gabriella scooted around her sister long enough to peek through the van's shattered window. She crawled back. "Yeah. I can't see Eli or the others."

Please God, let them be okay. Take me. Not them.

She popped off two more rounds. Five gone. A dozen left. "I need to get up on the dock, see if we can get into the warehouse."

"We'll be trapped in there."

"There'll be exits on the other side."

"We can't rescue our guys running away."

"We can't rescue them if we get caught."

"Go." Natalie eased up to the top of the dock. She propped herself up on her bad arm and fired.

Jesus, help me. Gabriella hoisted herself onto the deck and crawled toward the doors flat on her belly, like a worm. Any second a bullet would pierce her brain and splatter it all over the dirty rubber matting. Or sever her spine. She kept moving.

After eons, she could touch the door. She scrambled to her knees. Loath to lay the gun down, she stuck it in her waistband and used both hands to tug on it. The door creaked. It moaned. It screeched.

Finally, it moved a few inches. Then a few more.

God, is this Your idea of an exit plan?

Adrenaline and sheer terror combined to give her the strength of five bodybuilders. The door rose another two feet. She peered inside. Rows of boxes and crates. Front-end loaders.

A working warehouse. Storing what?

Gabriella whirled and did her commando crawl back through open enemy territory to Natalie. "We're in. Let's go."

"What? Are you planning to carry me?"

"It might sound romantic to die in a hail of gunfire, but I'd rather not." Gabriella leaned over and grabbed her arms. "We'll crawl together."

"We're not getting out of here. I'd rather stand our ground and go down fighting than get trapped inside."

"We don't have time to argue—"

The sound of high-powered engines roaring mixed with the gunfire. Metal smashed into metal.

"Is that help coming?" Natalie tugged free. "I can't see."

"Stay put." Still hunkered down, Gabriella hopped from the dock and climbed over her. She edged through the van's driver's-side door. AC would no longer be needed. It had been thoroughly aerated with bullet holes.

A WCSO armored SWAT vehicle blocked the van. Ricon had sent them on from the rendezvous spot. Sullivan's own guys would bring him down. ATF and ICE vehicles rolled in behind it. Chuck Jensen squatted behind a black SUV's bumper.

The cavalry.

She eased back from the van and crawled around the back until she could dodge between the van and the SUV. "Jensen!"

One fierce glance pierced her. "Stay down. Jake? Cavazos?"

"Eli's out there. I don't know about the others." Gabriella closed her eyes. *Please God.*

No other words came. None were needed. He knew her heart.

"Stop, stop, stop!"

A woman's screams tore through the air.

"Cease fire. Cease fire." A hoarse command from an unseen man. The volley of shots ended.

Silence followed so magnified it hurt Gabriella's ears.

Silence and sobs.

She crawled to Jensen's side. He grabbed a bullhorn from the SUV. "Lay down your weapons. On your knees. Hands behind your heads."

The few remaining men in camo did as they were told.

Weapons ready, WCSO SWAT officers and a horde of Feds descended on them.

Gabriella followed Jensen out. His weapon extended, he looked back and growled. "Stay."

"I have to get to Eli. I have to find Deacon and Jake."

"Not until we clear the area."

"Gabby!"

She raced back behind the semi. Natalie struggled to pull herself up. "We need to find them. Get my chair. Please."

"I'll get it. Can you wait while I search for them?"

"Bring them to me. And my chair."

"I will."

Adrenaline, already like a flash fire in her body, consumed Gabriella. She swallowed and gritted her teeth. Everything came down to this moment. One foot in front of the other. Step by step. *God, please, please.* Her mind wanted to run, but her feet refused to cooperate.

Dead or alive.

God, please.

The industrial park looked like a scene from a war movie.

Except the blood was real. The screams were real.

The sobs were real.

Her face sodden with tears, Sunny Mendez hunched over a huge mound of a man. She glanced up at Gabriella. "They killed Daddy? How could they?" Hiccupping a sob, she stumbled to her feet and grabbed at Gabriella's dirt-and-sweat-stained T-shirt. "You did this. You made them come. You killed him."

Precariously close to the precipice of fury, Gabriella peeled the woman's fingers from her clothes. Her stomach heaved with disgust. A lost child of God, absolutely. *God, forgive me.* "You killed him. He killed himself. By trafficking in illegal weapons. Do you know how many families have lost loved ones in Mexico because you funneled weapons into that country?"

Wasted breath. "Where's Eli? Where's Jake? Where's Deacon?"

"I don't know." Sunny pushed at Gabriella with both hands, her pink nails broken and dirty. "I hope you find them back there, dead. So you can know what this feels like."

A SWAT officer grabbed Sunny's arms and tucked them behind her. The zip ties clicked into place. Sunny screamed and struggled. "No, no, I have to stay with Daddy."

Gabriella backed away. Sunny thrust forward and spit on her. The eyes of a psychopath stared up at her. This woman was a skilled actor who had manipulated Jake for her own personal gain with no thought for the pain and suffering she caused him or others.

"God will forgive you. I hope I can." Gabriella turned and ducked past SWAT officers who handcuffed and moved prisoners to the other side of the vehicles to await transport. The Feds explored nooks and crannies, looking for runners. Other officers already cataloged weapons and dropped evidence tents next to expended cartridges.

Past bodies.

Kyle Sullivan had crawled from the van and lay facedown in the scraggly grass. Blood soaked the ground under him.

"Gabriella!"

"Deacon!" She jolted forward. Deacon leaned over a man who lay on the ground, legs intertwined with that of a man in camouflage and black army boots. Deacon had both hands on the man's chest.

Black jeans and a blue short-sleeved cotton shirt.

Nikes.

The sound of her own breathing filled her ears until her head might explode.

Eli.

She stumbled forward. "Eli, Eli?"

"We need an ambulance!" Deacon didn't look up. "Now!"

"We need an ambulance." She turned and screamed. "Get an ambulance. Now!"

"They're on their way." A man in an ATF jacket yelled as he marched a prisoner past them. "As many as we can get."

"Is he breathing?" She dropped to her knees. "Eli, talk to me."

"He's breathing." Deacon wiped at his face with the back of his dirty sleeve. "He asked for you a second ago."

"Eli, I'm here. Talk to me." She touched his bruised cheek. The dark stubble on his chin tickled her fingers. His nose looked swollen and crooked. "Don't you want to tell me I told you so or rant about how reckless I am or something . . . ?"

Anything.

He moaned. She bent so close her lips brushed his forehead. He smelled musty, like dirt and sweat. "Talk to me, love."

"Gabs, I'm sorry."

"It's okay. Just hang on. Help is on the way."

"Tell my son I love him."

"I will—what?"

"That's what I couldn't tell you." He coughed and groaned. "I have a son. You have to tell him."

Eli had a son. Nothing made sense. Too many missing pieces. Right now it didn't matter. Nothing else mattered but keeping Eli alive. "You'll tell him yourself. You're too stubborn to die."

"Jake? Is he too stubborn too?"

Please God, let that be true. Hope welled in Gabriella. She glanced around, but her brother didn't appear. "Is Jake here? Is he okay?"

"I moved him into the shade." Deacon's hoarse words came in ragged gasps. "He's okay. Weak, dehydrated. Beat up."

"You check on him. Tell him I'm here. Tell him Natalie's here. I'll stay with Eli. You have to get to her. She's going crazy out there, not knowing."

"Got it." Deacon removed his hands. They were red with blood. "Keep pressure on."

Gorge rising in her throat, she nodded and took his place.

"Mendez?" Eli struggled to sit up. Gabriella pushed him back down. The desire to lay next to him, to pour her blood into him overwhelmed her. "Did they get him?"

"He's dead. But they have Sunny." The woman had given the performance of a lifetime. A consummate actress. Angel-seductress-destroyer. "She's going to prison for a long time."

"The brother?"

"This one." Deacon knelt again. He untangled the legs of the man next to Eli with great care. The man stirred and moaned. "Pedro Mendez, Andy Mendez's brother. He's alive. We've got him, Eli. He'll pay for breaking into Natalie's house and terrorizing little kids. He'll go to prison for a long time."

A family of psychopaths.

Deacon hoisted himself to his feet and stumbled away. He looked ten years older than he had only a week earlier.

Before he'd met a cadre of people consumed by greed and willing to ignore the horrific human cost of their gun trafficking.

Eli didn't talk anymore, but Gabriella kept talking to him. "You have a son. That's so amazing. You'll have to introduce us. I can't wait to meet him. As soon as you're better."

A familiar dark, empty future loomed.

No. This time it was different. This time, she wouldn't run away. This time she would stay. And so would he.

CHAPTER 41

———

BEAT, HEART, BEAT. LET *his heart keep beating, God, please.*
Gabriella cradled her head in her hands and closed her eyes. Still, the
images and sounds bombarded her. Eli's blood soaked his shirt and
seeped into the ground. The EMTs who shoved her aside and worked
on him. Jake's battered face and emaciated body. Deacon carrying
Natalie to an ambulance. Eli's labored breathing. The screaming
sirens as the ambulance rocked and pitched over the gravel road.

The problem of where to go first from the ER had been solved. Eli
was in surgery. Jake now enjoyed a lovely room with a view. The doctor admitted him for observation after a few stitches, a tetanus shot,
X-rays, and a CT scan. They wanted him hydrated. They wrapped
Natalie's arm in a sling until she could see an orthopedic doctor for
more tests. She and Deacon went to tell Virginia the news.

Gabriella should've gone, but she couldn't move from the surgery
waiting room. She needed to be here. She breathed. It didn't help. Her
heart refused to stop pounding. Adrenaline still pulsed in her ears.
Her head throbbed. Her throat ached. People trailed in and out of
the waiting room, but no one bothered with the stinky, filthy woman
with tear streaks on her dirty face.

A throat cleared.

Until now. She straightened and wiped her dirty hand on her
equally filthy shirt. Chuck Jensen stood over her.

"How is he?"

"In surgery. The ER doctor said he found three bullet holes.

One through-and-through in his shoulder, another missed any vital organs. They'll have to dig around for the other one." She craned her neck from side to side. "It's not his first rodeo. He'll be bugging me for a ride home tomorrow."

God, please.

Jensen eased into the plush, green upholstered chair across from hers. "I don't know if you care at this point, but I thought I'd give you an update. You earned it. We've got Sunny Mendez in custody. Pedro Mendez, Andy's brother, is in surgery. They expect him to make it. He'll be arrested forthwith. We detained nine men on-site. Who knows how many escaped into brush country and crossed the river."

So they could continue their business of smuggling guns, drugs, and people. "Or through the tunnel."

"Exactly. It's an amazing feat, that tunnel."

Deacon had provided a thorough description. "It could've been Jake's burial ground."

"The voices on the tape belong to Andy Mendez, Kyle Sullivan, and Pedro Mendez."

"I thought I recognized one of the voices. I just wasn't sure until Sullivan hijacked us. Is Rincon okay?"

"Nursing a broken nose, two black eyes, and a concussion, but he'll live. He's just PO'd that he missed out on the big shoot-out."

"He had no idea Sullivan was dirty?"

"He says no. They didn't work closely together until the joint task force. LPD wanted to provide tactical support. Sullivan is talking to whoever will listen. He knows what they do to cops in prison."

"What's he saying?"

"He says Mendez had a merry band of thugs who raced around intimidating people as needed."

"In a black BMW."

"Yep. They killed Teeter and bombed the church. But the black pickup truck belongs to Sullivan. I'm betting my eyeteeth he pulled the trigger and killed the CI. He insists it was Pedro Mendez. It'll be interesting to see how Mendez tells the story."

"Pedro Mendez was the one who broke into our house?"

"Pedro, which explains why your sister described him as polite. The guy was an accountant with a clean record before he got mixed up his brother's business. He did Andy's books. Our background research shows he's been married forty-five years to the same woman. They have five kids and ten grandkids."

"I don't understand why Andy Mendez would go rogue after years in public service."

"Maybe Sunny will shed some light on that. They'll try to get her to cooperate. Right now she's shut up tight as a clam, waiting for her 'daddy's' lawyer. We'll question Pedro Mendez when he's conscious. Any one of the other men we arrested could turn state's witness for a reduced sentence. The Mexican authorities are investigating the property owner on the other side of the tunnel. It's an auto repair shop that rents moving trucks."

"Lots of in-and-out truck traffic."

"Yep. One of the men arrested was Manny Figueroa."

"Beto's uncle."

"Apparently, he wasn't happy just being a front for the moving of the guns to the border. He isn't talking, of course."

"He knows his son and the rest of the family will step in to keep his stores running."

"This won't even be a tiny blip in the gun trade."

The surgeon strode into the room. Jensen turned. Gabriella stood. The surgeon's mouth moved, but all sound had disappeared.

Jensen's arm went around her shoulders. He leaned closer. "He's fine. He'll be fine."

She shook loose from Jensen's hold. "Just say it again."

"He came through with flying colors." The surgeon—McKee,

McKinley, something like that—smiled. He looked twelve. "He's in recovery. When they move him to a room, you can see him."

Gabriella's legs gave out. She dropped into the chair.

Jensen loomed over her. "Can I get you a drink of water?"

"I need to tell his mom and dad."

"I'll go. You're white as a sheet. When was the last time you ate or drank anything?"

Her stomach roiled. "Natalie and Deacon are with Virginia and Xavier. Go tell them." She clasped her arms around her middle and willed herself not to vomit. She gave him the room number. "Tell Virginia to come to the surgery floor when she can. I'll meet her at his room when he gets out of recovery."

Jensen said something, but Gabriella didn't turn back. She had to get to Eli.

She raced through the hallways, only to twist and turn, tangled in red tape. She wasn't a relative. He was in ICU. No visitors. The minutes ticked by. Finally, the surgeon intervened.

Finally, she sat by Eli's bed, mesmerized by the simple rise and fall of his chest. The beep of the machines assured her he lived just as it had the first time they muddled through this together. Only this was different. This time she'd been there.

She touched blood on her shirt, dried to a crisp brown stain.

He lived. Jake lived. Deacon lived. Natalie lived.

Even she still drew breath.

She lifted his hand to her lips and kissed each finger. *Thank You, God. I could go on without him if that's what You wanted, but I'm so thankful You didn't make me do it. I'm trusting You for the next breath, the next step, the next day.*

Whatever he did, I forgive him. It doesn't matter what it was. Please forgive me for being a stiff-necked, hard-hearted, selfish child.

Eli's arm jerked. His eyelids fluttered. His head lifted. "Gabs, Gabby?"

His hoarse voice held a note of desperation drowning in a sea of undiluted fear.

"I'm here." She grabbed his hand. "I'm right here."

His head sank onto the pillow. "Bad dreams."

She squeezed his hand and let go so she could scoot a chair closer. Once seated, she took his hand again. "Rest. You're fine. So, tell me, why did you have a lighter in your pocket? Had you been smoking?"

"Seriously, you want to bust my chops about smoking right now?"

"Deacon said that lighter kept him from losing it completely." Gabriella smoothed her thumb over the scar on his palm. "You may never have been a Boy Scout, but you came prepared."

"How's Deacon?"

"He's fine. He's with Natalie. I don't even want to know what kind of medical treatment she's administering."

"Stop making me laugh." His eyes closed again. "Pops?"

"Doing better. Your mom wouldn't permit him to do otherwise." She rested her forehead on the cool sheets. *Thank You, Jesus.*

"When I was little, Pops used to tell me the story of Elijah. You know that story?"

She raised her head, stood, and touched his forehead. Cool. Heartbeat 78. Blood pressure 128 over 82. Better than hers. "Yes, I know the story. You should sleep."

"I was named for a powerful prophet who kept it from raining in Israel for three years. Pops used to tell me the story when I was little. God took Elijah up to heaven in a whirlwind right there in front of Elisha. My dad could tell a story."

Gabriella waited. Eli sharing a small piece of his childhood was a rare and precious gift.

"I was four. After he turned off the lights and closed the door—you know we didn't need night lights or the door open because God was taking care of us—I was so afraid God was going to swoop down and take me away, I hid under the covers. I was scared out of my mind."

His voice trailed away. His eyes closed.

"Sleep, love. You can tell me later."

"When I was stuck in that tunnel, I thought maybe He would take me up in a whirlwind. If He would even have me."

"You didn't think about what that would do to me?"

"I couldn't go because of my son. I prayed He would let me be the husband you need and the father he needs."

A son would take precedence. Gabriella had no children. Not yet. She and Eli had talked about children after he put the ring on her finger. Four or five, he said. Two or three, she said.

Someone had given him a son first.

Now, maybe he would let her in. Finally. She smoothed his sheets. "How old is your son?"

"Eight. He's eight . . ." Eli drifted away again. His breathing was still harsh, but his chest rose and fell. "Another time then."

She closed her eyes and willed the tears to disappear.

He would tell her when he was ready. Gabriella kissed his hand again and laid it back at his side.

Trust was a two-way street.

CHAPTER 42

WHEELCHAIR RACES WERE FUN. Deacon crossed the finish line—a grouping of love seats and overstuffed chairs at the end of the long hallway—before Natalie did in her rented power wheelchair. Having a doctor for a father really helped when it came to making things happen in the medical world. This fancy set of wheels didn't require the use of her fractured arm and easily broke the speed limit of six miles an hour. His run-of-the-mill manual chair was borrowed from the lobby when the nurse wasn't looking.

The nightmare of explaining to her insurance company the demise of both her chair and an exorbitantly expensive van only two years old would wait until tomorrow. Right now, her high, breathless laugh floating behind him was pure medicine for them both. Doctor's orders had been to drink plenty of fluids and rest for him and for her to see an orthopedist for her arm. Somewhere in those prescriptions were the words laugh, smile, and most importantly, kiss.

He maneuvered the chair into her space and accepted his prize. Natalie met him halfway. He leaned in for a soft, careful kiss on her swollen, bruised lips.

She backed away. "We need to talk."

"I'm busy being revived."

"You seem plenty revived to me."

He raised his forearm to his forehead. "I don't know, Doctor. I feel very warm."

"Deacon."

"Okay." He swiveled his chair toward the bank of windows that overlooked the medical center parking lot. In the distance a small pond sparkled in the late-morning sun. The last day of August. "Fire away. Oops. Poor choice of words. Newsroom humor."

"Humor is a defense mechanism." Natalie joined him at the window. "I've used it myself many times. Tell me what you're feeling."

"Like I dodged a bullet. Many of them, actually. Hundreds, maybe. I lived."

"It's okay to admit you were scared."

"I almost wet myself." He glanced at her profile. Bruises ringed her eyes. They looked dreamy and unfocused behind the spare pair of glasses Aunt Piper had brought along with clean clothes for all of them. An angry red scratch covered one cheek. The cut on her lip had started to scab. Still, she was the most gorgeous woman he'd ever met, and he'd just told her he was a coward. "I couldn't breathe. I felt sick to my stomach. I wanted to cry like a baby."

"But you didn't."

"In front of Eli, no way."

"Eli was scared too."

"It didn't show. He was too busy trying to find a way out. He got in their faces. He asked questions. He was a superhero."

"He's a police officer. It's what he does for a living. And he was scared. Only a moron wouldn't be."

"Why are we talking about this?" He didn't want to talk. He wanted to kiss. To inhale her scent. Touch her hair. He wanted to feel that alive. "Let's go get ice cream. Double scoops in waffle cones. Triple scoops, your favorite three flavors. What are your favorite flavors?"

"You can't keep it locked up inside. It'll eat you up."

"I don't need you to be my psychologist." He tugged her good hand from her lap. "How's the arm? Any pain? Do I need to kiss it and make it better?"

"Maybe you don't think you need a psychologist, but you do need a friend."

"Is that what you are? A friend?"

"I hope so."

"I was kind of hoping for more."

"Me too, but I need to start small. Can you understand that?"

"I do. I also know life is short. I've known that since I was eight, but the events of the last few days reinforced that knowledge in a big way." When his parents died, his life had changed forever. He no longer believed in fairy-tale endings. He understood loss in the way no child should have to understand. "I want marriage. I want kids. I want it all."

"Did you file your story?"

His job. If she couldn't let go of her distaste for his job, he would not get a happy ending. Once again. "What exactly are you asking me?"

"You borrowed a phone to call in a story and send photos to your editor before you would even let the doctors look at you. You interviewed Gabby. You interviewed me. You interviewed Jake. You interviewed Special Agent in Charge Jensen."

"I did my job."

"You wanted to break the story before your buddy Chris did."

"Chris broke the story here in Laredo. He's happy. He's my friend. I wanted to beat the national media." The adrenaline ebbed away. His head began to throb. "I rushed to file the story because that's how I keep my job. I need it. That's how I pay my bills. It's also what I do and what I am. Again, what are you asking me?"

"Your job is a huge part of your life. To Jake and Gabriella and me, this wasn't a story."

"If Eli weren't lying in a hospital bed, he'd be doing his job, too, regardless of his feelings for y'all."

"True."

"I'm a journalist. It's part of who I am." If she cared for him, she would want him to be himself. The guy who loved the thrill of the hunt for a big story. "Doing this job has been the center of my life for seven years."

"Having a family has a way of changing that."

"If I were a surgeon, for example, would this be a topic of conversation?"

She studied her hands in her lap.

"I'm sorry." *Alder, you idiot. Ease up.* "That was out of line."

"No. You're right. I brought the subject up. Paolo had a crazy schedule, but when he came home, he was home. He was present." She touched two fingers to her swollen lip. "Your world is foreign to me. TV photographers shot video of our car the night Paolo died. Stories ran on the ten o'clock news. They speculated about whether alcohol was involved. The next day, the paper ran a story—your paper. It was . . . invasive. Small children lost their father. Their mother was in the hospital for weeks, in rehab for months. It wasn't a story to me."

"Do you understand why it's news?"

"Not really."

"The hope is that people will learn something about the dangers of driving while intoxicated."

"Maybe. Or maybe mangled cars and flashing lights just make good video. If it bleeds, it leads."

"Give me time to convince you that there are members of the fourth estate who are more than ambulance chasers." He backed up and then edged closer so the wheels of their chairs almost touched. "Ask Gabriella. I'm very good in a debate. I know my stuff."

"We've been through a horrific experience together." Her words came slowly. "One filled with heightened emotions. If I were a psychologist advising me, I'd say go slowly, you two. You're from different worlds. Tread carefully."

"After what we've been through, my prescription is throw caution to the wind and live. Live and love."

"Throwing caution to the wind has its appeal. Are you sure you want to do that with a woman paralyzed from the waist down? It comes with a set of challenges you can only begin to imagine." Natalie's expression turned wistful. "I come with a boatload of baggage."

"Don't underestimate me." He swallowed the hard knot in his throat. "I know I'm not your first love. I know I'm not a surgeon. I'm not even brave. But I've been told I'm a decent guy. And I'm patient. I'm willing to wait until we're on the same page because you are worth waiting for."

"Let's try a first date."

"What do you mean? We've had several. A home invasion, a road trip, gun drawn in the middle of the night. We're on date four, at least."

"I'm serious."

"I know. And I'm serious when I say you're worth waiting for. I'll wait forever as long as you let me keep kissing you."

The sadness gone, Natalie grinned. "You are a decent kisser."

"Only decent?"

"Fishing for compliments?" She offered a knockout smile. "I might need to refresh my memory."

"Friends don't kiss."

"Purely for research purposes."

They kissed, a slow, gentle kiss that rocked Deacon down to the soles of his dirty New Balance sneakers. Her eyes closed, she leaned back and sighed. "Definitely decent. By the way, my favorite flavors are rocky road, cookie dough, and coffee with caramel and chocolate chunks."

"You bum." He wheeled around and shot down the hallway. "First one to the other end gets another kiss."

Which made them both winners in his book.

CHAPTER 43

———

ELI STILL SLEPT WHEN Gabriella opened her eyes an hour later. She touched his forehead. Cool. No pain lined his face. She brushed his lips with hers and slipped out quietly so she could speed walk to Jake's, the second of three hospital rooms occupied by people she loved. By God's grace all three would be around to annoy her and love her and fill her life with joy for many days to come. Her body felt so light, she might float to the ceiling any second. She pushed open the door to find Natalie and Deacon keeping Jake company. More people she loved.

"So you decided to grace us with your presence." Grinning, Jake pushed up against a pile of pillows. He was a pale, battered, bearded shadow of his former self. And that was only the outside. "I can't believe you guys called Mom and Dad over a little kidnapping."

"I can't believe you're taking up space in this hospital, you big faker." Gabriella threw the gauntlet down. Banter with her little brother. A dozen hours ago it had seemed as if that might never happen again. "You just want nurses waiting on you hand and foot."

"And someone to cook for me." Jake patted his flat stomach. "And bring me drinks."

Gabriella couldn't respond. The joy of seeing him alive took her breath away. She smoothed his sheets and adjusted his pillow until the tears were under control. "Don't you ever do that to me again. I think it's time for you to change jobs. Have you ever considered teaching law enforcement?"

"Or maybe I should become a chef." He grabbed her hand and

yanked, forcing her to sit on the bed next to him. "Would you give me a job?"

"In a heartbeat. We could be partners." Then she would never have to let him out of her sight again. She leaned closer. "How are you really doing, bro?"

His jaw worked. He shrugged. "Hanging in there."

"I'm sorry about Sunny."

"Me too. I'm an idiot."

"You weren't working her for information?" At most it had been a feeble hope. Her brother had a kind heart, not one that would go to any length to crack a case. "I figured if you really loved her, you would've told us about her. You were thinking about marrying her and you didn't even tell us or bother to introduce her."

"You were going through a bad breakup." He stared at the ceiling for a second, then met her gaze. "You're still conflicted about Mom and Dad. Natalie, you haven't exactly had it easy. I was going to tell you, but I kept putting it off. Besides, I knew you would be concerned about how little time I took to get to know her."

"So you had no idea she was involved?"

"Do you think I would've gone to Reverend Cavazos with her if I had?" He moved restlessly. "She was so sweet and kind and smart. The whole package. I couldn't believe I'd found her."

"She'd probably been fooling people her whole life. Psychopaths are like that. Right, Natalie?"

"We don't call people psychopaths." Natalie moved her chair closer to where Deacon sat hunched over his laptop writing with a rapid-fire hunt-and-peck style. "It's possible, though, that she has an antisocial mental disorder in which she is able to mimic acceptable behavior in order to get what she wants with no fear of the consequences of her actions. It sometimes manifests itself with violent social behavior. She was definitely a narcissist."

"A psychopath." Gabriella shivered. It wasn't the AC. The memory of the look of pure hatred on Sunny's face as she stared up at Gabriella would remain etched in her memory forever. "It ran in the family. Her dad, her uncle—they're intelligent, charming, and psychotic. How do people get like that?"

"There are reams of paper devoted to that subject." Her face lined with pain, Natalie rubbed her hand over her sling. "It's the nature versus nurture argument. In this case it could be both. They feed on each other. They were unnaturally close, and Sunny modeled her behavior on her father's and her uncle's. Who knows what skeletons are hidden in their family closets."

"And I introduced her to Reverend Cavazos." Guilt carved lines on Jake's battered face. "I feel so bad about the church."

"Don't. Eli and I carry that load."

"Nobody here is responsible," Natalie intervened. "A criminal threw that Molotov cocktail. Just like criminals killed Larry Teeter."

"Larry was a good guy just getting started. With a little more time, we could've been excellent partners." Jake sank lower in his bed. "We thought we were on the right track and the whole time Andy Mendez was wining and dining Rincon. Kyle Sullivan knew every move we made."

"They were hiding in plain sight." Deacon snapped the laptop shut. "Andy Mendez used a long and illustrious career as a patriot and a law enforcement icon to mask his new occupation. It's sad to think his service in Vietnam and the way he was treated when he returned sent him down that path."

"Many of our servicemen and women were treated badly when they came back," Natalie pointed out. "They didn't turn to crime and murder."

No one could argue that point. The room grew quiet. The image of Sunny standing in the South Texas brush in cowboy boots with an AR-10 cradled in her arms loomed in Gabriella's mind. She patted Jake's arm. "I'm really sorry."

"I'll get over it."

"At least we got the bad guys." Natalie sought Deacon's hand. Their fingers entwined. It was good to know that their relationship would now have time to blossom. "And you cracked the case."

"We got some of them, and because of that, we've stymied for two or three minutes the flow of guns into Mexico via Laredo to Nuevo Laredo. ICE will fill in the tunnel with cement." Frowning, Jake touched the bandage across his forehead. "The Mexican authorities will fill the tunnel in Nuevo Laredo. But this is just a hiccup in the gun supply flowing into Mexico. When one tunnel closes, another one opens. We take two straw buyers and one facilitator out of circulation, six more step up. It's lucrative for them and the cartels need the firearms."

"Job security." The sad truth. It would never end. It would never be over. Gabriella sighed and laid her head on her brother's pillow. "In case you don't hear it from anyone else, we're proud of you, little brother. You serve your country every day, and people don't appreciate what that means."

Natalie and Deacon joined in with a round of applause and loud hoots and hollers.

"Thanks, guys." Jake grinned his trademark lopsided grin. "Now bust me loose. I need out of here. I need real food, true sustenance. Carne guisada, tortillas, pico de gallo, *arroz con frijoles*—"

"Stop, stop." Natalie shook her finger at him. "The doctor wants you here for another night for observation. Maybe Deacon can run out and pick up takeout for us."

"Absolutely. I'll introduce you to my favorite restaurant."

"You could pick up the kids. I'm sure they'd love a visit."

"I haven't seen Cullen and Ava in forever." Jake's voice quivered. He wiped at his face. "I hope they're not too traumatized. I'm sorry about all this, Nat."

"They won't believe you're okay until they see for themselves."

Natalie wheeled over to the bed. She grabbed his hand and held on. "They'll be fine. We all will."

"Can you hold down the fort?" Gabriella hugged her brother's neck and slipped from his bed. "I need to make a phone call."

"Vic?"

"I already called her and filled her in on everything. She sends her love."

"Then who?"

"Mom."

Her siblings' hoots followed her into the hallway. *God, here goes nothing.* She took a breath and punched in the number.

Mom picked up immediately. "How is he? Is he is all right? We're at Heathrow, getting ready to board the aeroplane. We'll be in San Antonio tonight."

"He's fine. He's good, and Eli will recover too. I need to talk to you about something else."

"What is it, honey?"

"I'm sorry, Mom."

"For what?"

"For being an unforgiving turd."

CHAPTER 44

—

ONE APOLOGY DOWN, ONE to go. On the long walk to Eli's room, Gabriella rehearsed the words she would say. She prayed for his response.

His room was dark and quiet. Her head bowed, hands clasped, Virginia sat next to her son's bed. Gabriella slipped closer. She took Eli's hand and closed her eyes.

A few minutes later, Virginia sighed. "He's doing better."

"He'll be fine."

"I pray for God's will to be done, and then I tell Him what He should do." She breathed a soft chuckle. "I'm sure God is tickled by my audacity."

"A mother's love."

"A thankful mother who knows she has been blessed with the love of a good man and good children."

"When will you tell him what you told me?"

"When father and son are stronger." Her gaze, still clear and untroubled, met Gabriella's. "Xavier knows I told you. He agrees it was the right thing to do. Together, we'll tell Eli when he is well."

"I won't say anything until he brings it up to me."

"He will. I told Xavier I'd bring him a chocolate milkshake. I think he just wants me to leave him alone for a while." Virginia rose and gathered up her canvas bag covered with red-and-pink embroidered flowers. "Can I bring you something?"

"Deacon went for food." Gabriella hugged her. Virginia's scent was different from her mother's. Like Dove soap. "I'll come by to check on you later."

"Right now, it relieves my heart to know Eli is in your hands." She paused at the door and looked back. "Thank you for getting him out of there."

"It was a group effort."

Virginia smiled. "But you did it for love." She slipped away.

Eli stirred. "Mamá?"

"She went back to your dad."

He stilled.

"Are you up to talking for a minute?"

"To you, always."

Gabriella kicked off her shoes and scooted onto the bed next to him. Careful not to touch any of the tubes and wires, she slid her arm under his head and shoulders. She held him close. His warmth assured. "I love you."

"Love you too, querida."

"Whatever you did, whatever it was, I forgive you."

"I don't deserve forgiveness."

"You do."

Tears leaked from his eyes. She brushed them away. "You're the love of my life. Yesterday, you almost died for me."

"You, for me."

"Don't you think that's a sign?"

"Sí, mi amor."

Gabriella kissed his hair, his forehead, his swollen nose. His head lifted. Their lips met in a long, soft, bittersweet kiss. Pain, anger, bitterness, despair, uncertainty, they all ebbed. If not gone, they were the hard-earned building blocks of the foundation on which they would build a sturdy house. A house filled with the certainty that it was possible to know someone better than yourself and love them for who they were with all their sins, faults, and warts.

She pulled away slowly. "Do you trust me?"

"Sí."

"I trust you too."

"Marry me?"

"I will."

He sighed. "Finally."

"Is there something you want to tell me?"

His eyes closed. His chest lifted and fell.

Her future husband slept.

Gabriella curled around him and closed her eyes.

CHAPTER 45

———

THIS DAY COULDN'T GET any better. Gabriella pulled the Mustang into a parking space three spots down from Eli's Charger in Brackenridge Park. She grabbed her hair up in a ponytail, twisted a hair band around it, and smoothed a few unruly strands that tried to escape. The picnic basket on the seat next to her held thick roast-beef-and-swiss sandwiches on homemade rye bread with Eli's favorite spicy mustard, hummus and pita chips, double-chocolate brownies, sliced Granny Smith apples, Eli's Dr Pepper, and her choice of fizzy water. The suggestion for a picnic in the park after church had been his idea. The menu, hers.

The sun shone on a rare humidity-free, semicool October day in San Antonio. Maybe if Eli was up to it, they could take a walk. If not, they could feed the ducks at the river. Or sit on a bench and people watch. Or lie on the blanket and look for shapes in the clouds.

No pressure. No secrets. No tension. Six weeks into his recuperation, Eli still moved slower than he would like. He worked out with a physical therapist three times a week, saw the departmental shrink, and gave up smoking. For good this time, he insisted. He watched her cook. Sometimes he cooked for her. Or camped in the backyard with the kids.

Or played poker with Deacon, Jake, and his buddies from the PD.

Attending church together proved to be the cherry on top. For the first time in their relationship, he seemed at ease sitting next to her in the sanctuary. To her surprise he had a beautiful tenor that soared on the hymns he said reminded him of a childhood filled with such songs. Reminded him of his dad. The peace in his eyes assured her they were good memories. Today, he said he had an errand to run—doing what, he wouldn't say. Only that he had a surprise and she would like it.

The thought spurred her on. She grabbed the basket and plaid blanket and went in search of her future husband. The high-pitched sound of children laughing and screaming filled the air. Such a happy sound. The smell of fresh-cut grass mixed with the muddy scent of the San Antonio River. Happy childhood memories accompanied her as she walked across the street toward Joskes Pavilion. Eli sat, long jean-clad legs sprawled out, on a bench under an enormous live oak tree next to the old stone picnic pavilion. A bunch of kids chased each other around the playscape.

He looked like a man at peace. Her heart thudded. He looked good.

His gaze captured hers. He smiled. Her breath caught. Even better. "Hey."

"Hey."

"What are you thinking about?" She eased onto the bench next to him. "How many we'll have? Are you ready to change diapers? Or get up for three a.m. feedings?"

"All of that and more. I'm thinking four or five."

"More like two or three. We're old."

His arm came around her shoulders. He leaned in. His lips brushed her forehead. A tremor ran up her spine. The day turned warm. "How are you feeling today?"

"Ready for people to stop asking me that." His lazy smile took the sting from the words. "It's a gorgeous fall day. The sun is shining. I have no pain. I'm sitting on a bench in a park with the beautiful woman I love. I'd say I'm feeling really good."

"I promise I'll stop asking—eventually." Gabriella glanced around. "So I don't see a gift wrapped in fancy paper and topped with a shiny silver bow. What's my surprise?"

A young boy, maybe eight or nine, broke away from the kids playing nearby and loped toward them. "Papí, I'm thirsty."

He slowed to a walk when he saw Gabriella. His smile turned uncertain. Eli's arm tightened around her shoulders. "Samuel, come here. There's someone I want you to meet."

His expression bright with curiosity, the boy did as he was told. Warm brown eyes under a mop of curly brown hair. High cheekbones, full lips. Bronze skin. Tall for his age. He was the spitting image of his father. "Hello, I'm Samuel." He held out his hand. Perfect manners. Not so much like his dad.

Enchanted, she shook his hand. "I'm Gabriella."

"Eli is my dad." He smiled. He would be a heartbreaker someday. A miniature Eli. "He's a policeman."

"I know. He's my friend. I'm a chef. Do you like brownies?"

"Yes."

"Good. We'll have a picnic in a while."

"Okay. Are you my dad's girlfriend? Mamá says he's getting married."

Direct, also like his father. "I am. And we are."

"That's good, I guess. Mamá says you make him happy."

Mamá said a lot, but Samuel's intelligent eyes and serious demeanor suggested this child was wise beyond his years. Gabriella nodded and smiled. "And he makes me happy."

"Máma says adults are like that. I don't get it." Frowning, he studied his dirty Nikes for a second. "Girls are gross. Can I go play now?"

But still a little boy.

Eli handed a water bottle to his son. He cleared his throat. "Go."

Samuel gulped down the water, handed the bottle back, whirled, and ran.

Struggling to keep tears in check, Gabriella watched him go. "He's all you. Except the manners. That must be his mother."

Eli didn't answer. She leaned into his chest and stared up at him.

Emotion lined the contours of his sculpted face. His Adam's apple bobbed. He swiped his eyes on his T-shirt sleeve.

"You're a father, Eli."

"It's crazy. I know." He cleared his throat again. "Lily is a good mother. She's making sure he gets an excellent education. But a boy needs his father. I'm looking forward to teaching him to play baseball and basketball. She's had him in soccer, which is fine, but I'd like to do more. Next weekend I'm taking him to Laredo to meet Mom and Dad. We're going fishing."

"They know then."

"They do. My dad who isn't my dad."

Bless Virginia. It must've been the hardest conversation of her life, even harder than the one with Xavier all those years ago. "Xavier is your papí. He loved you and raised you and disciplined you. He fought for your eternal salvation. What child could ask for more of a father?"

"Things have been better between us since we talked."

"See, that's how it's supposed to work."

"He told me I'll make a good father."

"Of course you will. You had a good role model and you're a good man."

"I wasn't so sure when Lily told me about Samuel. It's hard for me to show my feelings—don't roll your eyes at me." He laughed and squeezed her hand. "I don't want to be that way with Samuel. I want him to know I love him. I want him to be better at showing his feelings."

"We'll work on that together. Right now, let's just enjoy the moment. You have a son."

"I messed up nine years ago, but now I can't honestly say I'm sorry." Eli sank back against the bench. His expression said he was a million miles and a hundred years away. "I was working under-cover in a sting designed to take down a gang on the south side that was running prostitution, drugs, money laundering—a full-service organization."

"Liliana was part of that ring?"

"By family. Not by choice. She was young and gorgeous—"

"I don't need *all* the details."

"I know. I just want you to see what I saw. I'm not trying to justify what I did. It was wrong. If the higher-ups found out I would've lost my job. Before the bust went down, I helped her get out. She left town without telling me about Samuel. I didn't see her again until last year."

"Why now? Why come back after all these years?"

"Her father was dying. Her mother needed her." His gaze followed Samuel, who swung gracefully across the monkey bars and dropped to his feet at the other end. "She had family business to deal with. She's divesting from some of her business interests. She's . . . branching out. She'll be traveling a lot for at least the next year."

"And now she wants you in Samuel's life?"

"She wants my influence." He snorted. "I know that's crazy."

"No it's not, considering the alternative."

"She wants to share custody with me, with us. I know that means she'll be in our lives permanently, but we have a son together." He withdrew his arm and clasped her hands in his. "Can you handle that? I know it's a lot to ask—"

"We're all adults—even if I haven't always acted like it." Her jealousy, suspicion, and mistrust had led her down a painful road that could've ended in permanent loneliness. She could've missed all this. "I owe you an apology for how I acted. I'm truly sorry."

"It was surreal. Having her show up at my door with Samuel. It opened old wounds and old feelings. I lost my bearings for a while. I couldn't figure out how to make it all fit together. My son, his mother, me. What did it mean for you and me?" His hands tightened on hers, then released. "I couldn't figure out how to tell you. I didn't want to hurt you, and I ended up hurting you worse. I did something stupid and then I compounded it by not owning up to it. Forgive me?"

In other words, they were both human. They messed up but, by God's grace, would get another chance. "Clean slate?"

"Clean slate."

"Ava and Cullen will love having a cousin to play with." She would love Samuel because she loved Eli. They were a package deal wrapped up in a bow. "We have an extra room at the house. He can stay with us when you're working—"

Eli's mouth closed over hers. The kiss reverberated all the way to the tips of her toes. She slid her hands around his neck and took control. Pent-up emotions exploded. Eli's hands tightened around her waist.

"Papí!"

They burst apart as if a grenade had exploded. His arms crossed, a scowl on his face, Samuel stood a few yards away. He marched over to Eli and whispered something in his ear and marched away.

"What was that about?"

"He said we're embarrassing him. That boys and girls don't do that in public. It's called PDA." Eli's grin stretched ear to ear. "We've just been called out by my son."

"Someday he'll be a teenager and we'll get even." Laughing, she studied the engagement ring on her finger. The diamonds and sapphires sparkled in the sun. She touched the cool gems with one finger. "We have the rest of our lives to embarrass him with PDA."

"Starting now. He'll just have to get used to it." Eli tugged the band from her hair so it fell to her shoulders. His hands cradled her head, his fingers intertwined in the long strands. His scent of Polo enveloped her as he lowered his head. His gaze locked with hers, telling her how much he wanted and needed her. Would always love her. The sounds of children playing and birds jabbering and cars crawling along the nearby street faded away.

"Just when I thought this day couldn't get any better, it did."

"I can't promise every day will be like this. We'll have good days and bad days. We both know that." His smile was sweeter than any culinary concoction she could create. "But what I can promise you is that we'll be in it together. Always."

He sealed the words with a soft, sweet, slow kiss.

God, let this day last forever and ever.

Amen.

A NOTE FROM THE AUTHOR

—

I LIVED IN LAREDO, Texas, from 1981 to 1987, working as a newspaper journalist. I also lived in El Paso, Texas, for a year and have lived in San Antonio, Texas, for almost thirty years. My experiences living so close to the U.S.–Mexico border and in a city that is a multicultural melting pot shapes my writing in this and other stories. However, I want to emphasize *Over the Line* is not intended to be a treatise on any political, economic, or social issues related to U.S.–Mexico border policies or relations. The opinions expressed by the characters are theirs alone, born out of their life experiences and values. I will keep mine to myself. The book was written in 2017 and early 2018, so any events or changes in laws and policy that have occurred since that time are not reflected here.

I have occasionally skewed law enforcement tactics and divisions to suit the needs of my story. The media outlets mentioned are real, but the journalists are fictional. As a young reporter, I did indeed frequent a pool hall with my media colleagues in Laredo in the early 1980s. We played pool every Thursday night at the Sky Lounge, owned and operated by Laredo police department officers. To be able to mine those rich memories for *Over the Line* was great fun.

On occasion, I created swatches of industrial park along the Rio Grande outside of Laredo where I needed them to be for my story. The statistics and other facts represent information available at the time the story was written and may have changed since then. While tunnels like the one in which my characters languish have and do exist along the U.S.–Mexico border, particularly in California, I'm not aware of any specifically being found in the Laredo–Nuevo Laredo area. I have done my best to be accurate regarding gun trafficking and types of weapons described. Any errors are my own, and I hope they don't impede your enjoyment of the story.

I love the multicultural heritage of my adopted home. Our lives are enriched by the ethnic flavors brought to our tables each day as we live side by side in a state over which six flags have flown. Our similarities will always be greater than our differences. For the record, I may not have been born in Texas, but I got here as fast as I could!

Above all else, *Over the Line* is a work of fiction intended to entertain, but also to make readers think about the importance forgiveness plays in our lives as we endeavor to live by the example Christ set for us. It is my hope I've succeeded on both counts.

Until the next story, may God bless and keep you.

ACKNOWLEDGMENTS

OVER THE LINE IS a story that's been percolating for years. I first started reading about gun smuggling into Mexico while still working in public relations. It took me back to my days as a reporter at the *Laredo News* and *Laredo Morning Times* in the early eighties. We were a scrappy bunch of journalists mostly from other parts of the country thrown together by our profession. We became a family. Those five years were among the best I've ever had. Young, full of ourselves, in love with journalism, and unencumbered by the realization that we would eventually get old and tired of low pay and terrible hours. Living on the border was a daily learning experience, like being embedded in another culture. I'm so thankful for the people I knew there and for what I learned about our multicultural heritage in this country. This book is dedicated to a small band of reporters with whom I sowed wild oats and managed to survive. I'm thankful for everyone of the Sky Lounge Thursday night pool crowd, but especially Joanne and Mike Cisneros, Larry Burns, Danny Hermosillo, and Shellee Bratton. Oh to be young again—or maybe not.

I also am indebted to Becky Monds for taking this chance on me in the romantic suspense genre and shepherding the book through the process of making it a better story. Where to cut and where to polish. Thank you, Becky, for your loving care. Thanks to Julee Schwarzburg for nitpicking the details into shape. Thank you for your patience. If you ever want to scream at my inattention to style, you never show it. My thanks to the entire HarperCollins Christian Publishing sales and marketing team for taking on the task of launching these books in a new genre (for me) and getting the book to a new audience. I so appreciate the effort. My special thanks to Allison Carter for working the publicity leads for *Tell Her No Lies*, which sets up the audience for this book and those to come.

As always, thanks to my agent Julie Gwinn for her feedback and support. To my husband, Tim, you are the best.

To my readers, thank you. Without you, none of this would be possible. Keep reading. Keep imagining. Keep delving into new worlds. They're the best kind.

Finally, thanks to my Lord and Savior, who makes all things possible, even when I don't deserve it.

DISCUSSION QUESTIONS

----

1. Gabriella has evidence she thinks proves Eli cheated on her. She doesn't want to forgive him until he tells her what he did and why. She wants to give him a chance to explain himself, but he refuses to do it. Does God expect her to forgive him anyway? Could you forgive him, if he were your fiancé? What does the Bible say about forgiveness?

2. Gabriella's mother had an affair with another man, and her parents divorced. She blames her mother and can't forgive her. Was it right for her father to divorce her mother for committing adultery? What does the Bible say about divorce? How is it viewed by society today? By the church?

3. Eli's mother, Virginia, reveals to Gabriella that Xavier is not Eli's father. She had an affair that resulted in her pregnancy with Eli. Xavier knows and he forgave Virginia. Could you forgive a spouse and accept his or her child as yours? Why or why not? What does God call you to do in this situation?

4. Gabriella feels responsible for her brother-in-law Paolo's death and her sister's quadriplegia because she served alcohol the night he died in a car accident in which he was the driver. Is she responsible, or is Natalie correct that as an adult Paolo was responsible for his own actions? What does the Bible say about alcohol? How does society view it? Do you believe avoiding alcohol is part of your Christian walk? Should it be?

5. Deacon and Natalie have different views on the role of journalists in reporting stories that affect the communities

in which they live. Deacon feels people have a need to know what's happening in order to make informed decisions. Natalie feels families shouldn't be subjected to the publicity. How do you feel about journalists covering DUI accidents in which people are killed, funerals of police officers, or protests against elected leaders? Do you think journalists play an important role in daily life in your country?

6. After innumerable shootings with hundreds of innocent victims, the United States and its citizens struggle with the role of guns in our society. Our Second Amendment rights versus our right to be safe in schools, in churches, at concerts, and wherever we socialize. Is there a deeper issue facing humanity when we resort to violence to solve our differences? As Christians, how can we work toward peaceful resolutions to difficult, often highly volatile, differences?

7. One of the most divisive issues to surface during the writing of this book involved separating migrant children from their parents when they were apprehended crossing the border illegally. Chris and Eli touch on it briefly at the Sunshine Lounge. Do you believe Christians should have a different view on this issue than nonbelievers? What would Jesus have done? How do you reconcile your political views with your Christian beliefs, or do you think that is necessary in your faith walk?

8. Law enforcement officers who are Christians may not support the laws they are required to enforce. What would you do in their shoes if your beliefs were at odds with your job as a sworn officer?

ABOUT THE AUTHOR

Photo by Tim Irvin

Bestseller Kelly Irvin is the author of seventeen books, including Amish romance and romantic suspense. *Publishers Weekly* called *A Deadly Wilderness* "a solid romantic suspense debut." She followed up with *No Child of Mine*. The two-time ACFW Carol finalist worked as a newspaper reporter for six years writing stories on the Texas–Mexico border. Those experiences fuel her romantic suspense novels set in Texas. A retired public relations professional, Kelly now writes fiction full-time. She lives with her husband, photographer Tim Irvin, in San Antonio. They are the parents of two children, three grandchildren, and two ornery cats.

Visit her online at KellyIrvin.com
Instagram: kelly_irvin
Facebook: Kelly.Irvin.Author
Twitter: @Kelly_S_Irvin